Eberhart Ghoηadz:
The Designer of Professional Sports on this Planet

J. A. Justice

ISBN 978-0-9841092-0-3

Eberhart Ghoηadz:
The Designer of Professional Sports on this Planet

Library of Congress Control Number: 2009906028

Published 2009 by:
SquidWorks, Inc.
855 N. Northwest Hwy.
Park Ridge, IL 60068 USA

Cover background image credit: NASA-JSC

In loving memory...

William & Delores

4

PREFACE

The story you are about to spend time with shall whisk you away to faraway worlds. Thriving worlds... where heroes and villains abound, forever striving to advantage both good and evil. Quickly find yourself immersed in a good versus evil struggle where occasional bawdy language and preposterous behavior progresses an engaging literary work considering the thoughts and perceptions of our own existence.

Eberhart Ghoṇadz: The Designer of Professional Sports on this Planet is rich in alien characterizations that sometimes humorously satires the human condition. Intertwining the adventure lay a surreal story of enduring sibling camaraderie that spans the universe. One set alien and the other human...both struggling with the rigors of growing up and the complexities of meeting and overcoming life's challenges.

The young aliens are no different from young humans. They do what young aliens do.... They get into mischief, act silly sometimes, pass alien gas, love their parents, come of age, fall in love, grieve over their dead, stand together against enemies, and try to contain their fear of the unknown while attempting to understand and embrace it. They live on a planet that has endured *Ocular Discrimination* and survived. Their heroes have championed the *Salary Disappearing Act* and have created *Don't Be Tired* plans to alleviate the lower-class burden. They think about using *Liquid*

XP27 Acid Formulate and try to understand why *Walkashan Gazeldas* hump *Utrovian* trees sowing their seed hundreds of times per span. And yes...the hero wonders why *Spot*, that wonderful little creature, had to get old and die.

The writing of this novel spanned many months. Consequently, the variation of mood may be somewhat perceivable in the writing. However, some areas of the story just begged for, and intentionally received, a little levity while other areas just would not tolerate it. The story was always allowed to lead. During the many hours of editing there has been a serious effort to maintain a consistent writing voice albeit imparting an unpredictable writing style that is unafraid to step off the path when it just feels right. It is humbling to realize one day that your views change so gradually over time that you almost do not notice.

I hope you will find this adventure interesting and entertaining. Further enhancing the reading experience, a sprinkle of artwork is included here and there. Finally, there is a substantial use of character dialogue throughout drawing you into the action, and hopefully, allowing you to feel and see the adventure. *I mean really*...if you just scan the pages, you may be able to hear an exciting voice vividly tell the story as you see it *live* in your mind's eye! That is how much I care about YOU, the valued reader! *–ENJOY!*

TABLE OF CONTENTS

CHAPTER ONE

THE INHABITANTS OF Uμ MPʹAR...

...The needs of the soul and the desires of the flesh are conceived as one and born identical twins. On occasion...they are so aligned in their purpose that neither shall betray the identity of the other....

"Sir, we believe she is being held, just below the surface, inside some type of sacrificial mausoleum." The intelligence officer continued to brief Sir Jacφb Puηt. He pointed at charts and maps detailing the surrounding structures. "...very strange, sir."

"Strange! How so, major?" asked Sir Puηt.

The officer moved slowly while listening through an earpiece to real-time intelligence reporting from an onsite team. He now was able to pull up infrared scans on the view screen. "There certainly appears to be a warm and living body within the crypt...."

"Yes, and...?"

"Sir, the seals...they are not broken!" The major became visibly uncomfortable as he again pressed the earpiece, listening intently. "...Atomic dating estimates the age of the seals well beyond... 5000 solacles.[1]" The expression on the major's face was one of disbelief.

"I see," responded Jacφb calmly. Jacφb quietly examined the scans closely. His thoughts focused on his father's words, *'...Though this house be chosen to deliver, wary the flesh sometimes shadows the soul. Allow not the adversary to field an unholy advantage.'* Looking up, "Is the rescue team in place?"

"Yes, they are in position and awaiting your order to execute."

Jacφb arose then straightened his uniform. "Please inform the commander... that I will be giving that order in person."

"...Sir!"

Jacφb exited the briefing room and moved smartly down the corridor. Stopping at a secured door, he punched in a key code and entered his quarters.

"Is she there?"

"Yes...I believe she is." Jacφb awkwardly kissed his wife. Now close, he whispered, "...how did you know where she was located?"

"I told you...the keeper of records disclosed that he had been coerced into keeping secret about a young female being held against her will inside the tomb." Perfidious touched his face and smiled while peering deeply into his eyes. "I'm so happy that you have found her."

"I must leave now. I will return when she has been released." He moved toward the door.

"...She has been waiting so long for you."

---

[1] Solacle -- solar cycle. Uμmpάr orbits the rad once every ninety Earth years.

Jacφb stopped briefly, without turning, and then exited through the door. Perfidious smiled....

The transport dusted-off with Sir Jacφb aboard. At high speed, the transport would arrive at the target location in a short time.

"Sir, we are well into our descent flight path," said the pilot. "Commander Akron will be waiting when we land."

"Very well, captain. Thank you for the update."

The transport came in low hugging the terrain and touched down quickly adjacent to the tomb. Commander Akron was waiting and did escort Sir Jacφb into the surface level of the structure.

"My team is four levels below, sir. The catacombs are quite extensive."

"I see, commander. Have other life signs been detected?"

"No, sir," Akron shook his head, "...just the one. Should we expect resistance?"

"Commander, it is prudent to exercise caution. Lead on...I'll follow you."

"Sir, this way," Akron motioned ahead.

As they trekked deeper into the tomb, the air grew increasingly stale while blending with a distinctly foul odor.

"...Weapons?" Sir Jacφb stopped and seemed to inhale deeply.

"Sir?" Now puzzled, the commander turned toward him.

"Your team...how are they armed?"

"Standard energy pulse weapons and staitho saber blades."

"Instruct them to ready their blades. The energy

weapons may be useless. There is an unusual ambient energy field, which may possibly be due to significant carbonite deposits." Jacφb now opened his eyes. He knew what might be coming. "We must go quickly!"

"Sir?"

"Lead on--Now!"

The commander complied. They quickly sped through winding corridors, down hard stone stairways, and through tight, knee-high crawlways.

"Here's a harness, sir. We'll have to repel down into the pit below." The commander and Sir Jacφb helped each other with the harnesses.

"Ready?"

"Yes...and commander..." Jacφb grabbed Akron's shoulder and turned him so that their eyes would meet. "Instruct your team to have their blades drawn when the crypt is opened."

The commander felt the seriousness of Jacφb's words--he nodded in the affirmative before jumping over the edge. Jacφb followed and soon both officers were touching the floor of the pit. After disconnecting their equipment, they moved toward the dispersed group waiting to enter the crypt.

"Commander," said the lieutenant in charge, "...there are additional heat signatures now. How can that be?"

"Steady, lieutenant. Instruct the team to ready their blades. The energy field surrounding the crypt may hinder the pulse weapons."

Sir Jacφb and the commander moved into position and the order was given to sever the seals.

[Pow, Pow, Pow, Pow!]

Small charges broke the seals allowing them to

fall away.

The lieutenant looked at the commander, "Sir?"

"Proceed."

Several troopers heaved the door ajar. The foul odor grew by a magnitude.

"Open it fully," ordered Sir Jacφb, "we must gain access!"

Suddenly, serpents slithered forth and attacked quickly. They wrapped around several team members and were squeezing the life from them. Forgetting their instructions, the team began firing their energy weapons. The bolts acted wildly, zooming in circles, striking other members of the team.

"USE YOUR BLADES!" yelled Jacφb. The energy field anomaly did disrupt the pulse weapons.

Finally, the serpents were subdued though several team members perished.

"Open it!" instructed Sir Jacφb.

The tomb cover was forced aside revealing a young female draped in silk-like robes.

"Colłiŋsía!" Jacφb touched her face. Her eyes opened sleepily. She gazed so innocently into Jacφb's eyes. "Allow me to help you, dear."

"Jacφb?" Colłiŋsía smiled. "Thank you."

"How does she know your nam--?"

"That's unimportant now, commander," said Jacφb. "We must leave quickly."

Colłiŋsía collapsed into Jacφb's arms.

"We'll strap her into the harness and hoist her up," said the commander.

The team moved as quickly as practical from the tomb. Now loading on the transport, the foul odor was oddly present.

She is mine, whispered the voice.

Sir Jacφb turned around quickly. Others appeared oblivious to the voice and were proceeding with the embarkation.

You have released me--thank you. Now let us discuss the rewards of service and the penalties for disobedience.

"...My lord! What have I done?"

"Sir Jacφb," said the commander, "...did you say something?"

"Eberhart's EdRep has lower marks this interval," said Hazăr. He flipped the pages and smiled. "He just keeps sinking lower." Hazăr seemed proud of his only son. "How the time has passed... [Sniffle] He's not my little shadow any longer." Stopping briefly to caress his wife's shoulder, he moved toward the viewport and peered out at the Uμmpάrian sky.

"I guess he'll be held back for another term." Tadφlŏn took a long leisurely sip of Utrovian tea. Immersed in the aroma, she smiled at her reflection while recollecting the difficulties Eberhart had adjusted to in order to achieve these results.

Since Eberhart's mother was an educator, he had a good reason for doing poorly in school. He certainly was her pride and joy. She looked down... A small nineteen-legged bug was patrolling across the table in front of her. At this moment, Tadφlŏn was being regaled with the thought of her efforts to help Eberhart succeed. She allowed it to pass unharmed.

Eberhart Ghoηadz was born in 18,761 on a small

world, 2764.3 million penãrds[2] distant from *Rectar 7*, called *Uµmpár*. With a population of only 13,785,962,548,793, everyone knew everyone else. He had only two parents and one sister. His father, Hαzăr, was a Trans-Dimensional Engineer. Hαzăr earned an income of seventeen thousand magnitudes of gold per solacle. His mother, Tadφlŏn, was a 20th level educator paid eight thousand magnitudes of gold per solacle. Dear Julíenηe was about the same age as he. They all lived as best they could in a small 25-room bungalow. Being cursed with prosperity--they hoped for a better life.

"Did you see Julíenηe's educational report?" Tadφlŏn handed the report to Hαzăr.

He thumbed the pages quickly already knowing what it would reveal. "I know...I'll talk to her about it." Again, he caressed Tadφlŏn's shoulders offering comfort though fearing rebuff.

"Talk?" she responds, "It's time for more than talk. Those high marks just can't be covered up with talk and good intentions anymore. No...Julíenηe isn't applying herself--we have to punish her this time!" Hαzăr's hands were quickly evicted and their offer refused. Tadφlŏn's pride became ensconced in a pool of self-pity that deepened with each successive educational report.

"...But honey--?"

"You butt-honeyed me the last review interval and I'm still sore--thank you very much," said Tadφlŏn, "and now her grades have gotten even higher."

"It's just a phase--!"

"What? ...a phase! At this rate, she'll graduate solacles ahead of the rest and be guaranteed a backbreaking salary besides... Damazar! I'm sending her

---

[2] Penãrd – unit of distance equal to one Earth mile.

shopping... alone!"

Hɑzăr was taken aback by her punishment decision. He opened his mouth and then bit his tongue to prevent further antagonizing his wife.

...Sounds like mom and dad are arguing again, thought Eberhɑrt as he watched the media viewer in an adjacent leisure alcove. Julíenŋe is going to really get it this time. What is her problem?

Eberhɑrt knew to stay clear of his mother when the EdReps came. Julíenŋe could never get it together and her EdRep was as a slap to their mom's face. Still, Eberhɑrt knew how demanding academia had become. Julíenŋe excelled in school causing her parents much shame. As a consequence, she received some very harsh punishment at times for this reason. This time, Julíenŋe brought home an educational report obviously saturated with high marks.

"JULIENNE," yelled Hɑzăr, "we want to talk to you!" Hɑzăr waited at the food prep's entrance keeping himself between his wife and his daughter. He had never envisioned parenting to be this difficult when he studied it briefly in school. Oh yeah...he now remembered dropping the class early--much too demanding.

"We've done enough talkin--!" A fire was building under Tadφlŏn with each passing zliton[3].

"Now dear...let's hear what she has to say."

Sounds came from the upstairs signaling that

---

[3] Zliton -- unit of time equal to one Earth minute.

Julíenηe had heard and was on her way down. A few zlitons passed before she skipped into the food prep area of the Ghoηɑdz' very spacious home.

"Julíenηe," said dad, "can you explain this EdRep?" Hɑzăr pressed the report to her face attempting to appear frustrated thus hoping to drain some of Tadφlŏn's anger.

"...I did my best, Dad," she answered. She allowed her eyes to dip toward the floor. "I just couldn't help unconsciously marking the correct answers on the exams...Honest!" Julíenηe tucked her knees slightly and toed the floor with her shoe.

"That was your explanation *last time*!" said Tadφlŏn. She stood up quickly from the table. "You keep this up and mark my word--you *will* graduate early!" Tadφlŏn pushed Hɑzăr aside and invaded Julíenηe's space challenging her reasons for yet another stellar performance.

"...Mommmm!" Julíenηe looked her defiantly in the face, "Don't blow an injector nozzle!" Julíenηe's eyes appeared now reddened and bloodshot. Hɑzăr had never witnessed the fire within his daughter. She definitely was Tadφlŏn's child.

"Don't you take that tone with me, young lady...I've had it with your superior educational performance!" Tadφlŏn stepped back-- [SLAP!] She slapped Julíenηe hard enough to knock her off balance. Julíenηe clutched her face. Her mother had never struck her before. Tadφlŏn was overcome with emotion. "...Twelve!"

"Whaaaat?" cried Julíenηe. She knew full well her punishment was going to be terrible.

"Next span," began Tadφlŏn, "...you are going

shopping.... You *will* purchase twelve new outfits." Tadφlŏn backed up and seated herself once more. She realized what she had done by slapping Julíenηe. Inside, she was already begging forgiveness.

"Daadddd!" moaned Julíenηe. Her eyes were pleading with him to intercede.

"Hone--," Hαzăr began to plead Julíenηe's case but to no avail.

"I told you--don't honey me!" said Tadφlŏn. "You heard me, Julíenηe. You had better get plenty of rest tonight. Now go to your room!"

Tadφlŏn took a final gulp of tea and looked down.... [SPLAT!]

"...just not FAIR!" said Julíenηe. She angrily stomped back upstairs.

"Don't you think that's a little harsh?" asked Hαzăr.

"Not as harsh as graduating early and having to carry thirty or forty mags of gold home every span."

She rose from the table, wiped her bug-bloodied finger on Hαzăr's shirt, and left the room.

Wow, thought Eberhαrt. He began to feel sympathy for his sister. ...She'll die! I've gotta help her...I guess?

Eberhαrt rolled over onto the floor looking for the comm. He needed to call in a favor. He spied the comm under an urn platform and began to roll-crawl, rocking from side to side with his hands clasp behind his back, to retrieve it. Picking it up and flipping it open....

No calls...it has been so long, he thought. When will the telemarketers ever call?

He punched in the location code and waited for a

response.

"Yeah."

"Hey, Cláron. It's Eberhart...."

"Hey," replied Cláron.

"Cláron, my friend, how's that AGV mod working out for you?"

"...Excellent, Eeeb! I raced her last evening--!"

"Uh...listen, Cláron. I need a little help...."

As Tadφlŏn had commanded, Julíenηe rose early and began dragging three bags of gold to the Trans stop located one penãrd from their home. Being early, the radlight reflected by the moons was still dim. She could see her dad watching from the illuminated upstairs glass port as she left.

This is not fair, she thought. ...Gold as currency--Damazar!

She proceeded to drag her shopping money across the street and through Foliage Park. It was the usual short cut to the Trans station.

"Ugh!" A sharp blow to the jaw sent her rolling into the brush.

[Smack, Kick, Kick!]

Julíenηe lost consciousness as the violent onslaught painfully proceeded.

The light was much brighter now. Julíenηe's eyes, puffily swollen, slowly opened. How long have I been lying here? Slowly, she stood up while leaning against a tree to steady herself. Why was I attacked? She was hurting terribly but began slowly trekking home. Blurrily glancing around, there was no sign of the gold. Enduring the pain as best she could, the fear of punishment for losing the gold dominated her thoughts.

She had become a victim of a revobbery![4] Her desperate physical condition was evidence of the brutal attack. As she neared home, she kept telling herself that no one could question the validity of her claim. She certainly did not want to be convicted of illegally getting rid of gold. She had made it to the door of her home. Turning the knob....

"OH MY!" gasped Tadφlŏn. Julíenη̡e pushed open the front door and fell to the floor. Rolling on the floor with her bloody face contorting, the pain appeared intense and unbearable--she just could not stop laughing!

Yes...Eberhαrt was so overcome with pity that he had rounded up some of his closest friends and they had moogled[5] Julíenη̡e while she was on her way to the shopping mall. Julíenη̡e came home without any gold or clothes. She was bruised and scraped from head to toe and just barely able to walk when she finally collapsed in the doorway. Gently rolling on the floor in excruciating ecstasy, Eberhαrt had never seen her so happy.

As time went on, Julíenη̡e's educational performance began to change. She was now doing almost as poorly in school as Eberhαrt. Later, Julíenη̡e became aware of Eberhαrt's involvement in the moogling. They grew closer together and their love for each other grew stronger. This camaraderie continued through eighteen solacles of junior high and into the sixth solacle of high school.

As people and things usually do, Julíenη̡e began to change. Eberhαrt noticed this but paid little attention until Julíenη̡e began to date. Females begin to mature earlier

---

[4] Revobbery -- reverse robbery. *Normally criminals force you to take their gold!*

[5] Moogle -- tough love, minus the snogging, by a significant other.

than males and Julíenη was no exception. Her body had begun to develop. Consequently, Eberhαrt became concerned about this because of his ignorance.

Some problems developed in the close alliance that had been the norm. Eberhαrt would wait until Julíenη was asleep and then place ice packs on her chest to reduce swelling. He would sprinkle shrinkabum[6] on her underwear attempting to draw up her hips. Eberhαrt even went so far as to hide the oooohvucchinis[7] that his mother brought home from the agro-market. With all the stories he had heard, the mere thought of her being lured into the fruit and vegetable laden porn industry spurred him to take action. However, all of his innocent efforts were to no avail, of course.

Julíenη began taking precautions. She routinely sprayed nipple de-icer on her chest and wore a pelvic dust mask to bed. She did these things rather than hurt her brother. It was not long, however, until Eberhαrt's own body begun to change. Julíenη began to notice his physical as well as his behavioral change. Eberhαrt would stare hopelessly at her female friends when they came over. She noticed that Eberhαrt would disappear for lengthy periods into the bathroom with the latest copy of *Gears and Robots* catalog. They were growing up and each of them knew it.

For several solacles things seemed to be going well. Then something happened in the east that shook the entire world of Uμmpάr deep in its bowls. It was announced on national view screen that, because of the

---

[6] Shrinkabum – latest craze targeting excessive junk in the trunk.
[7] Oooohvucchini – thingy-like fruit found only in the jungles of *Masturbia.*

recent war in that area, fossil fuel would be FREE! The nation reacted adversely. The economy soared while the price of food, durable goods, and most other merchandise plummeted. Eberhart's parents were immediately informed that their salaries would be increased by thirty-five percent and that there was absolutely no chance of a layoff for the foreseeable future. The planet's resorts were overrun. People began spending gold as fast as they could for fear of even lower prices. Vehicle sales rocketed and multi-billion magnitude gold homes could not be built fast enough to meet the demand. Eberhart feared that the end was near.

Like everyone else, the Ghoŋαdz' did as best they could under such poor economic circumstances. New vehicles were purchased for each family member and even a new multi-million mag gold home where they could be parked. It certainly was a desperate period in Eberhart and Julíenŋe's young lives. Until then, they truly did not fully understand the horrors of prosperity. Sadly, a desperate relative would soon exercise some very bad judgment.

Uncle Wolleïn Ghoŋαdz was imprisoned for throwing gold into the neighbor's waste containers. He was sentenced to four-hundred and seventy-five solacles in savers prison where he was forced to spend one thousand magnitudes of gold per span. His family was penalized as well. During his term in prison, the government would send an additional one thousand magnitudes of gold each quarter-solacle to his family. Wolleïn's wife, Wănzia, could not stand the shame. Overcome with depression, she decided to go to the wealthiest town on Uμmpάr and end it all. Subsequently, she was shot to death for putpocketing gold nuggets on unsuspecting victims. Eberhart never fully understood why his aunt committed suicide.

Eberhart often went to the square where his aunt had died. He felt so ashamed and coveted the ragged clothes that the upper-class wore. In *Penuriosus*, old vehicles and deteriorating homes were everywhere. The elite class surely knew how to live. The jealousy burned in Eberhart's soul as he watched children play with their sticks and old cans. He vowed to decrease the standard of living for all instead of an arrogant few. He thought to himself that the children playing were lucky enough to be born into poverty while he had to earn it. It was at that moment, on the eight hundred and sixty-fifth span of the solacle, that his destiny became clear. While he stood there, the sparse rays of radlight pierced the beautiful gray smog while his ears were being bombarded by the pleasant squeaking of the resident's pet rodents. His senses were being overcome as the brilliant smell of decomposing garbage filled his head with dreams of a glorious future. Ah, the hopes of the young.

Eberhart stood still for a while longer watching an old beggar in the center of the square. Piles of refuse decorated the bench where he sat. Overgrown vegetation provided a contrasting backdrop grossly illustrating the gentleman's dire circumstance. Eberhart's eyes would catch a random sparkle as the beggar's shoes glistened in the radlight. His tailored suit and manicured look was a frightful sight, no doubt, to these upper-class snobs. He was singing vibrantly and every now and again, a compassionate person would take a nugget of gold from his platinum cup. Eberhart would not forget this experience.

Julíenŋe finally amassed enough courage to invite her kisψm[8] over for consumption period. She had been planning this event for a long time. As she stood admiring the beauty of the meal table, she became overwhelmed with a feeling of pride. The tablecloth was a very faded purple and green. The edges were frayed much like the beard of a contestant for the Boolurian prison electric grid just moments after they had won. The washing that Julíenŋe had given it in sulfuric bleach had really done the trick. The candles were short from burning all morning. The center of the table was adorned with a bowl of withering fruit. She thought how brilliant she had been to put the fruit in the irradiator with the setting on incinerate to achieve this beautiful upper-class look. Sincerely wanting to impress her upper-class kisψm, Julíenŋe had stayed up all night turning the light switch in the meal room on and off in order to get the bulb to burn out. Ah, she was pleased indeed.

Julíenŋe knew that her mom had done her very best for this special evening as well. She had used her friend Toasta, who worked at Pyrotectic, to contact Drexall, at Radonseptic, to ask Bob, who did refuse landscaping, to send her the stale bread and rank meat that now lay decaying beautifully on the Ghoŋɑdz' humble table. The Ghoŋɑdz' would have really *put on the gazelda* for their upper-class guest if mom had swerved their vehicle a little sooner at the neighbor's pet.

Time was passing…she hurried upstairs to get herself ready for Jerẹmy Williams. Wow! She thought about him a lot…. Jerẹmy was a senior at school. At the

---

[8] Kisψm – unisex term; kissable, huggable, yum, yum, yummable-- *girlfriend or boyfriend!*

age of twenty-seven, he had been held back ten solacles for extraordinarily poor academic performance. This was understandable. His father had been held back in school for forty-three solacles--narrowly missing mandatory appointment to the national lawmaking body. There was little doubt that Jerẹmy was his father's son. Julíenηe admired how he studied very hard learning the wrong answers hoping to graduate near the bottom of the class. This would almost assure him of a dead-end, low paying job. However, she knew it was a very difficult endeavor.

[SCREECH!]

Jerẹmy looked at the very prosperous home his AGV had come to rest in front of. Inside were his potential lower-class kisψm, and likely, her parents. He hated these *meet-the-family* dinners. "Can't she just put-out without all these formalities?" he grumbled to himself.

It had not been an easy life for Jerẹmy. When you instinctively know everything from birth, the process of learning and applying the incorrect answer is a difficult task. Your brain demands that you reflexively give the correct answer. Learning the wrong answers and developing the mental frame of mind to apply them takes perseverance and a very strong discipline. Jerẹmy wondered if his ancestors could have ever conceived the problems they would create because of genetically engineered, innate intelligence. How could they have known...?

It all had started about 10,000 solacles ago. A researcher, Sharon Defoulgar, discovered that implanting genes of an experienced adult into an embryo yielded an offspring with the ability to learn at an accelerated rate. Indeed, the complicated implantation process encompassed three embryonic germ layers, and subsequently, the fetus. From the *ectoderm*--responsible for skin, feathers, hair, the nervous system, the *mesoderm*--forming such things as the skeletal, muscular, circulatory, and reproductive systems, and the innermost layer, the *endoderm*--responsible for the digestive glands, digestive tract, and lungs, Sharon performed a comprehensive holistic procedure before cerebral synapse coding of the fetus began. Her successful implantation technique enabled the brain to develop with instinctive intelligence as well as inducing other anatomical enhancements. (*...magnificent Bo-Bos and substantial Po-Pos became standard equipment!*) Even before this discovery, scientists had known for solacles that Uμmpάrian offspring were born with many natural instincts. However, it was not until Sharon Defoulgar pioneered the innate intelligence species evolution concept that embryonic and prenatal attribute manipulation rocketed into mainstream science.

After the government had given its approval to the *Defoulgar Procedure*, Sharon began teaching her technique to other scientists and doctors. Medical institutes sponsored by the government were built to perform the implantation. Special schools with advanced and accelerated learning programs were built for the *super kids*. Virtually every family could have their child engineered before birth. Moreover, since the government was subsidizing the innate intelligence program, they issued guidelines for the implantation process. The Department of Social Development studied and researched the future needs of society concerning professionals, trades persons, technical experts, and blue-collar workers. In the beginning, the quotas established for each area of expertise had to be met before free choice implantation was allowed. And so it was, solacle after solacle. Soon, the super kids began producing offspring and the advances in intelligence grew exponentially.

Over the solacles, the average intelligence quotient grew at astronomical rates. The implantation process was refined and re-refined to the point that pregnancy became a period of prenatal programming. All previously learned information was nano-compressed and free-electron transferred to the synapses of each developing fetus. Instinctive intelligence grew and began to solve the problems of Uμmpár.

Health, education, welfare, and economic problems were being dealt with. Almost all death causing health concerns were eliminated by 14355.3. There remained only one obstacle preventing the peoples of Uμmpár from realizing lifelong happiness.

From the time an Uμmpárian was born, their living cells were dividing, replicating, and replenishing a growing, maturing body. Meaningful Life--*a finite period where a soul-possessing body embraces emotional experiences while aspiring to become a loving and caring spirit, which shall transcend the corporeal form vindicating God's decision to continue the species.* However, at some point the cellular division slows to almost a standstill. The body weakens while cellular degeneration steadily increases thus spawning atrophy. Death--*a dreaded and sometimes sorrowfully agonizing end to the most wonderfully ambitious dream God does allow.* Finally, old age, the last known biological enemy of life, was dealt the final staggering blow.

On 14,360.3, Alberto S. Bunhold, M.D., PhD, X.X., X.Y., applied for a patent on a drug he named *BIRTHSTAR*. Birthstar is an enzyme derived from gold. When injected into the bloodstream it acts as a microbiologic key. The enzyme travels throughout the body resetting cells allowing them to begin youthful replication again. Skin cells, heart cells, brain cells, and every other cell begin to replicate just the way they did when the body was a few solacles old. In a matter of several spans, the youthful skin returns, the cardiovascular system is rejuvenated, the brain becomes sharp, alert, thirsty for knowledge, and sexual urge becomes dominantly aggressive. Birthstar became the fountain of youth.

By design, Birthstar was absorbed through the cytoplasm into the cell nucleus. Once inside the nucleus, the chromosomes, which store metabolic information about the entire cell, were modified. Consequently, when mitosis occurs, the identical daughter nuclei receive an identical number of *modified* youth enabling chromosomes. These new cells begin to replicate at a constant rate. Aging became a forgotten term. Subsequently, the word was deleted from all institutional dictionaries and is currently only listed in the *Political Promise Handbook*.

Economic, and especially, recreational concerns were the most difficult to manage. The plain fact was that the people of the world wanted MORE! ...More food, more sex, and more fun.

Scientists set to work satisfying these desires. Hybrid seeds were developed that would grow and produce on a regular cycle throughout the solacle. It was amazing, despite neglect or intentional abuse, the plants would continue to thrive and produce bountiful harvests. Furthermore, processing techniques made it possible for vegetation to be formulated to look and taste as any other food. Soon, ninety-nine and nine-tenths percent of all consumable foods were processed vegetation. Consequently, livestock became zoo residents and were bred only to prevent their extinction or the production of the occasional porn--uh…the occasional sexual education video.

Scientists went on to develop a technique whereby matter could be created from a single molecule. For instance, a single molecule of steel could be transformed into a magnitude of steel matter. This had made the supply of iron, jewels, and every other conceivable raw material inexhaustible. The one exception was gold. It seemed that the gold on Uμmράr was different from other indigenous minerals. Scientists were perplexed.

It has been said that most of the significant advances in science and a good deal of the major discoveries are the result of random accidents. The discovery of this particular technique was no different.

Dr. P. Narf Zepalisto and a colleague were experimenting with a DNA sample absconded from the tattooed backside of an uppity Marzusian cocktail waitress. They were hoping to prove once and for all that her waste products did possess an undesirable odor. During the cloning process that was supposed to produce a reasonable facsimile of this devilish, pulse-pounding, *I've got to get a new jar of Hydrozine Jelly*, little bitch beast's butt, the good doctor inadvertently bumped a flask of liquid XP27 acid formulate. (*You don't know what liquid XP27 acid formulate is? Well…, let me tell you that this is some kind of real high-tech juice, pal. No, sir, you won't find this little goo in just any space chemical supply and bait shop. It is THE #1 hair growth tonic in the galaxy.*) Anyway…as it turned over, the flask began to spew into the cloning chamber completely saturating the DNA sample, which at that particular moment was absorbing a great deal of Neutron particles.

[POW!]

Suddenly, one gigantic hairy buttocks appeared and began consuming poor Dr. P. Narf Zepalisto. Dashing to his aid, the loyal colleague, Haiymen Zhoyer, heroically attempted to rescue him.

"…GRAB MY HAND!" Haiymen attempted to reach him by dangling from a catwalk railing.

"I CAN'T REACH--!" Dr. Zepalisto disappeared briefly. "…NOOOO...THE MUSCLES--!" Dr. Zepalisto struggled with all of his might. "…THEY'RE CONTRACTING!"

Alas, unable to resist the cheeks of fate, Dr. Zepalisto slipped beneath the raging thong and was gone.

Some time passed and the advancement of science continued. The loyal colleague did refine the matter creation process, and subsequently, claimed it for his own. Rumor had it that he retired very comfortably on a small world somewhere in the Benzova sector with none other than the Marzusian cocktail waitress.

The standard currency, gold, was distributed purely as a method to tabulate consumption. Gold had to be spent! It became an illegal offense to give, destroy, or discard gold. The reasoning was that only through consumption tracking would all nations be made equal. This equality removed the threat of war because anyone, anywhere, could have anything. Commonsensical Uμmpάrians soon came to question where all the gold was coming from. It was widely known that gold could not be created from a single molecule as other matter. The government offered no explanation.

In no time, the beings of Uμmρár had food, goods, and currency beyond imagination. They now wanted recreation to relieve the boredom. Scientists were frantic with concern. How can you enlist competition among beings that are genetically, intellectually, and economically equal. New games were invented, but were quickly mastered by everyone through programming techniques. Participants instinctively knew how to play. It was a natural trait to know what must be done to win. Stalemate after stalemate resulted with any competitive game. Then a little kid revealed a shinning glimmer of hope.

During one research term, Barbara F. Vargarin was working on a prototype intelligence game that was designed to measure the minute differences in intelligence among several subjects according to their verbal and physical responses. Next to her was Lytelwon, her youngest daughter. Lytelwon became curious about what her mother was doing way up there on the desk. She began trying to get higher so she might be able to take a look-see. While trying to climb even higher...Oops! Lytelwon squashed Space Rocket's tale.

Space Rocket is the Vargarin's feline pet. It got its name shortly after it was discovered in the afterburner section of the neighbor's space & sport vehicle. Fortunately, Space Rocket narrowly missed being incinerated because of condensation in the solid core fuel rod. She only received minor burns and became a loyal user of liquid XP27 acid formulate.

Oh yeah, to continue... Space Rocket very

quietly and politely clawed the hell out of Lytelwon's leg. Space Rocket's polite action caused Lytelwon to gently nudge her across the room. However, in doing so, Lytelwon lost her balance and tumbled harmlessly to the floor, visibly angered and frustrated. Barbara looked down and asked if she had failed at her task.

The star imploded in Barbara's head! She would invent a game where the object is to lose! This would be extremely difficult for beings that reflexively answer and respond correctly. Barbara sat for zlitons, then spans, programming computators to analyze every possible piece of data available with the intent being to produce such a game. Time after time, the computator's final analysis would be--SOLUTION UNKNOWN. The construction, design, and format of such a game continued to elude her. Barbara kept reliving in her mind the time that Lytelwon had failed in her attempt to climb up on the table. "Have I missed something? Why did she fail in her attempt?" Barbara mumbled to herself.

Finally, after ten solacles of research, six husbands, and numerous accidents involving oooohvucchinis, Barbara gave up and retired at the age of twenty-seven. She authored a final report, which the *Institute for Hopeless Research* forwarded to the heads of government. The sad truth was apparent. In her report, she concluded, from her own research and the research of others, that presently living individuals did not have the capacity for failure. The government quickly labeled the report classified and sent Barbara to a retirement valley where she continues to act as a failure consultant to major political parties.

To the government, the meaning was clear. There could never be any competitive or challenging hobbies.

32

There could be NO fun. In true government form, an independent commission was appointed to study the problem and make recommendations. This commission was to be made up of the most intelligent individuals. However, because of innate intelligence, most intelligent meant everyone! Therefore, only those individuals with names beginning with the letter **X** and ending in **Z** would be appointed. Consequently, by selected appointment, a small committee of one million citizens was formed.

The committee dedicated itself to the task. They worked long spans stopping only for food, naps, and oral sex. They were relentless in their quest, but to no avail. The outcome after twenty solacles of study, eight billion magnitudes of fast food, and forty-nine trillion penãrds of dental floss was that the governments should institute a program whereby the inhabitants of Uμmρár would be taught to be failures. Only in this way would there be any hope of developing a fun past time.

The sad truth eventually leaked out to all nations. One lawmaker by the name of Olle Flutterbee, known to talk a lot when intoxicated, had a slip of the tongue. Panic began to spread throughout the planet's population. Heads of state converged and held twenty-two solacles of talks on the subject. All of which were shown on public view screen, naturally. Mr. Flutterbee never talked again. This was mainly because a Rak-O-Tron Neuter 7 chastity insert severed his tongue. A loving husband had insisted that his wife implant the device while he was away at a *Blind Faith and Trust* seminar. Nevertheless, it was determined that the beings of Uμmρár had to come full circle. From savage to supreme intellect, and now, they must somehow return.

A plan was formulated by Uμmρár's Educational

Institute and the News Media Conglomerate to inspire the beings of Uμmpár to be less intelligent. By unanimous decree—individuals who could display less intelligence and act uncivilized would be revered as more advanced, more successful, more stupid, and get more news coverage than anyone else gets! The privilege of uninhibited sex would be banned except for the new upper-class. Also, reproduction would only be allowed for individuals with I.Q.s of less than eight thousand. A timetable and schedule was developed to reduce the I.Q. standard each solacle. An individual would have to score less than the standard each solacle to continue to enjoy the new upper-class status and the accompanying privileges. As a final method of developing a cast system, the amount of gold individuals received would be proportional to their intelligence quotient. Therefore, striving for ignorance and poverty became the distinction between the upper, middle, and lower-class. Competition was again the norm. By knowing less, you could have less, which was proof to everyone that you were of the highest order of life and should be envied by your fellow beings.

The government placed paramount importance on inspiring the new upper-class to continue to become more ignorant and uncivilized. Indeed, the government taught by example:

- Grants were awarded to groups wanting to study the mating habits of furniture.
- The scientific community was charged with researching and developing the most ingenious weapons by which Uμmpár's inhabitants could destroy themselves and the planet if they so desired.
- Only one checkout window was allowed to be open regardless of the number of customers waiting to be

served.

- Space licensing facilities were ordered to instruct applicants that the government issued SoSo Planetary Security Card did not qualify as a form of identification.

- The planetary telecommunications company was broken up into 270,000,000 entities selling communication services by the zliton. Furthermore, the UIRM (Uμmpάrian Intelligence Reduction Ministry) was charged with simplifying the billing.

- The UIRM enlisted the Archival Encyclopedia Company to re-write the tax code and Brainteaser Industries to develop simplified forms.

- All medical doctors were instructed to encrypt instructions to pharmacists.

- The government declared yet another celebration span to honor military veterans while the veterans themselves were at work.

The most important government creation was sports. This added another reward for those that had attained the coveted status of new upper-class. Games of competition were held with the object being to lose. The team that lost awarded each being attending the game, *attendance was mandatory,* one thousand magnitudes of gold. Thus, another exclusive means by which the new upper-class could unload their gold, have less, and become more prestigious.

Jerẹmy thought how hard it had been for him to know this and still flunk one-hundred and eightieth millennium social sciences. He was overcome with a feeling of pride as he blew his nose on the doorstep and kicked on the door in true upper-class fashion.

[KICK, THUMP, KICK!]

Eberhart had heard the pounding and arrived at the front door nervous and somewhat apprehensive. He took in a deep breath, opened the large Tiluminum wood door, and stood in awe at the sight of Jerẹmy Williams.

Jerẹmy was wearing a dingy white tee-shirt slit up one side with a rather large purple, hand painted, letter 'F' on the front and back. It carried the *inspected by seven* sticker, which meant it was of the very lowest quality, further flaunting the true upper-class fashion statement. Eberhart's head tipped slightly forward so as not to look directly into Jerẹmy's eyes, which were partially masked by a malfunctioning pair of mirrored, personalized, designer, wire rim radglasses. Eberhart slowly moved his eyes down Jerẹmy's frame examining every microscopic detail while making his descent. Jerẹmy's pants were faded to a pale orange. The gaping holes in the thighs and knees were definitely designer. Eberhart just could not stand it any longer. His feelings of hate were welling up inside and beginning to burn deep in his soul. He hated Jerẹmy for being so gloriously ignorant.

"Uh, [eeeearrrtt!] ...welcome...please, come in." Eberhart strained hard and passed gas as Jerẹmy entered.

Ignoring Eberhart's pitiful attempt to show good breeding, Jerẹmy simply walked, his head bobbing to imaginary rhythm, into the living room and flopped down on the sofa. "Sure is new and clean in here," Jerẹmy remarked. He displayed a snobbish manner that made Eberhart's blood boil.

Eberhart hated modern society and especially this dorkaduzian. He hated striving for ignorance and he hated having to spend gold every span. Nevertheless, how could he change the way that things were?

Eberhαrt could see that his mom and dad were in the kitchen. Jeręmy's belching and flatulent attitude alerted them to the realization that their honored guest had arrived. In humble, lower-class fashion, the Ghoηαdz' walked into their lavish, horribly prosperous, living room and greeted their guest. Hαzăr stretched out his hand as Jeręmy rose from the sofa.

Jeręmy winked and said, "Hi," as he walked past Hαzăr toward Tadφlŏn.

She dropped her eyes and said, "Hello, Jeręmy ...Welcome to our home."

Tadφlŏn was dressed in the oldest formal attire in her wardrobe. Its woven, pink-flowered design clung to her well-proportioned attributes. Coming close, Jeręmy's hand grazed her left breast. He was orbiting dangerously close to the rad. Foolish bravado lured him closer. He slid smoothly around her on a film of atoms nearly able to massage his wildest dream against cheeks of unattainable reality. Eberhαrt noted the proud look on his father's face. Indeed, Hαzăr was pleased to see a young male of such breeding compliment his wife. Eberhαrt suppressed his laughter as Jeręmy's ego, inexperienced and grossly unprepared for the SHM effect[9], instantaneously vaporized.

After crashing back to rest, Jeręmy extended his neck and configured his mouth into sort of a diagonal, oval, oblong shape. "UUUUUURRRRRRRRRPPPPPP!"

---

[9] Smokin' Hot Mom Effect -- sophisticated sexuality that induces elevated heart rates, gushing adrenaline flows, reduced cognitive ability, and uncontrollable libidinal reflex.

bellowed Jeręmy. He let out a belch that could have been heard down the street except for the fact that everything always goes up the street. *It's the law!*

Jeręmy appeared to be feeling very secure in the way he had been displaying his superior breeding and character. He certainly displayed a sign saying he was a real catch of the millennium for Julíenηe!

[Thump, Thump, Rumble, Rumble!]

Julíenηe came stumbling down the stairs. She definitely was overdoing the clumsy routine. Eberhαrt could not believe his eyes as he watched her. Julíenηe was really trying to impress Jeręmy with her manner and outfit. She wore a hot, iridescent puce, sleeveless blouse with dingy white bra straps draping over both shoulders. Her skirt was bright yellow with what appeared to be ketchup stains on the backside. Descending from her knees was a pair of mismatched socks, which disappeared into a pair of six-patch tennis shoes. Teasingly, she flaunted her dirty, broken fingernails in Eberhαrt's face as she headed toward Jeręmy.

"Hey, Jeręmy …Wow, your team jersey looks like shitova!" Julíenηe cooed.

"Just got it this span…wanted to surprise you," Jeręmy said.

Jeręmy had a reputation as a fine athlete. His team, *Ignoramians*, had lost every game for the last three solacles. The gold that they had gotten rid of was reported to be of the highest proportion on record from any school team.

Hαzăr bellowed in a fashion that was courteous to their guest. "Let's eat!"

Heading for the table, Jeręmy tripped over the footstool. "Threw ours out two solacles ago…hazardous."

38

Eberhart reluctantly followed and sat down while the rest stood waiting until Jeremy took his place. After Jeremy sat down, he picked up a paper napkin and blew his nose then quickly discarded it over his left shoulder. Eberhart assumed this to be some type of good luck custom.

"What do you think about the upcoming game with the Lobotomies?" Hazăr asked.

At that moment, Eberhart's mind began to dream about how it might have been about 10,000 solacles ago....

"Well....Hello there, young person!" said the attractive lady.

"Hello," the little male said.

"Are you lost...? Well, you had better come in while I try to find your mother. What's your name?" asked the lady.

"Porky."

"Hello...Security? Yes...There is a young male here with me in 2069. Yes...Could you please? Yes...She is probably worried sick." Turning back to the little stranger, the lady stated, "Porky...Wow...Now that's a funny name. Why do they...?"

Porky began to fidget with her computator.

"Don't touch the computator!" she said sharply. "Why don't you sit over there until your mother comes...Okay?"

However, Porky continued to persist in his efforts to investigate the computator.

"I said don't...Get away from there! Do not press that button! NOOOOOO...," she groaned in horror as Porky pressed the erase, format, crash, and burn key. She screamed loudly not really wanting an answer. "DO YOU KNOW WHAT YOU HAVE DONE? That was a new formula for gene implantation! ...You little twerp!" She paced slowly rubbing her head with both hands. "I'll be a son-of-a... Now it's gone forever... Solacles of work...GONE because of a little kid... You little BASTARD!" She grieved as her legs began slightly buckling. "BASTARD! I just do not believe this shitova! A kid named PORRRKKKYY destroys my dreams." Sternly and sarcastically she asked, "Well, twerp...Why are you called PORRRKKKYY? ...some perversion toward PIGOT[10]?"

"Damazar, lady! ...Just touch your stupid gadget and you go-off on my ass!" Porky waved his hands purposely taunting Sharon. "Is God's little gift OTR[11]?"

Ah yes, Porky Greenbalm saves the future beings of Uμmpάr from the evil Sharon Defoulgar's innate intelligence.

Eberhαrt was deep in the zone and now chuckling wildly to himself.

"EBERHART...You haven't been paying any attention to Jerẹmy's opinion of the Lobotomies," Julíenηe said with a scorn.

"Oh, yes I was!" Eberhαrt snapped back at her quickly. "I...was just thinking about Jerẹmy's fine breeding. Yes...Jerẹmy's ancestors."

"Whicccchhhh onnnneesuurrp?" Jerẹmy asked while scratching his groin.

---

[10] Pigot -- Perfectly straight and optically flat, alien bacon.
[11] OTR -- Uh...go ask your wife or girlfriend.

"Why...Sharon Defoulgar, of course!" Eberhart was feeling much satisfaction as his eye pierced through Jeręmy's fading smirk. Jeręmy's family ancestry was said to include distant relatives of Sharon Defoulgar.

"I don't remember hearing that name before," Jeręmy said turning his head away.

"Oh yes...," said Eberhart, "she pioneered innate intelligence."

"E-BER-HARRT," Hazăr moaned sharply. "You have homework, I think! So, you may be excused."

"Okay, Dad," Eberhart said softly as he got up and left the room.

Eberhart slammed the door then leaped onto his bed. Landing on his back, he stretched out his arm and grabbed the remote control to everything. He loved being in his room. His bed was very plush and comfortable. In the corner was spot's old bed. After all these solacles, Eberhart could just never let it go.

[Click] The door locked. [Click, Click] The ceiling view screen came on and the lights went dim.

"...Countrymen we must be steadfast in the face of increasing prosperity. Only through the efforts of our children can there be security and peace for the future."

"You're such a jerk," groaned Eberhart as President Barnstrom's address continued.

It had been rumored that Barnstrom had cheated on the mandatory pre-election I.Q. exam. Anonymous sources had reported that a Walkashon gazelda had been seen with Barnstrom before the administering of the exam. Gazeldas, believed to be the most stupid of all living creatures, are pets of almost all politicians. It is said that gazeldas often sit for spans watching rocks erode in the wind. Modern history books came to conclude that most politicians believe that having a gazelda, as a pet, would help them to become more ignorant. Consequently, the rumor went that a gazelda took the I.Q. exam for Barnstrom. However, Eberhart did not believe this rumor. Eberhart truly believed that Barnstrom was a total idiot.

Barnstrom was responsible for the continuing burden of gold as currency. It was proposed at one time to have pieces of paper printed and used as currency. Barnstrom immediately labeled this proposal as intelligent and said it might even lead to commonsense. That's all it took because Barnstrom and others made it into office riding the *Commy* scare.

Eberhart sometimes envisioned himself as a commonsense person. How nice it would be to carry a piece of paper labeled 500 magnitudes gold *instead* of carrying 500 magnitudes of gold. Not to mention the steel reinforced suit pockets that were required to keep the gold from tearing through and falling on your feet. Trying to prove accidental loss of gold is a very difficult task. The only legally defined method of getting rid of gold is by spending it. That is the law! Yes...becoming a commonsense person might not be that bad. Eberhart decided that he must know more about this bunch of radicals.

[Click!] Two million channels and there still was not anything on the ceiling viewer worth watching.

[Click, Click!] "And so, one particle lays on another...," said the narrator.

"Oh great...The mating habits of dust particles," said Eberhart. "I forgot about the Tax Waste and Abuse channel." Eberhart rolled over and soon nodded off.

CHAPTER TWO

COMMONSENSE WITH AN AGENDA...

[Clack, Clack, Clack!] The gavel echoed.

"Will the CPU... please, come to order," commanded the moderator.

The CPU (Commonsense People of Uμmρár) were meeting to discuss research being done on a random orbit launch assigned to investigate trans-dimensional energy stability. It was theorized that by initiating the implosion of a star, the resulting increase in gravity would stretch the time continuum fabric enough for a small space vehicle to pass through. If this were possible, the past could be changed at the appropriate time to correct the wrongs that were done and prevent the discovery of innate intelligence. It was concluded that the random orbit launch assigned to investigate trans-dimensional energy stability would be Uμmρár's only hope of reversing the damage caused by innate intelligence.

"It sure is great of you to bring me to the Dells!" Julíenηe beamed. "Mr. and Mrs. Dell are sure going to be happy when they get home!"

Jeręmy wanting to do his part for lowering intelligence and creating poverty had taken it upon himself to go about helping one family each term. Going down his list of names in *Homes Available for Vandalizing* magazine, he would pick a name and live at their home for the duration of their absence. While there with his friends, if any, they would try to make the home a little classier. This time he decided to bring Julíenŋe along so she could feel the sense of satisfaction you get from helping others too. Gleefully, they began to redecorate the Dell's home. Jeręmy brought along a few friends and the necessary decorating tools.

"10 cases of Zordon?"

"Check."

"12 dzogmeat pizzas?"

"Check."

"10 bags of pretzelons?"

"Check."

"The Dell's neighbor, Mary?"

"Check."

Jeręmy, Julíenŋe, and friends began to eat, drink, and make merry all night long. Consequently, the decorating was almost finished by morning. Piercing through a small hole in the wall made by a misplaced erection owned by a young male with a severe nerve problem, came the first rays of radlight. Zordon cans and pretzelons adorned the floor. Julíenŋe's eyes were already open and a half-asleep Jeręmy noted her focused examination of his groin. She had given him the earring that now was lovingly attached to....

[Clop, Clop, Clop!] Sounds from outside ruined a perfect lovemaking opportunity.

"Wake up! Wake up, Jeręmy!" said Julíenŋe

excitedly. "Someone's coming up the side walk!"

The Dell's had been to see the new glass bottle-blowing exhibit in Trintova. It supposedly was an exciting tour. Mary had said how excited they had been to be invited to participate in such an erotic exhibition.

"Quick! ...Everyone out!" Jeręmy whispered.

Not wanting to wait around for the thanks and the tears of appreciation, they hurried out the side door that wasn't there the span before.

"Eberhαrt... [Thump!] Open this door!" Tadφlŏn banged the door impatiently.

"Yes, Mom."

"If you've been gumming up another ULTRO vacuum cleaner hose, you're going to get it!" warned Tadφlŏn.

He opened the door. "No, Mom...I've been watching the public monitoring system." He turned and pointed at the viewscreen. "Mr. Edsel, next door, has been trying to remove a sporickle from Mrs. Edsel's--!"

"I've warned her about those Vegetator brand fertility aids malfunctioning." Tadφlŏn shook her head. "Anyway, you've got company at the door."

His eyes widened. "Okay, Mom. I'll be right down!" Eberhαrt wondered who it might be. He quickly threw himself together and hurried downstairs to meet his guest.

"Eberhαrt?" asked the stranger.

"Yes...," said Eberhαrt. He immediately knew the well-dressed female was a lab technician. "Come in." Eberhαrt was wondering, what did she want of him? "May I...?" asked Eberhαrt as he removed his guest's white coat that had the words *Lab Tech* stitched in blue thread above the left breast pocket. Hanging up the coat, he noticed a book with gold lettering in the left pocket. Not wanting to be nosy, he quickly pretended not to see it. Turning to her, "How may I help you?"

The young stranger explained that she was from BlackStellar Labs, an institute dedicated to primitive study. They went into the living room and Eberhαrt motioned for her to sit.

"What does BlackStellar Labs want with me?"

"Well," she began, "we have been selecting new members for our R.O.L.A.I.T.E.S. project and your I.Q. makes you a prime candidate for future employment. You will graduate in a few terms. Is that true?" She asked while smiling brightly.

"Unfortunately...yes," said Eberhαrt. He tried not to stare while soaking up her beauty.

"I'm sorry...My name is Mμreeη." She apologized for not introducing herself earlier. "We would like for you to come up to our research facility on the first span of next term."

Eberhαrt felt as though he already knew her. Oh boy, he was hopelessly taken with her and would have gladly rode ten Sporehogs[12], fought three Mazurian yellow metal fish[13], and taught at least one Uμmpάrian politician[14] the definition of the word promise in order to see this babe again.

"What does this position pay?" asked Eberhαrt.

"Forty-five magnitudes of gold per term," she said.

---

[12] Sporehog -- pig-like beast, made up entirely of vegetable matter that can photosynthesize the hell out of you.

[13] Mazurian yellow metal fish -- goldfish with attitude.

[14] Uμmpάrian politician -- butt with vocal chords.

"...How much?" Eberhαrt could not begin to believe his ears.

Mμreeη repeated the rate of pay once more. Eberhαrt became very uncomfortable. Was distrust building in his mind? The minutiae of a stranger's compensation offer did deserve a higher level of scrutiny. ...Didn't it? Thoughts of illegality raced through his mind. Possibly, he would be involved with Nahrμvian gold smelters, Etheroznian video evangelists, or maybe even Quatojan insurance agents. Oh no! What had he done to draw upon himself such horrible prospective employers? What evil awaited him for such a pittance of a salary?

"Eberhαrt! Eberhαrt...are you okay?" asked Mμreeη.

"Yes...Excuse me... My mind was wandering," said Eberhαrt. "My I.Q. is over 9500...," he assured her. "That low pay is for someone graduating near the bottom of their class."

"That's it--you can take it or leave it," said Mμreeη smiling. "You are aware, no doubt, that it is against the law to refuse an employment offer."

"I'll be there," said Eberhαrt. He remained confused and very concerned.

Eberhαrt escorted Mμreeη to the door and handed her the lab coat she had worn. She could see his eyes glaring at the book in the pocket. Mμreeη quickly withdrew the book and tossed to him.

"Here...take a look through this before you come," said Mμreeη. Awkwardly, it bounced off his thumb and struck his nose. She giggled!

Mμreeη left while Eberhαrt, still smarting some, could not wait to investigate this strange gift.

R.O.L.A.I.T.E.S. Past, Present, and Future was the title printed on the front of the book in gold. Eberhart knew that this certainly was an illegal offense because the only legal use of gold was as currency. Nevertheless, Eberhart could not wait to start reading it, so he quickly sped off to his room before turning a page.

"Bye," said Julíenηe bounding from the vehicle toward the entrance to her home.

"SEE YA," said Jerȩmy loudly.

Jerȩmy sped away up the street at maximum thrust thinking about Julíenηe, sports, and his life.

"I'm an unhappy person," he thought aloud. "...But why?"

Sadly, Jerȩmy did not have a clue to his unhappiness. I mean the guy had everything cherished by modern society--a broken down home, an old vehicle, a test verified low I.Q., dirty fingernails, and a lower-class kisψm.

Why am I unhappy? What is wrong with me? Julíenηe...oh yeah, I really like her. Is she the only good thing in my life at this point? Do I really love her or am I infatuated because she still has that *New AGV Smell*? He asked himself these questions over and over again.

Cruising through the lower-class neighborhoods made him feel funny. Jerȩmy pondered his plight as he surveyed the neat, luxurious homes, the new vehicles, the well-dressed kids, and the nicely manicured lawns. It occurred to him that society had truly taken a dump on these people and he felt ashamed for feeling so unhappy. As Jerȩmy navigated through a virtual cesspool of prosperity, his mind drifted back to where it all started about 10,000 solacles ago....

"Yes...here he is," said the lady.

"We couldn't find his mother, Dr. Defoulgar," stated the security officer.

"Doesn't matter anyway...He just screwed up solacles of research." Sharon's voice sizzled with anger. "Take the little S.O.B. to detention until the police arrive."

"Yes, Doctor...Let's go kid," said the security officer. He pushed Porky toward the door.

After placing handcuffs on Porky, the security officer pushed and shoved him out of the lab and down the hall. All the while Porky Greenbalm was assessing the situation in his mind and was deciding on his next plan of action. Aggressively, Porky began resisting. He was hoping to delay their trip to detention just long enough for an escape opportunity to present itself.

"Stop squirming kid," said the security officer. "I'm from the CPU...I'm here to get you out!"

Porky ceased his resistance and began pondering this new development. Was the officer lying? Could this just be a trick to get him to divulge some critical information?

"What's your name?" asked Porky.

"Woodeye Williams," replied the officer.

"Woodeye?" repeated Porky.

"I know kid...but come on...you're basically named Oink!"

Yes, Jeremy had secret dreams about changing society. Unknown to him were the parallel dreams that he and Eberhart shared. One was poor, the other one rich, and both very unhappy with the present social norms.

[Chug chug, spit spit, rattle rattle, boom boom, Pissssssssssss!] Jeręmy's craft groaned and shuddered to a motionless state.

"Damazar...What's wrong now?" Jeręmy moaned aloud with frustration.

[Click click, earrll earrll, KaPOW!] The motors refused Jeręmy's requests to start or go any farther. He was becoming anxious while a dark gray was rapidly becoming the color of the cool evening air.

"That's all I need...To break down in a neighborhood of multi-million mag gold homes," mumbled Jeręmy. "Shitova...I had better leave this thing and get out of here."

Jeręmy slammed the hatch shut and headed off. Looking around, the nervous trembling was beginning. He walked as quietly as he could, stopping only to obscure himself when a face would appear in one of the many windows adorning the vast array of lower-class structures. Jeręmy had never felt so afraid when suddenly....

"Hey, rich kid," said the voice. A hand grabbed Jeręmy's shoulder. "You're a little out of your neighborhood aren't you?"

Scarily, other voices in the darkness began taunting Jeręmy. As he became more frightened, the warm aqueous liquid now trickling down his leg went unnoticed. He tried to muster all the courage within himself. After what seemed like an eternity, Jeręmy Williams uttered his first words.

"Cr-aft...bb-roke...dd-own...."

"What's in your pockets?"

"NNo-thing...."

Jeręmy continued to assemble every ounce of

strength he had within himself. Then, he quickly dispatched that strength to his legs, grabbed his backside, and ordered his feet to haul some ass. Frantically, Jeręmy ran as fast as he could, the muted darkness flowing smoothly around him. He sliced through the evening air not knowing where he was going or even if he could get there from where he was. He was truly scared. What would they do to him? ...Julíenꞑe! Why was he thinking of her now? The silence of the night, a passive comrade, allowed his ears to soak up the sound waves emanating from behind him. Almost instantaneously, the sound waves were analyzed by Jeręmy's brain and identified as footwear pounding the planet beneath him. Faster! Feet...go faster! Silence continued to remain a spectator permitting Jeręmy's ears to absorb an increasing amount of the sound waves. His brain quickly processed the waveforms, performed a trend analysis, and issued its conclusion--THEY'RE GAINING ON YOU!

"Ugh!" expelled from Jeręmy's lungs as he felt the solid planetary material suddenly rise up and abruptly end his journey.

"Stay down and you won't get damaged," ordered the voices.

Hands began tugging at Jeręmy's pockets. He began to squirm and battle what seemed like an endless barrage of extremities. Suddenly, one stronger than the rest collided with his head rendering him unconscious.

"...You, okay?" came a voice. "You, okay?"

Again, Jeręmy was touched by hands. However, this time they were gently patting his face as the voice continued to encourage him to respond.

"Jeręmy, are you okay?"

"E-ber-hart?"

"Yes, Jeremy ...Let me help you up."

Eberhart gently helped Jeremy to his feet. Jeremy was a bruised up mess of cuts and scrapes. The sluggishness of his movements and the way he flinched when trying to move indicated to Eberhart that he ached all over.

"Wow, you got it bad," said Eberhart holding in a chuckle.

Jeremy had been the victim of a bunch of robbers. His pockets were filled with gold. He even had a few bags tied around his neck.

"What happened?" asked Eberhart.

"My craft broke down," said Jeremy. His legs wobbled like gelatin, barely enabling him to stand.

"Come on," said Eberhart. He helped Jeremy to his AGV that was parked nearby. "Do you wanna go file a report?"

"No, it's not worth it," responded Jeremy. "I didn't see their faces and I'm not sure of how many attacked me."

"What are you ever going to do with all that gold?" Jeremy did not answer right away. He seemed to be contemplating more than just this one particular incident. The embodiment of innate intelligence and its impact on the complexity of his species' existence had brought his superior albeit fragile psyche to the brink. He stared off in the direction of the luxurious lower-class homes contemplating a philosophy derived solely to offset mistakes of arrogance and vanity. Finally, he turned back and stared directly into Eberhart's eyes.

"To the rad with it!" said Jeremy. He held up the bags of gold.

"Let's go get something to eat," he stated. "It's my treat! What's more? I want some good clothes; let's go shopping afterwards."

"They must have hit you pretty hard," said Eberhart totally surprised by these statements.

"Yeah, but I know what I'm saying," said Jeremy angrily. "I'm tired of being dirty, acting stupid, and not having a particle elimination chamber to go piss in!"

"But you've got it all, Jeremy!" Eberhart began to tease. "From birth, the entire population of Uμmρár strives to attain the status of the upper-class," said Eberhart in a jokingly, sarcastic tone. "Just kidding," confessed Eberhart. "I too am tired of the way that society has misjudged where we are, told us where we should go, loaded us onto transports, and sent us rocketing toward a destination of ignorance and poverty."

"Damazar, Eberhart! That is the longest sentence that I have ever heard. Especially, from someone that wasn't trying to sale me a used AGV or inspect my prostate with a two stage, self igniting, constant thrust, solar insertion device!" Jeremy was happily stunned by Eberhart's oration.

"Come on, let's shop till we drop and eat till we...uh... aren't hungry anymore!" said a laughing Eberhart.

CHAPTER THREE

THE DRUDGERY OF SHOPPING...

[Knock, Knock, KNOCK!]

"JULIENNE...WAKE UP, IT'S 90:30!" barked Tadφlŏn. "You have to go shopping with me this span."

"Wwhhhaaa...mmmmmnn...Okay, Mom," replied Julíenηe sleepily.

[Click!] Julíenηe pressed a button on the remote control to everything and the shower came on. [Click, Click!] The wardrobe closet opened up and the clothes rack slowly extended out.

"Hmm... What shall I wear?" Julíenηe thought aloud. "This red jump suit looks nice. No, we're not flying this span."

Julíenηe continued to ruffle through her vast array of body coverings.

How about my purple mini? she thought. "No. ...too early to show hair. Maybe this diamond studded bodysuit?" she mumbled sleepily. Julíenηe held up the suit in front of the mirror. "Mmmm... Yes, I like it!"

Julíenηe hung up her suit and went into the shower room. [Click!] Lying down on the shower bed, the jet streams of warm, slightly radioactive, cleansing liquid began moving over and under her nude body. The droplets of de-ionized liquid bounced off her soft tender skin. She easily began to relax while the waves flowed over the heightened nerve endings close to the surface of her body. She was still tired from the night before and was not really up to a full span of heavy duty shopping. This was supposed to be a thousand-mag shopping trip! As the liquid became a warmer and a more gentle spray, Julienηe closed her eyes and drifted off to a faraway place about 10,000 solacles ago....

"Quick--in here!" said Rosetta to the young kid and the security officer. "What took you so long?"

"I had to wait while my badge was checked and then I couldn't find the right lab," said Woodeye.

"The Enforcers just got here and they were headed for detention." Rosetta turned to scan the corridor.

"I'm sure glad to see you, Rosetta," said Porky.

"Yeah, you too," replied Rosetta.

"...you know Woodeye here?" asked Porky nodding toward Williams.

"Yeah...you do too! ...He's okay."

"No time for chit-chat folks...let's get going," said Woodeye interrupting them.

The three of them quickly exited the maintenance closet and hurried down the corridor to an air ventilation grating. Rosetta speedily unfastened the grating using an ERTD.[15] (*pronounced er-dee*) Porky and Woodeye set

---

[15] Earanium Radial Torquing Device -- screwdriver powered by an isotope of Walkashan gazelda earwax, which is always in the excited state.

the grate aside and the three of them slipped inside. Once inside, Porky and Woodeye pulled the grating up then back into place allowing Rosetta to fasten it again using her ERTD.

"We've got to get to the other side of this complex," Rosetta informed them.

"Wait! ...Sorry, it's okay. I thought I had lost the layout drawing of the ventilation ducts," said Woodeye. He handed the drawing to Rosetta. She quickly unfurled it.

"Okay...Yes...here we are at sub-level four," said Rosetta. "We need to get to this junction, turn here, then on to here, in order to access the elevator shaft," instructed Rosetta. She traced the proposed path on the drawing. "Okay...I'll lead the way."

"Wait!" Porky grabbed Rosetta's arm and whispered, "...you said I know him?"

Rosetta breathed a few words into Porky's ear and pushed on past to lead the way.

Slowly they began, Rosetta, Woodeye, and Porky. Three mercenaries, all were trying to extract themselves from the target area after successfully destroying the Innate Intelligence Project. They proceeded on as quickly and as quietly as they could. All the while, Rosetta noted that Woodeye was being overcome by the sweet smell of her perfume.

"Owwl!" she moaned. Woodeye nipped at her butt.

"Get going...Can't you crawl any faster?" needled Woodeye.

Rosetta ignored Woodeye's childish horseplay and picked up the pace. She knew that there still was danger ahead. They soon reached an intersection of ducts.

Voices were coming from the rightmost duct.

"You search sub-level four and we'll go to three," said the voice.

"Damazar...They must have made it to detention already," whispered Rosetta. "...This way."

The trio's knees were beginning to get sore as they continued to crawl toward their destination. They had been making their way through the duct for nearly one-hundred and forty-five zlitons. Although the duct's physical dimensions had not changed, the increasing fatigue was making it seem more cramped and confined. Finally, far up ahead, a light shown through a grid.

"There it is!" announced Rosetta.

The light came closer and closer as they crawled faster toward it. Their knees now aching and raw from the constant sliding against the metal wall of the duct did little to slow their relentless pace toward the grid. The light grew brighter and continued to illuminate the duct as they came to within a few penãr[16] of the grid.

"Okay...Let's rest," said Rosetta.

"What's on the other side?" asked Porky. He was the farthest away from the grid.

"An elevator shaft," answered Rosetta.

"Huh?" grunted Woodeye.

"We can get on top of the elevator here and ride it to ground level," explained Rosetta.

Rosetta took out her ERTD and quickly unfastened the grid. Quietly and gently, she passed the grid to Woodeye and then on to Porky. Rosetta peered down the elevator shaft spotting the elevator down below.

"Well? Do you see it?" asked Woodeye. He slid

---

[16] Penãr – unit of measure equal to twelve Earth inches.

up next to her.

"There it is," she said.

"How are we going to get down there?" asked Woodeye.

"We can jump to the cable and slide down...how else?" said Rosetta. She flashed a little grin.

"Oh yeah...Thanks!" said Woodeye. Woodeye leapfrogged over to the cable and slid down to the top of the elevator. "...Jump! I'll catch you!"

"Okay," replied Rosetta. She dropped her legs over the side of the elevator shaft. "Here I come!" Rosetta slid out of the ventilation duct while at the same time the elevator began to rise.

"Uhhh!" moaned Woodeye as she landed squarely on his chest knocking the wind out of him.

"Come on, Porky!" said Rosetta excitedly.

Porky leaped forward just as the elevator sheared past the duct opening. Landing on his stomach, his face mashed hard against her lower abdomen. She looked down at him and waited zlitons for him to look up. "Hey…are you injured or just doing a little research down there?"

Ah yes, thought Julíenηe, if only--

"COME ON, JULIENNE," shouted Tadφlŏn interrupting her dream. "You're just like your father...In the bathroom for zlitons."

"Yeah right, Mom," muttered Julíenηe shutting off the cleansing liquid. "Dad wouldn't be in the bathroom so much if you would stop your incessant nagging!" shot back Julíenηe.

"That's enough, young lady!" Tadφlŏn scolded her. "I DO NOT nag your father! I'm making him *better!*

59

Okay? So get yourself together--NOW!"

Julíenηe stepped inside the UV drying chamber briefly then hurried out to put on her diamond-studded bodysuit. After sliding into the suit, she sat down at the cosmetic station and began applying her make-up. She brushed a little green powder on her cheeks and then proceeded to paint her lips a brilliant orange. Then, using her rotary eyebrow trimmer, she began trimming the hair above her eyes. When she had thinned it to her satisfaction, she began to apply cosmetic adhesive under her eyes. Closing her eyes and tilting her head back to a forty-five degree angle, she began to sprinkle diamond dust onto the area where she had applied the adhesive. The dust settled onto the adhesive and formed sparkling triangles around her eyes.

"Hurry up, Julíenηe!" coaxed Tadφlŏn.

"Okay-- I'm coming!" replied Julíenηe sharply.

[Click!] The beauty station slowly withdrew into the wall as Julíenηe tossed the remote control to everything on the bed.

Tadφlŏn apparently was growing more impatient downstairs while waiting for Julíenηe to come down.

"Okay...I'm ready!" announced Julíenηe reaching the bottom of the stairs.

"It's about time--WOW!" said Tadφlŏn. "You sure aren't dressed for shopping," noted Tadφlŏn. "Do you have to show the entire planet how miserably prosperous we are?"

"Tough, Mom... I'm beginning to like being prosperous."

"Oh yeah...Well, we'll see when you're on your own and have to lug these heavy bags of gold every span shopping by yourself," stated Tadφlŏn. "Now come on and help me get these bags to the AGV."

Julíenηe helped Tadφlŏn carry bag after bag of gold to the craft and load it aboard. Poor Julíenηe was getting very tired after the fifteenth fifty-magnitude bag. Finally, the AGV was fully loaded and they were ready to embark on their span's worth of consumption.

"I hate shopping," moaned Julíenηe. "Why doesn't the government issue paper currency instead of having everyone haul around bags of gold?"

"Shut-it, Julíenηe!" Tadφlŏn quickly snapped. "Do you want someone to hear you?" asked Tadφlŏn not really wanting an answer.

"That's all we need is for someone to hear you and label us as commonsense people."

"Mom...but this is stupid!" said Julíenηe sincerely.

"Well...it's supposed to be!" replied Tadφlŏn looking very puzzled.

"Ah, Mommm...when are you ever--?"

"I DO NOT want to HEAR any more of that kind of TALK, young lady!" exploded Tadφlŏn.

"Okay, Okay...I'm sorry!" responded Julíenηe. She felt very frustrated.

The trip uptown to the shopping center usually took about twenty to thirty zlitons. The AGV was filled with gold, wrapped in silence, and likely would remain so for the duration of the trip. Julíenηe pondered the future while she observed the scenery embellishing their journey.

Traveling uptown was in and of itself not a bad experience. The Ghoηɑdz' resided in the country and the trip took them through some of the most beautiful territory on the planet. Cruising just about one-penãr above the planet at a speed equivalent to approximately 0.4 penãrds per zliton (ppz), Julíenηe really enjoyed scanning the planet for wildlife and observing the vegetation. Off at a distance, she could see herds of gazeldas mating, but wondered what humping Utrovian trees had to do with furthering their species. It has been said that the smell of the Utrovian tree arouses the creature and that one gazelda would sow its seed on the Utrovian tree hundreds of times per span. Scientists wondered what effect, if any, this had upon the tree and the beast.

Julíenηe especially liked the forests of Uμmpár. The Utrovian tree, which is the prominent variety of tree on the planet, was really her favorite. It is a very stately specimen. Reaching nearly three-quarter penãrd toward the heavens when mature, the Utrovian possesses a unique, however unfortunate, quality. Its bark is richly saturated with a substance known as Xenofolic Protein Acid, which is the main ingredient in XP27. When you consider the fact that XP27 is THE #1 hair growth tonic in the galaxy *and* Xenofolic Protein Acid is used in conjunction with Neutron radiation to create a mag of anything from just one parent molecule, you begin to fully understand the reason why this great towering specimen is being steadily harvested. ...Some say to the point where it may become extinct in just a few hundred solacles. Thinking about these things made Julíenηe sad.

The government had quickly discredited the CPU's research regarding the possible Utrovian extinction, but Julíenηe was convinced that their numbers were decreasing just from observing them daily on the way to the uptown shopping centers. Far off on the horizon, the dust billowed high into the sky. Julíenηe knew this was caused by the ten story high Utrovian automated harvesters that constantly and relentlessly roam the planet ravaging it of this precious resource. She wished that Xenofolic Protein Acid had never been discovered. She would have much preferred bald anything and mags of nothing than to see these beautiful trees, the antennas of the planet, steadily devoured by the Utrovian harvesters. ...Time passed quickly for her as she wondered about many things.

Closing rapidly on the Starfire Mall, the journey was nearing its end. Tadφlŏn soon began scanning for parking stations. She quickly slowed the craft to parking velocity and turned hard to snap up a pad vacated by another shopper. This was their lucky period. The pad was just steps from a traverse tube station. (*The traverse tube works much the same way as the delivery system at your local drive-in banking facility.*) Julíenηe could see that her mom was beginning to lose her anger and was beginning to feel somewhat happy by the time she had parked the craft and powered it down.

"That was great!" said Jerȩmy smiling.

"Who would've believed it?" said Eberhαrt shaking his head.

"What?"

"...You! The upper-class acting and eating like the lower-class," answered Eberhαrt.

"Well...I have to confess that I really don't like acting stupid," responded Jerȩmy.

"Well, I really don't like carrying 500 magnitudes of gold around with me every span either," countered Eberhαrt.

"Okay then...what are WE going to do?"

"Read this and find out!" Eberhαrt handed Jerȩmy the book given him by the cute lab tech.

"R.O.L.A.I.T.E.S... What's that?" Jerȩmy looked puzzled.

"Come on, let's go somewhere and you can read it," said Eberhart. He rose and tugged on Jerȩmy's arm.

Eberhart practically had to lead Jerȩmy to the AGV because he had become very curious and had already started reading the book. After they had entered the craft, Eberhart appeared to be thinking for a moment about where they should go to relax and talk about the subject that Jerȩmy was now so deeply engrossed with. Eberhart finally decided on the destination. He quickly powered up the engines and maneuvered the craft onto the planetary freeway. Within zlits,[17] the two hopped-up Zinctar Twin Reactor engines were at maximum thrust propelling them at 0.8 ppz toward Eberhart's, yet undisclosed, secluded hideaway.

They had been at maximum thrust for nearly twenty zlitons and Jerȩmy had yet to lift his eyes from the pages of that book. Eberhart seemed pleased that Jerȩmy found the book so interesting. Could it be possible that this once envied, once hated, upper-class creature and he might become comrades in search of a better way of life? Might it then be possible that they may even become friends? Eberhart pondered these things as he began easing up on the engines while reversing gravitational polarity in order to slow the craft to maneuvering speed. Their journey was nearing an end.

The craft turned smoothly toward the entrance of a yet to be harvested Utrovian forest. Eberhart was an excellent pilot and was able to maneuver the craft quickly through the forest bringing it to rest near a small white

---

[17] Zlit -- unit of time equal to one Earth second.

building that he had played around during his youth.

"Where are we?" Jeręmy finally looked up from the book. "It's scary here," continued Jeręmy while not quite sure what to expect.

"This is the place where I played as a child," answered Eberhart. "Dad and mom used to come here every term to church."

"This...is a church?"

"Yes...Not many people come here anymore," replied Eberhart. "I guess people became dismayed when term after term the church continued to give them more and more gold." Eberhart paced in a circle looking down or away, but not at Jeręmy. "I remember as a child that my mom and dad felt strongly about attending church, but came away feeling more hopeless and more prosperous than before they went. I believe that the church was meant to help lift your burden rather than add to it." Eberhart looked at Jeręmy. "Anyway, no one comes here anymore. No one...except for me that is. If only I could change...."

"So...are you going to join?" asked Jeręmy. He curiously awaited an answer.

"Yes...The CPU seems to have ideas that are logical and they may be able to do something with them," answered Eberhart after a moment of thought.

"This R.O.L.A.I.T.E.S. stuff is pretty scary," responded Jeręmy. "I mean...time travel and being able to alter the events of the past...Well, you know what I mean. What if they screw things up worse than they are?"

"I am going to BlackStellar Labs in a few spans," said Eberhart firmly while ignoring Jeręmy's concerns. "Go with me?"

"I don't know...," replied Jeręmy, "I could really

get into trouble."

"Come on," said Eberhart scrubbing his foot on the ground. "Or are you convinced that wearing old clothes and acting like a cocky idiot are really traits of a superior, civilized being?"

"Okay! Okay...I'll go with you," said Jeręmy finally conceding.

"Let's leave the gold here and look around," said Julíenηe. She scanned the parking area with a new sense of curiosity.

"Surely, you know that we can't leave gold unattended in the parking area," said Tadφlŏn.

"Well...I mean no one is going to take it, Mother!" argued Julíenηe.

"Don't get intelligent with me, young lady...If the authorities see this craft loaded with gold and find us wandering around, they might just think we're attempting to dump it," said Tadφlŏn. She continued to lecture Julíenηe about the finer points of the law regarding the transportation, security, and disposition of gold. "Do you want to carry and extra 500 mag fine with you this span? Well...do you?"

"No!" Julíenηe angrily answered.

"That's good! Now let's get our gold to the traverse station!"

Tadφlŏn extended the access incline and motioned for Julíenηe to help her unload the gold. Again, bag after bag, they carried their gold back and forth from the AGV to the traverse station. However, they were careful to stagger their trips. They did not want to leave any gold unattended. It is a very serious offense to abandon gold. The punishment is a long-term prison sentence or at least

66

a heavy fine. Finally, they had finished unloading. Tadφlŏn locked the AGV and returned to the traverse station where Julíenηe was keeping their currency company. Tadφlŏn kissed Julíenηe on the forehead for whatever reason. Next, she proceeded to select the consumption center level that the traverse tube would transport them to and stop.

Julíenηe was at least consoled by her mother's choice of level sixty-nine as their day's shopping level. Level sixty-nine boasted many a shop that catered to the upper-class. These shops were stocked with the latest hand-me-downs from other quadrants where the people were to ignorant to purchase such poor quality at extraordinarily high prices. However, in order to shop these trendy stores you must have a test verified low I.Q.

Intelligence Quotient Verification was another technological and social tool designed to keep the poor and the rich distantly separated. This meant you must possess a C.R.E.D.I.T.[18] chip in order to purchase anything in the trendy upper-class shops. Major companies authorized by the government issued these chips to a very select few. The requirements to receive such a chip were very stringent. The main requirement was a test verified I.Q. below 99. The second requirement was that your financial position was such that you had very few assets. If you met these requirements you could enjoy the privilege of not having to carry currency--gold, pay very high interest on your purchases--another exclusive means by which the upper-class was able to get rid of their gold, have less, and become more prestigious,

---

[18] C.R.E.D.I.T. -- Credentials Regarding Education and Detailed Intelligence Testing.

and get a membership credential at your favorite video rental center without a letter from your lawmaker.

"Look, Mom! …Another second-hand shop!"

"I see it...I heard that another one would be opening soon," responded Tadφlŏn.

"Let's take a look inside," said Julíenηe excitedly.

"Dear, you know that a credit chip is required to shop there," reminded Tadφlŏn.

"I do!" replied Julíenηe. "I've got Jeręmy's."

"What are you doing with Jere--?"

"Come on!" said Julíenηe. She pulled Tadφlŏn inside.

Tadφlŏn gave in to Julíenηe's enthusiasm and they both went inside leaving two push transports loaded with gold sitting next to the entrance.

"WOW...A MANUAL TUNER MONITOR!" said Julíenηe. "And Mom... Look over there...*Inspected by seven* is on every garment!"

Julíenηe was being carried away with the fact that they were rubbing dirty elbows with the upper-class. Unfortunately, Julíenηe and Tadφlŏn stuck out like an early morning gazelda penis preparing for a span's worth of Utrovian tree humping. Their clean, neat appearance and their fresh, recently manufactured, high quality apparel were a dead give away to the salesperson--they were hopelessly PROSPEROUS. The raggedly, fashionable saleslady spotted them immediately and wasted no time in letting them know that they were not welcome.

"I'm sorry, ladies...but you will have to leave," she said.

"We have a credit ch--," said Julíenηe.

"You...also have two transports of gold with a

security agent by them too!" said the saleslady.

"Oh my goodness--*the gold!*" Tadφlŏn grabbed Julíenηe and began dragging her toward the entrance. "That's ours, sir!" said Tadφlŏn excitedly. "A lady dropped her AGV access key and we were just returning it."

Tadφlŏn apparently hoped the security officer would believe her story and not fine them.

"May I see your I.Q. and Identity holocards?" The officer waited impatiently.

Tadφlŏn and Julíenηe began digging through their PECs[19] obeying the officer's request. Unfortunately, Julíenηe was so excited that she allowed Jeręmy's credit chip to fall out onto the officer's patrol cart.

"What's this? A credit chip...Hey!" The officer quickly concluded that these two ladies likely had stolen the chip.

Julíenηe realized her misfortune. Visions burst into her psyche--they would soon be on their way to prison if she didn't think of something fast.

[Sling...Smack! THUMP!]

Julíenηe had quickly piloted a bag of gold through 720 degrees of motion striking the officer quite firmly with it. This had a very negative effect upon the officer and cannot be fully appreciated by anyone who has never had fifty magnitudes of gold, traveling at two penãrds per zliton, impact with their face. The officer responded as expected. His teeth shattered while his jawbone crumbled. Shockwaves cascaded throughout his skeletal frame generating numerous micro fractures concluding with his body being recoiled backwards. Tadφlŏn was

---

[19] PEC – personal effects container.

speechless and Julíenηe was quite astonished. The superior strength and durability of the bag that held the gold was unbelievable!

"Let's get out of here!" advised Julíenηe picking up their personal effects.

"Huh...?" muttered Tadφlŏn.

"We've got to get out of here before more security arrives!" Julíenηe jerked her mother by the arm down the aisle. They ran as fast as they could frantically trying to avoid bumping into other security officers while locating the nearest traverse tube.

"Quick! Get in!" ordered Julíenηe. She firmly pushed a confused and disbelieving Tadφlŏn into the traverse tube.

"Julíenηe...Do you know what we have done?" asked Tadφlŏn.

"Mom...Don't lose it now! If we can get to the AGV and get away from this center, then we might make a clean escape."

The traverse tube whisked them away at high velocity toward parking pad 1467903, Z lot, aisle 19587, sector 5820, which was very close to *Clem's Space Chemical Supply and Bait shop*.

"Quickly, Mom," said Julíenηe. She pushed Tadφlŏn out of the tube and directed her toward their AGV. "...Access key?"

"What?" said a somewhat confused Tadφlŏn.

"Your access key...Get it ready!"

"Okay...Right!" Tadφlŏn was now finally getting a grip on the situation.

Julíenηe and Tadφlŏn hurried as fast as they could to the AGV being careful to stay out of the sight of the roving security officers. However, as Tadφlŏn fumbled

70

with the access key, the security officers were sweeping the area and quickly approaching.

"Hurry! Hurry!" begged Julíenηe.

"I'm trying, but the lock is...There...Got it!" said Tadφlŏn. They were very relieved that the access incline was extending.

Julíenηe and Tadφlŏn quickly entered the AGV and retracted the access incline. Frightened and excited, they both crouched low in the AGV and watched the security patrols roam the area.

"We're in one huge mound of shitova now! Thanks, Julíenηe," said Tadφlŏn angrily.

"I'm sorry, Mom...but I didn't mean for all of this to happen," responded Julíenηe. She was saddened by the recent events and by the fact that she had made her own mother a participant in a criminal act. "But I hate being labeled prosperous, Mom. We're no different except for the gold we have to carry and the clothes that we wear."

"I know, dear...I'm sorry too, but that's just the way society is now," said Tadφlŏn. She certainly understood the deep feelings that her daughter was having. "If you can't do anything about it you just have to accept things as they are."

Tadφlŏn continued trying to comfort her daughter while at the same time Julíenηe was mustering courage within herself. The realization of the criminal acts that they had just committed was beginning to sink in while the prospects of making a clean escape appeared to be diminishing.

Peering out the viewports of the AGV seemed to support her concerns. The area was a virtual traffic jam of security personnel. Julíenηe was now sure that escape from the consumption center parking area would be very difficult, if not impossible. Likely, she reasoned, that every craft would be stopped and possibly searched before they would be allowed to leave the area. For now, the AGV would provide a sanctuary for them to hide. Unfortunately, the parking area would later start to empty as shoppers ended their span's consumption and returned to their dwellings. Transportation vehicles still in the parking area would most likely come under greater scrutiny.

Tadφlŏn must have been evaluating the options that were available to them as well. She was nervously stroking Julíenηe's head. Julíenηe really hoped that a plan that didn't involve a lengthy prison term would present itself soon.

"Julíenηe...," said Tadφlŏn interrupting her daughter's sobbing. "Come on...You're my protector... Don't cry."

"I'm sorry, Mom...I'm so-oh sorry," responded Julíenηe.

"It's okay... Dry your eyes and put on your cerebral energizer," said Tadφlŏn in a comforting tone. "We've little time... I need you to concentrate that creativity you have hidden inside of you on a means of escape."

Julíenηe brushed away her tears, smiled at her mom, and stretched out on the floor of the AGV to begin contemplating their plan of action. She thought... What would Jerẹmy do if he were here? And, how would Eberhαrt handle a situation like this one? Julíenηe recalled how Eberhαrt had gotten his friends to moogle her that time when her mom had penalized her with extra shopping for doing so well in school. Eberhαrt always seemed to be there to help her. Julíenηe wished he were there now.

"And why not?" said Julíenηe as she activated the distress transponder.

"Julíenηe...What are you doing?" asked Tadφlŏn in disbelief. "You'll have every security officer in the area answering that distress call!"

Julíenηe had activated the universal distress transponder. This unique device was the latest in technology and the Ghoηαdz' family, of course, ordered it as an extra option on the AGV in order to spend a few extra magnitudes of gold. As a matter of fact, the emergency device was so new that it was more than likely that only a few AGV's were so equipped. Eberhαrt had jokingly told Julíenηe, "If you ever need help pulling your head out of your ass activate your distress transponder and I'll come a running!" Eberhαrt's craft was one of the few that were so equipped.

"Well, Jerẹmy, it's getting about time that we headed back," said Eberhαrt.

"Yeah...Let's get going."

Eberhαrt and Jerẹmy had been idling the time away at the church talking about the CPU, various theories concerning the void between politician's ears, females who do, and the ones that did. Both of them were feeling more confident about their future as they traveled up the access incline and into Eberhαrt's AGV.

"Ha...It's your little hose monster!" said Eberhαrt.

"What...What are you talking about?" asked Jerẹmy. He acted more than a little confused.

"It's Julíenηe...she's activated the distress transponder in the AGV."

"Maybe she's in trouble!"

"Nah... She's getting back at me...I told her if she ever needed help pulling her head out of her butt to activate it and I would come running." Eberhart laughed.

"Where is she?" asked Jeręmy as he secured his harness.

"Ah...Let's see...Okay she's at quadrant 2h3f, 1467903, sector 5820," replied Eberhart.

"Well? What are you waiting for?"

Eberhart quickly powered up the engines and engaged the thrusters to maneuver them out of the Utrovian forest. Once on the planetary freeway, the Zinctar Twin Reactor engines again were unleashed propelling them toward what they thought would be a few laughs and a good time.

"Okay, we're almost there," said Eberhart.

"She must be at the Starfire Shopping center," said Jeręmy.

"Don't tell me she activated the distress transponder just to get help carrying the span's worth of shopping," moaned Eberhart.

Eberhart cruised through the consumption center parking entrance well above the 0.1 ppz limit and began maneuvering through the maze of AGVs looking for Julíeηηe's. After becoming aware of the increased security traffic, Eberhart quickly brought the craft's speed within the legal limit.

"Damazar! What's orbiting with the security?" said Jeręmy.

"I don't know...but it's sure killing the area's space donut shop business," replied Eberhart with a smirk. "Hey...there's mom's AGV!"

"Look! Julíeηηe's waving," said Jeręmy. He tugged on Eberhart's shoulder.

Eberhart maneuvered close along side of Tadφlŏn's AGV as the access incline was extending.

"Hey, Julíenηe...Watch it! You want to get retro burned?" said Eberhart. He quickly powered down his engines.

[THUMP! THUMP!] Julíenηe began pounding on Eberhart's AGV until he had extended the access incline to let her inside.

"Retract! Retract! ...the access incline! Retract it!" cried Julíenηe excitedly.

Eberhart and Jerȩmy were quite bewildered with Julíenηe's behavior, but soon began to understand as she recounted her and Tadφlŏn's recent adventure.

"...And then I smashed him in the face with a bag of gold!" reported Julíenηe. Her arms were waving in a very animated fashion. "After that, we made a mad dash to the AGV. Then, with all the security, we were afraid to try and leave the parking area."

"Damazar...How's mom handling this?" asked Eberhart. He was somewhat shocked that his sister and mom were trying to flee from the authorities.

"At first, her mind seemed to go into hyperspace, but she actually is coping better than I am now," replied Julíenηe.

"What are we going to do? How are we going to get out of here, Eeeb?" Julíenηe peered deep into Eberhart's eyes waiting for an answer.

Silence filled the AGV as Eberhart and Jerȩmy looked at each other not wanting to believe the story they had just heard. Visions of prison, torture, heavy fines, and maybe even jury duty crowded their consciousness. However, a glimmer shown in Eberhart's eye and Jerȩmy smiled confident that a daringly dangerous, hopefully sex ridden, plan was about to be announced.

"I think I've got it," announced Eberhart.

Eberhart presented his plan to Julíenꞑe and Jerꬲmy. Julíenꞑe was skeptical, but Jerꬲmy seemed absolutely thrilled with it. Likely, because he and Julíenꞑe would be fleeing the parking area together, and Eberhart noted, she was wearing his favorite Uμμρárian tribal fragrance--*Ubangime #5*. Julíenꞑe and Jerꬲmy left Eberhart's AGV to inform Tadφlŏn of the plan. Shortly thereafter, Tadφlŏn exited her own AGV to pair up with Eberhart.

"Well, Mom? I see you've been instructing Julíenꞑe in the latest shopping techniques," Eberhart said then chuckled.

"Okay, Son...have your fun, but who'll neutron wash your clothes when I'm pounding asteroids?" responded Tadφlŏn. She cocked her head and rolled her eyes.

Eberhart again went over his plan with Tadφlŏn just to confirm her complete understanding. Then, he powered up the engines preparing for their departure.

"...And once you receive the signal from my distress transponder, launch toward home and DON'T SPARE THE ATOMS!" yelled Eberhart at Jerꬲmy as he pulled away. "Okay, Mom...Yell when you see an empty security vehicle," said Eberhart scanning the area.

"Right."

Julíenꞑe and Jerꬲmy made the best of their time together waiting for Eberhart's signal.

"Without a doubt, Jerꬲmy Williams...Are you sure you don't have gazelda blood in your veins?" joked Julíenꞑe. She playfully attempted to keep Jerꬲmy's hands at bay, but well…you know….

"One more time just in case you get caught and they ship you off to *Hastar 3* no penile colony for females," teased Jerẹmy.

Meanwhile, Eberhart and Tadφlŏn continued their search for an abandoned security vehicle.

"There...That one!" said Tadφlŏn spotting a security vehicle as the officer was leaving it.

"We'll park here just to make sure he's not returning right away," said Eberhart. He maneuvered his craft to the pad two spaces away.

Eberhart and Tadφlŏn sat patiently for several zlitons observing the security craft.

"Okay, Mom...See you in awhile," said Eberhart, breaking the silence.

"Be careful, Son. I'll be waiting." Tadφlŏn caressed Eberhart's face gently before he left.

Eberhart extended the access incline and stealthily exited. Tadφlŏn watched as he made his way to the security craft. After observing that Eberhart was able to gain entry into the craft, Tadφlŏn powered up the engines and maneuvered away.

Once inside the security craft, Eberhart began scanning the security channels hoping to gain some useful information.

"Vega SO318...Report," ordered the security controller.

"Now patrolling sector 5820...Negative sighting of suspects...Vega SO318 standing by," replied the officer.

Eberhart was now convinced that the security officials had only a sketchy identity match with his sister and his mom. Therefore, very confidently, Eberhart began to execute his plan. Eberhαrt set the security communicator to encrypt thus masking his voice and making it very difficult for the source of his transmission to be located. After calming himself, he began his transmission.

"May I have your attention, please!" he said. "The CPU has openly defied the lunacy of society...We have thrown away our gold and have eluded capture. We wish no harm to anyone...only commonsense. Therefore, we will surrender ourselves to the officers at the main security station. We have commandeered one of your security craft and are presently en route to that station."

After setting the stage for deception, Eberhαrt powered up the security craft and maneuvered it away from the pad slowly. As he had expected, a security check had begun already in order to determine the identity of the stolen security craft. He carefully listened to the security chatter then began programming the autopilot to follow a flight plan he hoped would decoy the security patrols long enough for friends and family to leave the consumption center without detection.

"...Positive identification. SO274 is to be intercepted and boarded," ordered the security controller.

"Damazar! That was quick!" Eberhαrt said to himself.

Eberhαrt headed toward his rendezvous with Tadφlŏn at increased speed. He maneuvered between the center's great structures in order to avoid meeting other security craft. Finally, Tadφlŏn's AGV was in sight. Eberhαrt continued to close on her at high velocity mentally preparing for what he must do. Within penăr of Tadφlŏn's AGV, Eberhαrt engaged the autopilot. Without delay, he secured himself inside the escape capsule.

Eberhart nervously, but firmly, grasped the eject lever then closed his eyes and pulled with all his might.

"SHI-TOOOO-VAAAAAA!" He screamed as the capsule separated from the craft.

Rockets immediately ignited on the escape craft propelling it at a ninety-degree angle to the security craft, which had made a hard turn to begin the preprogrammed flight plan. As planned, Tadφlŏn pursued the escape craft at maximum thrust. Eberhart nervously watched while the escape craft began to maneuver itself to what he hoped would be a safe landing inside a hospitable area. The craft banked hard and Eberhart could now sense the craft descending in order to land.

[Skiiiiddddd! Bump! Bang! Bump!] The craft ground to a halt.

"Damazar...What a ride!" said Eberhart as he dizzily emerged from the craft. "Clem's Coffee Bean & Seafood Warehouse!" read Eberhart on the sign. "Clem must have franchises all over the planet!"

Tadφlŏn had just touched down and was extending the access incline as Eberhart ran to join her. Once inside, Eberhart quickly slid into the pilot's seat and activated the distress transponder, which would signal Jerẹmy and Julíennẹ to begin their escape.

"Hold tight, Mom...We're gonna do a one-eighty and atomize this caffeine club!" Eberhart engaged the portside aft lateral thrusters while simultaneously igniting the two Zinctar Twin Reactor engines.

Eberhart's AGV reacted wildly, similar to an active fire hose, but without the twenty firefighters to hold it down. Flames from the Zinctar engines torched the area, sizzling four AGVs, frying two mags of Sodfish[20],

---

[20] Sodfish -- hybrid that looks much like a ball of grass.

and roasting enough beans for ten billion cups of coffee.

After some skillful wrangling, Eberhart was able to harness his engine's power and direct the craft toward the nearest center exit. Meanwhile, the decoy security craft was on its way to the other side of the center. Of course, the hope was that it would be pursued by enough officers to facilitate their escape.

"That's the signal!" cried Julienηe.

"Right...Let's go," responded Jerεmy.

Closely following Eberhart's plan, Jerεmy maneuvered the craft toward the exit at increasing speed. Julienηe watched as several security craft ignored them and continued on their way at high speed.

"It's working!" said Julienηe. "Eberhart's plan is working."

"Yeah...They must be after the decoy," said Jerεmy.

Jerεmy and Julienηe exited the center parking area without challenge. Once on the planetary freeway, Jerεmy accelerated to 0.5 ppz and headed for the Ghoηadz' dwelling with Julienηe cuddling by his side.

CHAPTER FOUR

A SPAN AT THE OFFICE
IN THE 188th MILENIUM...

Hɑzăr sat staring at the computator screen contemplating his life and his life's work as the Chief Trans Dimensional Engineer at FUTURE SPACE, INC. Future Space, Inc. is a company that specializes in creative space generation and space management. (*Space being storage space, merchandising space, living space, etc.*) As Hɑzăr's mind drifted, he thought about the evolution of the company, which strangely enough made him recall a little social history and its affect on Future Space, Inc. (*I mean... hey, this is my chance to fill you in on a little Uμmpárian history and planetary science. Besides, Hɑzăr has several zlitons before quitting time. He has time to really get some serious thinking done. ENJOY!*)

Uμmpár, because of the fact that its inhabitants have a life span of several hundred Earth years, is steadily being overwhelmed with structures, equipment, and *beings*. Space is the one element that both the upper and lower-class beings on Uμmpár were quickly running out of. Utrovian forests are currently being devoured so that the Xenofolic Protein Acid can be used to make magnitudes of everything, which will more than occupy the space vacated by the forest. Therefore, space management companies originated some solacles ago and continue to flourish. Future Space, Inc. was no exception. The rate at which the company had grown to one of the most successful space management entities was truly astonishing. Without a doubt, Ηαzăr Ghoηαdz was one of the prominent factors that contributed to that success. This is mainly because of the Multi-Warp, Infinite Loop Storage Structure that was designed by none other than Ηαzăr L. Ghoηαdz.

Though the MWILSS is the most advanced storage structure on Uμmpár, the operational mechanics are quite simple. A trans-dimensional phase generator is used to create incremental shifts in one of the most basic elements--*time*. Then, simultaneously and in full synchronization, the warp field generator creates a looping field for each shifted increment of time. The loop of time for each increment is precisely 2399.5 zlitons with 0.5 zliton spacing between shifted warp fields as a safety to prevent the undesirable effects of overlapping fields. *("Bob...I think the storage shed is on the blink again. Looks like Rover's molecules have combined with Aunt Martha's old end table--it's leaking splinters on the rug!")* Hence, storage space is sold or rented by 2400 zliton block. Once the storage structure is loaded, the contents are then projected back in time to a 2400 zliton period when the structure was empty. The stored inventory is then allowed to advance through time for

2399.5 zlitons and then is projected back in time 2399.5 zlitons to begin its advance again. Therefore, the MWILSS's storage capacity is determined by the number of 2400 zliton blocks it was allowed to sit empty before being put into service. ...An operational secret that is not known to anyone except Hazăr Ghoηαdz. Future Space, Inc. markets a ten and a twenty-increment unit. Sales are brisk. For each unit the buyer must accept ten-thousand and twenty-thousand mags of gold respectively. The ten-increment unit is the top seller.

The Ghoηαdz' were once more prosperous than could be imagined. Hazăr excelled in his academic studies after his parents left. He finally finished college at the age of sixteen unable to flunk his graduation exams. His only opportunity for employment was with extraordinarily high paying companies. He searched and searched using up the entire ten-span period allowed by law before an Uμmpάrian must accept employment. Finally, he felt the best he could do was to accept a position at a small start-up company called *Time Lag, Inc*.

The founder of Time Lag, Inc., Tim M. Archezon, had just invented the *PAST TIME* warp field generator. Mr. Archezon had been marketing his product to shoppers. The Past Time generator could produce a time warp field large enough to propel a single shopper and their gold back in time one hundred zlitons. This, he advertised, allowed the shopper more time each period to spend their gold thus making them less prosperous. The product was a big success. Uμmpάrians lined up to accept one thousand magnitudes of gold with each unit. However, because of the amount of time required by the Past Time generator to recharge its primary coils, only one field generation was possible each 2400-zliton period. Mr. Archezon realized that after the novelty diminished, the sales of his product would begin to decline because of its limited field generation capabilities. That was the reason he filed an application with the government, as required by law, for approval to hire a dimensional engineer.

The government began deciding how many employees are required by each company to produce their products or provide their services in the early 14000's. Any additional employees must be approved. It should be noted that proving the need for additional employees is both time consuming and difficult. In addition, for each individual employed, the company must accept ten thousand magnitudes of gold tax credit from the government for every one thousand revolutions of Uμmρár. However, the benefits of having employees far outweighed the government penalties. For instance, an individual unable to achieve a test proven I.Q. of three hundred or less could be put in top positions and paid unbelievable salaries. This allowed companies to unload their penalty gold and their standard gold tax refunds, which the companies must also accept from the government each solacle, on the employees. Indeed, this was not the best system, but was much better than the system that was used prior to the 14,000's--no system at all!

When gold became the standard currency on Uμmρár, many loopholes existed for unscrupulous employers to unload as much gold as they desired on their employees. It was common practice at that time for any company, bank, institution, and even government agency to employ large numbers of beings in non-essential, nonproductive, and often redundant positions with horrifyingly huge salaries that grew exponentially each solacle. In addition, criminal elements would use this tactic to flush gold through the system. Literally, the high wages paid in gold were breaking the backs of the average Uμmράrian. This abuse continued for many solacles until one average Uμmράrian, who happened to be a distant ancestor of the legendary red-eye, Freno Ziffnopho, pulled together a vast coalition of workers to fight these unscrupulous employers. In order to understand the factors that motivated Xandal Yetza Ziffnopho to take up the fight against employer oppression, you must first understand the significance of Freno Ziffnopho.

Freno Ziffnopho was a red-eye known to most beings on Uμmράr because of his crusade that brought the red-eyes and the yellow-eyes together. He was born in *Metapherous*, about the solacle 2052, some two thousand solacles before Sharon Defoulgar and innate intelligence. Metapherous was a region located on the solar radiated hemisphere of Uμmράr. Beings that were born on the near-rad hemisphere were just like the beings born on the far-rad hemisphere except for the color of their eyes.

The near-rad Uμmράrians had red eyes while the far-rad Uμmράrians had yellow eyes. In the early 1400s, the yellow-eyed Uμmράrians, or yellers, crossed what was then called *The Sea of Inferno* to explore the half of the planet closest to the *Rad*. At this time, the yellers believed this unexplored frontier to be uninhabited because of the extreme heat and radiation cast upon it by the Rad. Uμmράr rotates on an axis that is perpendicular to the Rad and revolves around the Rad once every ninety of Earth's years. Because of this orientation, the near-rad hemisphere maintains a minimum equivalent Earth temperature of ninety degrees-C and reaches a recorded high of one hundred twenty degrees-C during Uμmpάr's elliptical orbit around the Rad. For this one-half of Uμmpάr there is no night just blistering heat and brilliant light. In contrast, the far-rad hemisphere of Uμmpάr receives indirect light and heat from Uμmpάr's two quartz moons.

The quartz moons travel in elliptical orbits coming closest to Uμmpάr on the far-rad hemisphere. Because of the sizable one hundred and seventy-six thousand penãrd circumference of Uμmpάr, the dark periods are eight hundred zlitons while the light periods produced by the quartz moons are sixteen hundred zlitons in duration. Consequently, the far-rad hemisphere enjoys a temperature between thirty degrees-C and fifty degrees-C during Uμmpάr's revolution of the Rad. These conditions allowed the Uμmpάrians on the far-rad hemisphere to evolve practically identical to the Uμmpάrians on the near-rad hemisphere with the exception that their eyes were yellow.

The first yellers that encountered the red-eyes thought that they were inferior because of their exposure to the intense heat and radiation from the Rad. Many reds were captured and brought back to the far-rad hemisphere. Upon returning to their homeland, the yellers put the reds on display while the intellectuals of the period purported false analyses regarding the red's level of intelligence. For many solacles, the majority of yellers treated the reds in a degrading fashion. However, a minority of yellers were able to begin a movement to abolish these practices.

As technology advanced and knowledge was acquired regarding Uμmpάrian physiology, the anatomical truth that paved the way for the abolishment of these degrading and sometimes horrifying practices was discovered. Hinto Nafindixa, a celebrated healer and scientist, discovered the function of an obscure appendage-like organ. The organ, named Nafindix after Hinto Nafindixa himself, secreted a fluid that Hinto was able to clinically prove saturated the twenty-seven thyroid-type glands of an Uμmpárian preventing them from falling victim to radiation sickness. Hinto was also able to prove that once these glands were saturated with this fluid they produced a chemical he called *Zfreonyde*. The Zfreonyde entered the bloodstream and acted as a coolant for the Uμmpárian body when extreme heat was encountered. The anatomical truth became clear. The discovery of the Nafindix organ's function proved that all Uμmpárians could live on the near-rad hemisphere without any fear concerning the possible effects of heat and radiation. In essence, this proved that the red-eyes were not any different from the yellow-eyes with the exception of their eye color. The majority of yellers were shocked by these revelations, which came from one of their own. However, these discoveries did give the crusading yellers the ammunition they needed to get discriminatory laws rescinded and anti-discrimination laws passed. Uμmpár now appeared to be on its way to unification.

Government mandated non-discrimination immensely improved the livelihoods of the reds. However, the hatred that had instilled itself on both sides because of the atrocities that were committed by both the yellers and the reds did not surrender easily. During the solacles of healing, there always was an uneasy tension that flared at times resulting in senseless violence and death. This tension continued to be a barrier to complete unification until one red-eye came of age and entered the battle to end discrimination against anyone, anywhere, regardless of the reason. His name was Freno Ziffnopho.

In the beginning, Mr. Ziffnopho battled discrimination in the conventional manner. He lobbied for more stringent anti-discrimination laws and policies that favored the general sector that was victimized. However, the tension between the yellers and the reds did not lose its intensity. Certainly, the overt discriminatory practices disappeared, but the accusations of covert discrimination abounded. It was not until Mr. Ziffnopho's middle solacles that he finally realized that anti-discrimination laws and policies were not the complete solution. The tension continued to thrive and brutally continued to show itself at times. Mr. Ziffnopho reasoned for himself that the government could not be an effective diplomat charged with bringing the two sides together. Instead, the many laws and policies had forced the government to evolve into a referee, which served only to interpret the rules governing the conflict. Consequently, the government acting in that capacity made many bad calls against both sides. This realization brought about a turning point in Mr. Ziffnopho's life and his crusade.

Mr. Ziffnopho began his crusade anew with what he hoped was divine insight. He began his journey throughout Uμmράr encouraging the abolishment of any law, policy, or directive that favored any being positively or negatively solely because of their eye color. He diligently preached peace, education, moral values, understanding, and personal accountability. Mr. Ziffnopho professed his reasoning that there were no two identical anythings in the known universe and that total equality was an impossibility. He noted that the currently constant counting and tallying of how many yellers lived here, how many reds lived there, how many of both worked anywhere, what was the education level of reds, what was the education level of yellers, etcetera served only to fill up a scorecard of battle statistics. Mr. Ziffnopho believed that the questions being asked were valid, but that the designation of reds and yellers should be replaced with what they all were-- *Uμmpάrians*. It seemed to him that the very act of keeping and reporting statistics that made the distinction between Uμmpάrians, either as reds or as yellers, was in and of itself a source that encouraged continued division. Moreover, this was an unfortunate division between two groups of Uμmpάrians that were absolutely no different from each other except for the ocular anomaly.

Unfortunately, Mr. Ziffnopho's philosophy was not initially well received by either side. The reds believed him to be traitor to their fight for equality. On the other hand, the yellers discounted him as an opportunist trying to remain at center stage.

Both the red's and the yeller's beliefs were true of some activists at that time. These scavengers that crusaded for themselves, using the division between red and yeller as a vehicle to get to the pot of gold at the end of the rainbow, thrived on a continued conflict between the two. They used the conflict to gain power and influence within their respective groups. These unscrupulous beings were in many cases self-appointed and pursued their own agendas, which did not include bringing the reds and yellers together to live in peace and harmony. When an alleged act of discrimination or a controversial situation arose, the false prophets of unity spoke out inciting hatred by pouring salt on old wounds while trying to consolidate their positions and further their personal goals. Unfortunately, the masses were easily manipulated, and in all too many instances, struck out with senseless violence causing pain, suffering, and death with little remorse. Moreover, the planetary media piped this violence into every Uμmpárian dwelling so that each side could get angry or glad as they cheered their own side on. Sadly, each act of senseless violence served only to solidify each side's ideology and further the influence of the false leaders. The tension and hatred continued.

Mr. Ziffnopho refused to relinquish his philosophy of color blindness, peace, education, high moral standards, and personal accountability. He persevered and over time gained a substantial following of both the reds and the yellers that wanted to coexist in peace with an end to the violence and the continued division. He and his followers lobbied the lawmakers to remove favoring laws and the recording of statistics that noted the differences in Uμmpárians according to eye color. Mr. Ziffnopho's efforts over the solacles began to show positive effects.

Two hundred solacles had passed since Freno Ziffnopho had reached the turning point in his crusade and began it anew. Now, because of his personal sacrifices and the dedication of his followers, the reds and the yellers were coming together to live in peaceful coexistence. As it became obvious to all Uμmpárians that each individual directly controlled their own life and what they would make of it, the reliance on ineffective government policies ended. The success of each Uμmpárian depended on their individual self-discipline and motivation. Freno Ziffnopho had passed on leaving very little material wealth to his wife and only son. It was never his goal to be wealthy or famous though his name was embedded in the hearts of all Uμmpάrians. The unity and peace that all Uμmpάrians now enjoyed stood as a great testimony to his great courage, insight, and dedication.

Long after Mr. Ziffnopho's death and long before Sharon Defoulgar's innate intelligence, the one distinction between red and yeller faded away without notice. All Uμmpάrians now lived, worked, and played together in a harmonious fashion unimaginable just a few hundred solacles ago. Consequently, this state of togetherness led to a mingling of lives and culture. The trait that once caused so much pain, suffering, and discord had faded away. Solacles of mating between the reds and yellers had produced descendants with eyes that were an orange color. Unknowingly, Freno Ziffnopho had written the final chapter on ocular discrimination thus allowing nature the opportunity to gently close the book.

Now, hundreds of solacles later, Xandal Yetza Ziffnopho the great, great, great, great, great, etc. grandson, desired to follow in the footsteps of his ancestor. The working conditions for most Uμmpάrians were difficult at best. The conversion to gold as the universal measure of consumption and government mandated consumption requirements strained the relations between employee and employer. Yetza often thought of his great ancestor and his contributions to the beings of Uμmpάr. Yetza realized that innate intelligence was creating divisions that were different in nature from the ones his ancestor had faced, but these divisions would surely be just as difficult to close. Yetza could not fathom this striving for ignorance, the carrying of gold as currency, or the great intrusions by the government into the lives of all Uµmpάrians. Yetza was the only male in his family to receive his great ancestor's name. Freno's middle name was Yetza. This caused Yetza to feel obligated to uphold his ancestor's legend of great self-discipline, color blindness, peace, education, high moral standards, and personal accountability.

Xandal Yetza Ziffnopho's personal sympathy was now with the workers of Uµmpάr. He deplored the unspeakable ways that corporations exploited their employees to avoid the government mandated consumption laws. Yetza believed that if he could assemble a great coalition he might be able to effect the abolishment of the gold currency absurdity. Yetza made his first contacts with the workers that had the heaviest loads to carry. Executives were his first target. They were the ones with the heavy multi-thousand magnitude salaries and he hoped that they would be the most receptive to his ideas. Yetza held seminar after seminar preaching the concept of unity in numbers. Finally, Yetza was able to form the first worker's collective. U.A.B.S. or *United Against Back Strain* became the first organized body of employees. Initially, the membership was just about ten million. However, it wasn't long before the message of Xandal Yetza Ziffnopho had reached billions of Uµmpάrians.

The benefits of collective membership became known throughout the planet. The collective allowed the members to pay it dues. The workers could hold work stoppages thus providing themselves with extended periods without pay. In addition, the collective negotiators were able to keep their members on strike long

92

enough for the corporations to settle for no worker pay increase or even, sometimes, generous layoffs after a contract was signed. There was much resistance on the part of the corporations. They tried every means imaginable to shift their heavy gold load onto the employees, but the meticulous methodology of organized labor finally prevailed causing the government to step in and restrain the corporations from their gold pushing practices.

Detailed planning and precision execution of work stoppages proved to be the key. Work stoppages were timed to be when an employer had huge inventories on hand. During these periods, the employer could not unload his gold on the employees because they were not at work, nor did the employer have any manufacturing costs, and products that were in demand could be taken from stock. No employee costs, no manufacturing costs, and the customer could still be supplied! The employer was being stuck with huge amounts of gold and it was increasing. Enough was enough!

The corporations and the government were not happy with this situation. The corporations were not happy because the workers would not work and the corporations could not pay them. The government was not happy because the corporations maintained tremendous gold assets, and therefore, the government could not issue the corporations huge gold tax refunds. Not only were the corporations' assets growing, but also, were the government's assets. In effect, organized labor was stopping the government from wasting... uh... throwing away... uh... distributing... yes, distributing the wealth of Uμmpάr to the corporations to induce greater productivity. Something had to be done!

The lawmakers got together to formulate a solution to the problem. The lawmakers met three times per solacle totaling some thirty zlitons of intense brainstorming. Finally, law number 16,385,243.1, THE EMPLOYEE SALARY DISAPPEARING ACT, was passed. This law was one of the most comprehensive, far reaching, (*down through the employee pockets to the toe-end of their socks*) and controversial laws ever passed regarding employee income. The law itself was documented on the paper made from eight thousand trees; printed using the ink from many wells and weighed nineteen hundred and ninety-three magnitudes. Indeed, this was massive legislation meant to solve a weighty problem. The main points of the law were as follows:

- No employer shall unnecessarily hire Uμμράrians.
- No employer shall cause undue burden by paying unreasonable wages.
- For each employee, the employer must accept a substantial gold tax refund from the government.
- Employees working more than eight hundred consecutive zlitons on government related work may be paid time plus one-half.
- The employer may pay an executive not at work if the absence is deemed intentional.
- The employer may not pay a regular employee not at work regardless of whether the absence was intentional or not. The exception is when an employee is absent because of illness or injury then the employer may pay the employee at a reduced rate. This is to avoid undue hardship on the part of the employer.

Many points addressed the concerns of the employees. However, one point in particular was not well received by the corporations. The point is as follows:

- The employer must accept triple the amount of gold for products and services that the employer provides to the government.

The corporations lobbied intensely trying to get the E.S.D. Act amended to exclude the huge tax refunds that they must accept as well as the triple compensation for goods and services supplied to the government. However, the lawmakers remained firm and eventually all lobbying efforts were abandoned. Xandal Yetza Ziffnopho was pleased with the new law and felt that he could do more to lift the heavy gold burden off the worker's shoulders. Yetza encouraged collective leaders to increase dues and insist that the corporations set up what was known as D.B.T. plans or *Don't Be Tired plans*. These D.B.T. plans allowed the workers to unload a portion of their gold into a holding fund until they were allowed by law to stop working for good. The D.B.T. plans were very well received by the workers because it allowed them to lighten their take home load until the time came when they would not have to accept a salary. And, to the pleasant surprise of many employees, the gold in their D.B.T. plans would completely vanish before they were legally allowed to stop working.

Certainly, Xandal Yetza Ziffnopho had left his mark on the working class of Uμmpάr. Sadly, however, Yetza's life ended before he had realized his full potential. While strolling through the park, on his way to a posh hotel where he was to have announced his candidacy for a major political office, he was fatally struck by a bag of collective dues thrown by an unknown assailant. Government complicity was inferred, but never substantiated. Some experts have argued that too much currency was found at the scene for just one assailant. Likely, two bags were thrown even though only one empty casing was recovered by authorities.

Well, that is the story of how the government became involved in regulating employment.

Finally, the government approved Tim M. Archezon's application to hire an additional employee. The employee just happened to be a young husband and father, Hɑzăr L. Ghoηɑdz. Mr. Archezon spent many spans acquainting Hɑzăr with the PAST TIME warp field generator. Hɑzăr could easily comprehend the workings of Mr. Archezon's generator. Mr. Archezon could not believe his luck in finding such a useful employee to whom he could unload large amounts of gold. So true... Hɑzăr Ghoηɑdz, young and unable to flunk out in school despite the best efforts of the educational system and the learner's collective, was left wide open for heavy salary exploitation.

Hɑzăr became very interested in this particular field of trans-dimensional engineering. Hɑzăr spent a great deal of extra time examining the components of the PAST TIME warp field generator. Mr. Archezon gave Hɑzăr the task of improving the generator to the point where there was instant recharging of the primary coils making rapid warp field generation possible. Hɑzăr was more than happy to pursue this task though he did have heavier motives for doing so.

The amount of overtime that Hɑzăr was working was breaking his back and quickly filling up his home with gold. He and Tadφlŏn had also accumulated additional currency during their internships as mercenaries addressing space piracy. Therefore, he really needed to get rid of more gold than he had the time or the desire to spend. Hαzăr thought to himself that if he could just hide the gold somewhere and forget about it things would be okay. But...where could he hide the gold? Hαzăr theorized that if the PAST TIME warp field generator's primary coil could be made to recharge instantly, the generator could send an object back in time just as fast as the coils could recharge. Hαzăr further theorized that the time regression was directly proportional to the strength of the coil discharge. Finally, Hαzăr believed that the regression could be incremented and controlled. Therefore, Hαzăr began work on a new coil design and a device to increment the time regressions.

Hαzăr devoted himself to the work and Mr. Archezon was quite pleased with his progress. Hαzăr completed work on a perpetually recharging, super conducting coil. The windings were made of pure gold and coated with silver oxide. They were housed in a platinum case, which was filled with liquid helium. The redesigned warp field generator could effect a multi-solacle time regression repeatedly with only the initial coil charge. Hαzăr's unique design allowed a warp field the size of a three AGV garage to be generated while internally generating a smaller time regression field around the coil itself. Thus, when the coil was discharged, the larger field could send sizable objects back in time while the smaller internal field sent the coil itself back in time. The coil would regress back in time to a period when it was fully charged and then be allowed to progress through time again until another discharge was triggered. Finally, Hαzăr completed his design of a dimensional phase generator that could shift the time regressions in determined increments when working in full synchronization with the warp field generator. Hαzăr's project seemed to be nearly finished.

Quietly and without much fanfare, Hαzăr completed work on his prototype. Immediately, the testing could begin, and Hαzăr was excited about the prospects. Unknown to Mr. Archezon, Hαzăr took the unit home to conduct his tests. Late one night when Tadφlŏn and baby Julíenηe were sleeping, Hαzăr stealthily carried the unit to the AGV garage where he was currently storing fourteen magnitudes of gold. Once there, Hαzăr programmed the unit to send the entire fourteen units of gold back in time a period of one-hundred spans. Then he set the coil discharge rate at 2399.5 zlitons. After the gold had regressed one hundred spans, the unit would allow the gold to progress 2399.5 zlitons forward in time and then the coils would discharge sending the gold back in time 2399.5 zlitons to begin the cycle again. Thus, permanent gold storage without an atom of evidence left to prove it had ever existed. After rechecking the settings, Hαzăr energized the unit. The lights started flashing while his teeth started gnashing and I'll just be dog-goned if the blame fool thing didn't work. …Gone! …All of it! The entire fourteen mags of gold couldn't have vanished any quicker if it had been entrusted to the lawmakers. Needless to say, Hαzăr was beside himself.

Hαzăr was ecstatic at the seemingly complete success of his first test. So excited was Hαzăr that he began to jump up and down while laughing and giggling. Hαzăr was making such a stir that Tadφlŏn was awakened and came to the garage to see what on Uμmρár could be making him act this way. Was he having sex with one of those tickling hussies from Anus Three? Was his thing stuck in the vacuuming device while it was at full power?

"HAZĂR! WHAT'S GOING ON IN HERE?" yelled Tadφlŏn.

"I've done it," blurted Hαzăr.

"Done what? …Hey, where's all the gold?"

"It's gone," Hαzăr replied.

"Gone…Gone WHERE?" demanded Tadφlŏn.

"Back in time…I sent it back in time," said Hαzăr joyfully.

"What do you mean? …Back in time. How—"

"I used the Multi-Warp Loop Generator that I have been working on," said Hαzăr.

"Multi-What's it…?"

"Multi-Warp Loop--Hey wait a dab-blasted minute[21]," said Hαzăr realizing that not only did the fourteen mags of gold disappear, but so did his Multi-Warp Loop Generator.

The joy in Hαzăr's heart quickly melted away. He had overlooked one small flaw in his design. Hαzăr had forgotten to equip the generator with a fail-safe recovery device, which would have terminated the looping warp field and rapidly progress the unit to the present. Sadly, the unit, the gold, and Hαzăr's late night snack were gone forever, barring a malfunction, of course. Presently, the big question on Hαzăr's mind was what to tell Mr. Archezon. Possibly, he was a victim of revobbery by oozy, sticky little aliens that moogled him and made off with the gold *and* the unit. On the other hand, maybe …a

---

[21] Dab-blasted minute -- amount of time required by Uncle Dab to place one stick of dynamite in a place drilled in a rich seam of Bituminous coal, attach the blasting cap, connect the wires, ride the motor to the mouth of the mine, and shoot the seam.

malfunction, sir, and the unit along with my favorite Big Bang Era collection just disappeared! No, Hαzαr was Uμμpάrian and that meant he would have to tell the truth OR come up with a better story.

"Yes, Mr. Archezon... And when I came out of Clem's Donut Hole & Bait Shop some scoundrel had violated my AGV and stole the Multi-Warp Looping Generator," reported Hαzαr as seriously as he could.

"What kind of aliens live on this planet?" quipped Mr. Archezon quite astonished by Hαzαr's story.

"Don't worry, Mr. Archezon," replied Hαzαr. "I can have another unit built and ready for testing in a matter of spans."

And so, Hαzαr did set to work again building a new Multi-Warp Looping Generator. However, this time he designed the recovery module before any work began on building a new unit. The Multi-Warp Looping Generator became incorporated into a permanent structure and so what is now known as the Multi-Warp Infinite Loop Storage Structure was born. Consequently, Hαzăr received a sizable pay decrease and a huge pat on the back from Mr. Archezon.

"Damazar! ...It's time to go home!" said Hαzăr.

Hαzăr surprised himself that he had been dreaming for so long. He turned off his computater and left his office heading for home. He chuckled when he thought about the gold looping through time. He certainly was glad he no longer lived at that dwelling just in case the generator malfunctioned and the gold suddenly reappeared.

CHAPTER FIVE

Family fugitives...

Julíenηe and Jerȩmy had arrived at the Ghoηadz' dwelling. They were both excited at the recent events and somewhat worried about Eberhαrt and Tadφlŏn.

"Where are they?" ask Julíenηe with a sigh.

"Don't worry," replied Jerȩmy. "I'm sure they're okay."

[BUMP! BEEP!]

At that moment, Eberhαrt's AGV entered the Ghoηadz' parking bay.

"They're here!" Julíenηe ran to greet them.

"I told you that you shouldn't...worry," sighed Jerȩmy, but she was out of earshot.

Eberhαrt and Tadφlŏn exited the AGV and entered the dwelling after closing the bay doors. Eberhαrt was laughing while Tadφlŏn was still quite wound up after all of the excitement.

"Ah, come on, Mom," teased Eberhαrt. "If they catch you and Julíenηe I'll visit you in prison."

"Don't joke about this, Eberhαrt," said Tadφlŏn.

"Wow, we did it!" said Julíenηe joyfully.

They all sat down and calmed themselves as Julíenηe and Tadφlŏn recounted the events that led up to their having to flee from the authorities. As they laughed, joked, and relived their adventure it became obvious that they all were disillusioned by society's encroachment on their pursuit of happiness. One by one, each confessed a desire for a better life. A life free from absurdities such as striving for ignorance, carrying hundreds of magnitudes of gold around as currency, and the search for a politician with cognitive capabilities.

"I'm going to BlackStellar Labs in the morning," announced Eberhαrt.

"I've heard about that place," said Julíenηe. "The kids at school say it's a commonsense organization...Hey, can I go too?"

"Me too!" said Jeręmy.

"Sure." Eberhαrt was very pleased with their desire to go with him.

"Wait...Is that true about that place being a CPU organization?" asked Tadφlŏn.

"Mom, I really don't know... but I want to find out," said Eberhαrt honestly.

Just then, Tadφlŏn switched to mothering mode while completely forgetting about her own flight from the authorities.

"Eberhαrt, I don't want any of you to get mixed up with any CPU troublemakers," said Tadφlŏn.

"Mom--it's not illegal to be a commonsense being," replied Eberhαrt.

"You just close your mouth this instant," ordered Tadφlŏn. "I'm not going to let you make everyone think the Ghoηαdz' are swelling with intelligence!"

"But Mom--," started Eberhαrt.

"That's it, Eberhαrt!" Tadφlŏn was acting as though the recent events never occurred.

Tadφlŏn got up and headed for the kitchen to begin preparing Lunar Mountain Oysters, a favorite food of the Ghoηαdz family. Eberhαrt motioned for Julíenηe and Jerẹmy to follow him to his room.

Tadφlŏn held back her tears because she understood what they were all feeling. Tadφlŏn thought how society had made being prosperous a terrible thing. She knew in her heart that material things did not make anyone better or worse than any other. Indeed, the perceptions and collective classifications of society made the beings of Uμmpάr unequal. Tadφlŏn knew that they would always be lower-class. She also knew that she must act in order to protect her children's future.

"What do you think?" asked Eberhαrt.

"That's a wild plan," said Julíenηe.

"...you think they can do it?" asked Jerẹmy.

"...don't know, but I'd like to be in on it," replied Eberhαrt.

Jerẹmy and Julíenηe had finished reading the BlackStellar Labs project book that the lab tech had left. They both agreed to go with Eberhαrt and were quite excited at the prospects of being involved with such an adventurous project.

"I'M HOME!" Hαzăr had just returned from work.

"...IN THE KITCHEN," replied Tadφlŏn.

Hαzăr threw his bag on the sofa and headed for

the kitchen.

"So, what did you do this span?" asked Hɑzăr expecting to hear the same ol' same ol'.

"Well, let's see...," began Tadφlŏn.

Tadφlŏn continued to describe the events in every detail. Hɑzăr listened intently...raising an eyebrow every now and again.

"Just then...Julíenηe struck the officer with a bag of gold." Tadφlŏn made a swinging motion brushing Hɑzăr's head.

"How did you escape from the consumption center parking area?"

Tadφlŏn went on to describe Eberhɑrt's plan to decoy the security personnel while they all escaped. Hɑzăr was quite surprised at his wife's involvement. After sitting quietly for awhile, Hɑzăr confessed his own unhappiness with the current social conditions.

"I've been contacted by BlackStellar Labs."

"What about?" asked Tadφlŏn.

"They're in need of a trans-dimensional engineer. Particularly, one experienced with warp field generation equipment," he replied.

"When did they contact you?"

"Uh...some one hundred spans ago," replied Hɑzăr. "I've been working on one of their projects."

Hɑzăr and Tadφlŏn continued to discuss his project and her shopping center adventures. Eberhɑrt, Julíenηe, and Jerȩmy soon joined them. They each recounted their daring escape from the consumption center. Hɑzăr felt pleased that his family was able to elude the system and return home safely.

The evening passed quickly as well did the night--

500:30 came early. As a matter of fact, it came at 494:30 this morning. To continue to promote stupidity, the government decided to move time forward six zlitons on the second span of each term interval and that was what this span was.

Eberhαrt, Julíenηe, and Jeręmy had dressed, eaten, and left for BlackStellar Labs before Hαzăr and Tadφlŏn had awakened. All three were excited and clamored on about the adventures that they hoped awaited them. As Eberhαrt's AGV rocketed toward their destination, President Barnstrom was addressing the planet....

"...And I say to you we all must sacrifice. My tax refund plan will mainly affect the upper-class. For it is they who are most able to bear the extra burden...."

Eberhαrt, Julíenηe, and Jeręmy listened to Barnstrom's address concerning increased tax refunds and aid from neighboring planets.

"Who does he think carries the tax refund burden for the upper-class?" asked Julíenηe aloud.

"And what about that planetary aid..." said Jeręmy.

"Yeah...With the heavy burden that Uμmpάrians carry now, he wants us to accept an even bigger load," added Eberhαrt.

"For once I would like to see a President make his mark in history by caring for the health, welfare, and security of his own people," said Julíenηe.

"Never happen," said Jeręmy. "You wouldn't even get an honorable mention in the history books for satisfying the needs of the people who put you in office."

"You're absolutely right," said Eberhαrt. "Modern politicians desire to play on the planetary stage by formulating some peace accord between warring planets, which usually means that Uμmpár rewards them if they stop fighting for awhile."

"When will they ever understand," added Julíenηe. "...For a lasting peace to be palatable--you must hunger for it."

Time passed quickly as they discussed politics and society in general. Nearing the end of their journey, Eberhαrt and company had concluded that all politicians were decent beings with very good intentions though somewhat misguided.

"Hello," said the security officer, "Your name, please?"

"Eberhαrt Ghoηαdz."

"Please wait," said the security officer.

The officer entered the security station and proceeded to inform his superiors that visitors were at the front gate. After a few moments, the gate opened and the security officer again approached Eberhαrt's AGV.

"Go straight ahead to Bay Three and wait for an escort," instructed the officer.

Eberhαrt smoothly and skillfully maneuvered the AGV toward Bay Three. Upon reaching their destination, Eberhαrt was quite pleased to see the smartly dressed lab tech named Mμreeη waiting to greet them.

"Hello, Mμreeη," said Eberhαrt smiling brightly. "I brought my sister and a friend."

"That's okay," responded Mμreeη. "We encourage second-hand recruitment. Exit your craft and follow me."

A large overhead door opened and Mμreeη motioned for all of them to follow. Once all were inside, the door smoothly closed and they could feel themselves descending. After about five zlits, the door again opened and Mµreeη again asked them to follow. They proceeded down a corridor to a door, which bore the letters A.P.E.L.. Mµreeη then pressed a succession of buttons on a keypad that opened the door.

"Please, be seated," instructed Mµreeη. "You will be addressed shortly."

Mµreeη smiled at Eberhαrt and left. Eberhαrt was very infatuated with this person.

"I'm in love," stated Eberhαrt jokingly.

"You're in love, all right," responded Julíenηe, "...with anything that walks on legs and has hair between at least two of them."

"Eighteen to one-eighty--bionic, robotic, or humanoid...." Jeręmy doubled over laughing.

As the three of them continued to joke and laugh, partly to relieve their nervousness, a wall viewer came on. ...A stately being now appeared on the screen. He wore a monocle on his left eye and smiled brightly as he began to address them.

"Welcome," he said. "I am Sir Jacφb Puηt. You and your friends have been selected to participate in a bold adventure aimed at rescuing the people of this planet from the social absurdities that now exist. As I am speaking to you, an implosion capsule is rocketing toward Sigma Nine-thousand. Sigma Nine-thousand is a star currently withdrawing into itself. It will begin to implode upon contact with the capsule. We have calculated that the implosion will begin after another sixty-four spans have passed."

Eberhαrt, Julíenηe, and Jeręmy exchanged glances at each other as they listened to this almost unbelievable plan. Up until now, it really seemed like fantasy rather than fact.

"...A specially designed spacecraft is being readied to launch and rendezvous with the star at the height of its implosion when its gravitational force will be increasing exponentially. The spacecraft will rocket toward this star at an ever-increasing velocity. The extreme gravitational pull will cause the spacecraft to reach a velocity of one-point-one times the speed of light. At this point, the spacecraft will be one span away from colliding into Sigma Nine-thousand. Consequently, the spacecraft will have achieved a velocity that will allow it to exit conventional time and space beginning the journey back to a period in our history before Sharon Defoulgar's innate intelligence ever existed.

It is my hope that you will agree to participate in this bold and daring adventure. If so, then you shall pilot this spacecraft into the unknown regions that exist beyond conventional time and space. Your mission will be to prevent Sharon Defoulgar from perfecting innate intelligence. The details of this mission will be further explained, but first you must decide upon whether or not you will participate. Thank you."

The screen went blank as Eberhart, Julíenηe, and Jerεmy sat staring at each other. Fear, excitement, and curiosity flowed through their veins as they contemplated the question that Sir Puηt had put before them. The door behind them opened and Mμreeη entered the room. They watched her as she scanned their faces for clues to their innermost feelings concerning what they had just heard.

"I'll show you to your quarters," said Mμreeη.

Mμreeη led them out of the room and back to the elevator. Once inside, they felt themselves briefly ascend. The door opened to a long corridor. Just outside the elevator, the trio could not help but notice the large sixty-four illuminated on the corridor floor.

"Please, follow me," she said while motioning with her hand.

As they walked, they could see into many of the units. There seemed to be a male and a female inside all of them.

"This is your unit," said Mµreeη nodding to Jeręmy and Julíenηe.

"Eberhαrt," said Mµreeη pointing across the hall to another door. "This unit is ours...."

The span had passed quickly. Tadφlŏn could hear Hαzăr's AGV entering the parking bay. She had picked up some Arturian food on the way home from work and was preparing the table for their meal together.

"Tadφlŏn," said Hαzăr entering through the door, "I'm home!"

"How was your work, dear?"

"Terrible," replied Hαzăr. "I got paid this span and my back is killing me."

"Come to mama," cooed Tadφlŏn in a teasing manner. "When are they ever going to cut your salary? I mean you put in long spans and are productive." She rubbed his shoulders and then said, "You deserve it."

"I wish!" responded Hαzăr while turning on the televiewer.

Hαzăr settled in on a program where a flashy dressed, silver haired evangelist was asking for commitments to further one of the many religions on Uµmpάr.

"...I know my friends that times are hard. I know that burdens are heavy, but I can feel that there is someone out there wanting to accept a five-thousand mag pledge...."

"One zlit of sowing and thirty zlitons of reaping," said Hαzăr sarcastically. "That's all these guys want to do is to give someone their gold. Why don't they take some of mine for a change?"

"Come on now, honey," said Tadφlŏn trying to soothe him.

"Well, damazar...How can the government let these beings get away with giving their gold away?" said Hαzăr showing much frustration. "I'll bet that THEY don't have to go out and spend gold every span," he continued. "And you know how Xlim and Zilly Rae Fakers lived!" Hαzăr shook his head. "I'm sorry...." He apologized for allowing the troubles of life to dampen their evening together. "...And your work? Did everything go okay?"

"Compared to last span...I would have to say that everything was terrific," said Tadφlŏn chuckling.

Hαzăr and Tadφlŏn spent the evening talking and cuddling. Just, basically, being an old and very happily married couple. With the children staying at BlackStellar Labs for awhile, the chance had come for Hαzăr and Tadφlŏn to rediscover each other. Ah yes... this evening was sure to outshine a dwarf star.

"Let's get some sleep," said Mμreeη turning down the light. "...lots going on next span."

The room surrounding Mμreeη and Eberhαrt was quite small. It was filled with one parallelogram bed, a ceiling televiewer, a shower room, and a dressing station.

"I feel like I know you."

"You do, kind of...," responded Mμreeη. She

turned toward him. "I sat across from you in a nano-economics class a few solacles back."

"That's right! I remember now," said Eberhart, "I asked you out on a date!"

"You most certainly did not!" Mμreeη sat up and gave him a disappointing look.

"Yes, I did! You said, 'Absolutely NOT!'"

"You asked me to go with you to your friend's AGV race on the night before finals and... I said absolutely not because of that."

"I was over-the-edge about you then...you know?" he said.

"Eberhart, I was always around, but I just couldn't seem to get close to you--until now. I am still very much attracted to you." Mμreeη lay back down and turned her back toward him. She was feeling just a bit embarrassed about disclosing her feelings.

Eberhart lay pondering this new information. He now understood why he had been paired with Mμreeη. She chose him! He chased sleep, but found himself awake and watching her, fully absorbing her beauty, way into the night. Indeed, Mμreeη exhibited beauty like an autumn forest--both natural and breathtaking. Her eyes radiated a lovely and inviting orange aura. Her hair was chopped and somewhat bowl-cut in front. Her skin was smooth and her body was well proportioned. Eberhart guessed that she was approximately 5.8 penãr tall and weighed about one-hundred thirty magnitudes. Yes, to Eberhart, she was gorgeous. Yawning at last, he finally drifted off to sleep enjoying just being near her.

"Time to get up and get going," said Mµreeη whispering in Eberhαrt's ear.

Eberhαrt opened his eyes to see Mµreeη hovering slightly over him. Waking, he gazed first at her face and then to the small galactic tattoo on her naked breast, he realized that she was completely nude. Eberhαrt became quite nervous at this new development. Knowingly, Mµreeη began stroking his chest lightly. Eberhαrt focused his willpower on trying to control his body's hi-frequency quivering. Finally, her tenderness soothing his anxiety, they came together, still trembling, in a fashion that only people in love can.

Being lower-class, Eberhαrt had never dreamed that lovemaking would be this good or that he would ever have had the opportunity to enjoy it so freely. Now overcome with desire, their bodies surrendered to bold explorations guided by tender caresses. Slowly, with purpose, they ramped up their passion. Grinding together sensually...firmly pulling and pushing, twisting and turning...their lips sweetly dissolving into passionate kisses. Mmmm...this bonding, designed by deity and engineered by destiny, began to cure....

[Knock!]

"Are you ready?" asked Mµreeη standing in Julíenηe and Jeręmy's doorway.

"Yes," replied Jeręmy, "we're almost ready."

Everyone had now assembled in the corridor. Mµreeη once again escorted them to the door labeled A.P.E.L. Once inside, they were invited to sit. The viewer came on and they were again addressed by Sir Jacφb Puηt.

"I trust that you all slept well," inquired Sir Puηt.

112

All nodded but sat quietly.

"I'm sorry," said Sir Puŋt. "Please feel free to speak. I am able to both see and hear you."

"We slept wonderfully well," beamed Eberhαrt.

"Good... good," responded Sir Puŋt. "Have you made a decision?"

Eberhαrt, Julíenŋe, and Jerẹmy looked at one another and smiled. Then Eberhαrt spoke....

"Yes, we have, sir," said Eberhαrt.

"...And will you join us in our adventure and quest for a better life?"

"Yes, sir...We will," answered Eberhαrt with Julíenŋe and Jerẹmy nodding.

Jacφb began to explain the intricacies of the mission. He encouraged their questions and effort during the upcoming training and mission preparations.

"Excuse me, sir," interrupted Eberhαrt, "what does A.P.E.L. stand for?'

"Artificially Programmed Edible Life-form," replied Sir Puŋt.

Jacφb went on to explain that if the mission went according to plan, the A.P.E.L.'s function was to add a piece of grey matter to Sharon Defoulgar's brain allowing her to foresee how future society would turn out. It was hoped that the A.P.E.L. would successfully alter her innate intelligence technique with the aim of avoiding the present period's problems. Of course, for all of this to happen, the voyagers must precisely rendezvous with Sigma Nine-thousand just as its gravitational force is paramount, pass successfully through the time continuum breach to the correct historical period, find Sharon Defoulgar, motivate her to ingest the A.P.E.L., and return. ...Farfetched? ...Hopelessly impossible? Maybe....

However, Eberhαrt and company were certainly going to give it their best shot.

Time passed quickly as Mμreeη, Eberhαrt, Julíenηe, and Jeręmy trained and prepared for the mission. Of the utmost importance were the times they spent learning all of the spacecraft's unique instruments and the procedures that they must precisely follow. The time for their departure was quickly approaching.

"Have you seen Julíenηe and Eberhαrt lately?" asked Tadφlŏn.

"I saw Eberhαrt a few spans ago...No, many spans ago come to think of it," answered Hαzăr.

"I'm getting a little concerned," said Tadφlŏn.

"Yeah," replied Hαzăr, "I'm a little worried myself."

"I'm going to call the authorities," announced Tadφlŏn.

Hαzăr was about to voice his misgivings concerning the involvement of authorities, but Tadφlŏn was already reporting the disappearance of their children.

"They're sending an investigator over," said Tadφlŏn terminating communication with the U.F.B.A..[22]

"I don't know if involving the government is a good idea," responded Hαzăr looking more worried than before.

"What do you mean, dear?" asked Tadφlŏn perplexed by his statement.

"Well...I mean...do you remember where we used to live after we first were married?" began Hαzăr. "Do

_____

[22] U.F.B.A. -- Uμmpάrian Faith Based Agency

you remember that night in the AGV bay when I was screaming?"

"What are you getting at, dear?" asked Tadφlŏn very confused.

[Knock, Knock, Knock!]

"U.F.B.A....Open up!"

"Damazar," said Hαzăr, "they're here already!"

Tadφlŏn opened the door to three plain suited agents wearing large helmets with the initials U.F.B.A. printed on the sides.

"Mr. and Mrs. Ghoηαdz?" asked the first agent.

"Yes," replied Tadφlŏn, "come in."

The three agents entered the Ghoηαdz' dwelling and secured the living room. They wasted no time in beginning their investigation. As Hαzăr sat quietly, the agents asked many questions and documented Tadφlŏn's story.

"Mr. Ghoηαdz," said the agent, "do you have anything to add?"

"No," answered Hαzăr. "What my wife has told you is about it."

Just then a forth agent entered through the door and called the senior agent aside. After a brief conversation, the senior agent returned to speak with the Ghoηαdz'.

"Mr. Ghoηαdz," he began. "You and your wife lived in the Julious sector many solacles ago."

"Yes," responded Hαzăr.

"Well, sir, we've been investigating a mysterious gold appearance at what was your old address," said the agent. "Seems a few spans ago, the current owner's AGV, wife, and pet were injured when a large stack of gold bars appeared out of nowhere."

"So?" shrugged Hɑzăr. "What does that have to do with our missing children?"

"You're one of those time travel engineers aren't you?" pressured the agent.

"Well, I do work in the field of trans-dimensional engineering," stated Hɑzăr becoming obviously nervous.

"I mean that you could probably send things away in time," said the agent. "Things like gold...maybe even children!"

"Just what are you implying?" Hɑzăr was now visibly angered.

"You know it's a federal offense to do away with gold, and children too for that matter, if the purpose is to reduce your salary," continued the agent steadily pacing in front of the Ghoηɑdz'.

"Do away with our children...reduce our salary...What is going on?" Tadφlŏn was more confused than ever.

"You two will have to come with us," said the agent.

"What do you mean? Why?" asked Tadφlŏn.

"I meeean... you two are under arrest for the suspicion of willful child losing and salary evasion," stated the agent bluntly.

"Hɑzăr, what's going on?" asked Tadφlŏn, completely stunned.

The agents quickly ushered Hɑzăr and Tadφlŏn away to the Interrogatorium.[23] Once there, the Ghoηɑdz' were confined to await questioning.

"I'm scared," confessed Tadφlŏn.

---

[23] Interrogatorium -- A place where they put you under hot lights and try to get you to spill your guts--*a Tanning Salon with attitude.*

"Don't worry, honey," replied Hαzăr trying to calm her fears.

Two others were confined in the next cell. Obviously, they did not care for each other's company. In fact, Hαzăr and Tadφlŏn were unable to get any rest that night because of their fighting and bizarre activities.

"Baaah! Baaaaah!" cried one.

"Hαzăr…what are they doing?"

As Hαzăr and Tadφlŏn sat quietly, the two Uμmpάrians next to them did behave very, very badly for the duration of the sleep period.

"Wake up!" sounded a voice.

"Mr. Kiaser, you're being released into your mate's custody," said a burly and gruesome looking guard.

"Bub, are you all right?" she asked.

"Honey," said Bub as he smirked at his cellmate, "no more Marzurian ale for me!"

Hαzăr and Tadφlŏn quietly monitored the Kiaser's as they were escorted out by the guard. This should have been of some small relief, but other concerns now commanded the Ghoηαdz' attention.

"WHEN ARE YOU GOING TO LET US OUT OF HERE?" screamed Hαzăr not really expecting an answer.

"Stop screaming," said Tadφlŏn trying to ease Hαzăr's frustration.

"Baaah! Baaah!" came the cry from the next cell.

"Be quiet you disgusting person! You--!"

"Mr. and Mrs. Ghoηαdz," said a voice interrupting Tadφlŏn's verbal assault on the adjacent cell, "you're being released into my custody."

117

A security guard in very threatening attire forcefully unlocked and opened the cell door.

"What about our children?" Hαzăr demanded with the bravado only a worried father could display.

"This way, please," continued the guard giving Hαzăr a stern, but respectful look.

The Ghoηαdz' complied and followed the guard down a series of dimly lit hallways all the while fearful of what now lay in store for them and their children. They passed through doors, down then up lift stations, and through pungent smelling corridors. They went over, then under, and around checkpoints to what Hαzăr knew was the underbelly of shadow government corruption clothed as national security. Hαzăr was getting just a little bit pissed off at this run around.

Their trek ended at a small waiting room where there was a very sinister person seated with his head buried in a stack of papers. The Ghoηαdz' were becoming more fearful of this seedy character as the guard proceeded to lead them directly up to the official.

"Here they are, Mr. Gharthy," said the guard.

The guard turned and walked out of the room. The official looked at both of them for what seemed like sixty zlitons and then smiled.

"Mr. and Mrs. Ghoηαdz," he said, "...please, be seated. I'm Mizol Gharthy from U.C.O.M.[24]"

"Pleased to meet you, Mr. Gharthy," said Tadφlŏn nervously. "What's this all about? ...Why are we here?"

Gharthy gave Tadφlŏn a stern look. "Well, Mrs. Ghoηαdz, you and your lovely little family are in a teenie weenie bit of trouble. Did you know that your children

---

[24] U.C.O.M. -- Uμmpάrian Covert Operations Ministry

were members of the CPU?"

"Our kids?" Tadφlŏn asked.

"Now calm down, folks," commanded Gharthy. "Come on and admit it...you are well aware of your children's CPU activities. ...And isn't it true that not only your children but yourselves as well are COMMYS?"

"WE DON'T KNOW WHAT YOU'RE TALKING ABOUT!" Tadφlŏn rose from her seat.

"You mean that your kids DO NOT work for BlackStellar Labs?" Gharthy said with a glare that put Tadφlŏn back in her chair.

"Well, yes...maybe," replied Tadφlŏn with a more subdued tone while turning her head to the side.

"Mrs. Ghoηαdz, BlackStellar Labs is nothing but a mere front for the CPU and I'm going to prove it!"

Gharthy's eyes glowed red with the crazed look of a near-rad lunatic.

Tadφlŏn rolled her eyes at Hαzăr who had been remaining conspicuously quiet. Hαzăr offered no response and continued to sit quietly.

"Now, if you and your husband would just sign this confession, things would become easier for all concerned," said Gharthy as he pushed the document in front of them.

"A confession of WHAT?" demanded Hαzăr finally breaking his silence.

"Well, Mr. Ghoηαdz...you *can* talk," said Gharthy in an intimidating manner. "Always mistrusting the government aren't you?" continued Gharthy. "Why...you're the typical Commy, Mr. Ghoηαdz! ...bet you even want to read it before you sign it. As a loyal government employee, I am hurt! Please folks, just trust me and SIGN IT!"

Mizol Gharthy was a crafty and persistent government official. He alone had done more to create a fear of commonsense people than any other individual had. Hαzăr knew this. He also knew that they must play along and wait for a chance to escape.

"Why didn't you say you were a FOR REAL government agent?" said Hαzăr appearing to cozy up to Gharthy. "Why...we'd be happy to do whatever the government wants."

Then Hαzăr, to the disbelief of Tadφlŏn, signed the document.

"Hαzăr...what are you doing?" asked Tadφlŏn. "We ARE NOT commonsense people!"

Hαzăr, looking now at Tadφlŏn, clasped her hand and displayed a twinkle in his eye that gave her a feeling that everything was okay.

"What's this? Ballbuster," said Gharthy, "What's a Ballbuster?"

"...THIS!"

Hαzăr's foot proceeded to accelerate on a collision course with Gharthy's groin, which culminated in a spectacular explosion of pain and suffering on the part of Mizol Gharthy.

"Let's go," said Hαzăr to Tadφlŏn as Gharthy buckled and took up a fetal position on the floor.

"Ouch!" said Tadφlŏn. She followed closely with Hαzăr.

"Wait! The guard is in the hallway," whispered Hαzăr. "Quick--take off your suit," said Hαzăr.

"What? So, this is what turns you on...you little muff hound," breathed Tadφlŏn jokingly as she complied.

He ignored her comment. "Quickly, run out into the hallway and then run back here!"

"...But I'm naked!"

"Tadφlŏn!" whispered Hαzăr, "Shut up and go!"

Tadφlŏn made a dash for the hall. As she turned quickly to return, she slipped and made a very audible "SPLAT" as she hit the floor. The guard, taken by surprise, could not believe his eyes. Cautiously, looking around as if to ensure they were alone, he crept forward to get a better look. A little grin appeared on his rugged, severely battle damaged, face. Then, the guard broke into a full-fledged, sex crazed, *ain't had none in a zliton*, gallop.

"Oh goodie, oh goodie...gonna get me some Uμmpa-tang!" (*Sorry... We are not on the planet Poon!*)

As the guard streaked after Tadφlŏn, who had now regained her footing and disappeared from the hall, his face collided with a rather heavy chair. His body and thingy in hand, however, continued on for another hundredth of a penărd before falling to the floor and flopping around in what can only be described as a very painful and lewd manner.

"Let's go," said Hαzăr hurriedly.

"Where are we going?" Tadφlŏn asked as she quickly drew on her suit.

"BlackStellar Labs," replied Hαzăr. "...We've got to find the kids!"

"Hurry...I'm right behind you!"

Hαzăr and Tadφlŏn made their way down the dark corridors being careful to avoid detection.

"Quick! ...up there," said Tadφlŏn pointing at the ventilation grating.

"Good idea," said Hαzăr. "I'll boost you up."

Carefully and quietly, Hαzăr and Tadφlŏn made their escape. Unfortunately, U.C.O.M. agents were in close pursuit and could be heard on every level.

"Hold on...we're almost there," said Hazăr.

Hazăr and Tadφlŏn exited the ventilation ducts at the AGV parking garage.

"Quickly," said Hazăr, "this one's not secure."

"I'm in," confirmed Tadφlŏn. "Punch it!"

Hazăr quickly maneuvered the AGV out of the garage and headed for BlackStellar labs. Looking back, Tadφlŏn informed Hazăr that U.C.O.M. was in close pursuit. Hazăr put the AGV into a hard turn narrowly missing two gazeldas attempting sex with a mailbox.

"Look out!"

[CRUNCH!]

Just as Tadφlŏn screamed, the Ghoηadz' vehicle impacted with the side of a U.C.O.M. vehicle crunching hard. The impact drove the mobile handsets into the agent's ears.

"They were just saying on the viewer that these mobile handsets could cause brain damage," said Hazăr solemnly.

The Ghoηadz' AGV sustained minor damage and they continued on... quietly humming a dial tone.

"There it is," said Hazăr pointing to the entrance to BlackStellar Labs.

Stopping just in front of the gate....

"May I help you, sir?" asked the security officer.

"Uh...Yes, we are here to pick up our son," replied Hazăr with Tadφlŏn nodding in support. "His name is Eberhart Ghoηadz."

"Wait here, please," directed the guard.

After appearing to communicate with someone, the officer returned to the Ghoηadz' AGV.

"Straight ahead to Bay Three and wait," the guard instructed.

Hαzăr nodded in the affirmative as the gate opened allowing them entrance to the facility grounds. Their craft slowly maneuvered past various complexes that caused the Ghoηαdz' to wonder what BlackStellar Labs was really about. Arriving at Bay Three, the Ghoηαdz' turned on the media receiver and waited as instructed.

"Are you lonely? Do you need someone to talk to? Are your pockets full? Then dial 1-900000000000-UNLOAD…We've been waiting for you! …Ahhh…Eeee…Oooh BABY! …Call Now!"

"…I can feel someone out there needs to accept a gold donation. …Why not call now and make a commitment."

"Broadcast leeches," said Hαzăr finally. "Let's go!"

"They said wait here," responded Tadφlŏn.

"…For what! …U.C.O.M.," retorted Hαzăr.

Hαzăr extended the ramp and encouraged Tadφlŏn to go with him in search of their son. Carefully, they investigated each structure looking for an entrance.

"No doors…Nothing," said a bewildered Tadφlŏn.

"Look," said Hαzăr.

An overhead door was opening. Muffled voices and unusual sounds of movement could be heard.

"What's in there?" asked Tadφlŏn.

"Come on," invited Hαzăr quietly.

Hαzăr and Tadφlŏn slid up next to the door. Peeking around the opening, they could see some activity around a hover vehicle. The vehicle powered up and started toward the door. Hαzăr and Tadφlŏn concealed themselves and prepared to enter the facility. As the vehicle exited, they entered and moved nonchalantly toward an interior doorway.

Passing through the unlocked door, they made their way down a corridor. Sounds were coming closer to them. Hαzăr quickly directed Tadφlŏn through another doorway shutting the door behind them. Quickly, they proceeded forward. Suddenly an alarm began to sound. Thinking they had been detected, they moved even quicker toward a lift. As the lift door closed behind them, the alarm sound became muffled.

"What did you do?" asked Hαzăr.

"Whaaa--" uttered Tadφlŏn.

"This thing is moving," said Hαzăr.

"I didn't touch anything!" replied Tadφlŏn.

The lift had begun descending with steady acceleration. The Ghoηαdz' remained quiet, held hands, and allowed sex crazed notions to dirty dance in their heads.

"We've stopped!" Tadφlŏn's voice broke the silence.

Hαzăr moved closer to the door. As the door slid quietly aside, Hαzăr was confronted by the most hideous a creature he had ever seen....

"...Mother Gluteus?" said Tadφlŏn quite surprised.

"You still married to this poor excuse for a gob of Tirallian dung?" quipped Tadφlŏn's old nanny.

"Tirallian dung," snapped back Hαzăr. "Why you mutated Dorkaduzian waste sucker. You--!"

"Meltdown you two," interceded Tadφlŏn. "We're looking for our children...not trouble."

"Yes," said Hαzăr. "Where are Eberhαrt and

Julíenŋe?"

As Hɑzăr and his nanny-in-law stood snarling at each other, they were joined by others.

"Welcome...I am Sir Jacφb Puŋt," said a uniformed gentleman.

"Tadφlŏn...Honey...This is my husband," announced Perfidious. "I'm no longer...Mother Gluteus."

"Not now, dear," said Jacφb, "the countdown has commenced. Follow us."

"Where's our children?" demanded Hɑzăr growing impatient.

Sir Jacφb acted as if he had not heard a word and moved smartly away from them with Perfidious in tow. The Ghoŋadz' followed the Puŋts to a large bay. As the Ghoŋadz' looked on as lights were flashing, people were busy monitoring instruments, and doing whatever people do in a Time Vessel Launch & Recovery bay. Impatiently, the Ghoŋadz quizzed their hosts about Eberhɑrt and Julíenŋe. Suddenly, the muffled alarm became very distinct and urgent.

"Sir," said a well-dressed female security officer, "the upper levels are being penetrated!"

"What's going on?" asked a concerned Tadφlŏn.

"U.C.O.M. agents that were following you likely have entered the complex," said Sir Puŋt.

"That heap of Woolosian waste has led them here!" barked Perfidious.

Perfidious sneered at Hɑzăr thus insinuating that their impending confrontation was certainly his fault. Hɑzăr quietly responded in kind with the typical elevated middle fingers and the ever famous, "I got your Woolosian waste right here!" crotch grab.

Yes... There were no molecules of love wasted

between these two. Hɑzăr's dislike and mistrust of Perfidious went back to the early spans of Tadφlŏn's and his courtship.

CHAPTER SIX

An ideal family unit...

"Daddy...this is our next door neighbor, Hαzăr Ghoηαdz. He's here to help me flunk random mathematics," said a young Tadφlŏn to her father.

It had been Tadφlŏn's sixth span at Ignoranium High. Her father, Sάgαçion, had been unexpectedly transferred to Lobotma, a second quadrant village in the near-rad hemisphere. This had been a difficult move for Tadφlŏn. She had lost her mother just last term to *phototrophosis*, a supposedly extinct viral infection where photosynthetic bacteria become trapped inside of an organic host. In order to escape and access light, which is used to convert carbon dioxide and water to food, the bacteria consume the organic host leaving no trace of their existence. Achates Mythosa, the family physician and life-long friend of Sάgαçion, attended to the family's needs. Tadφlŏn was confident that her mother received the best care available. Still, sometimes she thought her father did not display the grief she would have expected. Now, here in a strange new place, she was just trying to fit in.

"Where did you live before coming to Lobotma?" inquired Hαzăr.

"Prystine," replied Tadφlŏn.

"You're kidding...Right?" said Hαzăr disbelieving.

"What do you mean?"

"Come on...You don't expect me to believe that you gave up a life in Prystine to come and settle in Lobotma," replied Hαzăr.

Tadφlŏn offered only a puzzled look.

"You really don't know where you are now...Do you?"

While looking around as if to see if anyone was watching, Hαzăr pulled Tadφlŏn very close and brought her up to speed on her new home.

"Listen, Tadφlŏn...People don't just move here from places like Prystine," Hαzăr said. "If you really lived in Prystine...You're being dealt with."

"Dealt with?" responded Tadφlŏn.

"Lobotma is nothing more than a rehab village for those with I.Q.s too high for their own good," answered Hαzăr. "What does your dad do for a living?"

"Why...he's a perpetuity scientist," responded Tadφlŏn. "Why do you ask?"

"That makes sense," admitted Hαzăr. "He must have discovered something that has made the Controllers nervous."

"I don't understand, Hαzăr."

Hαzăr took her hand and held it gently then looked into her eyes. "...You're so refreshing. I hope we can be something more than just study partners."

128

Tadφlŏn blushed slightly and smiled without responding. She already knew in her heart that Hαzăr and she were destined to be together.

"Uh hmm, uh hmm!" grunted Perfidious.

"You mind your manners, little mister," she commanded. "…and missy you'd best beware of the low-life parasites that thrive around here."

The sinister, middle-aged nanny appeared from nowhere to intervene on their personal moment and then was gone.

"Low-life…parasite!" whispered Hαzăr. "Who the heck was that?"

"That's my nanny. Dad's new employer sent her when we were being relocated," said Tadφlŏn. "The government assigned her to us."

"That's scary," said Hαzăr. "I already do not like her. Wait a zliton…Your dad works for the government?"

"Yes," replied Tadφlŏn. "That's why we're here. He was randomly selected for HRP. You know…the Hemispherical Relocation Program."

"The Hemispherical Relocation Program," repeated Hαzăr. "What's that?"

"I really don't know much about it," admitted Tadφlŏn. "All I know is just after I lost my mom, the government notified us that we had won the Planetary Lottery. Magnitudes of gold began arriving at our doorstep. …dad became worried. As part of the prize, we were uprooted from Prystine and moved here."

"I don't think I have ever heard of a Planetary Lottery," said Hαzăr.

"Anyway, Hαzăr…meeting you has been my first blessing since this nightmare started," confessed Tadφlŏn softly.

Hɑzăr and Tadφlŏn sat holding hands as if they had known each other from birth.

Just through the doorway, in plain view, Perfidious scorned as she spoke into a planetary communication device. "...I know that you desire their union...but I sense a troublesome combination with these two. I--I'm sorry...yes, I understand!"

"You had better keep an eye on that kid, Mister Academis," advised Perfidious. "He will be an undesirable influence on your daughter."

"Undesirable to whom?" asked Sάgaçion. "I think Tadφlŏn rather likes him."

"Mind my words," grumbled Perfidious as she went on about her business.

Sάgaçion peeked around the corner into the study observing his dearest and her new friend. Sάgaçion knew that Hɑzăr was now something special to Tadφlŏn. Her heart was revealed by the sparkle in her eye. Feelings of love was evidenced by the way she held his hand, the way she seemed to glow as he looked at her, and the way she laughed softly seeking not to betray these moments of happiness.

These past spans had been most difficult for Tadφlŏn to endure. Losing her mother.... Sάgaçion wanted to confide in Tadφlŏn the truth, but he dare not for fear of their safety. He welcomed her respite from grief and resided to do what he could to protect her new friendship.

"Uh hmm, Hɑzăr is it?" said Sάgaçion loudly before entering the room. "I'm Tadφlŏn's father, Sάgaçion. I work with your father, Vęríle," he continued. "Would you like to stay for dinner?"

130

"Oh yes, Hɑzăr," added Tadφlŏn, "Please?"

"Sure ...yes," replied Hɑzăr. "Thank you, sir."

"I'm off to inform Perfidious," said Sȧgaçion then he left them.

Tadφlŏn smiled and shrugged her shoulders at Hɑzăr.

"I think he likes you," she whispered.

Typically, the revelation that a father actually likes the boy his daughter is dating dissolves that relationship faster than a... well... an anti-relationship pill--what else? However, the Academis family was far from typical. Sȧgaçion knew his daughter's judgment was always heart-felt and sound. As for her part, Tadφlŏn had only known love, caring, and respect from her mom and dad. An ideal family unit... or so their genetic designers thought.

Yes, Sȧgaçion and Tadφlŏn's mother, Vĕracítii, were engineered beings. Their designers intended that they would mate and begin to produce a family unit that would accept the current social structure without question. With controlled childhoods, the future Ghoηadz couple grew up as next-door neighbors. They attended school with other engineered couples in a community created for this particular purpose. The Controllers hypothesized that genetic programming and a steady feeding of institutionalized propaganda would produce adult Uμmpȧrians that would accept their decrees without question. Their hypothesis was flawed....

"Everyone ready?" asked Sir Jacφb.

"Yes, sir!" answered the crew as they boarded the spacecraft that bore his name.

They had practiced for this event and now all was

131

proceeding as planned. Although hurriedly, the crew moved into their positions and immediately began take-off procedures. Eberhαrt and Mµreeη looked at each other as all of their hearts began racing with the final countdown moments rapidly approaching. They all knew the importance of timing. A fraction of a zlit delay could mean they would miss the targeted time period or even worse... be vaporized by the imploding Sigma Nine-thousand.

Launch personnel could be seen scurrying around the craft. Preparations for launch were almost completed. The clock was counting down and the crew was getting edgy. Still, the opportunity to alter history and delete innate intelligence could not be ignored. What would it be like without innate intelligence? Would they all suddenly become stupid? Millions of thoughts were passing through their heads.

"Nine!"
"Eight!"

"Seven!"

[BEEP! BEEP! BUZZZZ!] sounded an alarm.

"Sir! Security has been breached!" said the launch technician.

Yes, the U.C.O.M., acting on what they had pieced together from their lengthy interrogation of Hαzăr and Tadφlŏn, were storming the BlackStellar Lab complex. The U.C.O.M. was unaware that the U.F.B.A. already had a deep cover operative inside.

"SIR! THEY'RE ABOUT TO GAIN ACCESS TO LAUNCH CONTROL!" frantically shouted the technician.

"Transfer the alternate data pack and launch!" commanded Sir Jacφb.

As the commandos blew the door, the technician downloaded the most recent calculations concerning the implosion of Sigma Nine-thousand and the alternate data pack.

"Download comple--!"

A wink of an eye later, the technician lay dead from laser fire. However, the spacecraft was already belching fire as vertical take-off engines began pushing the ship away from the planet. Within zlitons, the main engines fired. The craft ascended rapidly, gaining speed, and was soon beyond the view of the naked eye.

Sir Puηt, his wife, the Ghoηαdz', and the rest of the CPU team escaped via secret tunnels from the control room. However, Eberhαrt and the rest were just vaguely aware of what had transpired during the zlitons before their launch.

"Too soon..." murmured Mμreeη to herself.

"What?" Eberhαrt asked.

The craft continued to shake and groan as its structure, aided by an inertial compensation field, struggled to adjust to the increasing velocity. The crew was held firmly in their seats reluctantly accelerating with the ship. Their appointment with destiny... would they make it?

"MUREEN!" said Eberhart loudly.

"WHAAATTT?" came the somewhat vibrated response.

"What do you mean? ...Too soon!" repeated Eberhart.

"I mean...or I think I mean...we launched before we should have," replied Mµreeη.

"What will happen now?" asked Julíenηe.

"I don't know...Maybe we will miss our targeted time period or," Mµreeη swallowed deeply, "...plunge into Sigma Nine-thousand!"

The craft's speed continued increasing as it raced toward Sigma Nine-thousand. The inertial compensation field was fully generated and steady. The crew had calmed and was busying themselves with all the instrumentation.

"How long before--?" began Jerẹmy.

"Two spans," replied Mµreeη reading his thoughts, "...before the implosion capsule will contact Sigma Nine-thousand."

"What can we do?" asked Julíenηe.

"Pray and prepare ourselves for our tasks ahead," said Eberhart trying to instill a sense of calm and duty.

A mere speck in the universe during a wink in time, the spacecraft continued to speed toward its destination and its appointment with fate.

"Aft thrusters, two-Z burn," commanded Mµreeη.

Jerẹmy responded and ignited the aft thrusters for two zlitons. This, the final course correction, assured them of arriving to meet with their destiny as planned.

"Switching to artificial navigation," announced Mµreeη.

With their course corrected, the computater would now guide the spacecraft and its occupants to a rendezvous with the past or, quite possibly, death.

The craft's speed was surpassing fifty thousand penãrds per zlit when the crew began their sleep period. Looking out the forward viewport, the darkness was speckled with tiny lights. Some appeared to streak by them while others appeared to be waiting to meet them. Fear and anxiety filled their hearts and was contained only by their shared hope of achieving a success that would release their people from an unbearable existence. Each pondered the unknown and dreamed of what might await them.

Ságaçion kept a keen eye on the instruments all the while thinking of his beloved Vĕracítii. Many spans had passed since she had entered stasis allowing her thoughts to be sent back in time to derail the innate intelligence program. He could not contain his emotions...he was nothing without her. How long could he... would he... deceive Tadφlŏn? His heart broke for her. Vĕracítii and Tadφlŏn were oh so close. Still it was Vĕracítii's wish that she not be told for fear of what might happen if Tadφlŏn had a slip of the tongue.

"You haven't said a single word, Ságaçion." Ovalŏn broke the silence.

"I'm sorry," he said, "I was thinking of Vĕracítii."

"I know, dear. I can't help but think of Vẹríle all

the time."

Ovalŏn had been patiently caring for the trio for spans now. Watching, worrying, and loving them. Her husband lay in stasis next to Woodland Williams and Věracítii Academis. These three brave individuals, whom for a brief period would not be missed, accepted the opportunity to undertake this daring mission to alter history.

Ságaçion, a perpetuity scientist, had made a significant discovery some time ago--thought waves of the brain were *never* lost. He discovered that brain waves originating hundreds of solacles ago were still traveling in space. More importantly, these waves were a tether, a direct link to the past. All that was needed was a device to receive them.

Ságaçion developed a means by which to attract and filter these waves. He theorized that the magnitude of these rhythmic fluctuations of electric potential could be sent through a coil creating a brain wave magnetic field. Furthermore, he theorized that by sending his own brain waves through a conductor cutting across this field would result in an induced electromotive force traveling back to the source. Indeed, the link to the past was complete. This basic theory became known as *The Ságaçion Principle of Trans-Temporal Telepathy.*

For spans, in the lab where he worked in Prystine, he would filter and play the thoughts. Ságaçion would connect himself to the brainwave transporter and send his thoughts via a single wave pattern back to the source. In doing so, he suddenly would just awaken in someone else's body in another time period. It was unbelievable! Ságaçion refined his instruments and began documenting periods in time by determining the age of the waves he was filtering. He developed computater programs to document and catalog wave patterns by time period, gender, frequency, and so on. Finally, he came across the thought waves of individuals from Sharon Defoulgar's time. Working with his good friend and colleague, Vẹríle Ghoηαdz, a plan was struck to attempt the alteration of Uμmρár's past. Unfortunately, these activities had been noticed by the Controllers. Ságaçion knew they were about to step in and shut down his project. He could not delay setting up a shadow mobile lab.

Not wasting any time, Ságaçion, Vĕracítii, Vẹríle, and Woodland began planning their most daring historical intervention. The mobile lab was in place and a period of time was selected to coincide with vacations so as not to raise suspicions about these missing individuals. No one else could know. Not even Tadφlŏn. At the appointed time, the plan was executed. As feared, the Controllers stepped in and did terminate the formal project. Consequently, Ságaçion was informed that he had won the planetary lottery and relocated. Now in Lobotma, the mobile lab was home to the trio that has risked their lives in an attempt to eliminate innate intelligence. They have yet to awaken signifying that their mission has yet to be completed.

"Do you think they're safe?" she asks.

"I don't know...I pray they are," he replied staring into the thin air.

"When will we know? When will they come back?" Ovalŏn became saddened.

"Now, now...don't cry. When they have completed the mission they will awaken on their own," said Ságaçion touching Ovalŏn's shoulder as he lovingly brushed Vĕracítii's face. "We must patiently wait and minister to our loved one's bodies until their thoughts return." Ságaçion's emotions pooled and tears trickled down his cheek.

[VAVOOM! ...FLASH!]

"What was that?" Julíenηe, waking much later than the rest, was now shocked to full consciousness.

"The implosion capsule has now contacted Sigma Nine-thousand!" announced Eberhαrt. He was already glued to the scanner observing the event.

"Switch on the monitor," commanded Mµreeη.

The screen was tremendously bright with the light emitted from the implosion of Sigma Nine-thousand. Quickly, however, the light began losing its intensity very rapidly. Other lights emitted from neighboring star systems could now be seen. And, as expected, the lights could be observed moving closer to the imploding star because of the tremendous gravitational forces that were now being forcefully applied.

"What's happening?" asked Jerẹmy.

"Sigma Nine-thousand is now contracting into itself," answered Mµreeη, "As its implosion continues, the gravitational forces will increase dramatically."

The star was compressing and everything around it was being drawn into it. Eventually, even light would not be able to escape the ever-increasing gravitational force.

"Speed--point nine LS," said Eberhαrt.

The spacecraft was glowing from the friction produced by the particulate matter being encountered as it rapidly closed on Sigma Nine-thousand.

"Light Speed!" announced Eberhαrt, his heart thumping against his chest.

138

Though the outermost layer of five glaciated heat shields was performing superbly, particulate was vaporizing from the spacecraft surface and the temperature inside the craft was increasing.

"Fourteen zlitons to warp!" said Μμreeη with a noticeable tone of uncertainty. "Begin time tracking preparations." Μμreeη seemed to struggle to remain focused on the procedures that would ensure their safety and success.

Jerȩmy began to power up a device that had been invented to calculate time passage as a body travels in excess of 1.86 x 10E5 penãrd/zlit. Theoretically, this device would track time passage and allow them to slow to sub-light speed and exit the time distortion at the appropriate period...theoretically.

"I can't get any power to the Emsicube module," said Jerȩmy.

"Try the breakers," instructed Eberhαrt.

"12 zlitons," droned Julíenηe.

"It's the time inverter transducer...I think," said Jeremy.

"Let's pull it apart," said Eberhart. He hopped out of his seat to help.

Eberhart and Jeremy began to frantically remove the fasteners that held the T.I.T. in place.

"Eight zlitons to warp."

"This one's stripped," said Jeremy. He was fumbling with a bolt.

"Use grips!" barked Eberhart.

"We have to get it fired or we're dead!"

"Four zlitons."

"Got it!" said Jeremy.

As they pulled out the T.I.T. it now became visible that a wire had arced and burned.

"GET ME THE FUSATRON!" yelled Eberhart.

Mμreeη lunged for the tool compartment and fumbled for the fusatron so that Eberhart could fuse the wire together. They were all starting to feel a little panicky as what might be their destruction was drawing near.

"Two zlitons."

"CATCH!" shouted Mμreeη.

Eberhart intercepted the fusatron and turned to administer it to the joint formed by the two wires that Jeremy had now mated together.

"Damazar! Jeremy--stop shaking!"

"One zliton!" sounded Julíenηe who now was fixated on the atomic clock.

Sigma Nine-thousand was growing closer and closer.

"THIRTY ZLITS!" Julíenηe's voice crackled indicating that she was now being overcome with

140

emotion.

"Just a bit more," said Eberhart.

"Fifteen zlits...We're not going to make it!" said Julíenηe.

"YOU'RE TOO LATE!" screamed Mµreeη. The cockpit began creaking from the increased gravity that was now trying to crush the hull of the ship as it was being drawn closer to oblivion. "YOU'RE TOO LA--!"

"GOT IT!" Eberhart slammed the transducer in place.

"POWER UP NOW!" yelled Jerẹmy.

"TWO ZLITS!"

"ONE!"

"WARP!"

The cockpit returned to its normal state while the monitor went blank. Everyone sat in silence. There were no sounds from anything except....

"Look," said Jerẹmy. He now pointed at the Time Correlator.

The time increments were counting backward at an increasing rate. As the realization of actual time travel was becoming evident, a nervous but restrained fear came over them.

"We're going backwards," announced Eberhart. He was somewhat dazed by the words he had just uttered.

"18700... 18000... 17000..."

Eberhart stopped saying the numbers aloud as they all looked on.

"Are we really going back in time?" asked Julíenηe.

No one responded. It seemed as though the reality of the moment had them all in a firm grasp. Their minds were too busy trying to sort out their lives and what was going to happen to them now.

"13500..." resumed Eberhart. "12500... 12000... 11000... 10000... 9000..."

Suddenly, the ship began slowing as was also evidenced by the Time Correlator.

"8900...."

"Look...the Time Correlator has almost stopped!" noted Jeręmy seeming to expect something ominous to happen when it finally did.

Everyone's eyes were fixed on the digital readout as it finally stopped.

"Sensors have detected a small planet 950,000 penãrds ahead bearing 8491 mark 2," announced Mµreeη.

"Can you get an atmospheric assessment yet?" asked Eberhart.

"Not yet," replied Jeręmy, "we're still too far out."

"...damage report?" ordered Eberhart.

"We were shaken up badly but diagnostics are not reporting any failures. The heat shielding has very minor damage, navigation appears to have lost two percent calibration, engines at ninety-seven percent, and the rest of the systems are nominal," reported Julíenηe.

"All right," said Eberhart. "Good job, you guys."

The *Sir Jacφb Puηt* sped toward what its crew believed to be a very young Uµmpár. A strong sense of excitement was taking hold as they realized the significance of their success thus far. To journey through time and stand on the doorstep of their distant past... it felt like a dream.

"The atmosphere is suitable for our life form," said Jeręmy.

They now were within close visual range of the

142

planet.

"Wow!" uttered Mμreeη. "Look at all that water."

The little blue planet was covered by water with a centralized landmass. It appeared to be well prepared to support a variety of life. The atmosphere was thick with mostly nitrogen, some oxygen, and a small quantity of other gases.

"I...," started Jerẹmy, who was still gazing at the Time Correlator, "guess we should prepare for a landing."

"I agree," said Eberhαrt calmly and, more importantly, confidently.

The mood had turned. They had made it... so far. Anyway, they were now officially time travelers and that was a fact.

"Let's get our butts down there!" said Mμreeη in an eager and adventurous voice.

They all took their positions again and buckled up.

"Okay...fire thrusters on my mark," commanded Eberhαrt. "Two, One...MARK!"

The rockets fired for a few zlits to reduce the ship's speed.

"Orbit is decaying and we will enter the atmosphere in two zlitons," said Mμreeη.

The ship streaked across the alien sky hurrying to keep an appointment with destiny. Locating a large clearing, the crew gently guided their craft to a landing area. Leaves were flailing and the dust billowed as the *Sir Jacφb Puηt* touched the ground.

"Okay...We've landed," said Jerẹmy.

"Check all systems and cut power," commanded Eberhαrt.

As they proceeded to check and power down the flight instruments a pair of eyes were closely watching from beyond the ship. The crew of the *Sir Jacøb Puŋt* reviewed their instruments and stood quietly at the viewport looking at the beauty of this strange world.

CHAPTER SEVEN

PARADISE GONE ASTRAY...

"What now?" Julíenηe had asked the sixty-four thousand mags of gold question.

"Well, the atmosphere registers as hospitable to our life form," said Mµreeη. "Let's go out and take a look around."

They individually secured their stations and offered each other subdued praise for accomplishing the mission thus far. Eberhαrt finished examining the instruments determining the status of the ship. Before departing the confines of the *Sir Puηt*, the crew ingested an anti-bacterial compound that should protect them from possible unknown contagions. They all milled about the doorway of the ship waiting for Eberhart to complete the necessary tasks. After a brief period, Eberhαrt began making his way toward them.

"Ready?" asked Eberhαrt. He scanned the faces of the crew. "...Then let's go."

The outer door swung out to contact the surface. Eberhαrt paused at the door absorbing the landscape and carefully reviewing the sensitron's readings. As they left the craft, they turned to their ship to adjust their individual homing receivers. Each silently admired the scarred beauty of the ship that had delivered them to this new world. Somewhat awed, they turned to continue their mission and headed for a nearby hill to observe their surroundings.

"Sir Puŋt," said Eberhart.

"What?" asked Jerẹmy.

"Sir Puŋt," said Eberhart again, "We have left the door open on the ship."

Eberhart reveled in the beauty of their ship. The *Sir Puŋt* was somewhat majestic against a backdrop of greenery and a pearled blue sky.

"It'll be okay," said Jerẹmy. "We're too far away to go back and close it now."

A shadowed figure moved deliberately through the foliage. Quietly and carefully, the shadow drew closer to the landing site. The opened door of the ship and the crew's departure had not gone unnoticed.

"I didn't think our planet had this much vegetation in 8761," said Jerẹmy.

"I didn't think so either," agreed Mµreeŋ. "...But it is beautiful."

"Remember everyone...we've got only six spans to find Sharon Defoulgar and compel her to ingest the A.P.E.L.," said Eberhart.

"That's right," said Jerẹmy. "We must find Sharon, get her to eat the A.P.E.L., return to our ship, blast off to rendezvous with another imploding star, and time warp back to our own period. ...A virtual piece of cake!"

"All of which, if all goes well, will have only

taken a fraction of a zliton," finished Mµreeη.

Eberhαrt eyed them both.

"What?" Jeręmy threw up his hands and was playing innocent.

Eberhαrt grinned, shook his head, and off they went. The crew of the *Sir Puηt* had barely entered the forest when their unknown host crept to the ship.

"Something is wrong," announced Jeręmy. He appeared confused as he tapped lightly on his instrument. "I'm not detecting a significant number of life forms." Jeręmy looked around. "...Plants and vegetation are all wrong for the 8700 period."

"What are you getting at?" Julíenηe questioned. She pursed her lips at him.

"I'm only detecting two humanoids in sensor range," reported Jeręmy. "I can't get a fix on their position because of a strong interference."

"Sensors are displaying odd, but very strong, signals. ...Like a very strong force of some kind," said Mµreeη. Mµreeη walked in a circle around the rest of the crew scanning and frequently adjusting the sensitron.

"Can you determine an origin?" asked Eberhαrt rotating from left to right trying to locate the source.

"No...However, these readings are....Wow! ...They're off the scale!" said Jeręmy.

"I've never seen anything like it," agreed Mµreeη. "The sensitron can't identify the type of energy or its source."

"Let's split up and scout a radius of about one penãrd from the ship," said Eberhαrt.

"We'll meet back at the ship in two spans," added Mµreeη.

They all nodded in agreement. Jeręmy and

147

Julíenηe headed off in the direction of the life force signals. Eberhαrt and Mμreeη proceeded toward what may be the strong force origin. The crew walked for some time.

"I'm a little nervous," confessed Julíenηe.

"It's going to be okay," comforted Jerεmy now taking her hand and gently squeezing it.

Julíenηe looked at him briefly and returned the squeeze. Jerεmy was satisfied. Up ahead they could see a clearing surrounded by beautiful flowers and fruit trees.

"It's ...beautiful," said Julíenηe somewhat awestruck.

"Come on," said Jerεmy, "...let's check it out."

Drawing closer to the clearing revealed even more wondrous colors. Fruit trees hung full with yellow, red, orange, green, and rainbow colored delights. The ground was covered with plush, soft green vegetation. The air breezed fresh and clean. Musical melodies wafted to their ears from camouflaged creatures within the lush vegetation and from the winged sirens being caressed by the wind. *Flora* and *Faunus* certainly had been directed to put their finest work on display.

"Wow," whispered Jerεmy.

"I feel so..." started Julíenηe. She spoke softly so as not to disturb the wonder.

"...content." Jerεmy correctly read her thoughts.

Gracefully descending to the soft green surface, Jerεmy and Julíenηe were being subdued by spiritual ecstasy. Nowhere in their world had they felt as they do now. They gently caressed each other as they lay looking toward the sky. A refreshing breeze enveloped them with happiness.

"The signal seems to be divergent to the entire area," said Mµreeη. "What was that sound?" Mµreeη suddenly felt peculiar. ...a stinging sensation in her lower leg. The rigidity of her legs dissolved and she stumbled slightly.

"I am unable to precisely locate a source as well," agreed Eberhαrt. He turned around. "Are you okay?"

"Yes, why wouldn't I be? Just a little fatigued. Uh...did you hear a hiss or something?" Mµreeη subtly quizzed Eberhαrt.

"No, I haven't heard anything. Listen, we've been hiking sometime now in this direction," said Eberhαrt. "Let's circle back and sweep the area again."

"Then maybe we can rest and take sustenance," said Mµreeη. "I'm tiring quickly for some reason."

Eberhαrt gave Mµreeη an agreeing nod and they moved on. After an extended walk, they had covered a sizable area. Mµreeη was now visibly fatigued.

"Okay, Mµreeη," said Eberhαrt, "let's rest here and have some food."

"Needn't ask me twice," replied Mµreeη. She sank quickly to the plush surface.

"We have three energy bars, grain loaf, water, and Utrovian tea."

"I'll have an energy bar and some tea," responded Mµreeη.

"Thank you," said Mµreeη as Eberhαrt served her.

"Sure you're okay?" inquired Eberhαrt. "...You're rubbing your leg."

"Oh yeah...scratch, I think...I'll put something on it. Anyway, this snack will pick me up--I'm sure." Mµreeη gave him a smile. She did not want to show him the spot on her leg that now burned like fire.

"I'm quite puzzled," confessed Eberhart, "there should be significant life already on this planet."

"I agree," said Mµreeη. She motioned for him to wait until she swallows. "...the 8700 period boasted much animal life as well as a significant Uµmpάrian population. They would have been backward and primitive still using wheels, fossil fuels, atomic energy, and battery operated sex toys, but...."

"...they should be here," said Eberhart.

"Yes," said Mµreeη, "...it's a mystery." She gazed at Eberhart for a zliton...he blurred a little. "I'm getting soooooo sleepy."

"Lay back and close your eyes for awhile," advised Eberhart. He now was stretching out himself.

As the tired couple nestled in close together, the rad concurred and began to set. A picturesque sight if ever they had seen one. It was truly beautiful. However, neither had noticed that there was only one moon and it was getting pitch black. The Uµmpάr they knew had two moons that reflected light to the far-rad hemisphere. Therefore, there was never any complete darkness. Just a few hundred zlitons of dusk on the far-rad hemisphere as each quadrant lost sight of the two moons. The near-rad hemisphere saw the rad constantly.

"Jeręmy, I can't see you anymore," said Julíenηe.

"I've never seen it so...black," responded Jeręmy. He was trying hard to see his hand waving in front of his face.

"Are we going to be okay?" ask Julíenηe curiously.

Jeręmy found her in the darkness and pulled her close, "Of course...don't worry."

"It's so...without light," said Julienne.

Jeremy released her briefly and found his pack.

"Is this better?" asked Jeremy. He snapped and shook a lumen cube, which glowed green.

"Yes, thank you! You're so thoughtful."

The lumen cube illuminated a small area around them.

The crew of the *Sir Punt* settled in for a little sleep period. The next span, when it was hoped the light would return, the exploration would continue. For now, however, all would rest and maybe even dream....

"There will be guards at ground level checking the elevator," said Rosetta.

"What are we going to do?" asked Porky.

The elevator steadily ascended floor by floor toward ground level. The trio brainstormed loudly, bantered chaotically, all the while dynamically designing and heuristically adapting the plan to escape.

"Go...Go now!" instructed Rosetta.

"Okay ...don't push," replied Porky. He dropped into the elevator from the access panel.

"Don't worry," said Woodeye, "...it's going to work."

The elevator slowed and came to a stop at ground level. The door opened, and as expected, security was waiting.

"Gotcha!" said one guard arrogantly.

Seizing Porky quickly, the two guards did not want to waste any time searching the elevator. They realized their mistake when suddenly....

[Smack, Smack! Thump, Thud!]

The guards dropped like heavy bags of dirt.

151

Rosetta and Woodeye had descended from the top of the elevator taking them from behind. The plan had worked flawlessly. Dragging the guards to a nearby storage room....

"So far so good," said a relieved Porky.

"...Looks like there's a security vehicle unattended." Woodeye looked at Rosetta out of the corner of his eye.

"I see it," replied Rosetta. "Don't they know that vehicle theft is on the rise?"

The trio joked quietly and made their way out of the building and into the vehicle. Porky worked his magic decrypting the access key and they were off. The mission was successful so far. There remained one more hurdle to reasonable safety--escape the near-rad hemisphere.

"How much farther?" inquired Woodeye.

"Not long," responded Rosetta, "...we'll have to ditch this ride soon."

"How are we...Uh...What's the plan to get us out of this quadrant?" asked Porky.

"Who said we're trying to get out?" responded Rosetta mysteriously.

Porky raised his eyebrows as he looked curiously to Woodeye for insight into Rosetta's last statement. The craft banked hard and slipped quickly into a transit tunnel. Surely, a collision would be imminent.

"Okay, everyone get out here," ordered Rosetta

All exited and made their way through the transit tunnel. A distant light was growing brighter as they penetrated deeper into the underground system.

"It can't be much farther," assured Rosetta. "The maintenance tunnel has been shut down for many, many spans, but my access key should still work."

"We're heading toward the underground maintenance service tunnels," realized Woodeye.

"The transit service tunnels?" asked Porky.

"No. The gold mine service tunnels," answered Woodeye.

Before innate intelligence, gold was so rare no one had ever heard of it, thought Rosetta. Only a scarce amount of gold was ever discovered on Uμμράr. Strangely and suddenly, a few mines sprang up. All of them except one were located in the far-rad hemisphere. The mines were claimed by the government, which had its power base in the near-rad hemisphere. Commonsense historians believed that tunnels were bored to connect the mines together thus permitting the redistribution of assets from the far-rad mines to the only near-rad mine. The government maintained the clandestine operation that stole thousands of magnitudes of gold from the unsuspecting far-rad inhabitants, or so it is believed. Contradicting this theory, however, is the fact that the far-rad mines were never exhausted of gold. They continue to provide an astonishing amount of this once unheard-of mineral.

"There!" exclaimed Rosetta. She pointed to a shadowy opening in the transit tunnel wall.

"Yes...I see it," said Woodeye. "It must be the service entrance...Hurry!"

The light from the oncoming transit capsule was rapidly growing brighter. Just as they entered the service alcove, the quad-segment transit capsule whooshed by sucking them back out into the tunnel and tumbling them some distance from the entrance. Luckily, they were only bruised and made their way back to the service entrance.

"Okay, we're in," announced Rosetta as the door

latch released. "Careful," she whispered. She eased open the door. "It's clear."

[KaBlam! KaPow! BOOM!]

"What the heck was that?" blurted Porky as he ducked for cover.

"One less security vehicle...," replied Rosetta, "I think?"

The service tunnel was dimly lit and the trio made their way cautiously toward what Rosetta's map detailed as a distribution node. Distribution nodes were points at which gold laden transport capsules were unloaded. Since the capsules returned to the far-rad hemisphere after loading/unloading, the trio hoped to stow away on a capsule headed back to the other side of the planet.

"Restricted access," said Woodeye. "Let's hope your access key works again."

"All right," said a relieved Rosetta as the latch released.

The trio had gained access to a corridor leading to the transport docking station. They hoped that the station would be unattended at this time. Moving slowly, they crept down the corridor to an elevator. Without words, Woodeye and Porky looked to Rosetta for guidance.

"Okay, let's go." Rosetta entered the elevator.

"Where does this lead?" asked Porky.

"The mine and transport pathways are on lower levels," replied Rosetta.

"Let's hope that no one is around," submitted Woodeye.

The elevator doors opened on the first level below where they had got on.

"Stay here and hold the door," said Rosetta.

"Where are you going?" asked Woodeye.

"I'm not sure if this is the correct level," responded Rosetta. "I need to take a look."

Porky and Woodeye held the elevator as Rosetta slipped away down the corridor and through a doorway.

"I sure hope this map is correct," said Rosetta to herself.

She crept quickly down narrow corridors to where she began to hear sounds--voices to be precise. Rosetta had located a docking station on this level. Unfortunately, there was a security checkpoint nearby. Rosetta, down on all fours, moved quietly hoping to recon without being detected.

From behind several storage containers, she observed uniformed security milling around and playing grab-ass. They must be waiting for a transport to arrive, she thought. ...Why so many? She began to crawl a little closer in order to hear what they were saying.

"Did you see the size of that thing?" said one security guard.

"I know...I had heard that these gold transports were huge, but I had no idea they were that big."

"How much can they hold?"

"I don't know, but they have been unloading it nonstop for forty-five spans!"

What transports were they talking about? she wondered. What could hold that much cargo? Rosetta slid backward retracing her path. She must get back to Porky and Woodeye to report what she had heard. Shitova, she noticed that she had unknowingly broken three nails. That pissed her off!

"Look what we got here," said an arrogant guard.

Rosetta was taken by surprise when she had backed out into the corridor.

Rosetta wasted no time in introducing their nadz to her boots. She moved as if her ass was covered in rocket fuel and an igniter was clicking behind her. She definitely did not want to be burned.

"GET HER--!" shouted one guard as he was booted.

Rosetta kicked, punched, twirled, and otherwise beat the shitova out of these guys. Unfortunately, she had missed someone.

[ZZZZzzzzzzz!] The laser hummed as it burned into her shoulder.

Rosetta came to rest on the ground with that terrible stinging pain that only a burst from an *interlaced, modulated frequency, disrupter/laser* could deliver.

"Do you think you got it all?" asked Woodeye.

"Huh? Got what all?" replied Porky, not understanding the question.

"The innate intelligence data....," clarified Woodeye. "Do you think you deleted it all?"

"...can't be sure," confessed Porky. "There was a significant amount of data on Sharon's computater. She told me that was all of it, but...."

"But what?" asked Woodeye.

"The computater had been hacked by a HEINIEAC 7000," replied Porky.

"HEINIEAC?" Woodeye kind of snickered.

"I know...it was the butt of many jokes when it was first introduced. HEINIEAC--Highly Electronic Intelligent Node Isolation Effecting Aggressive Control-- The most sophisticated data acquisition and control system ever developed," said Porky. "The system kernel had logged a previous event detailing an intrusion by an

156

HEINIEAC 7000...It was data mining for innate intelligence data!"

"What are you saying?" asked Woodeye. "Do you mean there might be a backup of the information?"

"What I'm saying is," replied Porky, his face now slightly worried. "...A HEINIEAC 7000 was performing dedicated mining specifically looking for innate intelligence data. And...I don't know if it was successful."

Porky turned, peering into the corridor scanning for Rosetta. Time passed slowly. Both Woodeye and Porky were becoming concerned when Rosetta failed to return.

"Too long," mumbled Porky. "Rosetta has been gone too long."

"Yeah, I agree," replied Woodeye. "Let's go."

Porky and Woodeye set out to search for Rosetta.

Traversing the path they believed she had taken put them within earshot of a security detail...and a captive.

"Shhh...quiet," whispered Porky while pointing to the obvious commotion.

Porky and Woodeye watched helplessly as all but one security guard accompanied Rosetta onto a security transport. They crept closer only to see the transport depart into one of several transport tunnels.

"Where are they taking her?" asked Porky.

"I don't know," responded Woodeye. "Let's go ask."

Springing out and onto the one remaining guard, Woodeye pounded him almost senseless.

"What's their destination?" Woodeye asked the guard.

The guard offered no reply.

Woodeye held the guard down and nodded at Porky.

[ZZZZzzzz!] The laser whined as Porky blasted the guard's leg.

"I'm not going to ask you too many more times," said Woodeye very impatiently.

"Station 13 for interrogation," confessed the reluctant guard. "She may have been involved in the theft of some important data."

"Theft...data?" said Woodeye. "What data?"

Woodeye applied pressure to the guard's injured leg with his foot, but the guard did not possess further information. Woodeye and Porky secured the guard and searched the station. They found a tunnel map and an access key for the transports. Their next destination was station 13.

The birds were singing beautifully as a nearby brook babbled rhythmically. The greenery, with its wonderful sprinkle of colors, was slowly giving up the dew that glistened ever so slightly. This might well have been the most wonderful awakening of nature the crew of the *Sir Punt* had ever been privileged to behold.

"Oh my goodness," breathed an awakening Julíenηe. "...Have you ever seen a more beautiful place?"

"Unbelievable," agreed Jeręmy.

The two sat in awe trying to take in the unparalleled beauty that surrounded them. Simultaneously, Eberhαrt and Mμreeη were awakening to this new world as well.

"Eberhαrt...," Mμreeη pushed and playfully poked

a sleeping Eberhαrt. "Wake up!"

"Is it time to go home yet?" said a not quite awake Eberhαrt. "You're up early."

"This place is just so very relaxing I've been jotting down a few thoughts," replied Mμreeη.

"...Thoughts?"

"I'm composing a short poem, silly. So strange...the words just came to me."

"Let's see--!" said Eberhαrt. He made a grab for her pad.

"Sorry," laughed Mμreeη. She dangled it while keeping it from him, "...not done yet!"

The two of them arose to enjoy this refreshing new morning that was offered.

"It's so beautiful," said Eberhαrt as he offered her an energy bar and some tea.

"Lct's eat and begin exploring," suggested Mμreeη.

"Agreed."

Eberhαrt and Mμreeη finished their meal and were off. They traveled through the most delightful gardens before starting toward the rendezvous point. While on their way, they began to see a darkened area not far away. It was in stark contrast to the wonder and beauty they had enjoyed thus far.

"What do you think is over there?" asked Eberhαrt.

"I don't know but we should investigate," said Mμreeη.

"We're running late." Eberhαrt felt uneasy about going there.

"Let's check in with Jerẹmy and Julíenηe," said Mμreeη, "...they can meet us there."

"I'm not sure we should go there," said Eberhart.

Ignoring Eberhart's reservations, Mµreeη was already in contact with the others and giving them directions. Eberhart became slightly frustrated and a little concerned at Mµreeη's eagerness to explore the darkening.

"They're on their way," said Mµreeη.

"Mµreeη!" Eberhart grabbed her arm, "...We must be careful."

"We will...silly!" Mµreeη pecked a kiss on his cheek and started off.

Jeręmy and Julíenηe nibbled their breakfast as they walked making their way toward the darkening. Drawing closer, they both were becoming increasingly unsettled.

"This doesn't feel right," said Jeręmy.

"I know," agreed Julíenηe. "This place doesn't belong here in the midst of such beauty."

As both halves of the *Sir Puηt's* crew converged on the darkening, they met.

"Oh Mµreeη, you would not believe the beautiful place where we slept last night," said an excited Julíenηe. "Mµreeη," repeated Julíenηe after being ignored.

"We should continue on," said Mµreeη as if oblivious to the others.

Mµreeη moved off briskly. After Eberhart, Jeręmy, and Julíenηe exchanged puzzled looks at her behavior, they began to follow. Mµreeη pressed them all on at every chance. She appeared hurried and in search of something.

"What's the rush?" Eberhart was trying to break the ice with her now cold persona.

160

"If you don't want to go then STAY BEHIND," said Mµreeη harshly.

Eberhαrt stopped in his tracks, pausing and looking at Julíenηe and Jeręmy who were just as surprised as he was at Mµreeη's tone.

"Something's not right here, guys," said Eberhαrt.

"Agreed," said Jeręmy as Julíenηe nodded.

"We can't let her go alone," said Julíenηe.

"Okay," said Eberhαrt, "...but let's stay alert."

They followed Mµreeη into a dense forest at the edge of the darkening. Mµreeη had gotten far ahead of them. They could still see her, but just barely.

"MUREĚN," called Eberhαrt, "...WAIT UP!"

They could see that she stopped briefly and then continued. After moving quickly for some time, they had caught up with her. Relieved at finding her, the slithery creature moving away went unnoticed.

"What are you doing with that here?" asked Eberhαrt.

Mµreeη sat staring at the A.P.E.L. that she held in her hands. Her eyes were glassy while she gazed into it as if it was a crystal ball.

"MUREĚN," said Eberhαrt. He spoke loudly while kneeling to touch her hands.

"What?" Mµreeη now shaking her head. "Where are we?"

"What do you mean?" asked Julíenηe. "Don't you remember coming here?"

"Why do I have the A.P.E.L.?" asked a confused Mµreeη.

They recapped the story of their trip to the darkening and her determination to get there including her harsh responses.

"I'm so sorry," said Mµreeη. "I only remember waking up. ...And my leg. It's so sore." She now freely exposed the reddened albeit diminished wound she had suffered the span before.

"Why didn't you say something?" Eberhart applied a little first aid.

"I don't like this place and our time is running out," said Jeręmy.

"I don't like it either," agreed Eberhart, "...there's an evil here."

Suddenly, a slithering serpent appeared, surprising them all. It appeared to single out Eberhart by approaching him and preparing to strike.

"What is it?" asked Julíenηe.

"A fallen angel," muttered Mµreeη.

"What?" Jeręmy did not fully hear her.

The snake coiled tightly and struck out fiercely at Eberhart. Sensing the evil, Eberhart stepped aside quickly thus allowing the serpent to fall harmlessly to the ground.

"Watch out, Eberhart!" Julíenηe became stricken with fear.

"EBERHART!" yelled Mµreeη, "...CATCH!"

Mµreeη tossed Eberhart the knife given her by her father. Just as he secured the blade in his right hand, the serpent had already coiled and was striking again. Eberhart caught the serpent in his left hand and held it firmly just below its head. For a brief moment, Eberhart looked deeply into the eyes of the serpent. It became hypnotic....

[SLICE!]

Eberhart severed the head of the serpent and dropped it to the ground. A steamy, foul odor emanated

162

from the lifeless creature. To the surprise of the crew, the serpent decomposed quickly and was gone.

"Let's get out of here," said Julíenηe nervously.

"Yes," agreed Eberhαrt.

Jerẹmy, Julíenηe, and Mµreeη moved toward the direction they had come. Eberhαrt stood alone surveying the darkening. Defiantly raising the knife he had wielded against the serpent, Eberhαrt knew greater battles with evil awaited him.

Mµreeη stumbled. "Are you okay?" asked Julíenηe.

"Yes, I'm just tired."

"She has been quite fatigued lately," confessed Eberhαrt to Jerẹmy.

"What do you think is the problem?" whispered Jerẹmy.

"I don't know, but with the wound on her leg and her actions this span...I'm concerned about her," confided Eberhαrt.

"Is she okay to travel now?" asked Jerẹmy.

"Who cares!" announced Julíenηe to the surprise of her colleagues. "I mean...don't you feel it? This place is wonderful!"

"Feel what?" Eberhαrt looked at Julíenηe expecting some type of clear explanation.

"That light, airy, contented feeling," said Julíenηe.

They were at the boundary edge of the darkening and the wonderful gardens they had previously explored. The darkening had seemingly depleted their spirits and now the wonder of the gardens was having the opposite effect.

"One thing's for sure--we are in the wrong time period," concluded Eberhαrt. "I wonder.... Maybe we are even on the wrong planet!"

"I think so," said Jerẹmy. "We had better continue back to our ship."

"Yes," said Eberhαrt. "We must prepare for lift-off."

"WWHHYY?" said Julíenηe and Mμreeη simultaneously.

"Can't you feel the heavy load of cares and troubles leaving you," said Julíenηe with a sincere astonishment that they were contemplating leaving.

"Ah...I feel so freeeeee," Julíenηe danced around as if she was riding on air.

"Come on, let's go," said Eberhαrt.

"I'll help Julíenηe," said Jerẹmy.

Eberhαrt grasped Mμreeη as Jerẹmy took hold of Julíenηe and began their journey back to the ship. Julíenηe and Mμreeη were not alone in their feelings. Eberhαrt and Jerẹmy could feel a sensation of total peace and tranquility sweeping through them as well. With the females more securely in tow than their own feelings were, Eberhαrt and Jerẹmy continued in the direction of the ship. They grew closer and closer to the clearing where the ship had touched down. There seemed to be a slight darkening of the sky as if their presence was somehow contaminating the planet. Eberhαrt noticed the definite difference in the sky. He thought about how peculiar it was now for the area where they had landed to appear to be the center of increasingly grayer skies.

"Hey...look at that, Eberhαrt." Jerẹmy was pointing to the darkening of the clearing where their craft was.

"Yes," responded Eberhαrt, "I see it."

They continued as the grayness of the sky began

to engulf them as well. Though the brilliant colors of their surroundings were now transformed to black and white, they were close enough to see the ship.

"Look!" said Jerẹmy. "There appears to be someone leaving our ship!"

"I see!" said Eberhαrt.

Loosening their grip on the females, who were just now returning from their most pleasant inner journey, they began racing toward the ship. As they slowed to approach their visitor, still unaware of their pending arrival, the others finally caught up with them.

"It looks like a naked female! ...I think," said Jerẹmy.

The four crept increasingly closer to the ship and their unexpected visitor. Their guest appeared to be at ease as she inspected the exterior of their craft. Unlike the Uμmpάrians, the native of this world was small, thin, and short. Her well-defined structure moved gracefully as if it too was floating on air. She possessed two eyes, a centered nose and mouth, two ears, two breasts, two arms, and two legs. Her skin was the color of the rainbow. However, it appeared to be fading to gray as everything else was.

Suddenly, their visitor noticed the crew of this strange ship approaching.

"Hey...Hold it! Don't be afraid...," said Mμreeη. She spoke in a more soothing and concordant voice.

Though startled, this terrestrial being did not attempt to escape the crew's presence. She stood stately and erect just staring at them without uttering a sound.

"Who...Who are you?" asked Jerẹmy.

The creature continued to stare at them as if to consume all that they were. The crew could sense their souls were being touched and felt comforted.

Eberhart moved closer and caressed her arm most gently. The being slowly raised her head to examine Eberhart's face.

"I'm Eberhart," he whispered softly.

As Eberhart gazed into her eyes, her face flowed into a smile. She extended a hand to touch his. Moving slowly, her fingers probed the texture of his skin while her eyes shined brightly with innocence. Eberhart turned to look at the others. He searched for words to describe this...this spiritual interaction now taking place. What was happening? He had never experienced such feelings of.... What was that...in his mind? It was barely noticeable. Yes, a whisper. Eberhart listened with his mind. He wanted...needed to hear.

...Tellurian, whispered the gentle voice.

Jerẹmy noted Eberhart's look of hypnosis. Not wanting to take any chances, Jerẹmy felt compelled to intervene.

"Eberhart...EBERHART...Time is exhausting quickly." Jerẹmy firmly raised Eberhart's awareness.

"Hmm... Yes," said Eberhart slowly.

Mμreeη caressed Eberhart's arm and tugged firmly dissolving the interaction.

"Eberhart! What are we going to do?" asked Mμreeη.

As if a magic spell had been broken, Eberhart, aided by Mμreeη, sluggishly moved away from the petite female and toward the *Sir Puηt's* crew.

"We've came back too far in time," said Jerẹmy. "We likely are on the wrong planet!"

Eberhart's awareness increased as he struggled to digest Jerẹmy's words. Julíenηe and Mμreeη both rang in

166

with their own concerns albeit no one offered advice on how to proceed. Eberhart beheld the faces of his comrades that now looked to him for wisdom and leadership. The feeling of responsibility that they had placed on him was overwhelming. How should he react? What should be their next move? ...Time was running out!

Eberhart moved smartly toward their ship and entered. Zlitons past before he exited the craft and extracted what may have been an act of desperation from Mµreeη's pack.

"You're not--," said Julíenηe. "I mean that's not Sharon!"

"Well," said Eberhart, "if this is the wrong planet it will not matter to our future."

No one offered a response though each face questioned his statement.

"On the other hand, if we're just too far back in time... Surely Sharon Defoulgar will be her descendant."

Eberhart looked at each one of them offering them their chance to convince him otherwise.

"...But Eberhart," said Jeręmy. "The A.P.E.L. is programmed with information to show Sharon how the future would be with innate intelligence. This female... alien being... whatever... likely would not understand, much less change, the future."

"Jeręmy," answered Eberhart, "...that is true. However, we...the four of us...." Eberhart paused and looked at each of them silently asking for understanding. "...have the power to program the A.P.E.L. and change the future ourselves."

"What exactly are you suggesting?" asked Mµreeη.

"Like Jeremy said, she likely would not understand the current programming of the A.P.E.L.," said Eberhart. "Therefore, any enlightenment would be thus wasted."

"So?" said Julíenηe.

"So...we must program the A.P.E.L. with more basic step-by-step instructions, so to speak, to govern future evolution on this planet."

Silence spoke softly as the crew became aware of the responsibility that Eberhart was asking them all to accept.

Mμreeη looked at Eberhart. "Are you saying?"

"Yes! We will be the architects of the future of this world and possibly our present," announced Eberhart. "Come on...we've got enough entry terminals in the ship for all of us. Let's get started!"

The crew entered the *Sir Jacφb Puηt* one-by-one. Their host observed their every move as if trying to understand why these alien creatures had entered her world.

"How should we start?" asked Julíenηe.

"We must break this down into manageable parts," answered Eberhart.

Eberhart looked at each of the crew, thought for a moment, and then began delegating their individual responsibilities to the project.

"Jeremy," said Eberhart, "you will work on health and welfare. Julíenηe...you will outline the educational and religious structure."

"But Eberhart, I do not know--!"

"Yes, you do," responded Eberhart trying to instill confidence in her. "And you," he said nodding at Mμreeη, "will be responsible for all aspects of science,

168

mathematics, and universal logic."

"What about you?" quizzed Jeremy.

"I know," said Mµreeη, "Eberhαrt will design recreation."

"Eberhαrt Ghoηαdz-- Have Jockstrap... Will Travel," said Julíenηe laughing.

"Finance too!" included Jeremy.

"Especially finance," agreed Mµreeη, "We don't want gold being heaped on us from all sides anymore."

"I had almost forgotten about that," confessed Eberhαrt. "This place does seem to lift your burdens and wipe them away."

Eberhαrt stood thinking for a moment. "I think that I can kill two gazeldas with one A.P.E.L."

To work they all went. The crew was enthusiastic about their individual responsibilities for determining the future of this planet's inhabitants and possibly their own. Diligently they pondered and pecked at their terminals as their host observed them unaware of the scope of the work being done.

A substantial interval of time passed. Each of the crew thoughtfully and seriously put their heart and soul into designing their particular aspect of the project. Their future and the future of millions would be affected by their actions this span. This realization weighed heavy on each of them. Quietly, each stopped and sat silently observing their comrades.

"Everyone finished?" asked Eberhαrt softly. "Let's hope we've done our best."

They all nodded in the affirmative thus giving their approval for Eberhαrt to finish the task. Eberhαrt pressed a single button to upload the thoughts, wisdom, experience, and best wishes they all hoped would be enough to secure a brighter future for them all. The A.P.E.L. responded by random illuminations across its exterior. Then, after a period, the A.P.E.L. paled thus signaling that the process was complete.

"That's it," concluded Eberhart.

"Not a moment too soon," said Mµreeη. "We've only four spans to lift off and rendezvous with Vendar Three."

"Now all we have to do is get her to eat it," said Jerȩmy.

"Not here--," said Mµreeη, "we can't give it to her here. We must get her away from the ship before liftoff."

"You're right," responded Eberhart. "The rocket blast might damage her."

"Wait," added Jerȩmy, "we must first show her what to do with it."

"I know!"

Julíenηe quickly pulled out an oooohvucchini and walked up to their young friend. Julíenηe began licking the fruit. Then Julíenηe raised it to her nose.

"Ummm...gooood!" Julíenηe motioned for her to observe.

Julíenηe slowly drew the fruit into her mouth and took a bite all the while holding the A.P.E.L. up for the young female to see. She seemed to understand and to their surprise....

"Fooood?"

The *Sir Puηt's* crew looked at each other, laughed aloud, and said in unison, "Yes... fooooood!"

"Julíenηe," whispered Eberhart, "take her to that tree by the garden."

"We've only a few zlitons," announced Mµreeη.

"Hurry, Julíenηe!" encouraged Jerȩmy.

Julíenη proceeded to take their new friend by the hand and gently lead her to the tree as instructed. Placing the A.P.E.L. on the tree, their young host stood motionless while observing Julíenη and the strange item now offered. Julíenη knew she must go now because the time for their departure was approaching. She took the female's hand and placed it on the A.P.E.L. After flashing a caring smile, she hurried to the ship and the crew made ready to liftoff.

"Power up all systems," said Eberhαrt.

"Systems on," responded Mµreeη.

"Let's go," said Eberhαrt. "We have an appointment to keep."

The ship rose slowly from the planet. The foliage bowed and waved as if to say--so long. The crew once again took in the breathtaking beauty from the viewports.

"She's not eating it," said Jerємy.

Their new friend, awed by the ascent of the ship, had placed the A.P.E.L. back on the tree.

"Julíenη," said Eberhαrt, "take the handset and project your voice to her."

"Take the Ah-pel," said Julíenη.

"Jerємy, illuminate the A.P.E.L. with an ion beam," said Mµreeη.

A translucent, orange-red beam stretched from the ship to contact the A.P.E.L. The puzzled female once again turned her attention to the glowing item on the tree. Picking up the A.P.E.L., she looked once more toward the ship.

"Eat...Eat...Ummm...Good." Julíenη spoke using a soothing voice to encourage her to eat it.

The calm, young female seemed to understand. She began licking and then started nibbling on the strange fruit the visitors had given her.

"Yes! Yes! ...SHE TOOK A BITE," shouted Julíenη.

"Four, three, two," counted Mµreeη.

"Engage main thrusters," said Eberhαrt.

The ship ascended rapidly as their young friend watched. Soon it had vanished.

"Ah-pel," she said.

"One...Engage main drive."

"Main drive engaged," said Jerẹmy confirming.

"We're on schedule," said Julíenη.

All sat quietly monitoring their instruments. There seemed to be an uneasy feeling in each of their stomachs. Each one of the *Sir Puηt's* crew was hoping that what they had done was just and correct. They would ensure the course was set and all systems were nominal before entering stasis.

CHAPTER EIGHT

GOING HOME...

The room appeared to be spinning. The faces of her captors were melting then stretching and then distorting some more. What was going on? Have they drugged me? What planet am I on? Ságaçion... Where are you, Ságaçion?

"The drug's just now taking affect, Sir," said the female tech dressed in a white jumpsuit of sorts.

The Sir was a tall male with grotesque scarring to the left side of his face. One eye had been dislodged and then surgically reinstalled. The muscles apparently had healed incorrectly, which caused the eye to pull out of alignment. This gentleman did not smile and appeared not really to have a reason to do so.

"Begin the questioning," said the Sir.

"She's not quite ready--," started the interrogator.

"BEGIN AT ONCE," ordered the Sir.

"Yes, Sir! At once, Sir!" The interrogator jumped with fright.

[SLAP!]   The interrogator slapped her face smartly.

"WAKE UP!" said the interrogator.

[SLAP! SLAP!]

"Wake up! What is your name?"

"Where am I--?"

[SLAP! SLAP!]

"Wrong answer! What is YOUR NAME?"

"Vera...Uh...Rosetta," she replied.

"She's being untrue," said a timid looking individual that was closely monitoring the instruments tethered to her scalp.

[SLAP!]

"LET"S   TRY   AGAIN!" screamed the interrogator.

The Sir motioned for the jumpsuit dressed tech to administer an additional dose of the truth drug. Rosetta's vision blurred substantially.

...Ságaçion? Is that you, dear? Her mind begged for her beloved. Her thoughts twirled in a surreal world of torment and ecstasy. Barely realizing her dire situation, Shitova! ...They've pumped me full of *Truthsayer*. I can't help, but...must not answer.

"PROCEED," commanded the Sir.

[SLAP!]

"...Your NAME?" The interrogator knew that he must extract the information that the Sir wants or die.

"Roset--,"

[SLAP, SLAP, SLAP!]

"No, no, no...Your name! What is your NAME?" asked the interrogator again.

"...Věracítii," she mumbled dizzying with the drug. The tech monitoring her nodded.

176

"That's good, Věracítii. What were you doing in the tunnels?"

"Escaping from near-rad...." Veractii slumped under the drug's influence.

"Why were you trying to escape this hemisphere?"

"...destroyed innate intelligence project. [Painful groan!] Ughhh...needed to escape."

"She's lapsing in and out of consciousness, Sir. We've overdosed her with--!"

"HOLD YOUR TONGUE," barked the Sir.

The Sir paced slowly around the room. All eyes dipped toward the floor as he neared any of the room's occupants. He casually played with his disjointed eye. Slowly, he fingered the moist gelatin-like bulb in a circular orbit about its socket. This involuntary tendency unnerved the hardest of the interrogators. Obviously, this helped him to plot his evil strategy.

"Allow her to rest until I return." The Sir walked smartly from the room.

"Let's get her on the table there and lay her down," instructed the interrogator.

Meanwhile, Porky and Woodeye had commandeered a transport and had begun their search for Station 13.

"Stay to the right at the intersection," instructed Porky. "This map shows station 13 at about fifty penãrds from our current position."

"I sure hope they don't hurt her," said Woodeye.

"I think Rosetta can take care of herself," said Porky with a comforting tone.

Porky and Woodeye streaked through the transport tunnels at breakneck speed. Fortunately, there had been no other vessels using the tunnels. They wondered if the guard they had disabled had been found. ...And if so, had the alarm been raised? Still they pressed on though talking very little. Passing by a facility that looked totally out of place, the duo saw a very large space transport landing. They wondered what I.T.S. stood for. However, the focus was the rescue of their colleague and then to escape the near-rad hemisphere.

The Sir entered the room. "Let us begin again."

The interrogator motioned for help in getting their captive back into the chair and re-attached to the polygraph-type instrument. She was still out of it. Her body was still quite limp and unresponsive. Still, the Sir had ordered them to begin. They dared not to disobey him. The interrogator tenderly cleaned and applied the electrodes to her scalp and chest. She must be more forthcoming with information or the Sir will extinguish her life force, the interrogator thought.

"Vĕracítii...Can you hear me?" asked the interrogator.

"What were you doing in the near-rad hemisphere?"

"...Destroying innate intelligence project," she replied in a half-conscious whisper.

"Were you successful?"

The Sir momentarily stopped pacing the floor, but continued to twirl his eye.

"...Yes," she whispered.

The interrogator looked first to the polygraph tech monitoring her and then to the Sir.

178

"She believes that the project has been destroyed, Sir," concluded the interrogator.

"We must be sure," said the Sir motioning for an additional dose of Truthsayer.

"Sir," protested the interrogator, "...she is of no value dead!"

[SLAP!]   The interrogator was knocked to the floor.

"DO NOT LECTURE ME ON HER VALUE!" The Sir flashed a look that caused the interrogator to fear for his continued existence.

"I'm sorry, Sir," whimpered the interrogator now humbling himself.

"Ask her how it was destroyed," commanded the Sir.

The interrogator gained some composure and approached their captive once more. Quickly, he checked the dilation of her pupils in order to gage her level of consciousness.

"Věracítii...Věracítii...How did you destroy the innate intelligence project?

"Porky...deleted...," she said and then trailed off.

"Was the information destroyed?"

"...yes," she responded, drunkenly slurring her speech.

"How was the information destroyed?"   The interrogator again checks her pupil dilation. "How did Porky delete the information?"   The interrogator pressed her to answer noting the Sir's impatience.

"...Porky pretended to be lost and when Sharon was distracted he...," she paused passing from consciousness. "...Porky hacked the computater and deleted all traces of the data with a triple hard storage...wipe filling the storage addresses with random...characters."

"Where is Porky now?"

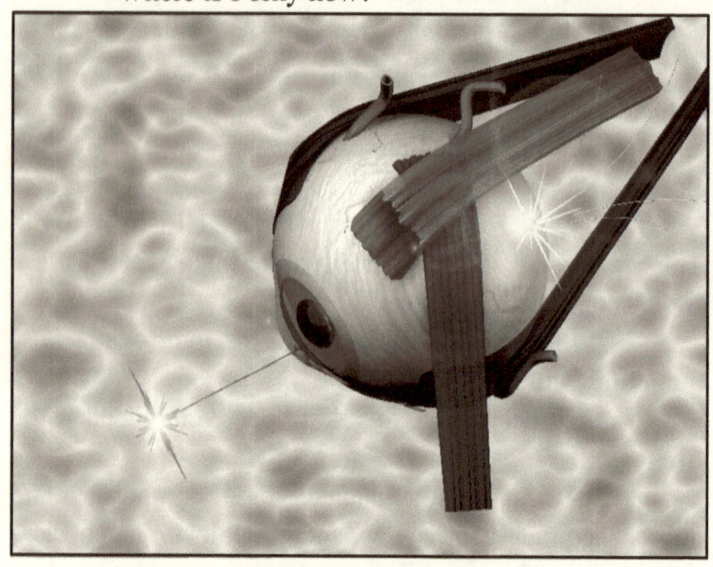

[ZZZZzzzzzzz!] The laser pierced the dangling eye of the Sir causing him to clutch his face. [ZZZZzzzzzzz, ZZZzzzz!] The Sir went down stunned, as did the geeks.

"I'm right over here!" Porky and Woodeye burst into the room with guns a blazing.

"What have you done to her?" Woodeye pressed his weapon to the interrogator's temple. "We will NOT be taking prisoners!"

"I only gave her Truthsayer," replied the interrogator glancing at the now exploded eye of the Sir. "She will recover."

"She had better," threatened Porky waving his laser pistol. "Remove her restraints. NOW!" Porky barked and the interrogator jumped.

"You will help us get her out of here. Do you understand?" said Woodeye.

"Yes, I will help you," agreed the interrogator.

"Ah, I feel sick...." Rosetta moaned.

"Don't try to speak, Rosetta," said Porky. "Save your strength."

"Her name is not Rosetta," said the interrogator as he helped carry her to the transport.

"What are you talking about?" asked Woodeye.

"Her name is not Rosetta...While under the Truthsayer she said her name was Věracítii."

"It's not important," said Porky after noticing Woodeye's puzzled look.

"What do you mean?" asked a still puzzled Woodeye.

"I'll tell you later." Porky quickly shifted his eyes to the interrogator.

Woodeye understood that Porky did not want to talk in front of the near-rad interrogator. He would accept that for now though he was really starting to think that Rosetta and Porky had secrets between them.

"This is as far as you go," said Porky. He secured the interrogator's hands and locked him in the storage room.

Making their way with Rosetta in tow, the trio had made it to the stolen transport. After quickly getting Rosetta aboard, Woodeye eased the transport into the launch tunnel and headed for the far-rad boundary. It was silent for a long time as the transport swooshed smoothly through the tunnel at high speed.

"Well," said Woodeye not being able to hold back his curiosity.

"Well, what?" asked Porky.

"Who is she? Who are you?" Woodeye's face grew solemn.

"We are from the future," confessed Porky.

"I don't understand," said a now confused Woodeye.

Porky went on to explain the principle of trans-temporal telepathy. Porky confessed that his real name was Veríle. Woodeye became even more confused when Porky offered....

"You are also from the future! For whatever reason, your thoughts have interlaced with Woodeye of this period."

"My thoughts...are from the future?"

"Yes," answered Porky.

"Ridiculous...I know who I am," said Woodeye.

"Your name is Woodland Williams and right now your body is stretched out on a padded table alongside Věracítii and me. Your thoughts are being linked to this person's thoughts in this period. Search deep in your mind and you will see the truth."

Silence filled the transport as it sped through the tunnels. Woodeye had engaged the autopilot while Porky was tending to Rosetta's needs. Her vital signs were stable and it appeared she would recover as the bio-interrogator had said. Poor Woodeye sat thinking about this new revelation when he suddenly realized...it was true.

"We are all neighbors in...Prystine," mumbled Woodeye. "Ságaçion Academis pioneered trans-temporal telepathy."

"It's good to have you finally with us, Woodland." Porky patted his back.

"My host's mind is very clear. I was as a voyeur just watching as the events took place. It was intoxicating!"

Woodeye sat quietly reviewing his thoughts on the recent events. Porky, turning to check on Rosetta from time to time, monitored the transport's instruments. Without further delays, they should cross the hemispheric boundary in two to four spans.

Did I delete it all? Who was controlling the HEINIEAC 7000? Please...oh please, let this be a successful mission. Porky was full of doubt. They would not know for sure until they could get to the far-rad hemisphere where they would release their hosts and disconnect their thought waves. Would they just wake up back in their own bodies as Ságaçion had said? If history were altered... Would there still be bodies waiting for their return?

"Dad, Perfidious has been rummaging through mom's stuff," said Tadφlŏn.

"Rummaging... What do you mean?" inquired Ságaçion.

"I left for school the morning of last span. Half-way there I remembered that my project folder was still in my room. So I returned to get it. When I was going upstairs, I heard someone in your room. I thought it was you so I went to look and say, *hi*. When I got to the door, I could see that Perfidious was going through the storage bins containing mom's personal items. She appeared to be collecting samples of mom's... undergarments."

"Undergarments?" Ságaçion was puzzled.

"Yes. Items like bed clothes, underwear, she even took mom's hair brush!" The anger was beginning to swell inside her.

"Honey," said Ságaçion gently brushing a tear from Tadφlŏn's face, "I'll get to the bottom of this. Don't worry. But until I do...we must keep a watchful eye on Perfidious."

Ságaçion reasoned that Perfidious must have been trying to collect any biological samples that Vĕracítii had left behind. Why? ...DNA examination? Possibly. They must be trying to determine Vĕracítii's health status. They suspect! Has something in the past tipped them off?

"Please come back to me," whispered Ovalŏn as she stroked Vẹríle's face. "I don't care about innate intelligence or Sharon Defoulgar. I don't care about any of it. ...Just you!"

"I love you too," said a waking Vẹríle Ghoηαdz.

Tears began to gush from Ovalŏn's eyes as she realized that her prayers were being answered. Vẹríle, Vĕracítii, and then Woodland began to awaken. Though somewhat disoriented, they were returning from their unbelievable journey.

"Don't sit up too quickly, my love," said Ovalŏn helping a determined Vẹríle to rise.

Ovalŏn tended to the others ensuring that they felt comfortable. She patted their faces with a damp towel. She was so happy.

"We have to go!" Ságaçion entered the mobile lab as the trio became fully awake. He could not resist hugging and kissing one of his two purposes for living. He too was so glad they had returned.

"Perfidious has been looking for biological specimens on Věracítii's clothes. It can only mean that the Controllers suspect that her death may have been a hoax. I'm sure they are searching for further evidence. Achates, the attending physician, has been detained for questioning. We must inform our loved ones and escape."

"Was the mission a success?" asked Věríle.

Ságaçion looked down avoiding direct eye contact.

"Honey...Ságaçion?" said Věracítii.

"No...we failed," answered Ságaçion. "It appears the Controllers were one step ahead of us."

"What do you mean?" asked Woodland.

Ságaçion went on to tell them that he suspects that the Controllers realized their plan early on and had used his discovery concerning brain wave perpetuity against them. Ságaçion reasoned that while he was refining the telepathy process, the Controllers were conducting parallel experiments. He now was convinced that the Controllers had dispatched agents to strategic points in Uμmpár's history to protect their interests. Unknowingly, he has helped them solidify their control on the psychological and sociological aspects of life on Uμmpár. How could he have been so blind? With the vast resources at their command, the Controllers could dispatch a legion of agents throughout all of Uμmpár's history utilizing his principles.

"Is Tadφlŏn okay?" asked a now worried Věracítii.

"She is fine, my love. She is with Hαzăr. We shall visit our love ones and leave Lobotma," said Ságaçion.

"Visit...Why do you say visit?" asked Věríle.

185

"Our children are safe. The Controllers know that they were not involved in our plan. In addition, the Controllers still want our children to be together. This ensures their continued safety."

"What are you saying?" questioned Ovalŏn.

"We must leave them," said a tearful Věracítii. "They will be much safer if we leave them here to continue with their lives."

Very sadly, they all agreed. Now it was time to get the heck out of Labotma. Another period, the battle could be engaged again. For now, they must escape and preserve their lives.

"She was going through mom's stuff." Tadφlŏn walked around the room and then sat down on the edge of the bed.

"What do you think she was looking for?" Hαzăr followed and sat down next to her.

"I don't know. I told my dad...he said he would get to the bottom of it."

"Where's your dad now?" Hαzăr gently placed his hand on hers.

"I don't know...I really miss my mom." Tears filled Tadφlŏn's eyes.

"I know."

"Oh Hαzăr," said Tadφlŏn gently kissing his lips, "I love you."

"I love you too." Hαzăr gently returned her kiss.

Just then, the door opened to Tadφlŏn's room.

"I'm sorry for barging in, sweetheart," said Sάgaçion, "...we have to talk."

A figure caught Tadφlŏn's eye entering the room just behind her dad.

186

"MOM?"   Tadφlŏn jumped up and ran to Vĕracítii. Tadφlŏn paused to just look at her smiling face.

"Hello, my sweet child. ...I've missed you so," whispered Vĕracítii.

Tears welling, Tadφlŏn embraced her and held her oh so tight. "I love you, Mom."

Vẹríle and Ovalŏn Ghoŋadz now entered and surprised Hɑzăr. Sɑ́gaçion proceeded to bring Hɑzăr and Tadφlŏn up to speed. Vĕracítii and Vẹríle recapped their experiences while attempting to eradicate Sharon Defoulgar's innate intelligence.

Hɑzăr and Tadφlŏn were blown away with this revelation. Unbelievably, their parents were engaged in activities that undermined the Controllers of Uµmρɑ́r. Sɑ́gaçion advised that they were not safe staying here.

"We'll pack now," said Tadφlŏn. "It won't take long."

"My dearest," said Sɑ́gaçion, "they do not suspect that you or Hɑzăr were involved. We must keep it that way."

"I don't understand." Tadφlŏn started to protest.

Vĕracítii moved close to Tadφlŏn and touched her face. "You and Hɑzăr will be safe here. We--Woodland, Vẹríle, Ovalŏn, your father, myself--must distance ourselves from you in order to protect you."

"But Mom...[Sob] I just got you back," said Tadφlŏn.

"I know, dear...You shall always have me and I you. You must trust us."

Vẹríle and Ovalŏn hugged and kissed their son. Sɑ́gaçion promised that they all would be reunited again. He asked Tadφlŏn and Hɑzăr to be strong and to always take care of each other.

With one last hug and kiss. "Do not lose faith in us. We love you and we will be with you always. This I promise you." Ságaçion kissed his daughter's forehead and dried her tears. Věracítii bid her adieu and then they were gone. Tadφlŏn and Hɑzăr consoled each other while trying to make sense out of it all.

Many spans had passed since that terrible period in Tadφlŏn and Hɑzăr's lives. Perfidious would continue to intrude on their happiness. Nonetheless, she and Hɑzăr were meant for each other and that was that. Therefore, this span, they would be joined in holy matrimony. Their parents would be so proud she thought....

We are oh so very happy for you, my dearest, whispered the voice in her head.

Tadφlŏn froze in place. Was this wedding jitters? She had never....

You are okay, sweetheart, whispered Ságaçion in her mind. We promised that we would be with you always and we shall. We love you deeply and wish for you and Hɑzăr the happiest future together.

Where are you? thought Tadφlŏn.

We're fine sweetheart...but we must continue to stay in hiding for now, whispered Věracítii.

How do I hear you?

The Ságaçion principle of trans-temporal telepathy, whispered her father.

He is a genius, you know, said Věracítii.

When will I see...hear from you...How do I contact you? Tadφlŏn's mind was buzzing with questions.

We'll be checking in on you from time to time dearest. ...and we will be together again. Until then, we want you and Hαzăr to build a wonderful life together and make us some wonderful grandchildren!

Mom, Dad...I love you.

And we love you so very much, Tadφlŏn. Now go be happy and enjoy your life together with Hαzăr.

It was undoubtedly the most wonderful wedding gift Tadφlŏn could have hoped for. Her parents were alive and well. They were with her and in her thoughts. She would have to read up on the trans-temporal telepathy thing her dad invented. She did hope, however, that they wouldn't be watching all the time though. Tonight she and the love of her life were going to…well…do wedding night stuff!

Many, many solacles passed…. Hαzăr and Tadφlŏn had produced two wonderful children who were now grown. Just fully grown and out there, somewhere, trying to save the people of Uμmpάr….

"We must proceed to the alternate site," instructed Sir Jacφb Puηt.

"What alternate site?" asked Perfidious sternly. "You have never mentioned an alternate site."

Unceremoniously, Sir Puηt paused looking at first Hαzăr and Tadφlŏn and then to Perfidious. He motioned subtly to two CPU agents traveling with them and then drew his weapon.

"Ah Perfidious," started Sir Puηt, "...of, relating to, or marked by perfidy; treacherous. Your name defines your existence perfectly. From the very first zliton you met Sάgaçion Academis, the purveyors of evil you serve have been known to us. Your complicity in continuing the wickedness of the Controllers was expected. And now...for the countless lives destroyed and the hopeful dreams that can never be...you will be held to account."

Without hesitation, Sir Jacφb Puηt discharged his laser pistol burning a hole through her head. It was like the cutting of a puppet's strings. She collapsed to the ground in an animated display of rag doll physics. Sir Puηt mumbled a prayer for God to have mercy on her soul and then he walked away. Hαzăr and Tadφlŏn were somewhat stunned. Hαzăr paused over her remembering her cruelty and trying to forgive....

"BITCH!"

Transports were waiting for them to get aboard. The alternate site was supposedly located in the near-rad hemisphere. Archived data modules rescued before the CPU facility was overrun were being loaded onto the transports. Sir Puηt had been hurriedly put on the first transport by his CPU escorts. Hαzăr and Tadφlŏn were being directed to the second transport. As they were boarding, Sir Puηt's transport came under attack and a firestorm started breaking loose. They could see that the transport got hit but was able to escape. And now their transport was being fired on. The pilot was hit!

"HAZĂR! THE PILOT IS SLUMPED OVER THE CONTROLS!" screamed Tadφlŏn.

Hαzăr quickly dashed forward to the cockpit with Tadφlŏn hot on his heels. Quickly, they relocated a very dead pilot to the rear of the transport. Others trying to make their way to the transport were being attacked.

"What are we going to do?" asked Tadφlŏn. She tried to contain her excitement.

"If we can get to the others they might have a chance to get aboard," replied Hαzăr.

Tadφlŏn looked at Hɑzăr and her eyes seemed to say--Let's do it! She did not know why but Hɑzăr gave her a little smile that said everything was going to be okay. It seemed to calm her. Hɑzăr powered up the transport and it lurched toward the small group being attacked. He skillfully placed the transport between the attackers and the CPU techs.

"Quick, open the door," said Hɑzăr.

Tadφlŏn was already moving when his request was being made. She stumbled when an energy bolt struck the side of the transport. She could see that the techs were returning fire as best they could with their small energy weapons. Tadφlŏn regained her balance and opened the door to the rush of techs very happy to see her.

"Bless you, dear," said a thankful tech entering the transport.

"LET'S GO," yelled Tadφlŏn from the rear of the transport.

Hɑzăr double-checked over his shoulder for the love of his life before punching the thrusters. The transport groaned to life swerving around and over BlackStellar Labs. The attackers continued to fire from the ground, but they were not prepared for aerial pursuit. Hɑzăr quickly maneuvered the transport out of their range.

At Hɑzăr's request, Tadφlŏn contacted the first transport thus updating their situation. Sir Puŋt's transport transmitted scrambled navigation instructions to their transport. Hɑzăr engaged the autopilot as instructed. Hɑzăr and Tadφlŏn looked lovingly at each other and held hands. The autopilot assumed navigational control of the transport and began executing the programmed flight path to an undisclosed location.

192

CHAPTER NINE

Hijacked...

[BEEP, BEEP, BEEP, BUZZ, BUZZ!] The alarm sounded as the stasis capsules began the process of waking the crew.

"Ah, that was quick. What the...," Jeremy was speechless.

"Oh yeah ...this never is pleasant. Whoo...Who are you?" asked Mµreeη.

As the crew awakened, they became aware of their visitors. Let us say recruiters to be exact. Franchise recruiters that cruise the warp stream looking for unsuspecting travelers like the crew of the *Sir Puηt*. Ah yes, Eberhαrt recognized this motley bunch. They appeared to be Nahrµvian gold smelters. However, when Eberhart looked around he didn't see the *Sir Puηt* loaded down with gold. Quite odd really, he thought.

Nahrµvians melt the gold, which is toxic to them, and cast it into figures of their god. After hijacking a ship, they force the crew to accept their golden deities. The Nahrµvians believe that getting rid of gold cast in the deity form is not only proper but also holy. Except in this case, there was not a single speck of gold aboard. What was going on?

"I am Urφch of the holy planet of Nahrµvia," said the biggest one. "You are now the property of the Rhyuoph Hazardous Waste Services Corporation of Nahrµvia.

"Your ship will be escorted to our opportunity center located in this quadrant," added another one of the recruiters, "where your training will begin."

"What? What the gazelda dung is the Waste Services a go-go?" said Eberhαrt with a noticeable snarl.

"Yeah," added Julíenηe, "and what training are you Uµmprats[25] talking about?"

"Your training," growled Urφch, "...will encompass all necessary tasks required to maintain quality housekeeping in many sensitive facilities."

"Yes," snickered his second named Toiletro, "you're going to receive a franchise enabling you to maintain several of these facilities for practically no compensation. In fact, you are going to pay Rhyuoph Corp. for the privilege of working."

"You know that doesn't really sound that bad," admitted Jerẹmy.

"On Uµmpάr they force you to take compensation for peeing," agreed Mµreeη.

Eberhαrt looked at Jerẹmy and Mµreeη as if to say--Have you two been sniffing liquid XP27 acid formulate or what?

---

[25] Uµmprat -- rodent-like creature native to Uµmpάr, which scavenges waste treatment facilities. It is said they can eat ten times their weight in shitova every span. They commonly are used by medical facilities to leach politicians who are full of it!

194

"These are sweat shop slave masters that you have to pay to do their bidding," said Eberhart harshly.

"He's right," whispered Julíenηe. "These types of franchise corporations exploit planetary beings that are desperate to own their own solar business."

"We must look for an opportunity to escape before the chargebacks start arriving," said Eberhart.

"Chargeback...What's that?" asked Jerẹmy.

"Well, after working your tail off to satisfy a customer, the franchise corp. will distribute your compensation minus numerous franchise fees. Then, when your customer doesn't pay, you are issued a chargeback."

"What do you do?" asked Mµreeη quietly.

"There's not much you can do. You can call the franchise corporation to inquire, but they may give you the run-around. In any event, these corporations are out to get customer contracts. Consequently, they will bid the work for next to nothing to get them," said Julíenηe.

"Okay, then," whispered Jerẹmy, "it's our duty to issue this corporation a chargeback that they will never forget."

"Now you're talking," smiled Eberhart.

The crew of the *Sir Puηt* quietly considered how to franchise a little justice in this quadrant. Eberhart reasoned that since they had not been able to return to their own time period these thieves operated to the opposite extreme when compared to the norms on Uµmpár. Where on Uµmpár you would be given unbearable compensation, here you are barely compensated. Gees, there must be a middle ground on some other planet.

"Toiletro, bind their hands," said Urφch and then turned toward the bridge. "...take the helm."

"Yes, sir," replied Latrína.

Both suspected pirates obeyed without question. Latrína appeared to be at home behind the ship's controls. Eberhαrt became impressed with her ability to quickly identify critical systems and execute space maneuvers. Urφch hovered close by the *Sir Puηt's* crew as if he expected them to rebel. Mμreeη nudged Eberhαrt directing his attention to the primitive pulsed-energy weapons that the pirates were carrying.

"What species are you?" asked Urφch. "Latrína says she has never seen controls like these on your space vessel."

"We are from the planet, Uμmpάr," responded Julíenηe.

"I do not recognize that name," admitted Urφch. "What star system?"

"Eureka," replied Jerξmy.

"Preposterous," snapped Urφch. "That star system is located on the far boundary of the mapped universe--tens of billions of light-solacles away. Do not attempt treachery."

"We're not lying," said Jerξmy.

"It's of no consequence where you are from," said Urφch. "You are now in the service of the Franchise in the Lotzaphii galaxy. ...for the rest of your natural lives!"

With that said, Urφch evilly smiled at them and moved off to confer with Latrína and Toiletro. The crew of the *Sir Puηt* watched their captors' every move trying to glean information that might help them to escape. Urφch appeared to be somewhat cozy with Latrína. Mμreeη again nudged Eberhαrt pointing out how Latrína's body

196

language gave away her familiarity with Urφch. They were lovers! Eberhαrt smiled approvingly at Mμreeη for her meticulous observation.

The *Sir Puηt* shuddered slightly as thrusters fired. The crew understood this to mean that they had entered planetary orbit and were preparing to descend to the surface. The crew was unable to free themselves thus far. They hoped that on the surface an opportunity to escape might present itself. The ride was getting a little bumpier indicating a landing was soon imminent.

"...Lieutenant Pisoph requesting landing vector."

"348.7," responded the surface controller.

Again, the *Sir Puηt* groaned slightly as they felt it roll into a new heading. The thrusters again continued to fire adjusting attitude and stabilizing the ship along the new flight path. Urφch patted Latríηa's shoulder signaling his approval of her piloting skills. Toiletro seemed to busy himself with sensor sweeps. Eberhαrt had noticed this earlier but had not paid much attention to it. What was he looking for?

"Anything?" asked Urφch.

"No, sir," replied Toiletro, "sensor sweeps have been clear."

"Very good, keep scanning," instructed Urφch.

"What are they looking for?" whispered Jeręmy.

"I don't know," replied Eberhαrt. "...Galactic law enforcement?"

"...A reasonable assumption," said Mμreeη.

The vibration increased dramatically as the *Sir Puηt's* thrusters fired with great force cushioning their landing. Latríηa powered down the systems and communicated this action to their ground controllers. Even with the systems off, their captors remained seated while quietly conversing giving an occasional look over at their captives from time to time.

"We're still moving," noted Julíenηe.

"Yes," agreed Eberhαrt. "They're parking the ship. Possibly, we're being moved below the surface."

"Why?" quizzed Jeręmy, "...and what's with the constant sensor sweeps?"

"They apparently have enemies," replied Eberhαrt. "The enemy of mine enemy...."

"...yes," added Julíenηe.

Some time had passed before the ship came to rest. The recruiters now arose and began preparing to disembark.

"All right...the joy ride is over," said Toiletro. He moved cautiously while helping the captive crewmembers to their feet.

Urφch and Latríηa flanked the captives with their weapons drawn. Toiletro opened the ship's door and began herding the crew out of the *Sir Puηt*.

"Okay, let's move...," moaned Toiletro. He roughly poked and pushed the crew out of the ship.

"...Down to the end of the bay to await a medical exam," instructed Latríηa using her weapon to point.

"Can't have you aliens bringing a contagion into our training facility," said Toiletro.

"That was amazing how you were able to learn our ship's controls so quickly," said Eberhαrt complimenting Latríηa.

"Shut up and keep moving," commanded Urφch. Eberhαrt noted a tinge of jealousy in his voice.

Eberhαrt nodded for the others to comply as he led the way. At the end of the bay was a comprehensive medical station. Eberhαrt and the others were instructed

198

to strip off their garments for the exam. Мμreeη again nudged Eberhαrt pointing out how the female techs were laughing while looking at him and Jeręmy.

"Why are they laughing?" Eberhαrt asked the examiner.

He smiled and then said, "They are wondering how you satisfy your females with just one sex organ!"

"Very well, I thank you," spouted Jeręmy. "Uh...How many do you have?"

"Nahrμvian males have three. ...quantity matters as well," said the examiner proudly. "Now please enter this chamber for decontamination."

The medical examiner ushered them into the decontamination chamber for the standard quarantine period. Although they enjoyed being together and naked, they decided to use this time to formulate additional strategy aimed at self-preservation.

"What if they separate us," asked Julíenηe.

"Remember that each of us has a passive neuro-transponder woven into the cortex of the brain," said Мμreeη. "The Puηt's locator can identify the signal within a one-hundred thousand penãrd radius."

"Besides," said Eberhαrt, "they will keep us together for the training period...I hope."

The vapor entered the chamber unnoticed quickly relaxing and then inducing sleep in the *Sir Puηt's* crew.

"I don't know about this bunch," confessed Toiletro.

"I agree," said Latríηa, "They smell like trouble. The technology on their ship is very advanced."

"We'll put them through the training program," said Urφch. "They will serve the franchise or die."

"I don't like it," said Toiletro. "We should just issue them chargebacks and dump them in the asteroid belt."

"Yeah," agreed Latrína slapping Toiletro's hand.

"You have your orders! Now carry them out," commanded Urφch.

"Aye, sir."

The transport had traveled thousands of penãrds thought Tadφlŏn. Eberhαrt and Julíenηe.... She missed them. She wondered where the alpha site was located. She also thought it was quite strange that their view screens and viewports had been turned off and sealed. Obviously, someone did not want them to see anything outside the transport. She could feel the subtle course changes and increases in velocity. The air pressure had been elevated and the nitrogen mix had been adjusted. Evidently, the desire was to allow a richer oxygen atmosphere within the transport. The subtle changes registered by the ship's instruments confirmed this. Were they leaving Uμmpár? This ship was capable of travel within the solar system. Tadφlŏn knew that Hαzăr probably was already spinning up many new scenarios. What planetary bodies, asteroids, or moons were close by? Was the alpha site located off Uμmpár?

Tadφlŏn sat up, partially awake, looking fuzzily through her eyelashes. She was hoping to rest and reclaim some strength before they arrived at who knows where. She could not help noticing Hαzăr. He would glance at her lovingly as he believed that she was asleep. He was troubled, she thought. She could see that he busied himself with observing the instruments and indicators. He was restless. Why? And...what was that with the

200

summary execution of Perfidious? Many questions still unanswered. Was that what was bothering Hɑzăr, she wondered? What about their children? Were they all right? Would they be able to return to Uμmpάr in the correct time period? Tadφlŏn felt helpless.

I believe the Ghoηɑdz' were shocked by your execution of Perfidious, said the unseen shadowy figure.

"Possibly," responded Jacφb. "It was necessary you know."

In what way? questioned the figure.

"Perfidious had achieved her purpose and was no longer valuable. She had served the Controllers well after Sάgaçion and Vĕracítii disappeared. Hɑzăr and Tadφlŏn were joined and produced offspring," said Sir Puηt.

True...Yet you have placed their offspring in harm's way needlessly, said thc figure beginning a critique.

"An acceptable risk," said Jacφb. "They may yet be successful."

Ah, yes...the A.P.E.L. I had almost forgotten about your...the CPU's... desire to rule Uμmpάr. If the mission is successful, the CPU becomes the dominant force on Uμmpάr, teased the shadow. ...seems that commonsense would be compromised.

"Commonsense requires modification," responded Jacφb. "It is flawed in its truest form."

How so? asked the figure.

"Commonsense is...*common*!"

I see, responded the shadow. You believe an uncommon sense is required as well. ...One for which to guide the commonsense. It's a most interesting concept.

"Sir, did you say something?" asked the co-pilot.

"No...Uh...just thinking out loud," replied Sir Puηt, "...just thinking out loud."

The co-pilot rose and made his way back to the cockpit from the rear of the ship.

"He's talking to himself again," said the co-pilot to the pilot.

"He has a lot on his mind now," responded the pilot, "...maybe you'd be talking to yourself too."

"It's more often now...it's weird...you know?" said the co-pilot. "Even the security detail is starting to freak a little."

"We'll mention it to the doctor when we arrive...Okay?"

"Agreed," said the co-pilot.

"Ah...how long have we been asleep?" murmured Eberhαrt.

"I don't know," replied Mµreeη.

Our gang awoke to a new environment. They were in a large complex that reeked of spent plutonium and rotting flesh. As they looked around, they noticed several pieces of equipment and several radiation suits.

"We're inside an old breeder reactor facility!" said Eberhαrt excitedly.

"Radiation suits," said Mµreeη, "...put them on-- NOW!"

The crew became aware of the seriousness of their situation and quickly donned the hazard suits. After each member finished checking the other's suit for proper sealing, the crew began to look around. Hundreds of old fission fuel rods were stacked with some in a haphazard fashion. ...Shitova! What were they doing there?

"Good morning!" A voice blared through the loud speaker. "Welcome to the Rhyuoph Corp. radiation cleanup training facility."

"We could have died in here if we hadn't awakened!" said Eberhαrt.

"You did awaken and you're not dead," replied the voice from the speaker. "Now your training in hazmat housekeeping can begin."

"We're not going to clean--!"

"Ah, but you will," said the voice they now recognized as Urφch. "You see those radiation suits you have on are made from a dissolvable synthetic material. Currently, the radiopacity[26] is sufficient to protect you. However, after about one span, radiolysis[27] will begin and they soon will allow x-rays and other radiation to pass through--to you! I suggest that you listen carefully and pay close attention to the training instructions you are about to receive."

"It would seem that we are captive students," admitted Jerẹmy.

The crew looked at each other now understanding the consequences of inaction. As the speaker instructed, the crew listened and learned. In short time, they were quickly operating the radiation scrubbers and fuel rod vacuums. Urφch was sincerely impressed. He had never had such an astute group of trainees. They were going to produce extraordinary fees for the Rhyuoph Hazardous Waste Services Corporation of Nahrμvia.

After nearly a span, the crew had decontaminated the facility to well below dangerous levels. Urφch congratulated them on their efforts and directed them to

---

[26] Radiopacity -- the ability to block electromagnetic radiation.
[27] Radiolysis -- chemical breakdown via radiation.

the decontamination showers and some earned food and rest.

"This is gazelda dung," moaned Jerȩmy. "How are we going to extricate ourselves from this deadly training ground?"

"Uh, you done complaining, *teenie weenie?*" teased Eberhαrt. He nodded his head thus nudging Jerȩmy's attention to the video surveillance.

"So I'm a small pain in the ass!" replied Jerȩmy. "...Yeah, I'm done."

Eberhαrt chuckled as the crew headed for the showers where they tried to wash off the sweat of their labor. Once out of the shower, they found fresh garments with the franchise logo imprinted on them. Toiletro was waiting with armed guards to escort them to the eating area. The crew followed without incident. They were tired and hungry.

The eating area was large enough to feed hundreds of trainees. When the crew arrived, they noted about fifty or so trainees already eating. They could not help but notice the way they ate. They were like animals that were infrequently fed. Spontaneously, a fight would break out over a morsel of bread. The guards would quickly subdue the fighters by electrifying their franchise training garments. Urφch liked his trainees to be hungry and obedient. The crew filtered through the line collecting their meager portion of food that looked and smelled like Uμmprat droppings. The crew decided to settle at a table where a small male and female were eating.

"You don't want this," said a trainee. He took the small female's bread.

"And you don't need these!" She instantly buried her small foot into his genital area.

204

The bread-stealing trainee doubled over and dropped to floor curling up like a noodle.

"Get out of here!" The small male growled as he began stomping the extremity of the now injured trainee.

"Uh...are these seats taken?" inquired Eberhαrt. He watched the injured trainee crawl away.

The scrappy duo offered only a look of indifference, which was a good enough invitation for the crew to sit.

"I'm Eberhαrt and these are my traveling companions-- Mμreeη, Julίenηe, and Jeręmy."

"Hey," said the crew.

Silence ensued for several zlitons.

"Uh hmmn...We're new here. I mean...uh...we were recently hijacked," clarified Eberhαrt.

"They've had us cleaning in the reactor facility," said Julίenηe. Julίenηe, being ignored, looked at Eberhαrt and raised her eyebrows.

After several zlitons of silence, the male spoke. "I'm Jet Scoe and this is Alli Oosh."

"Our pleasure to meet you, Jet, Alli," said Eberhαrt nodding and smiling. "We're from Uμmpάr."

Immediately, Jet and Alli perked up and looked at each other. "Where are you from?" asked Alli displaying a little more friendliness.

"Uμmpάr," replied Julίenηe. "Heard of it?"

"Uμmpάr is in the Eureka star system," said Jet, "ninety-two billion light-solacles away."

"So you have heard of it," said Jeręmy jokingly.

Jet and Alli's eyes met briefly for a conference. "We can't talk here."

"Where?" inquired Eberhαrt.

"Your next training session will be in the Level IV Bio-Weapons training facility. We'll meet you there," answered Alli.

"Wait," said Mμreeη. "Where are you from?"

"We're Tellurians," said Alli. Both Jet and Alli rose to leave with their training group.

"Tellurian," said Eberhαrt. "Where have I heard that?"

"We'll be landing soon, Hαzăr," crackled the voice from the communicator.

"Very good." Hαzăr looked over at Tadφlŏn.

"Your viewports will be opening soon. You must switch off the autopilot at that time and follow us to the landing zone," instructed Sir Puηt.

"Understood...."

As Jacφb had said, the viewports opened and the view screen cameras were functioning again. Hαzăr disengaged the autopilot to take manual control of the transport. Looking out just ahead, he could visually see Sir Jacφb's transport. Hαzăr utilized sensors to maintain a pursuing flight path. This certainly could still be Uμmράr, thought Hαzăr. There were two moons glowing in the sky and the terrain looked familiar. Still...something feels wrong.

"Where are we?" asked Tadφlŏn assuming an alert posture.

"I really don't know," admitted Hαzăr. "The view screens just came back on."

"Do you think we are still on Uμmράr?" Tadφlŏn surprised Hαzăr with the revelation that she too suspected an off-world second site.

"You never cease to amaze me with your intuitiveness," said Hαzăr with a smile, "and...I do not know if we are still on Uμmρár."

Tadφlŏn took Hαzăr's hand as they followed Sir Puηt's transport to the landing zone and possibly to some answers to their questions.

"We're approaching the landing site," said Hαzăr.

"I see it," replied Tadφlŏn.

Sir Puηt's transport was headed for a clearing just ahead. It appeared to be vacant of any structures. Indeed, the landscape was aesthetically pleasing. The clearing was surrounded by a lush green forest sprinkled with a breath of colorful wild flowers. Beyond this were rolling hills with majestic mountains in the distance. Hαzăr wondered where on Uμmρár this could be. Still, the absence of hostiles was very welcome.

"Straight ahead, Hαzăr," instructed the voice from the communicator.

"Acknowledged--straight ahead."

As Hαzăr and Tadφlŏn watched with surprise, the transport in front of them vanished as it entered the clearing.

"What the--!" said Tadφlŏn.

"Cut your speed ten percent," instructed the transmitted voice.

"Confirmed...cutting speed ten percent," said Hαzăr.

Though somewhat befuddled, Hαzăr proceeded ahead toward the area where the first transport had vanished. Suddenly, they entered some type of energy field, which was devoid of solid objects and completely filled with darkness. After a brief period holding the instructed course, a huge city of complexes appeared.

Hαzăr and Tadφlŏn could now see the first transport and quickly adjusted their course to follow it.

"Very good, Hαzăr, Tadφlŏn," said Sir Puηt over the communicator. "Welcome to Sedition Outpost Alpha."

"Wow!" exclaimed Tadφlŏn.

Looking out their viewport in all directions revealed a vast city. Hαzăr estimated it to be the size of Prystine, which had a population of just fewer than forty million. They seemed to be taking the scenic route passing by numerous coliseums, stadiums, libraries, shopping centers, office complexes, residential structures, and recreation parks. It was an amazing trip around the city. Periodically, Sir Puηt would announce a location of interest over the communicator.

"Well, what do you think?" asked Sir Puηt.

"Amazing!" said Hαzăr.

"Unbelievable!" added Tadφlŏn.

"Glad you approve. You'll get a chance to see more of it. I promise," responded Sir Puηt.

"Look over there," said Tadφlŏn pointing at a military-type facility.

Thousands of soldiers could be seen on parade. It was like an invasion force being readied for deployment. After the awe had subsided, Hαzăr and Tadφlŏn looked at each other with a combined sense of apprehension.

Hαzăr skillfully followed Sir Puηt's transport to a landing area on the far side of the military-type structure. Hαzăr set the transport down gently and began de-energizing systems while awaiting further instructions.

"Exit the transport and you will be escorted to a briefing area where your questions may be answered," announced a voice from the communicator.

208

Noting that the announcement did not come from Sir Puηt, the Ghoηαdz' along with other passengers exited the transport and complied. Looking up at the structure, Hαzăr guessed it to be about thirty stories high. As they paused to take in all that was around them, the obvious questions about how all of this could be cloaked puzzled Hαzăr.

"This is amazing," confessed Tadφlŏn. "How could they build all of this and keep it a secret?"

"I really don't know. ...but I'm already thinking about it."

Their escorted journey took them along wide paths through scenic gardens to an entrance to the facility. Everyone proceeded in through security screening equipment and an examination by security personnel. Once inside, security separated Hαzăr and Tadφlŏn from the others. Subsequently, they were led to a great hall where Sir Puηt joined them.

"Welcome! Welcome to Sedition," said Sir Puηt with pride.

"Thank you," replied Hαzăr and Tadφlŏn in unison.

"This is a very large city," said Tadφlŏn.

"How did you keep it hidden away from view?" inquired Hαzăr.

"So many questions," responded Sir Puηt, "...all will be answered in due time...in due time. For now, please follow me."

Sir Puηt led them to a lift, which took them to the very top of the structure. They exited through additional security into a huge viewing area complete with optical enhancers to scan the entire city. It was obvious that Sir Puηt was just a little vain in his pride for this city. Hαzăr and Tadφlŏn noted how he glowed as he pointed out areas of interest. He seemed to gloat when detailing the plan he designed that led to the building of this outpost and particularly its ability to remain undetected.

"What's wrong?" asked Hɑzăr.

"Nothing," replied Tadφlŏn, "...seems I'm getting a splitting headache."

"Not to worry, dear," said Sir Jacφb. "This and other areas of the city are shielded against trans-temporal telepathy. The interference waves being emitted sometimes induce a mild mental discomfort."

"Jacφb," said a young female, "I was worried."

The young visitor, somewhat older than Eberhɑrt, hugged Jacφb and spoke with him quietly for a few moments before being introduced to Hɑzăr and Tadφlŏn.

"This is Hɑzăr and Tadφlŏn Ghoŋɑdz."

Hɑzăr and Tadφlŏn nodded and offered their hands in a gesture of friendship. The young female smiled brightly at them while accepting.

"May I introduce, Cołłiŋsía Verŋa Puŋt...my little sister." With that, Cołłiŋsía politely curtsied.

"Hello," said Cołłiŋsía politely. "Have you come to help my brother battle the Dark One?"

"...Dark One?" inquired Tadφlŏn.

"Cołłiŋsía," said Sir Puŋt, "...would you please go and prepare suitable living arrangements for our guests."

"Of course," replied Cołłiŋsía. She gracefully excused herself.

The Ghoŋɑdz' looked at Jacφb with facial expressions that exuded questions about the Dark One. Jacφb astutely began to circumnavigate Cołłiŋsía's disclosure while providing scant details concerning the Dark One. Hɑzăr and Tadφlŏn politely withdrew their inquiry after realizing that Sir Jacφb was not going to provide any substantial background information at this time. Time gently passed as Sir Jacφb detailed a little more about the R.O.L.A.I.T.E.S. project.

"Ah Cołłiηsía," said Sir Jacφb. He diverted their attention to his sister's return.

"Your living space is ready," said Cołłiηsía.

"Thank you, my dear," said Sir Jacφb. He waved his hand inviting the Ghoηɑdz' to follow their escort.

The Ghoηɑdz' silently offered their thanks and followed as requested. Hɑzăr noticed before leaving that Jacφb, appearing deep in thought, turned to look out over the city.

"How long have you lived here at Sedition Outpost Alpha?" asked Hɑzăr.

"How long?" repeated Cołłiηsía. "I was born here."

"Just when was Sedition founded?" asked Tadφlŏn.

"28842."

"Excuse me!" blurted Hɑzăr. "Did you say 28842?"

"That's over 10000 solacles into the future," said Tadφlŏn.

"Certainly you joke…" laughed Cołłiηsía. "We have just celebrated the passing of 28865!"

Hɑzăr and Tadφlŏn were unable to speak. Looking at each other in disbelief….

Why are they so surprised by the date, thought Cołłiηsía? Could it be possible that they were from another time? If so… When? Cołłiηsía had never been away from Sedition and certainly was not aware of what may be happening on their world. This was just too much to comprehend. What has Sir Jacφb been telling them? Was Jacφb keeping secrets from her? My dear brother is so protective....

"Who is the Dark One?" asked Hαzăr.

"I'm sorry," replied Cołłiηsía. "Jacφb has asked me not to speak of this one to you."

"We just want to help," Tadφlŏn assured her. "...Please tell us as much as you can."

Tadφlŏn's motherly love shown through soothing Cołłiηsía's concerns in a way she had never experienced. Cołłiηsía had never known a mother or a father. She was told that her parents had died in an earlier conflict and that she was Jacφb's only relative. Consequently, she had never experienced the parental love and caring that radiated so naturally from Hαzăr and Tadφlŏn.

"We must talk elsewhere." Cołłiηsía dismissed their escort and motioned for Hαzăr and Tadφlŏn to follow.

"Where are we?" asked Tadφlŏn. "My headache is returning."

"This is one of several libraries," replied Cołłiηsía. "It is safe to talk freely here. Jacφb and I spend much time here as he instructs me in the history of Sedition and the struggle that has consumed him."

Basking in the warmth of these new feelings Cołłiηsía disclosed all that she knew. The ominous Dark One came to be known many solacles ago when Jacφb suddenly began conversing, seemingly, with himself. Though most all that were aware of those singular conversations passed it off as stress or the intense responsibility of Sir Jacφb's position. The Dark One was believed by Jacφb to be a projected sentient presence that

212

at first appeared spiritual in nature. Later, Jacφb came to understand that the presence was a trans-temporal tool being utilized in an attempt to transform Uμmράr into a society whereby resistance to the desires of the Controllers did not exist. In other words, someone was trying to manipulate the past to achieve a desired affect for the Controllers. Jacφb had told Cołłiŋsía that it was better to collaborate and keep the Dark One close in an attempt to identify the manipulators. Subsequently, Jacφb had confided in her that the Dark One's plans were more sinister than just the controlling of Uμmράr.

Cołłiŋsía went on to say the R.O.L.A.I.T.E.S. project was an attempt to induce the manipulators to reveal themselves. The mission to enlighten Sharon Defoulgar about the futility of innate intelligence was really a tempting opportunity for the manipulators to intervene in a much earlier stage of Uμmράr's history. It was hoped that during this intervention their true form and intentions would be revealed. Cołłiŋsía said that there was an element of danger in the R.O.L.A.I.T.E.S. mission. However, Jacφb had taken every precaution to safeguard the crew.

"Wow," stated Tadφlŏn.

"How are we going to not think about this once we leave this protected area," asked Hαzăr.

"Drink this," said Cołłiŋsía. "All of the fluids dispensed in the city contain an isotope that directly interferes with temporal telepathy making it virtually impossible for our thoughts to be collected. Jacφb constantly encourages me to drink."

"Doesn't the Dark One suspect something?" asked Hαzăr. "I mean…not being able to collect thoughts might raise some suspicions."

"For whatever reason, this city's location naturally inhibits temporal telepathy to some degree according to Jacφb," replied Cołłiŋsía. "The isotope in our fluid supply slowly decays emitting high speed beta anti-particles causing electromagnetic interference. It is an additional layer of protection as are the safe areas where temporal telepathy is completely suppressed. The manipulators are tolerant of our privacy concerns though they continually attempt to circumvent these safety precautions."

"It gets quite complicated," said Hαzăr. "Considering what you have told us, I am very concerned about the safety of our children and for the rest of the Sir Puŋt's crew."

"I understand," replied Cołłiŋsía. "The A.P.E.L. that the crew took with them will act as a lightening rod attracting the temporal telepathic efforts of the manipulators. It is hoped that the manipulator's temporal telepathic connection will be permanently addressed to the planet that the *Sir Puŋt* was destined for."

"But that planet was a very young Uμmράr!" exclaimed Hαzăr.

"Not exactly…," responded Cołłiŋsía.

CHAPTER TEN

THE ADVENTURES OF
JET SCOE AND ALLI OOSH...

The sun's rays beamed brightly through the trees spraying photons of light on everything. Seemed like just another glorious morning in just another average mid-western town. The birds were chirping while the calm of the night dissolved into the bustling activities of townsfolk on their way to work and to play.

[Beeeeeeep, BURRMMMMP!]

"GET OUT OF THE STREET YOU CRAZY KIDS!" screamed the irate driver.

Two bicycles, swerving in and out of in-town traffic, made their way out of town to a secret location. Peddling through the trees, past the old pond, over the meadow, and into foothills to the cave where their lives had been transformed not so many months ago were two brave young people known as Jet Scoe and Alli Oosh. A brother and sister team of would-be planetary heroes or at the very least--small town good guys. Arriving at their

215

destination, the duo took great care to hide their green-powered transports before entering the only Earth outpost of the TIA. (Temporal Intelligence Agency) Using sophisticated biometrics to enter their secret outpost, they descended below the surface to an arrangement of communications, surveillance, TV watching, snacking, and game playing gadgetry.

"Well...school's out for summer," said Alli with that look in her eye that Jet knew all too well.

"Okay, what have you got us hooked up with this time?" said Jet shaking his head.

"Ah, not too much," said Alli slyly. "...But read this!"

Alli went over to a console and pulled out a copy of a periodical dated June 10, 3160.

"You know we're not supposed to be using the temporal microfiche viewer without permission," said Jet a little disappointed.

"Listen...we agreed to work with the temporal investigators months ago after we discovered their presence here on Earth," said Alli. "They gave us the viewer, all of this equipment, and we haven't heard from them since."

"Soooo," moaned Jet.

"Sooo, we can't just sit here all summer long doing nothing," continued Alli. "So I thought I would contact them. And...I did!"

"You contacted the TIA and you didn't even let me in on it."

"I know Jet and I'm sorry," said Alli. She dropped her head while looking at Jet out of the corner of her eye.

"Ahhh...we're supposed to be tight," said Jet.

"They gave us a MISSION!" said an excited Alli.

"They WHAT!" blurted Jet with eyes big as melons.

"They sent us this communiqué," replied Alli. She handed Jet the document. "They've instructed us to scan the 32nd century periodicals for environmental anomalies."

"Anomalies?" asked Jet. "What kind of anomalies?"

"Just read it." Alli pointed at the message. "They suspect trans-temporal hazmat dumping."

"Trans-temporal hazmat dumping?" Jet scratched his head.

"I know...our first assignment," beamed Alli. "Isn't it so exciting?"

"What have you found?" asked Jet.

"I found this," said Alli. "A paper dated 6/10/3160 reports extraordinary appearances of hazardous materials seeping forth from beneath major population centers. It goes on to say that scientists were baffled as to the simultaneous appearances all over the entire planet."

"What does it mean?" mumbled Jet.

"It means that someone is going to violate the temporal dumping code and make Earth a planetary toxic waste site," argued Alli. "That's what it means."

"I guess now we have to file a report or something?" concluded Jet.

"Agreed," said Alli. "We know the format. Let's work on it today and send it off."

"Wow, Alli," confessed Jet, "this is kind of exciting!"

"I know...Let's get to it."

Jet and Alli busied themselves writing out the report and then coding it for transmission to the Milky Way TIA communications node. Just to double check their research, Jet and Alli scoured the thirty-second century periodicals again using the temporal microfiche viewer.

"Wow…according to this, at least a dozen sites start oozing toxic materials within a period of a month," said Jet reading the periodical again.

"Okay…It's coded," announced Alli. "Are you ready?"

"Ready," replied Jet. "Let's transmit it."

Alli fed the report into a facsimile type reader that literally chewed it up and spat it out as confetti. Of course, it was transmitted as well. The lights flashed in a manner signaling that the transmission occurred and a readout declared it to have been received by the communications node located somewhere out there in the galaxy.

"Well," sighed Alli, "I guess now we wait for any reply."

"Do you think there will be a reply?" asked Jet. "I mean maybe all they wanted was for us just to research the periodicals and that was it."

"Sheez, I hope that wasn't it," responded Alli. "I'm hoping for an off-world, off-time period…oh whatever! I just want to be involved."

"It's getting late," said Jet, "we had better go."

"Yeah, let's go."

Heading to the lift for their ride back to the surface Alli and Jet detoured into the sub-surface hangar. Jet and Alli would spend hours in the spacecraft simulator practicing to fly the *Tellurian*. That was what Ságaçion and Věracítii had named it. They had said that Earth's inhabitants were Tellurian and so they thought it a fitting name for Earth's first intergalactic spacecraft. There it sat, a few feet away, looking somewhat ominous. Jet and Alli loved to sit in it just dreaming of their extraterrestrial jaunts throughout the galaxies. Though Jet and Alli spent countless hours flying the *Tellurian* simulator, they were unable to get a single instrument lamp to flicker in the real thing. The *Tellurian* could only be activated by a remote transmission from the TIA. This Jet and Alli deduced was a safeguard to prevent them from rocketing around the solar system to who knows where. Still… it was awesome just to be inside this intergalactic bad boy!

"Someday," said Jet, "we'll get the signal and we are going to light up the night sky with this beast."

"You know it, bro," agreed Alli, "but for now…we've gotta blow."

"Good one, sis," said Jet slapping Alli's hand.

The rocketeering hopefuls made their way back to the surface where their two-wheeled chariots awaited. Jet and Alli seemed to have great fun together unlike typical siblings. It seemed the secret of the extraterrestrial beings that they shared help to bond them tightly. They each felt a supreme purpose for being.

Arriving back at home, they saw mom in the kitchen readying supper while dad was reading the paper. Jet and Alli were blessed with wonderful parents that cared for them deeply and they knew it. It was funny how Ságaçion and Věracítii, two beings from another world, were not much different from their own parents. Ságaçion and Věracítii spoke as proud parents of their own children and exuded values that seemed common among decent

God-fearing people. Alli remembered how they had spoke of Tadφlŏn, their daughter, her husband, Hαzăr, and their grandchildren. Their grandchildren were on a mission to end tyranny on their home world of Uμρár while helping beings from other worlds. It was overwhelming at times thinking about all that they had come to know in such a short time.

"Supper's ready, you two," said mom. "Now go wash up--right now."

"Right, Mom," said the duo and off they went.

The evening went along nicely. Jet and Alli's mom had prepared a pot roast with potatoes, carrots, corn on the cob, and fresh corn bread. It was a great end to a terrific day. After hugs and kisses, Jet and Alli retired to showers, teeth brushing, prayers, and bed. They couldn't sleep, however. They were just so wound up that Jet in his room and Alli in hers kept their communicators on all night.

[Bzzzzzzzz, BZZZZZZZZZ!] The annoying clock sounded.

"Jet!" said Alli shaking him somewhat roughly. "Wake up!"

"What...What's going on?" responded a sleepy Jet.

"Come on! ...The communicator is flashing!" whispered Alli.

With that said, Jet's eyes opened wide and he bounded from the bed to have a look for himself. Sure enough, his communicator was flashing as well. This could only mean that they had another communiqué waiting at the TIA outpost. They were very excited though they tried to remain composed through breakfast so they could be excused from the house.

"You two sure rose quickly this morning," noted dad aloud.

"What have you got planned for this day anyway?" inquired mom.

"Nothing much," replied Alli coolly.

"Yeah..." said Jet. "We thought we might go by the carnival that opens today and look around a bit."

"That's right," said dad, "it's over by the school."

"I want you two to be careful," insisted mom. "No talking to strangers and don't go off by yourselves."

"Right, Mom," agreed Jet giving mom a little smile.

"No problem," said Alli, "we won't."

After being excused from the breakfast table, Jet and Alli packed a little for their day. A few snacks, drinks, a video game, and they were off. Once again, peddling through the trees, past the old pond, over the meadow, and into the foothills to the cave where an adventure beyond their wildest dreams or nightmares was starting to unfold.

"Come on...hurry!" encouraged Alli as she was entering the cave.

"I'm right behind you, sis," responded Jet.

Hurrying through the cave to what seemed a dead end, Alli felt carefully for the recess where a combination of biometric scanners would allow them access to the TIA outpost lift. Within seconds, the stone moved aside exposing the lift doors where another redundant security screening was required. After successfully passing this layer of screening, the lift doors opened and they entered.

The doors swished shut and yet another layer of screening was required before they would be allowed to descend.

"I guess you can never be too careful," said Jet. They exited the lift into a lower level anteroom.

"Guess not," responded Alli.

They moved quickly to the communications area where the communiqué was awaiting them. At last, with excited breathing becoming audible, they were within inches of their second communication from the TIA.

"Go ahead," encouraged Jet, "...read it!"

"Okay...here we go," replied Alli. She carefully picked up yet another historic document.

After moments of silence while Alli quietly reviewed the document....

"Well...? What does it say?" inquired an impatient Jet.

"It says...," started Alli, "Agents Jet Scoe and Alli Oosh, Tellurian TIA Outpost #7948356241, Milky Way Galaxy. Your recent research report detailing unexplained toxic appearances has been reviewed. Ignoring a few misspelled words, (*Damazar! Even off-worlders bitch about spell'n. Stay in and EXCEL in school, kids!*) the content is regarded as excellent fieldwork. Therefore, as the reporting field agents you are hereby offered first refusal of an off-world temporal intelligence gathering assignment. If--?"

"Did you just say...OFF-WORLD?" yelled an excited Jet.

"Yes! It says an off-world temporal intelligence gathering assignment!" repeated a gleeful Alli Oosh. "There's more... listen. If you accept, the appropriate arrangements will be made to transport you to the nearest

TIA facility where orientation for your specific assignment will be administered."

"Wow, Alli," started Jet, "off-world orientation! How sweet is that?"

"Quiet, there's more," nudged Alli. "DISCLAIMER: During this assignment certain physical, emotional, and spiritual attributes will be required. To be specific, you may be required to walk, run, crouch, crawl, slump, stoop, lift, push, pull, wave, swing, jump, hop, skip, touch, feel, taste, smell, talk, whisper, listen, read, write, and think. Additionally, you may laugh, cry, sympathize, empathize, love, hate, display anger, display bravery, act vengeful, compliment, criticize, judge, condemn, scream in terror, scream in pain, be silent, and remain calm. Furthermore, you likely will pray for help, deliverance, mercy, forgiveness, salvation, death, and the many blessings you may or may not receive. Finally, this assignment may require you to be subjected to extreme sensory inputs. Although, because of your status as temporal agents, you cannot experience death, the full range of physical, emotional, and spiritual stimuli may be endured. Therefore, it is assured that you have never experienced anything like this ever before." (*Lawyers obviously were not exterminated by a meteor shower as was once believed. They escaped natural selection and moved into other more lucrative areas of endeavor.*)

Jet listened intently to Alli as she read aloud. This is what *he* heard....

"DISCLAIMER: During this assignment you will utilize all of your physical, emotional, and spiritual resources. It is most likely that you will have to act aggressively using your newly acquired physical attributes to subdue the enemy and extract the required information.

Using your superior skills to operate advanced spacecraft, you likely may intercede in explosive space combat situations that possibly may result in commando style raids to save innocent aliens while blowing the hell out of god-awful ugly creatures that are intent on destroying life, liberty, the pursuit of happiness, baseball, and mom's apple pie. Furthermore, your spiritual skills may require you to offer words of remembrance as you stand pissing on the graves of these heathen bastards that have dared to terrorize the God-fearing inhabitants of our blessed star system. You Tellurians are unique in all the universe and we salute you for the acts of bravery and compassion as well as the extreme alien ass-kicking you are about to perform. THANK YOU!"

"That's just unbelievable," mumbled a daydreaming Jet.

"I know," replied Alli. "I'm a little scared too."

"Scared?" responded a now alert Jet. "They need us and we just can't say no, Alli. Can we?"

"Nah...I guess not," replied Alli. She had reservations.

"All RIGHT!" Jet high-fived a more subdued albeit happy Alli Oosh.

"How do we respond, agree...you know...How do we say--WE ACCEPT?"

"Well, it says," began Alli. "You have six spans-"

"What's a span?" asked Jet.

"In parentheses it says six Tellurian days," responded Alli. "I guess a span is like one of our days. Now...where was I? ...you have six spans to reply. If you accept, there will be further instructions transmitted."

"What are we waiting for?" Jet urged a positive answer, "Let's accept!"

224

"Cool your jets--Jet! They are giving us six days," said Alli. "Let's at least sleep on it. Okay?"

"Okay." Jet did not hide his disappointment.

Jet and Alli both read the communiqué at least a dozen times each before leaving. Both were very excited though Alli, being a little older than Jet, was cautious. The thought of the unknown--aliens, possibly hideous creatures, pain and suffering--it was overwhelming. Jet on the other hand was so wound up that he spent a good amount of time this day in the *Tellurian* spacecraft simulator dreaming of space battles and the like. Initially, Alli was the one seeking adventure when she had contacted the TIA. And now, Jet was the one overjoyed at their chance to experience the adventure of a lifetime.

Jet and Alli peddled quickly back into town heading for home. They were all wound up at this latest bit of news.

"I just can't believe that we are finally getting a mission," said Jet.

"Yeah," responded Alli, "it's probably an easy training mission just to break us in."

"Yeah."

Bouncing off the grass and onto the pavement of the grocery store parking lot, the hunched silhouette of the local gang of bullies became visible. Jet and Alli tried to quickly alter their path--it was too late.

"Where are you two headed this late in the evening?" said the gang leader. Billy Bob Beaston slid his bike in front of them and caused them to stop.

"Home," said Jet, "you know...that thing you crawl out from under each day."

B.B. Beaston did not laugh even as his gang chuckled.

"Shut up!" said B.B. looking at his gang. "...morions."

"That's a sixteenth century soldier's helmet--MORON!" said Alli.

"She's mocking you, B.B.," said one of his gang.

"Yeah, B.B. You gonna take that?" said another.

B.B. dropped his bike and began heading in Alli's direction.

The other members of his gang were cheering him on with a chant. "Beat her up, break her legs, stomp her fingers till she begs...Beat her up, kick her ass, push her face into the grass...Beat her up, burst her nose, the blood's now spattered to her toes...Beat her up, smash her teeth, all that's left is place the wreath...Beat her u--!"

[SMACK!]

Jet being all wound up with this off-world mission stuff lunged off the seat of his bike striking B.B. in the jaw. As they both tumbled and rolled head over heels, B.B. began to whimper. Standing up, Jet displayed his bravest *I'm gonna stomp the crap outta you* stance. Unbelievably, the much bigger B.B. began spitting out a tooth...no...teeth...into his hand. Tears were running down his cheek as he backed off crying, "Guys...I need a doctor! [Sob!] Guys...don't leave...I need a doctor!"

B.B. was left to fend for himself. His gang had fled when all the teeth spitting and blood spattering began. Climbing back on his bicycle, "We're not done here...You better start looking over your shoulder."

Jet and Alli remained silent. Luck was with them so far--no need to push it. B.B. rode away.

"I don't believe what you just did!" said Alli laughing and hugging Jet.

"I really don't believe what I did either," confessed Jet. He suddenly got the shakes. "Did you see how the blood just poured from his mouth?"

"You were awesome, bro!" said Alli. "...Thanks."

"You can thank me by helping me stay away from that guy," said Jet. "You know he won't forget. What am I going to do?"

Jet's moment of bravado had ended and now he realized that paybacks might be a bitch.

"You two are late," noted mom as Jet and Alli entered through the kitchen.

"Hi, Mom," said Alli giving mom an unexpected hug before heading upstairs.

"Hey," offered a subdued Jet as he followed Alli upstairs.

"GET WASHED UP, YOU TWO," yelled mom shaking her head. "Supper will be on the table in just a few minutes."

"Okay," sighed dad now entering through the kitchen door, "...the lawn is cut, the garbage is on the curb, and I'm in need of a hug."

"Supper is almost ready," said mom as she kissed dad lovingly. "Hit the showers--you stink!"

The evening supper was just great--as always. Jet and Alli seemed to enjoy it just a little more today. The family talked and laughed as mom and dad recapped their day and quizzed Jet and Alli about their day at the carnival.

"Jet...you're quiet," said dad. "What's up?"

"Ah, Dad," began Jet, "I had a run in with B.B."

"You should've seen him," said Alli.

Alli recapped the encounter being careful to leave out the off-world mission stuff.

"...and POW! Jet knocked his teeth out!" said Alli. "B.B. began spitting blood and his gang ran away...It was great!"

"My word," said mom. "He might need a doctor...I had better call his mom right this instant."

Mom got up and headed for the phone while Jet and Alli just looked at each other. Why was she so concerned with B.B.?

"Jet," said dad, "just because you can lick somebody doesn't mean you should."

"Daaaad!" uttered Jet.

"I know...I'm sure proud of you for sticking up for your sister. ...But don't go looking for trouble, Son. Trust me on this. When I was young...I was a hell-raiser too. ...It got me into a lot of trouble. I've lost teeth, suffered broken bones, and almost never got the chance to marry your mom. She was afraid of me. People thought I was a troublemaker."

"Well...were you?" asked Alli.

"No," said dad, "...not really. I just didn't know how to make real friends. I was always afraid people would laugh at me so I acted tough and that got me into a lot of fights."

"So, what happened? ...Mom take the fight outta you?" said Jet jokingly.

"In a way," said dad. "I got sweet on her and she wouldn't have anything to do with me. Until...I started bringing her flowers. I knew she liked flowers. She was always picking them and carrying a bunch home. So, I started bringing her flowers. The other kids began to laugh at me. I was tough, mean, and certainly not used to

228

that. Nevertheless, I cared more about your mom than I cared about the laughing and that taught me a little humility. After awhile, when I didn't beat anybody up for laughing, the kids started talking to me. They weren't afraid anymore. I soon found out that I liked playing and be friendly more than fighting. I certainly liked your mom and I knew she wouldn't even talk to me if I didn't behave. I'll bet B.B. just doesn't know how to make real friends. Maybe you should show him."

"Whaa--?"

"Well, B.B. is all right according to his mother," said mom returning to the table. "I told her we'd pay for any medical bills if he needed a doctor. She said that those were baby teeth anyway and probably were already loose. I'm sure glad you didn't hurt that boy too bad."

"Mom...that boy is as mean as they come," said Alli. "It was him and that gang of his that started it anyway. ...serves him right!"

Mom seemed to ignore what Alli said. She had made up her mind that any fighting was a bad thing. Finally, after a long silence, she spoke...

"You know Susie called," said mom.

"Oh yeah," replied Alli, "...What'd she want?"

"She said you were supposed to meet her at the carnival," mom said with a raised eyebrow.

"Whoops," said Alli looking at Jet, "I completely forgot. Jet and I were on the Sling and Puke ride almost all day. ...weren't we?"

"Oh yeah...I haven't been slung and puked like that in I don't remember when," confirmed Jet. "It was great!"

"Well, I'm done," said Alli quickly. "May I be excused?"

"Uh, me too," said Jet.

Mom nodded as Jet and Alli grabbed some cookies and headed upstairs.

"That was strange," said mom aloud.

"What dear?" mumbled dad while attempting to eat supper and read the evening paper simultaneously.

"Something tells me that Jet and Alli didn't go to the carnival today," replied mom.

"Ah honey," said dad, "...they're kids. You know how their minds change in a blink of an eye. They may have been there and then gone to some other friend's house."

"Maybe," said mom. Her eyes stared off out the window, "...and about this fighting. What has gotten into them? Are we bad parents?"

"Of course not... They're being kids and they do what kids do while growing up. You know how I was...."

"...That's where they get it from--You," said mom, "I should've known!"

"Whaaaaat!"

Jet and Alli did their best to proceed about their normal routine of showers, teeth brushing, and prayers before bed. They both were somewhat anxious and excited. The events of the past two days were unprecedented in their lives. Consequently, the momentous decision before them was unprecedented in Earth's history. Jet and Alli were the first humans to make contact with extraterrestrials. If they accepted the TIA's assignment, they would also be the first humans to leave the solar system, to cooperate with sentient beings from other worlds, to eat alien food, to crap on alien soil, to.... The list of firsts overwhelmed their thoughts. The

230

sad part--their adventures might never be known on their own planet--bummer. In any event, the opportunity was just too significant to ignore. Their minds raced for sometime before sleep crept in and stole their consciousness.

"BREAKFAST!" yelled mom, "COME ON BEFORE IT GETS COLD!"

"Alli, Alli," said Jet shaking his sister, "Wake up! We've overslept!"

The excitement for the past two days had been keeping them up late talking and comparing daydreams. Understandably, the body can take so much stress and strain. Fortunately, both kids really needed the extra rest and there was really no harm done. They both quickly pulled themselves together and went down for breakfast where dad and mom were already enjoying the morning.

"Well," teased dad, "...glad you could join us!"

"Good morning," said Alli.

"Morning," added Jet.

"You guys seemed to sleep well," said mom. "Stay up late?"

"Not really." Alli tried to derail the 20 questions. "...Just happened."

"Yeah, I think the alarm clock dozed off," said Jet jokingly.

"What's on your guys schedule today?" inquired dad.

"More carnival?" interjected mom. She kind of glanced over in their direction letting them know she was suspicious.

"Uh...We thought we might just ride around today," said Alli.

"Yeah, you know...maybe we'll hook up with Susie, Jake, or some other kids," said Jet.

"Anyway, it's summer," continued Alli, "...we're not keeping a structured routine."

"I see." Mom coolly peered over her coffee cup.

"We might even be back for lunch," said Jet. That revelation earned him a little kick from Alli under the table.

"Uh...Not likely though," recanted Jet, "but hey...it's summer. Anything can happen!"

"Right," retorted dad. He nodded at mom excusing himself *and* his coffee to the porch.

Jet and Alli successfully fended off mom's cross-examination of yesterday's carnival discrepancies. They knew that mom had sensed a certain level of deception and now they must be increasingly discreet in fulfilling their duties as Earth's only TIA agents.

So once again, it was through the trees, past the old pond, over the meadow, and into foothills to the cave where their adventure awaited them. Entering and descending below the surface, the teenage Tellurian TIA agents checked for additional messages and then settled in to make a very important decision.

"So let's transmit a message that we accept the assignment," urged Jet.

"Are you really sure?" asked Alli. "It may be very dangerous!"

"Listen, sis," said Jet, "...you said it yourself... Someone is going to try to turn our planet, our home, into one big toxic waste dump. We must not allow that to happen."

"Oh, you're gooood," said Alli. Jet had just quoted her to win the argument.

232

"Then you agree," said Jet smiling.

"Yes, I agree," replied Alli with a grin. "When you reference such intellect...of course, I agree. We must do whatever it takes to defend Earth in the past, present, or future."

"All right! Let's draft our acceptance."

Jet and Alli documented and filed their reply saying that they would accept the assignment. This time, however, they did not have to wait a day for another response. Within minutes of their transmission, the communication terminal spat out a succinct instruction-- ENTER THE TELLURIAN IMMEDIATELY AND PREPARE FOR DEPARTURE!

"Enter the Tellurian immediately," repeated Alli. "What about telling mom and dad? I'm sending another message...."

"Alli, they said immediately," noted Jet.

Alli ignored her younger sibling and sent another message asking for guidance on family goodbyes, what clothes to bring, etc....

"Look!" said Jet pointing to another communiqué being printed.

"ENTER THE TELLURIAN NOW -- DO NOT DELAY!"

Jet took Alli by the arm and began dragging her to the spacecraft. Alli began to get teary-eyed. The realization that she and Jet were leaving not only their home, but also, their planet for the first time was very emotional. Jet's excitement had not yet allowed him to think about missing his family.

As they entered the underground hangar, the spacecraft was coming alive. Lights came on, whining sounds of systems, engines, whatever.... This beast was waking up! The instruments were flashing and the readouts were... well... reading out. Jet and Alli entered the craft where they stood briefly in awe as the displays illuminated. The lights flashed while the holographic being began addressing them. THE HOLOGRAPHIC BEING... WOW!

"...now seeing me...you undoubtedly have been offered and accepted an assignment of great importance. We realize that you may have many, many questions. They will be addressed in due time. For now, you must follow my instructions as I prepare you for departure. Please do not hesitate for this craft's departure is imminent. This craft operates exactly as the simulator you have utilized during training. Please proceed to the piloting seats and secure your restraints."

"She looks so completely...real!" noted Alli. The holograph of a uniformed, young woman seemed to follow them as they complied.

"I know--isn't this just too much?" replied Jet.

"This ship is equipped with inertial suppressors for extreme velocity changes. However, they may not be useful for collisions, explosions, energy weapon attacks, and etcetera. After we have departed this planet, I will begin your orientation with the basic knowledge my programmers have prepared for you. The sub-light journey to the nearest TIA node will take approximately 2.3 spans. This time will be utilized to prepare you for some things you have never experienced before."

"Systems are coming up green...," said Alli.

"...just like the simulator. Way cool!" added Jet.

The holographic instructor continued. "Please examine all the instruments and ensure that all systems have revived from hibernation. Ensure that their display

234

color is green thus signifying that they are operating within normal parameters. A yellow color is still acceptable for departure. Amber or red signifies a malfunction has occurred and the automated repair system requires activation. Yes, this craft can repair itself given enough time to do so. Unfortunately, all systems are included in the previous hibernation cycle. If all is well, the automated take-off may be activated allowing us to depart. Oh yes, Alli...."

"Whaaa-she called me by name!"

"...my programmer thought you might be somewhat concerned about leaving home. He advises--do not be sad. You shall return to your family a stronger, more intelligent person enjoying a greater appreciation for your family and the life you have been blessed with."

"Uh, hello," said Jet. "What about me?"

"You can't talk to a hologram," retorted Alli. She completely missed it...Jet was just poking fun at her.

"Oh yeah," responded Jet. He turned his attention back to the instruments.

The hologram continued to instruct Jet and Alli as their craft began to move. Slowly, the *Tellurian* inched upward with steady force from vertical thrusters. Jet and Alli monitored a video screen to see if the path overhead was clear. As the craft rose higher, the access doors began moving aside to allow the *Tellurian* to leave its underground sanctuary and begin a journey to the far side of the Milky Way. Steadily and with increasing speed, the spacecraft left Earth's atmosphere on an exciting voyage to an unknown adventure.

"This holographic instructor is really cool," commented Jet. "I have never endured this much instruction before and liked it. For some reason I am enjoying learning about the TIA, this ship, and alien etiquette."

"I have to agree," added Alli, "I feel the same. It's almost as if I've always known this stuff. Pretty cool...when you think about it."

"This ends our instruction until you awaken after your required sleep period. The ship is performing within normal parameters and is following the preprogrammed course. The galley is fully operational for your nutritional needs. The forward observation area is available for relaxation while your personal sleeping quarters are ready as well. I wish you bon appétit, good evening, and good night."

"Wow, let's go check it out," said Jet jumping up. "I'm hungry."

"Hey look," said Alli. She was pointing at the food prep unit. "It's flashing--PLEASE MAKE YOUR SELECTION."

"Cool! What are the choices?"

"Hamburgers, fries, shakes, potatoes, roast, beans, corn... you name it," replied Alli. "The list keeps on going!"

Jet and Alli ate a wonderful meal together. Heeding nature's call, they found the washroom and their quarters. The closets were fully equipped with apparel for each of them. They explored everywhere on the ship then performed their routine of showering, teeth brushing, prayers, and preparation for bed. Though they were tired from an exciting day, they could not resist lounging in the forward observation area. Quietly, Jet and Alli sat beholding the stars. Some appeared to fly by while others seemed to sit waiting for them to catch up. It was amazing.

[CHIRP, CHIRP, BEEP, BEEP, BUZZ, BUZZ!] sounded the wakeup alert.

The holographic instructor had returned and was waiting for Jet and Alli to awaken. As Jet and Alli came forth from their quarters, the onboard sensors detected their movement and the hologram began to address them.

"Good morning! I hope your rest was adequate. Please proceed to take nourishment and report to the observation area so that your instruction may continue."

Jet and Alli mumbled their good mornings at each other and headed for showers and the galley. The selection for breakfast was just astounding and equally delicious. Jet and Alli proceeded to the forward observation area. There they seated themselves in the plush accommodations and continued to enjoy the drinks they had brought from the galley.

"Ah, good morning again," said their holographic instructor. "Taking up where we left off... The TIA endeavors to restrict access to temporal pathways."

Charts, maps, and graphs were being displayed aiding the instruction.

"Various temporal loops in local timelines have been accessed for fun, profit, or convenience for many Earth years. These local manipulations have not been considered harmful. Consequently, the TIA does not scrutinize these incursions closely. Recently, the TIA has come into intelligence that suggests that some of these localized temporal loops have been used to camouflage temporal pathway access points. We now believe that these access points are being used for increasingly illegal activities. One activity in particular is the illegal dumping of hazardous materials on unsuspecting timelines in distant galaxies. Your research has suggested that your own planet may yet fall victim to this crime."

Jet and Alli, still waking, did their best to absorb all this new and fantastic information.

"Your assignment after proper orientation as well as accelerated physical, mental, emotional, and technical training will be to infiltrate a known franchise we believe to be utilizing access points for illegal hazmat dumping. The goal of your assignment is to identify the entities that facilitate the shipment, their drop-off point, and the entities profiting directly from the illegal disposal of the toxic materials."

Jet and Alli had consumed and retained much of the information delivered to them. Their journey of the past two spans was ending with their destination now within view.

"Jet," said Alli pointing at the small planet-like body now visible.

"Do you think that's it?" asked Jet. "Is that the TIA node?"

"I guess so," replied Alli.

"We will be preparing to land at our destination shortly," announced their holographic instructor. "You should take care of your bodily needs at this time and take your places on the bridge."

Jet and Alli took up their positions as the autopilot flawlessly navigated toward their destination. They now could clearly see that they were approaching one large asteroid among many larger ones in this area. Drawing closer to the moon sized body, the *Tellurian* named spacecraft adjusted its attitude to approach the surface. The inertial suppressors worked wonderfully. Jet and Alli

238

noticed no change while the craft quickly decelerated, rolled slightly, raised its nose, and appeared to be heading for a surface landing. Looking out the viewports, Jet and Alli watched the surface speed by as the craft turned and rolled into a canyon. At high speed, the spacecraft proceeded on the flight path where a cave-like opening became visible. Without any reduction in velocity, the spacecraft disappeared into the asteroid's body. Once inside, the pathway became illuminated and the craft began slowing to be received on a clearly marked landing platform just ahead.

"Look," pointed Jet, "...we must be landing there!"

"I see it," replied Alli. "This is just way cool!"

The *Tellurian* swung gracefully around touching down on the pad exactly as it should. As clamps secured the craft, the platform began to descend to a lower level.

"When we have descended to the sub-surface hangar please remain at the bridge awaiting my instructions," announced the holographic instructor.

The platform had completed its descent with a slight jolt. Clanging, banging, and hissing sounds were audible signals that the platform was being secured, doors were closing, and a breathable atmosphere was being supplied.

"The hangar is now secure," stated the instructor. "A TIA welcoming agent will arrive shortly to escort you. It has been my pleasure to instruct you during this journey and I look forward to our next interaction. Good bye!"

Jet and Alli could hear the outer door open and the access incline extend. Very soon, an alien would greet them. They were both just so nervous at this encounter.

"Welcome to TIA in the Milky Way," said the agent. "Please follow me."

Jet and Alli were somewhat surprised because other than being somewhat taller and larger boned, the female agent was humanoid in appearance. They held each other's hand and followed close behind her. She led them off the ship and through numerous layers of security to a lift, which took them deeper into the asteroid. After descending several levels, the door swished open to a busy atmosphere of other agents. All appeared humanoid. The new arrivals were ignored for the most part, though some of the agents offered greetings. Apparently, a periodic arrival of trainees was nothing new here.

"Ságaçion? ...Ságaçion Academis?"

"Alli...hello," responded Ságaçion smiling. "Hello Jet... It's wonderful to see you again."

"Hey, Ságaçion," said Jet smiling. "It's good to see a familiar face."

"Indeed," replied Ságaçion, "that's why I'm here. When I was informed that you and Alli would be going on assignment I wanted to be here to greet you."

"Is Věracítii here too?" ask Alli.

"You bet I am," said Věracítii now entering the area.

Alli and Jet gave Věracítii a hug as they smiled and laughed with their friends. It was good to see them in these strange new surroundings. Alli hoped they could spend time with them learning the ropes so to speak.

"Okay, you two," said Ságaçion, "we are going to get you settled in and fed. Then it's...let see if I remember...."

"A routine of showers, teeth brushing, prayers, and bed," said Věracítii.

240

"Yes, that's it," said Ságaçion smiling. "Let's go!"

Jet and Alli were feeling quite good about this adventure so far. They have traveled possibly millions of miles, landed on an asteroid inhabited by alien temporal agents, and were received by aliens they had discovered on earth. They have consumed alien food, crapped in alien toilets, showered with alien water, watched an alien entertainment display, and had slept in alien beds. They had quite a bit to feel good about.

Waking early, the duo were fed and taken to the training areas. They were introduced to electro-stimulation of the synapses and a rigorous physical training program. All of which, was specifically designed to augment their cognitive ability as well as their strength and stamina. Also, alien psychologists interviewed them and did start their emotional control training. Finally, they were given cerebral enhancers to permit accelerated learning. After a few spans, the training affects were more than noticeable. Jet and Alli's cognitive abilities excelled, their strength and endurance increased ten-fold, and each had achieved a heightened sense of their emotions. All was going very well. Jet and Alli were happy though they missed their family.

Numerous spans had come and gone while Jet and Alli's training was nearing its conclusion. Each able student had mastered alien-style self defense, significantly increased their knowledge base, and mastered the control of their emotions. Today, the assignment particulars would be presented.

"Good morning, Jet, Alli," said the lead instructor.

"Good morning, sir," they responded.

Entering a conference room setting, Jet and Alli were seated awaiting the mission briefer. They poked and teased each other in a fun way. They had grown closer as brother and sister and as a team.

"Good morning," said the briefer upon entering. "Please direct your attention to the screen." The briefer walked to the viewer and began the presentation.

The screen illuminated to surveillance of a spacecraft being loaded with slimy green toxic waste. The scene cut to the same craft in a different location off-loading the hazmats into a storage facility. After the craft had left, the facility vanished and so did the hazmats. Time-lapse surveillance later captured the storage facility reappearing without the hazmats.

"This appears to be a temporal access point. We believe hazmats are being shipped and dumped presumably into other timelines and other worlds," said the briefer. "The surveillance footage just presented was anonymously supplied to us. Therefore, we do not have any idea where this facility is located."

"Was there identifying markings on the storage facility or on the spacecraft?" ask Alli.

"None that could be found," replied the briefer. "The data module was apparently preprocessed and blanked out identifying information. The supplier's intent was to turn us on to the crime while not implicating the company where they likely worked."

"So what's the plan to catch these bad guys," asked Jet enthusiastically.

"The plan that involves you two," said the briefer, "...is one of reconnaissance."

"Recon--," said Jet.

"You and your sister," said the briefer, "...will act as stranded servants on a Tirallian resort ship. The planned journey will take you into the Lotzaphii Galaxy where it is likely, we hope, you will be hijacked and placed into the service of the Rhyuoph Hazardous Waste Services Corporation of Nahrµvia."

"Whoa," said Alli interrupting. "What's this servant and hijacking thing about?"

"Yeah," added jet. "Let's just storm in there, weapons blazing, and take this group of dung sucking thugs down!" Jet was on his feet and arms were waving as the adrenaline flowed.

"We cannot blaze our weapons or make a storm," said the briefer somewhat frustrated. "We must not let them know that they are a target of our investigation. It is hoped that while you are in the service of the franchise you will gain knowledge into the location of an access point and possibly identify the entity operating the illegal operation."

"Let me get this straight," said Alli, "...you are going to get us shanghaied so that we can spy from the inside. Yes?"

"What means this--sheng hi?" inquired the briefer looking at Jet.

"We know that you have concerns," said Ságaçion who now entered the room. "Your safety, the safety of all our agents, is of great importance. There can be no guarantee that you will not be harmed. However, one attribute of being a temporal agent is that there will not be lasting effects."

"I don't understand," said Alli.

"What I mean is," began Ságaçion. "When your mission is complete you will be transported back to your home world and resume your life there beginning at the moment you left."

"You mean that no matter what happens," quizzed Jet, "it will be as though it never happened when the mission is over?"

"Yes," replied Ságaçion. "The experiences will be remembered in a non-harmful sense so that you may gain greater knowledge adding to your skills as temporal agents."

"Cool...like we're invincible," mumbled Jet starry-eyed.

"Be careful," advised Ságaçion, "these experiences that you may endure will be very real at the time and may be deathly frightening. You must act to protect yourselves always. ...UNDERSTOOD?"

"Yes, sir," replied the duo.

"Very well," concluded Ságaçion. "Your ship leaves the next span. ...Jet, Alli, you are to be an integral part of our efforts to protect innocent beings no matter where they are in time and space. We...Veracitti and I... are so very proud of you. We thank you for your efforts and await your successful return. Good Luck!"

"This way please," instructed a female agent. She motioned for them to follow.

Nodding their goodbyes to Ságaçion, Jet and Alli were led away by the agent. Jet and Alli spent the next quarter-span being outfitted with the proper attire and makeup. They had previously been exposed to the Tirallian culture during training, which had prepared them for their acting debut. The female dominated Tirallian culture was based around pleasure giving. Be it physical, emotional, spiritual or a combination of all three, the Tirallians were renowned for their abilities in this area.

The Tirallians were bi-pedal creatures. They were somewhat petite and bore a humanoid resemblance. The males were fully equipped with tentacle-like sex organs and were legendary throughout many galaxies for their skills inducing exponential orgasmic reactions in male and female alike. Contrasting, the Tirallian females were legendary in their insatiable physical needs that males of most species could not satisfy. Their beauty supplemented by bodily aphrodisiac production kept the Tirallian females in a heightened state of sexual awareness, which captivated the attention of any male and most females within close proximity. Of course, Jet and Alli were inoculated thus protected while being in close proximity to Tirallians. Furthermore, the Tirallians were a private species and did not engage in PDA, *public displays of affection*. Consequently, there would not be any embarrassing moments for Jet and Alli.

"Okay, good luck you two," said Věracítii as Jet and Alli entered the Tirallian craft.

"You nervous?" ask Alli.

"A little," replied Jet. "Not about the mission though."

"What then?" pressed Alli.

"I...just don't want these Tirallian females to hurt me," snickered Jet.

"Oh PLA-EASE," responded Alli pushing a laughing Jet against a bulkhead.

The Tirallian ship departed as scheduled to begin its journey through the Lotzaphii Galaxy where the likely hijacking would occur. The trip at high warp cruising speed would take about twelve spans. Typically, Tirallian ships were barely faster than light speed. However, this ship had been retrofitted with a detachable high warp modular engine. It would be detached and jettisoned before entering the Lotzaphii Galaxy so as not to raise any suspicions.

"Wow," whispered Jet as they walked around with their serving trays. "This is what I call a luxury spacecraft."

"It sure is fancy," replied Alli. "Look at all those statues and fountains."

"I know," said Jet, "...pillows everywhere and what about this music? ...it's kind of a mesmerizing, cool beat."

Jet and Alli played their parts well as indigenous help providing for the comfort of the Tirallian guests. During their journey, they dispensed food, drink, snacks, reading material, pillows, and smiles to many of the six thousand guests aboard the Tirallian luxury ship. The time passed quickly while Jet and Alli played their parts and actually came to enjoy the interaction with the aliens, which was friendly and always pleasant. ...This was about to change.

The modular engine had been jettisoned several spans ago and now the Tirallian pleasure ship was deep inside the Lotzaphii Galaxy.

"What was that?" said Alli as the ship shuddered abruptly.

"I don't know," replied Jet. "Let's go see the captain."

The corridors leading toward the bridge became congested with guests nervously wondering what had happened. They bantered loudly with questions! Had there been an accident? ...An onboard explosion? ...A collision? ...What? Jet and Alli were permitted on the bridge by the captain.

"Okay, you two," said the captain, "looks like we're about to be boarded. That ship out there just exploded an energy capsule off our port."

"What should we do?" asked Alli.

"Go back below and carry on with your duties," replied the captain. "I'll escort our guests around and I'm sure they'll notice you."

"What makes you so sure," asked Jet.

"Pirates don't kidnap Tirallians for slave labor," responded the captain. "However, you're not Tirallian."

"I see your point," said Jet.

Jet and Alli went on serving the ship's guests. The captain eventually made his way along with their new guests to the entertainment decks. Jet and Alli could see the Nahrµvians. It did not take long for the Nahrµvians to notice them as well.

"What are you two doing here?" asked a large Nahrµvian.

"Our ship became disabled and the Tirallians rescued us," replied Alli feigning a smile.

"We are trying to repay them by helping serve their guests," added Jet.

"I see," grunted the Nahrµvian and walked away.

Jet and Alli could see that the Nahrµvians were keeping an eye on them while they talked amongst themselves.

"I'm a little nervous now," confessed Jet.

"Me too," responded Alli. "Those brutes look like they're up to no good."

The captain was seen once again entering the entertainment lounge where the Nahrµvians were becoming quite loud and obnoxious. Moments passed before the captain could be seen escorting the Nahrμvians away.

"Whew," said Jet with a sigh of relief. "Maybe they're leaving."

"I don't think so," replied Alli.

The sound of weapons fire was now audible and several Nahrμvians had returned to the entertainment lounge where they began to break things and push the guests around. The captain backed by Tirallian security returned as well. This seemed to quiet things down a bit.

"We'll leave...but those two come with us," said one Nahrμvian.

"If you want to travel this galaxy without further incident," said another, "you will release these two into the service of the Franchise."

The captain, convincingly hesitant, argued against their demand before finally agreeing to turn Jet and Alli over to them. The captain watched as the Nahrμvians took the young Tellurians and left by shuttle. Once the Tirallian ship was safely out of the Lotzaphii Galaxy, the captain would file his report with the TIA. Jet and Alli were now captives of the Rhyuoph Hazardous Waste Services Corporation of Nahrμvia.

CHAPTER ELEVEN

Hazmat dumping
for fun and profit...

"What are you thinking about, Eeeb?" whispered Julíenηe.

Rolling slightly over, Eberhαrt gave his sister a little smile from the small bed where he lay. The cell, quarters, or what have you, was not very large. At least they were grouped together in one place. Mμreeη and Jerεmy were sound asleep, which is what Eberhαrt and Julíenηe should have been doing.

...Seemed like a dream, Eberhαrt thought. Here, in another time, in a seemingly cruel place, Eberhαrt was thinking of mom and dad. He wondered what was going on back on Uμmpάr. Were their parents okay? Were they thinking about him and Julíenηe? He was sure they were probably worried sick. ...How could he have allowed his crew to get sidetracked here with these Nahrμvian pirates? What has happened to their ship--the *Sir Puηt*? Why was he here? Was it fate? ...And what is with that Jet and Alli? Why did he feel a certain bond with them? ...Three sex organs! Wonder what that's like? ...How can they bring this cruel franchise to its knees? ...And his beloved

249

Spot, that wonderful little creature he cared for as a child. So playful...Why did he have to get old and die?

"Nothing," replied Eberhart very softly.

"Good dreams," whispered Julíenηe. She closed her eyes.

"I'm so tired," said Alli, "How much longer do we have to suffer in the service of the franchise."

"Not much longer," replied Jet with an understanding look in his eyes. "We just need to recon this training planet for a few more spans before the authorities can make their arrests."

"What if we can't gather enough evidence?" ask Alli, "I mean so far they're guilty of kidnapping, hijacking, space piracy, slave labor trade, and being just plain mean and gosh-awful ugly. Sadly, these acts are tolerated in this solar system."

"We know this franchise utilizes captured slave labor in the guise of owning your own business to perform hazardous material cleanup throughout the galaxy. ...Right? What we do not know is where the hazmats are shipped. We must find this out for the sake of all the planets."

"I know," said Alli. "This mission has just been so long and difficult to endure. ...I know that being temporal investigators may take us to different time periods and might place us in all sorts of dangerous situations. Nevertheless, I gotta to tell you, bro...for our first assignment...this has been a terrible experience."

"It has been horrible," agreed Jet. "However, these new arrivals from the Eureka star system are different. They're from Uμμpάr! Sάgaçion is from that planet. I think they will help us."

"I sure hope so," said Alli. "I guess we'll find out when we disclose who we are at our rendezvous."

Just then, several trainees swung open the cell door. The look in their eyes seemed to say that this mission was going to get a lot worse before it got better.

"Well...you two look kind'a cozy," slurred one brute of a creature. "We thought your female might want to experience some pleasure with creatures better equipped than you."

"Back off Boolurian dung suckers," growled Jet.

One brute moved toward Alli. Jet spun and sliced with a sharp tool he had been saving just for today. As the creature's life fluids spewed forth, the others paused briefly. Alli, seizing the opportunity, leaped onto the largest one and began to tear at its eyes and ears. Jet twirled and sliced deep into the third creature before being slammed hard against the wall. The creature bashed Jet even as its own internal organs spilled forth from the wound he had inflicted. The first creature, still clutching at its severed parts, began to thrash wildly at Jet as well. Alli was slung off and bounced painfully at the feet of the creatures delivering deathblows to Jet. They were inadvertently trampling her as they continued their onslaught. The largest creature once again grasps Alli and tosses her effortlessly aside. He moved on her as she fought furiously to protect herself.

"You will be given ample time to eat," said Urφch, "...then it's off to the bio-weapons cleanup training facility."

With that, our gang was ushered roughly into the eating area once more. Nahrμvian thugs pushed and shoved them down the chow line where they gathered portions of food they thought they could swallow without actually tasting. Looking around and trying to appear ambiguous in their seat selection, they scanned the area for Jet and Alli.

"There," whispered Mµreeη.

Spotting Alli sitting alone, the crew steadily moved closer to join her. Eberhαrt kept a watchful eye all around believing that they were under surveillance most all the time. As they drew closer, the swollen eyes, cut lips, and bruised body of the petite young girl aroused a fiery anger in them all.

"Where's Jet?" whispered Eberhαrt to Alli.

"They intentionally left our cell door unlocked last night and several of these pieces of shitova came in and roughed us up," began Alli. "Jet took quite a beating. He was unable to get out to eat."

"Did they...?" ask a tearing Julíenηe.

"They tried," interrupted Alli. "Jet had a sharp piece of metal. He sliced and stabbed as hard as he could. I did my best as well. There was blood everywhere and I was screaming and fighting with all my might...." Alli began to tremble as she relived the nightmare.

"Easy, dear," comforted Mµreeη.

"Finally, the one named Latríηa burst in. She shot two of them while the big one named Urφch strangled the other one. Latríηa brought some first aid supplies and told me to attend to Jet. Later, I could hear horrible screaming. Urφch was torturing the guard that had left our cell unlocked. The guard begged for mercy. ...he received none."

"At least they saved you," mumbled Jeręmy.

"They saved us because we are the property of the franchise," said Alli angrily. "We can't service their

252

contracts if we're crippled or dead." Alli tensed with emotion.

"Listen...they're sending us to the weapons cleanup training facility this span," said Eberhart.

"We'll be there," replied Alli. "We have much to discuss. We'll stow away on a shuttle and gain access to the facility. Therefore, do not look for us...we'll find you."

"Will Jet be up to it?" asked Jeremy.

"My brother is a true warrior," stated Alli firmly. "He will be there."

Toiletro approached their table and ushered Alli away with her group. Though the Nahrµvians were ruthless, the franchise did not condone brutal acts against the helpless unless there was a fee to be collected.

"Time is up," growled Urφch. "Your training awaits you. Now--MOVE!"

Urφch, backed by several armed Nahrµvians, escorted the *Sir Puņt's* crew to the transports for their journey to the bio-weapons cleanup training facility, which was located on the other side of the planet.

"Where are you taking us?" asked Eberhart bravely.

"Shut up!"

[Thump!] One of the Nahrµvians struck Eberhart hard with the butt of his weapon.

"The Level IV training facility is extremely hazardous. Therefore, it is located a good distance from our welcoming center," began Urφch. "The training center is being made quite hazardous as I speak in preparation of your arrival. During these next few spans, you will learn how to quickly evaluate the hazard level, specify then acquire the appropriate cleanup equipment, decontaminate the facility, and dispose of hazardous biomaterial. ...Questions?"

"Who's administering the training?" inquired Jeręmy.

Urφch just looked at him oddly as if to note the irrelevance of his question. "Your close attention to the training video is quite important. You will be left completely alone to view the training materials and proceed with the cleanup. Because of the hazards involved, Nahrμvian personnel will not be supervising you directly. The reason being--trainees often make mistakes...*and everyone dies.* I will return in three spans. If you are alive *and* the facility has been decontaminated to acceptable levels, then you will be extracted."

"...if we're not alive?" asked Mμreeη.

"Then you will be eventually cleaned up by a more studious group of trainees," replied Urφch with a grin.

"If not Uμmράr...then where?" asked Hαzăr.

"Billions of light-solacles from Uμmράr lies the Milky Way Galaxy," began Cołłiηsía. "Jacφb located a very young planet where it seemed that life was just beginning. He embarked on an elaborate subterfuge to deceive the Dark One into thinking this was a very young Uμmράr. Jacφb crafted the A.P.E.L. to embody the foolishness that exists on Uμmράr such as using gold as hard currency for general commerce. Jacφb has been unable to identify the manipulators utilizing the Dark One. Therefore, he has hoped to divert their attention away from the true Uμmράr to this other planet by inducing the effects on their society that he knows the Dark One is attempting to impose on Uμmράr."

254

"So this trip to change DeFoulgar's mind about innate intelligence was really about using the A.P.E.L. to impose the same cruel and unjust social structure on an unsuspecting world," recapped Hɑzăr in a very fiery tone accompanied by animated gestures.

"Our children were put in harm's way so that we might cause unknowing beings to suffer the same horrible social cast system that now exists on Uμmρár?" questioned Tadφlŏn irately. "That's incredulous! Unbelievable!"

"It does sound illogical and--?"

"Illogical," said Hɑzăr, "It's immoral! The people of Uμmρár have suffered for solacles with a social structure that has impugned their intelligence and broken their backs--literally."

"I do not understand your resistance to my brother's plan to save your world," submitted a confused Cołłiŋsía.

"Your world," repeated Tadφlŏn, "Isn't it *your* world too?"

"I have never been away from Sedition," confessed Cołłiŋsía. "This is my world."

"Then you do not have any idea of the pain and suffering that your brother is trying to impose on these unsuspecting beings," stated Tadφlŏn.

"Come with us back to Uμmρár, Cołłiŋsía," said Hɑzăr pleading. "Let us show you the absurdity of existence that should never be endured by any species."

"Please," said Tadφlŏn, "...then you will see why it is so important for you to dissuade Sir Jacφb from perpetrating this injustice on another world."

"I will consider what you have said," agreed Cołłiŋsía. "Now you must go to your quarters and get settled in. We shall see each other again at the evening meal. Please follow me."

The Ghoηαdz' were surprised and greatly concerned at this revelation. It was inconceivable that anyone would want to inflict an Uμmpάrian-like social structure on another world. What could Jacφb be thinking? Were they missing something? Hαzăr knew they must first convince Cołłiηsίa that this would be an unconscionable act inspired by Jacφb's self-righteous illegitimacy.

"I guess we're supposed to go inside," concluded Julίenηe.

"Urφch said the so called training video is just inside that entrance," said Jerȩmy.

"Room 14A," added Mμreeη."

"Let's go," instructed Eberhαrt taking the lead toward the entrance. "...be aware that we likely are under remote surveillance. Let's keep an eye out for that."

The reluctant group proceeded toward the level IV bio-weapons training facility to begin their unwilling indoctrination into the art and science of bio-weapon hazmat cleanup. Many containers were staged at the facility to provide storage as the facility was decontaminated.

"Think they have enough containers to hold all the hazmats." Jerȩmy jokingly pointed at the enormous supply of containers.

"They do appear to have over-purchased for just a training facility," admitted Eberhαrt noting that all the containers were new.

"Over here," said Julίenηe, "I've found 14A."

"Okay guys, let's get these suits on," instructed Eberhart. "I don't want to take any chances."

Eberhart knew that getting their suits on was a priority because of the unknown levels of contamination at the facility.

"Good," praised Eberhart. "Let's find the instruments and determine the level of contamination."

"I found them over here," said Mµreeη. "There's a video display data pack as well."

They settled in to view the training material, which identified the instruments and explained their uses. Some of the instruments appeared quite old and certainly were of questionable calibration. The video outlined the training program along with what should be accomplished in three spans. Determine the toxic level, rough decontamination, finish decontamination using vacuums and scrubbers, irradiate decon equipment, toxic scan of facility, log cleanup, await inspection, and be extracted.

"Seems simple enough," said Jerεmy.

"Uh hmm," Eberhart pretended to clear his voice as he pointed out a surveillance camera and then proceeded to bash it with a scrubber wand.

"Let's secure this room," said Eberhart.

A close sweep of the room did not reveal any further surveillance equipment.

"Okay, let's be careful where we talk," said Eberhart.

"What about Jet and Alli?" asked Mµreeη.

"They said not to look for them," commented Julíenηe. "They will find us."

"True," said Eberhart. "For now, let's get on with the task at hand and point out anything that may look out of place."

They all nodded in understanding and began the daunting task of cleaning up the facility. Fortunately, powered lifts and moving equipment were appropriately staged and ready for use. The instruments recorded very high levels of various bio-weapon hazmats. Eberhαrt scanned continually waiting for Jet and Alli to arrive.

"I wonder who gets the job of spilling these containers back out again to mess up the place for the next training group?" asked Jerεmy aloud.

"No one," said a voice that was not of the group.

They all turned to see Jet and Alli by an access tube. They were motioning for the group to follow them.

"Let's go," instructed Eberhαrt.

Eberhαrt, Julíenηe, Jerεmy, and Mμreeη followed the young Tellurians to an area of the facility where the toxic levels were the highest.

"We can speak freely here," said Jet.

"The high levels of Carbonite 14 residue disrupt audio/visual equipment," added Alli.

"You said no one spills the hazmats out again for new trainees," said Julíenηe. "Then how does it become so contaminated?"

"All the new barrels," said Eberhαrt, "...this is a dumping facility."

"Yes," responded Alli. "Let us fill in some blank spots."

"The Rhyuoph Hazardous Waste Services Corporation of Nahrμvia is a front for an illegal hazmat dumping operation extending across several galaxies," began Jet.

"...and timelines," said Alli.

"We believe that trainees are brought here to cleanup hazmats that are illegally dumped," said Jet.

"Once cleaned up and placed in containers, the hazmats are shipped to another location where they are placed into a Multi-Warp Infinite Loop Storage Structure."

"MWILSS," said Julíenηe, "our dad designed that."

"Your dad is Hɑzăr Ghoηɑdz?" asked Jet.

"What's your mom's name?" asked Alli.

"Uh, yes and Tadφlŏn," replied Julíenηe.

"You're from the future."

"Wait a zliton," said Eberhɑrt. "How did you know?"

"Well, it's a long story," said Jet.

"We have made the acquaintance of one Mr. Sɑ́gɑçion Academis," announced Alli.

"How do you know grandpa?" asked Julíenηe.

"We'll talk as we go," said Alli,

"...but the TIA--," started Jet.

"TIA?" asked Eberhɑrt.

"Listen...we're temporal investigators," said Jet.

"Sɑ́gɑçion sent us here to identify the who, what, when, where, and how with regard to this hazmat dumping," said Alli.

"Using this MWILSS, as you call it, the bad guys have adapted it to access the timelines," said Jet.

"Yeah...and they're using it to dump this crap on our home world in the future," said Alli.

"I'm not fully up to speed yet," confessed Eberhɑrt, "but if you're following grandpa's instruction, then I know you are doing the right thing."

"That said," concluded Jerẹmy.

"How can we help?" rang in Mμreeη.

With more talking, questions, answers for questions, and so on, the past and present came together.

It seemed that Jet and Alli were correct in their belief that Eberhart and his gang would help them. Jet and Alli would be missed before long, so they must move forward quickly. Completely cleaning up the facility was their first priority. They must ensure there would be a large quantity of toxic hazmat barrels for pickup.

"Please, if you would follow me," said Cołłiŋsía upon entering the room.

"Cołłiŋsía...Have you thought about what--," said Hαzăr.

"Please...I said I would consider what you have said. ...and I am. For now, however, let us have a meal together with my brother. He so wants to help his people. It is I that urge you to open up your minds."

The Ghoŋαdz' looked at each other and bowed their head slightly as a sign of consideration for the young female. Cołłiŋsía led them through the vast hallways to the lift where they ascended once again to the viewing area. Passing through numerous security checkpoints, the wary guests arrived to see a feast laid out in their honor.

"Welcome again," came Sir Jacφb's greeting. "Please," waving his hand, "be seated."

Sir Jacφb held the chair for his sister then seated himself. There must have been ten courses of Uμmpάrian favorites. The Ghoŋαdz' proceeded to indulge themselves because you never turn down a free meal, and it had been quite some time since they had eaten.

"Cołłiŋsía tells me that you do not agree with the intent of the R.O.L.A.I.T.E.S. project," said Sir Puŋt unexpectedly. "I'm sorry...Cołłiŋsía and I keep no secrets between us. She has told me of your desire for her to see and live as an Uμmpάrian for herself."

260

"Uh...Well, yes," offered Hαzăr who was caught off balance by this revelation. "We believe that it would be horrifically wrong to subject another species to the absurdities that now are mandated on Uμmpάr."

"You see, sir," said Tadφlŏn, "you lured our children into a mission that may cost them their lives under false pretences. Even worse, you have made them an accessory in committing the same heinous act of social degradation that they have endured and vigorously despised for all of their lives." Tadφlŏn became animated as her emotions swelled. "...For you to use the victims of Uμmpάr's social tragedy as the messengers of exactly the same evil is shameful. It is a slap to the face of every Uμmpάrian. You must not do this! No one should *EVER* do that to anyone."

"My brother would never inflict the hardships you speak of," argued Cołłinsía. "He is good and kind. He is trying his best to defend Uμmpάr from the evils of commonsense!"

"Evils of commonsense," said Hαzăr, "...is that what he has told you?"

"That will be quite ENOUGH," ordered Sir Punt raising his voice. "Cołłinsía, you may be excused child. You should not have to listen to the ranting of the disgruntled lower-class!"

Cołłinsía chose to remain seated.

"Disgruntled...LOWER-CLASS!" yelled Tadφlŏn. "Good people have died fighting the evils of the class system on Uμmpάr--you son-of-a-Tirallian whore!"

"SILENCE!" ordered Sir Punt. "You think it is just so easy...managing the societies of many worlds. There is sickness, pestilence, true poverty, and war, which the inhabitants must endure. ...All of which are absent on

Uμmρár--if you haven't noticed. I became involved with the CPU while still very young. Their songs of fairness and logic did make good commonsense. It was not until the Controllers took me to other worlds and allowed me to see the foolishness of commonsense did I turn away."

"So you admit collusion with the Controllers," commented Hαzăr.

"Collusion," repeated Sir Puηt, "fraudulent secret agreements, illegal activities...I don't call my relationship with the Controllers--collusion."

"Then what do you call-- the selling out of your own people while aiding in the subversion of the inhabitants on other worlds?" questioned Tadφlŏn.

"Out there," began Jacφb, "an unknown number of civilizations are going to use good commonsense to facilitate their very own extinction. Their commonsense will tell them that they must enjoy the freedom of will. They must always pursue their own happiness. Their individuality must always be preserved. The Controllers opened my eyes to the absurdity of the *one*. The preservation of the one person, the one people, the one planet, or the one galaxy does not enjoin the unity of the plural universe. Beings using commonsense within this vast universe are killing themselves for the one extra credit of currency. The commonsensical entrepreneurs are exhausting the resources of their one planet, their one solar system, their one galaxy, their one timeline. They do this for the selfishness of the one."

"You're delusional," submitted Tadφlŏn.

"The Controllers seek to unify the many," said Jacφb. "They seek to provide fairness for the many by controlling and counting consumption. The Controllers...seek to unify the many by removing sickness and replacing it with a very long lasting health. The Controllers...seek to unify the many by removing the struggle to achieve a higher I.Q. by providing it to the many from birth. THE CONTROLLERS...seek to unify the many by removing the stigma of poverty by using gold as the currency so that prosperity is the real burden."

"I have never heard the oration of so much gazelda shitova," uttered Tadφlŏn. "We want our children back safe and sound or I am going to kick the *one* ass-- YOURS!"

With that, Hαzăr lunged to his feet and stripped the weapon from the nearest of Jacφb's many bodyguards blasting away disabling two more. Tadφlŏn followed his lead by putting Sir Jacφb's throat on the pointy end of an eating utensil.

"You are going to take us to the location where our children are due to arrive," said Tadφlŏn now pressing the utensil firmly enough to draw blood.

"You had better pray that they return quickly and safely," said Hαzăr. He pressed the gun barrel into Jacφb's side.

"Cołłiŋsía!" barked Tadφlŏn. "Do you know where the ship is supposed to return?"

"...Yes," she replied, "I'll take you there. Please do not hurt him."

Tadφlŏn gave Cołłiŋsía a reassuring look only a mother can display attempting to calm the frightened young female. Cołłiŋsía took the lead and ordered the guards to stand aside and provide for their transportation to the landing area located not far away.

The hallways seemed long as they carefully made their way out of the building with Sir Jacφb as their hostage. It seemed like an army of his guards escorted them. Cołłiŋsía urged all of the guards to restrain themselves. For a young person, having never left this city, she was acting very wisely with consideration for all. A transport was waiting when they finally exited the building. Carefully, Tadφlŏn backed into the transport still holding the utensil to Jacφb's throat. Hɑzăr's finger never left the trigger nor did the gun barrel ever leave Sir Puŋt's chest. Once they all had entered, the transport's door closed and it lifted off for their destination.

"Please," said Sir Jacφb beginning to beg, "...you don't understand."

Sir Puŋt offered to now enlighten Hɑzăr and Tadφlŏn.

"We were being observed back at the dinner table," said Sir Puŋt. "You must now listen to me!"

"What lies have you prepared for us now?" asked Tadφlŏn.

"Your father, Sɑ́gaçion, suspected Perfidious as a spy for the Controllers immediately," said Sir Puŋt. "Consequently, he felt it might be to our advantage to allow her to operate as they desired."

"I don't understand...You're saying my father was with the CPU back then," questioned Tadφlŏn. "You're lying to save your one ass."

"Not with the CPU as it now exists, but as a supporter of the use of his principles to advance commonsense wherever possible," replied Sir Puŋt.

"Us," stated Hɑzăr.

"Yes," confirmed Sir Puŋt.

"Us...I don't understand," said Tadφlŏn.

"You see, your father suspected the watchful eye of the Controllers at all times. All the while, the plans

264

that were being made and carried out to derail Sharon Defoulgar's innate intelligence was just...."

"Boilerplate?" said Hαzăr softly.

"Indeed," replied Sir Puηt.

"You're saying that my father always knew that the mission to alter history would fail," said Tadφlŏn. She looked at Hαzăr for confirmation to an unbelievable story.

"Well, let's say that your father believed that if it didn't fail that would be great," confirmed Sir Puηt. "However, if it did fail...all would not be lost."

"Our parents collaborated in this...the most complex of a deception to ensure that the Controllers would not prevent our union?" asked Hαzăr.

"Eberhαrt...Julíenηe," said Tadφlŏn staring at Hαzăr.

"Yes," said Sir Puηt. "They are the beginnings of a new race of Uμmpάrians that shall forever embrace commonsense and the principles of justice, liberty, and the pursuit of happiness for all species--not just the one."

"An elaborate deception," said Tadφlŏn.

"Yes," responded Sir Puηt.

"The altering of history, the stopping of Sharon's innate intelligence, the R.O.L.A.I.T.E.S. project...All were combined to form an elaborate deception?" asked Hαzăr.

"Unbelievable I know! Yet thanks to the insightfulness of your parents and Sάgaçion's utter genius, tens of millions of commonsense families were permitted to unite and produce offspring. Sάgaçion's principles of trans-temporal telepathy spread the word of a disastrous future. It became known that without the help of thousands of communities just like Prystine our society was in great peril. Communities where the Controllers attempted brainwashing were fertile ground for the truth.

The Controllers had put in place an elaborate infrastructure to manipulate the inhabitants. Ságaçion's principles made it possible to warn everyone to this evil and allow them to choose. The people chose goodness, freedom, and commonsense."

"What about Eberhαrt, Julíenηe... the A.P.E.L.?" asked Tadφlŏn.

"When will they return?" asked Hαzăr.

"I can't say for sure," admitted Sir Puηt. "Though their ship has been programmed to land at the alternate site if their mission was not successful."

"What happens if their mission is successful?" asked Tadφlŏn.

"Well," began Sir Puηt, "if they are successful...the people of Uμmpάr shall owe them much."

"You just stood in there extolling the virtues of the Controllers' wisdom," said a very suspicious Tadφlŏn.

"Are you now telling us that was an elaborate show too?" asked Hαzăr. "Will the real truth please STAND UP!"

"At this point, sir," began Tadφlŏn, "all we know is what you have said. ...and your story continues to change. What do you think, Hαzăr?"

"I agree," replied Hαzăr. "You lost our trust awhile back and we're not prepared to give it again so quickly. You just keep us safe while we wait for our kids."

"Please," said Cołłiηsía, "...you must trust him."

"Cołłiηsía," said Tadφlŏn, "...you still have our trust. Please help us to find the truth."

"I shall," she replied. Cołłiηsía was now somewhat relieved, "...and it shall vindicate my brother."

"We hope so," added Hαzăr.

266

The transport arrived at the landing area where it was hoped Eberhαrt and the crew of the *Sir Puŋt* would return safely. With their escort, the worried parents led Sir Puŋt into the facility still maintaining their weapons at the ready. Sir Puŋt ordered the guards to leave. Hαzăr, with Cołłiŋsía's help, secured the level.

"Okay...since we may be here for a little while, Jacφb," said Tadφlŏn, "why don't you tell us your story again."

"First," said Hαzăr looking at Tadφlŏn, "...let's hear everything you know about the Dark One."

"We can't locate them anywhere, sir," said the Nahrµvian guard.

"Bring me the person that supervised the transport loading at the bio-weapons facility," commanded Urφch. "Lieutenant Pisoph! What is the status of the trainees now at the bio-weapons facility?"

"Sir, the surveillance equipment is down at the facility," announced Latríŋa.

"What did you say?" growled Urφch. "...When?"

"We're not sure," replied Latríŋa now stiff at attention. "Sometime last night."

"TOILETRO," yelled a very angry Urφch. "Ready my transport. We leave for the facility immediately."

"Yes, sir! Right away!"

"If we have allowed spies into this training facility, the Controllers will rip me into shards and feed me to the wasteland creatures," said Urφch exuding concern.

"Don't worry," offered Latríŋa, "we'll find them."

"If they are not found," growled Urφch turning toward her, "...some of you will not live to hear of my death!"

"Understood, sir," she replied.

"Sir! Major Itrule reporting!"

"Major--where are the two small Tellurians?" asked Urφch.

"I don't know, sir," replied the major. "We've been searching for some time an--!"

"WHAT? YOU ARE JUST, AT THIS VERY ZLITON, ALERTING US TO THEIR ABSENCE! ...AAGGGGGHHHH!" Urφch drew his weapon and blew the major's ear clean off.

"Lieutenant!" barked Urφch.

"Sir!" she replied.

"Let's go...The rest of you...help the major clean up this mess before I return."

Urφch's transport blasted off heading for the training facility. Two other armed transports had been dispatched and were already landing.

"You heard me," commanded Urφch, "I want them alive and unharmed. So get in there and find them."

"Sir, do you think that it is wise for them to go in now?" queried Latrína. "There has not been a hazmat scan yet. The facility may still yet contain deadly toxins."

"Then scan, lieutenant!"

"Yes, sir--," responded Latrína.

Urφch's transport touched down and he, Latrína, and Toiletro subsequently entered the facility.

"There is no sign of the Tellurians or the Uμmpárians," said the colonel in charge.

"Look at this place," mumbled Toiletro, "...it's spotless!"

268

"I have never seen a facility decontaminated to this level," added Latrína. "The scan shows it to be 99.9998 percent free of toxins."

"That's unbelievable," said Urφch. "...Why?"

"Sir?" asked Toiletro.

"Nothing," said Urφch. "...continue sweeping the facility."

"Sir," whispered Latrína, "the next pickup and shipment is about a quarter-span away."

"We shall proceed on schedule," ordered Urφch. "Now stop talking and find those trainees."

"Several solacles ago I began to sense a presence weaving in and out of my thoughts," began Jacφb. "I first thought it was just fatigue, but later I became concerned that I was beginning to lose my sanity. A voice that unnerves me, even now, continues to question my decisions while probing my reasoning."

"Did you seek help?" asked Tadφlŏn. "Did you consult with medical professionals?"

"No," replied Jacφb. "I think I realized from the start that the subtle attempts at manipulation were real and external. The moniker *Dark One* was begun by close personal guards or assistants that noticed my conversations with myself usually took place in dimly lit areas. I suppose I tried to hide these peculiar interludes by lingering in the shadows."

"My brother has endured this cognitive struggle for quite some time in an effort to lure the adversary into the light." Cołłiηsía lovingly held Jacφb's hand.

"Taking what you have said at face value...," Hαzăr was not quite convinced that Jacφb was being truthful. "...What have you learned about the Dark One after these many solacles of coexistence?"

"Coexistence?" repeated Sir Jacφb now becoming somewhat defensive. "You make it sound traitorous...What have I learned? I have learned that I am fragile but indestructible, ignorant though insightful, weak however empowered, humble but arrogant, and somewhat hateful though I am truly loved." Jacφb was looking at Cołłiηsía as he spoke holding her hand so gently. "I have learned Mr. and Mrs. Ghoηαdz...," began Jacφb. His face became more confident albeit confessing. "...that there exists an evil that has never been imagined. This evil is so virulent, so destructive, so subtle, and so all consuming that our best efforts as a singular species will never eradicate it. We are seeded with it from the point of our conception and provide it a fertile host enabling it to grow and influence those close to us."

"You're rambling, Jacφb," said Tadφlŏn, "...focus a little on what this evil is."

"I don't know exactly what it is," replied Sir Puηt. "Its characteristics are greed, bigotry, war, exploitation, prejudice, and the craving for power to name a few. I don't know what it is, where it is, who it is, or how to destroy it." Jacφb buried his face in his hands appearing lost in emotion.

"What do you know?" retorted Hαzăr, annoyed by Jacφb's philosophical effusion.

"I do know that this evil is the root cause of the social absurdities on Uμmpάr," said Jacφb looking sternly at Hαzăr. "and I do know--where it desires to infect sentient beings!"

Hαzăr's obvious disdain for Jacφb had now been dealt a possibly fatal wound. Hαzăr's lip softened slightly as Jacφb elaborated on events that led to the discovery of this evil and its beginnings. Tadφlŏn still very much concerned about Eberhαrt and Julíenηe desired a more straightforward plan of action that resulted in Eberhαrt and Julíenηe returning safely as well as Uμmpάr's absurd social directorate being replaced.

"As the manipulators allowed me access to other worlds," began Jacφb, "...utilizing Ságaçion's Principle of Trans-Temporal Telepathy, I began to systematically search for a world where this evil did not exist. Solacles passed and the manipulators expected me to aid them in cementing their grip on Uμmpάr's future. The manipulators installed me as the leader of the CPU in order to expose those on Uμmpάr that might ultimately resist their plans."

"So you were working all along for the Controllers while attracting followers," said Tadφlŏn. "How could you sell out your own people?"

"You just don't understand!" responded Jacφb sharply. "The manipulators have been directing a multi-galaxy cartel of profiteers and rogues for several hundred solacles and they are not even aware that the Dark One is influencing their behavior. I have engaged in a strategic battle to destroy the Dark One in its infancy."

"Possibly, Jacφb," suggested Hαzăr, "...you have enjoined a battle of futility while ignoring the opportunities to prevail in the smaller conflicts that might have liberated the hearts and minds of your fellow Uμmpάrians. And just maybe, Jacφb, this evil you speak of has already consumed you using your own vanity and belief that you alone can defeat it."

"Preposterous," replied Jacφb. "The R.O.L.A.I.T.E.S. project shall deliver a decisive blow to the Dark One. The A.P.E.L. shall enlighten the inhabitants to the evil that is yet to spawn on their planet."

"What are you talking about?" asked Tadφlŏn.

"Once ingested, the A.P.E.L. will begin to enlighten its host to the existence of the Dark One and the evils that may ensue," said Jacφb.

"So you've collaborated with the Controllers for solacles helping to create an unbearable social structure on Uμmρár. You've betrayed the identities of countless individuals that desire the use of good commonsense. You've created the vast city of Sedition so that genetic creations can grow up without the love of parents. You've located a world where this evil did not exist. Now you are endangering our children and others on a mission to this world, in another time, to infect the natural evolution of a species with the knowledge about the Dark One," lectured Tadφlŏn. Her voice was ever-increasing.

"You are the Dark One," said Hαzăr sorrowfully. "Can't you see that in your own vain crusade you have carried out the agenda of the Dark One as its proxy?"

"No! You're wrong," mumbled Jacφb trying to constrain his thoughts. Jacφb wanted them to fully understand, but he must continue the charade.

Cołłiŋsía fainted unexpectedly. Hαzăr caught her and eased her into a chair.

"What happened?" Tadφlŏn gently touched Cołłiŋsía's forehead and examined her pupils.

"I don't know," replied Hαzăr. "Do you think our pressing Jacφb has upset her enough to cause this?"

Tadφlŏn shrugged her shoulders and slipped into mothering mode to comfort the stricken young female.

Do not believe them, Jacφb, whispered the Dark One. They are confusing you. They are just trying to stop you from fulfilling the heroic journey to save your people.

"That's right," said Jacφb. "You're trying to stop me from helping my people. You're trying to sabotage the mission. He's right...you're all against me."

"Who is right?" asked Hαzăr.

"Yes, Jacφb," said Tadφlŏn, "Who?"

"How did you get in here?" said Jacφb to the Dark One. "This facility is shielded from you."

Hαzăr and Tadφlŏn looked on as Jacφb carried out an animated conversation seemingly with himself.

"JACΦB!" cried Tadφlŏn, "STOP IT! There's no one here."

Jacφb realized what he was doing. He turned and looked at each of them while his mind tried to hide from the Dark One. The thought that he may have betrayed so many was seemingly more than his psyche could bear. He wanted to tell them. ...To make them see. ...On a field chosen a long time ago, the final battle was about to begin.

You thought you could hide your thoughts from me, teased the Dark One. I am forever with you, Jacφb. You willingly allowed me into your heart and provided me with such fertile soil to grow and bear fruit. You chose me above yourself and your people. You have been a loyal follower denying yourself the love of family and friends in order to serve me.

"I have never served you," Jacφb said aloud. "I have manipulated events in order to save my people."

Save your people or rule over them? said the Dark One with obvious swagger. You have spent solacles serving me while searching the universe for a world that I was unaware of. I must admit when you finally found the Tellurian world I was taken aback. I generally believed my reach was universal. If it had not been for you that world may have gone unnoticed. The A.P.E.L. shall deliver this world to me. For this favor, Jacφb...I thank you.

"No, it's not true," said Jacφb tearfully. "You're just trying to deceive me. No...I won't believe...."

"Jacφb," said a tearful Cołłiŋsía now awakening, "I'm here...please let me help."

"My dearest, Cołłiŋsía," wept Jacφb, "I'm so sorry. ...So very sorry. I've betrayed you, my people, and myself while being so presumptuous as to think that I alone held the key to the Dark One's destruction. The Dark One has used my arrogance to enslave our society and infect the hopes and aspirations of others as well. ...Please, please forgive me."

Jacφb fell to his knees appearing to weep with the realization that he had endeavored in the service of this horrible evil his entire life. Cołłiŋsía knelt to comfort her brother and wept with him. Hɑzăr took Tadφlŏn by her hand and softly caressed it as they came to understand just how filthy the rags of self-righteousness could be. Their hearts remained heavy with concern for their children.

CHAPTER TWELVE

TIME TO GO HOME YET...

"The I.T.S. transports are arriving, sir," reported Latrína.

"Very well," replied Urφch. "Get those containers aboard and make ready to receive the shipment."

"Yes, sir."

Several I.T.S. *Werkorse* class vessels were arriving. They touched down and workers began to load the containers onto the first vessel. Another vessel was staged to offload the next shipment of toxins for trainees to clean up. It was quite a profitable operation for the franchise. Numerous trainees, working for zero compensation, would decontaminate the dumpsite by loading the hazmats into containers, which would later be retrieved and taken to a temporal access point for disposition. The franchise received payment for taking the toxic shipment and the dumpsite cleanup. The pickup was free. It was a real hazmat laundering operation.

"LIEUTENANT!" yelled Urφch.

"Yes, sir," replied Latrína. She quickly arrived and stood at attention.

"The escapees!" barked Urφch. "Report!"

"Sir," began Latrína, "...the search continues. The escapees remain at large. We have begun sensor sweeps of this quadrant. If they are here, sir...we will find them."

"You had better, lieutenant," growled Urφch. "DISMISSED."

The lieutenant hurriedly left to personally supervise the search for the missing trainees. This was not going to look good on her record. Meanwhile, Urφch was still puzzled about the cleanliness of the facility. Why had they been so meticulous in the cleanup of the bio-weapons facility if they had planned to escape? Did they back track to retrieve their ship?

"MAJOR!" yelled Urφch. "Ready my transport...I depart immediately for the welcoming center. Inform Lieutenant Pisoph of my whereabouts."

"Yes, sir," replied the major. "Immediately!"

Urφch's transport lifted off destined for the franchise's welcoming center. Possibly, the escapees were trying to get their ship back. Meanwhile, Latrína was notified. She had very little positive results to report and was continuing the planetary scan, which might take several spans to complete. She informed the major that it was unlikely that the escapees planned to remain on the planet for very long. How could they leave?

The I.T.S. transport loaded with numerous full hazmat containers had long sense departed. Its destination was a temporal access point at an undisclosed galactic location. No one but the transport captain knew the destination coordinates. The ship's navigation was programmed and encrypted by the captain at some point in their journey. I.T.S. also rotated their captains often to prevent their presence in any one sector from becoming too routine. It should also be noted that captains were retired, *permanently*, after a few trips.

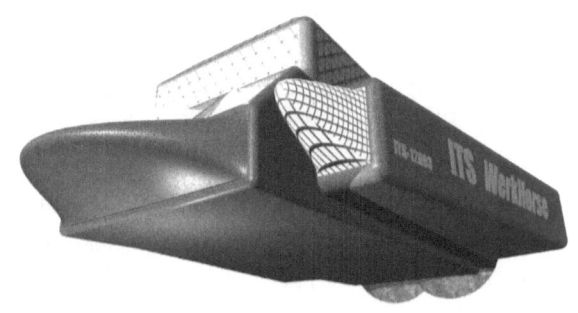

"Yuck, this thing stinks," mumbled Eberhart to himself. He was peering slightly from his home of nearly a span. After seeing no one around, he exited the hazmat container that he had stowed away in to get aboard the I.T.S. Werkorse. Quietly, Eberhart made his way through the ship's hold searching for the others. Oh my, there are thousands of containers here, thought Eberhart.

"Julíeηηe...Mμreeη...Anybody?" He whispered into his communicator, "...Come in!"

"Pzzzt! Pzzzt! Eberhart...over here," whispered Julíeηηe.

"I thought I wouldn't find anyone for awhile," said Eberhart.

"I don't know where the others are...I can't get my communicator to work," reported Julíeηηe. "We'll just have to keep looking."

"Agreed...." Eberhαrt and Julíenηe continued their search.

It seemed like an ocean of shipping containers. Where did all of these hazmats originate? Obviously, the Lotzaphii Galaxy has more than one hazmat pickup site. Eberhαrt kept whispering into his communicator hoping for a response. Eberhαrt and Julíenηe finally met up with Jet Scoe and Alli Oosh.

"Sheez, are we glad to see you guys," whispered Alli as she hugged Julíenηe. "We've been searching for zlitons for you guys. The C14 is disrupting our communicators."

"I know," replied Julíenηe, "...ours too. Guess we underestimated the hold of this transport."

"Yes," said Eberhαrt, "...but the extra cleaning to add more Carbonite 14 to the cargo allows the path of this transport to be tracked for some time."

"Oh yeah," said Alli, "Carbonite 14 has a half-life of like--forever."

"We were able to get a message to the TIA," said Jet. "They will be looking for the C14 trail. They can trace it back to the franchise's training center."

"Are we safe with so much C14?" ask Julíenηe.

"There will not be any lasting affects if our exposure is less than 30 consecutive spans," replied Alli, "...and C14 has no cumulative health effects."

"Hey, guys!" Jeręmy and Mμreeη were making their way toward them.

"Hey," said Eberhαrt. "Glad we're all together again."

After some pleasant reunion moments that included kisses, hugs, an ass squeeze here and there, the gang set about planning a strategy to identify the temporal access point and prevent this transport from dumping its cargo on an unsuspecting world somewhere in another timeline.

"These transports typically have a small crew compliment," offered Jet.

"Yes," said Alli, "...particularly on a dumping trip to a secret location, the fewer the better."

"That makes sense," said Eberhαrt. "Fewer crew members mean fewer leaks about the access point whereabouts."

"What do you know about its potential location?" asked Julíenηe.

"Well, the TIA believes that it is entirely possible for the access point to be off-world," replied Alli.

"Off-world?" repeated Jerεmy.

"Yes," said Jet. "It could be on an asteroid, moon, or even...."

"A mobile platform," finished Alli.

"On a mobile platform," said Mμreeη. "That would be hard to locate."

"Yes, it would," said Alli. "What's worse...there could be several."

"We need to locate a master distribution record," said Eberhαrt.

"Do you think they would even have such a record, Eeeb?" asked Julíenηe.

"Absolutely," responded Eberhαrt. "Even thieves perform necessary accounting in order to get paid."

"I see," said Alli. "In order to provide proof for payment they would need to keep a verifiable record for a certain amount of time."

"I think so," confirmed Eberhart. "...and where would be the one place to keep it?"

"At the transport dispatching location," said Mµreeη. "They would need to know where their transports are and where they have been in order to submit billing."

"Wow," said Eberhart. "That nano-economics course is finally paying off!"

"Shut up!" responded Mµreeη pushing Eberhart playfully then hugging him.

"Okay, gang...What is our action plan?" asked Jeręmy.

"First, we'll need to ensure that this transport doesn't leave its destination," said Eberhart. "It's our only way back to the dispatch point."

"Right," said Alli. "We can split up with some of us staying aboard to keep the transport from leaving while some of us are sabotaging the access point."

"Julíenηe and I will secure the transport," offered Jeręmy. "We can cause a few containers to explode at just the right time. They won't want to leave until it's safely cleaned up."

"Good idea," said Eberhart. "The rest of us will exit the transport and search the facility for maps, records, etcetera before sabotaging it."

"We will need weapons," said Jet smiling.

"I'll bet there's an armory of sorts on board," said Eberhart. "Let's find it. We'll meet here in 60 zlitons."

Our heroes start off in several directions to find the armory and possibly some kick-ass BFGs. The

280

Werkorse class design included two enormous cargo holds, three decks, engineering, propulsion, and the bridge. This craft was built for heavy hauling with *Muletech III* ion drives for long journeys and two *Hyper-Ejaculatronic* impulse engines to get the load moving quickly from a stand still. Indeed, this class of carrier made up the backbone of the I.T.S. fleet of transports.

My dearest, Tadφlŏn, whispered the voice. ...Tadφlŏn!

Who's there? asked Tadφlŏn silently in her mind.

It is I, replied the whisper, ...Mom!

Mom, thought Tadφlŏn. Is it really you?

Oh, my dearest...I have missed you so, whispered Věracítii.

Oh Mom, replied Tadφlŏn, I've missed you so very much. When will I see you? How is dad? Where are you?

So many questions, whispered Věracítii--soon, wonderful, with you always....

Oh Mom, smiled Tadφlŏn in her mind.

Listen carefully, whispered Věracítii. You and Hαzăr must leave now for the Milky Way Galaxy.

"What?" mumbled Tadφlŏn aloud.

"I didn't say anything, dear," replied Hαzăr.

"I'm sorry, Hαzăr," said Tadφlŏn. "I was thinking aloud."

Mom, continued Tadφlŏn in her mind, the Milky Way Galaxy is light-solacles from here! That's where Eberhαrt and Julíenηe were destined.

That is why you must leave now, said Věracítii. They will need you in the not too distant future. Please, Tadφlŏn... you must trust what I say.

281

How? ask Tadφlŏn. We do not have a ship that can make that journey in a lifetime.

Ask Jacφb about the *Cołłiŋsía One*, said Věracítii. It is warp stream capable and very fast. You are three spans from the *Arturian* wormhole. It is a direct passageway. Hurry! Please...the Milky Way Galaxy and the third planet from the rad. Go now!

But mom, started Tadφlŏn, Mom? Mom!

"JACΦB!" said Tadφlŏn grabbing his shoulder, "Where is the *Cołłiŋsía One*?"

"How did you know abou--?"

"We don't have time for questions," said Tadφlŏn. "Take us to it--NOW!"

"Tadφlŏn," said a concerned Hαzăr, "what's going on?"

"We'll talk on the way, dear," replied Tadφlŏn. "...the kids need us!"

Tadφlŏn forcefully ushered Jacφb to his feet even as Cołłiŋsía protested slightly. Jacφb led them back to the lift where they had entered. After entering a code, submitting to several anatomical scans, and reciting a poem to satisfy the voice recognition, the lift began to descend. Down went the lift for what seemed like several zlitons. The door opened to a vast hangar where, as Věracítii had mentioned, a ship christened *Cołłiŋsía One* sat in indescribable beauty.

"My mom says this ship is warp stream capable and very fast," announced Tadφlŏn.

"Seems your mom is very well informed," replied Jacφb.

"Our children need us and we need your ship," said Tadφlŏn forcefully.

"What are the security codes?" asked Hɑzăr bluntly. "Do you want to redeem yourself somewhat? Give us the codes--now."

"Of course," said Jacφb, "...of course."

Hɑzăr, Tadφlŏn, Jacφb, and Cołłiŋsía entered the ship so named after the latter. As the engines came online and the systems powered up, the *Cołłiŋsía One* prepared for departure.

"Opening hangar door," said Hɑzăr, "...and engaging vertical thrusters."

With Tadφlŏn in the pilot's chair Hɑzăr carried out the duties of co-pilot without hesitation knowing full well that his wife was one awesome pilot.

"Okay," said Tadφlŏn calmly, "prepare for warp travel."

The inertial suppressors allowed the *Cołłiŋsía One* to accelerate from slow to go in a fraction of a zliton while keeping everyone's internal organs in the correct place. Attaining a very high speed within the warp stream afforded them the luxury of traveling great distances in very short periods. Thankfully, the warp stream was just out of phase with time and space permitting them to travel in more or less a straight line to their destination. ...Even if that straight line went through planets, rads, asteroids, and so on. Quite remarkable really! The projected travel time to their destination was about three or four spans.

"Lieutenant Pisoph," said Urφch into the communicator, "...Report?"

"Here, sir," responded Latrína. "There is no sign of them, sir. I think they've already left on one of the I.T.S. transports."

"I have come to the same conclusion, lieutenant," agreed Urφch. "Return to the welcoming center immediately. We shall pursue the werkorse laden with the hazmats."

"Yes, sir."

Urφch had no real way of knowing which vessel provided unknowing transport for the escapees. However, his gut feeling said it was the hazmat transport. Still bothering him was the extreme level of decontamination that the escapees performed on the bio-weapons facility before leaving.

"Lieutenant Pisoph," called Urφch into the communicator once more, "Latrína... come in."

"Yes, sir," she replied.

"Latrína," commanded Urφch, "perform a C14 scan on the bio-weapons facility as you pass by on your return path."

"C14 scan, but--?"

"Just do it!" commanded Urφch.

Zlitons passed as Urφch awaited confirmation of what he feared. He thought it clever. The welcoming center was not the place to be.

"Toiletro," said Urφch, "make the Uμmpάrian craft ready for departure immediately."

"Yes, sir," replied Toiletro.

"Lieutenant Pisoph reporting," crackled the voice from the communicator.

"Yes, Latrína," said Urφch more casual now. "What have your scans shown?"

"Scans show a Carbonite 14 trail a penãrd in width from the bio-weapons facility into space," announced Latrína. "I can only assume that it is coming from one of the transports."

"As I suspected," thought Urφch. "...Set down at the security hangar where the Uμmpάrian craft is secured."

"Yes, sir," she replied.

Urφch accompanied by a personal guard headed for the *Sir Puŋt* housed at a security hangar nearby.

"Pisoph reporting," cried Latrína, "Urφch! ...come in!"

"Go ahead," answered Urφch speaking into the hand held communicator.

"Galactic security forces are landing, as I speak, at the bio-weapons facility."

"Ignore them," ordered Urφch, "...continue to the security hangar."

"Yes, sir. We'll be there shortly."

Suddenly, weapon blasts erupted from around the corridor's corner taking out one of Urφch's troopers.

"RETURN FIRE," yelled Urϕch as he drew his weapon discharging it numerous times while diving for cover.

"You--," ordered Urϕch, "stun grenade--NOW!"

Executing Urϕch's orders immediately, the major tossed two *BriteLite* stun grenades down the corridor. They exploded with a devastatingly intense light and a static discharge field that rendered the Galactic security forces unconscious. Urϕch jumped to his feet pulling a subordinate with him. They could hear an increasing level of weapon's fire as they made their way to the security hangar.

"Go!" said Urϕch. He now was pushing the trooper toward the *Sir Puηt*, which was powered up and ready to launch.

"Where's Latríηa?" asked Urϕch as he entered the *Sir Puηt*. "...Latríηa?"

"Here, sir," she replied. She smoothly stepped forward into his loving embrace.

"Thought I'd lost you," whispered Urϕch. He pulled her close.

"Never," she whispered back.

"Get us out of here, lieutenant," ordered Urϕch aloud.

"Yes, sir," replied Latríηa. She quickly jumped into the pilot's seat.

The *Sir Puηt* was not an attack craft, but it could haul alien ass if it need be. ...And it need be! Latríηa punched the thrusters and the *Sir Puηt* lunged through the hangar doors narrowly missing two security assault craft that were landing. Galactic Security craft in orbit spotted them and gave pursuit. Latríηa was an unbelievable pilot and the *Sir Puηt*, being from the future, had a little extra

286

sub-light get up and go. Evasive maneuvering to avoid torpedoes and laser bursts sloshed the crew a little. And dang, those inertial suppressors don't help much with a concussion blast from a nearby torpedo explosion.

"They're falling behind, sir," reported Latrína.

"Outstanding, lieutenant," said Urφch. "...Course 8491 mark 2. We'll take a wide arc around the galactic forces and follow that C14 trail."

"Yes, sir," replied Latrína, "...course entered."

With security forces moving in on the franchise's training center, Urφch could not be happier to be on his way out of the Lotzaphii Galaxy. Incidentally, he didn't feel bad either about that operation being closed down. The Rhyuoph Corp. sucked!

"Hey," said Mµreeη. "We had no luck."

"Well, we found two stun grenades and a knife," replied Julíenηe as she and Jerẹmy held up their find.

"Hey, guys," said Jet, "...over here!"

"Did you find something?" asked Eberhαrt.

"Follow us," said Alli proudly.

Climbing through two maintenance shafts and crawling through three ventilation ducts, the gang exited onto the bridge level deck. Quietly, Jet and Alli led the way to where the ship's master armory was located.

"The lock requires a keycard," said Mµreeη.

"No problem," said Jet. "Sis, would you please."

Alli pulled a keycard from her pocket, swiped the access panel, and the door opened.

"Sweet, Alli," said Eberhαrt. "Where did you get the card?"

"We found the captain's quarters while crawling through a duct," she replied, "...spotted it on his desk. The rest is well...ya know."

"Look at all this firepower," said Jet. Oh boy, he had that gun tote'n look in his eyes.

"Cool energy blaster," said Jeremy.

"Okay, guys," warned Eberhart, "don't get crazy with this shitova!"

"Don't worry, Eeeb," said Julíenŋe. "They're just having a little fun."

"Besides," said Alli, "these are all stun weapons."

"Say again," said Jet.

"See the sign over there in twenty-two languages," said Alli. "I.T.S. does not permit the storage of lethal weapons on company transports."

"Maybe so...," replied Eberhart. He now was pushing Jeremy's gun out of his face, "But I believe the symbol on this weapon means kill."

They all took a closer look at the hand blaster Eberhart was holding. The weapon bore a symbolic icon depicting an alien torso with smoke coming from where the head should be thus indicating that some of these weapons might indeed be deadly.

"Again," said Eberhart, "treat these weapons with care and respect. Above all...do not shoot yourself!"

"Gotcha." They all nodded with a little more reverence.

"Okay, let's get quietly up to an observation area so we can see what's going on," said Eberhart.

"Crew quarters are on the deck below us," said Alli. "...Some have viewports."

"Great," replied Eberhart. "We'll follow you."

Alli led them quietly back to a maintenance shaft accessing the deck below. Each one carefully descended the ladder exiting on the lower deck.

"Wait," whispered Eberhart, "...someone's coming."

Eberhart and Alli dissolved into an alcove while the others kept quiet in the maintenance shaft.

"Okay," said Alli, "it's clear."

They carefully proceeded past the crew's quarters checking doorways as they went. For a large transport, the crew's quarters were very small. Finally, a doorway was unlocked. They quickly entered it to get out of the corridor. Fortunately, this crew quarters was equipped with a viewport allowing the gang to watch the stars go by.

"It's so beautiful." Julienne was looking out the viewport.

"We have a pretty good view from here," commented Jeremy.

"Yeah," agreed Jet, "...looks like we're overlooking the forward areas."

"Great," said Eberhart. "We should be able to see the platform or whatever as we approach it."

"Guess once this is over you guys will be going home," said Jet.

"Yeah, I guess," replied Eberhart.

"Think you'll get over to our part of the universe sometime?" asked Alli.

"You never know," said Julienne smiling, "...ninety-two billion light-solacles is not that far away."

Alli began laughing and they all joined in. You can never have too many friends even if they are far away.

"Sir, the C14 is reading off the scale," reported Latrína.

"Good," replied Urφch. "We're very close now. With luck we should catch them soon."

"Is this ship armed?" asked Toiletro.

"Seems there are forward and aft laser cannons," replied Latrína.

"That's not much," said Urφch, "...but it will have to do. If we can get close enough, taking out an ion drive will bring them to a crawl. We can board them and search for the escapees."

"With the welcoming center overrun with security forces," began Toiletro, "...might we not be better off heading back to Nahrμvia?"

"How will you ever work again?" said Urφch. "...With your record showing you permitted detainees to escape, your place of work was overrun with security forces, and you were unable to recapture the escapees. Come on Toiletro...have a little self-respect."

"Sorry, sir." Toiletro hung his head.

"We're going to clean up our reputations first," said Urφch, "...then return home as heroes and defenders of the workplace."

"There it is," reported Latrína. "Scanners show it to be five million penãrds out."

"Very good," said Urφch, "...less than a span before we overtake them."

"Something else, sir," added Latrína. "Scanners show another contact nine million penãrds out."

"It's an access point!" said Urφch. "Can we get more speed?"

"...A what?" asked Toiletro.

"Speed, Latrína?" said Urφch.   He ignored Toiletro's query.

"She's at maximum sub-light speed now, sir."

"Can we engage the warp drive briefly?" asked Urφch.

Latrína paused and did not respond immediately.

"Lieutenant," said Urφch, sounding a little impatient.

"Sir," replied Latrína, "...this craft does not possess warp capability."

"What?" responded Toiletro.   "How did they get from the Eureka star system to the Lotzaphii Galaxy without a warp drive?"

"Indeed...." Urφch pondered many things.

The *Sir Puŋt* cruising at its maximum sub-light speed was overtaking the I.T.S. Werkorse. Urφch worried that the Werkorse might reach the access point before they could overtake and board it. If indeed, that other contact was an access point and not some other vessel. Urφch considered the possibility that Galactic Security Forces had already plotted the C14 trail and projected an intersection to interdict the transport. That's what he would have done. Could this craft successfully defend itself in battle with security forces? ...What about an access point this far out? Weren't the access points on moons, asteroids, or planets? Intel had never suggested otherwise. ...How would he deal with Toiletro when the time came? ...Were the Tellurians safe? Were the Tellurians and Uμmpάrians working together? And... What of Jacφb Puηt? He must be on the transport as well. ...He felt it. He must follow the *Believers* instructions. This had been a really dung laden assignment. ...Except for Latríηa Pisoph. How would he tell her? Would she still care for him? She is just too hot! ...And he was deeply in love with her. Damazar....

"Seems the ship may be slowing," said Eberhαrt.

"How do you know?" ask Jet.

"I don't," replied Eberhαrt, "...but look!"

Eberhαrt pointed out the viewport at what appeared to be a distant light. A light that was flashing!

"Well," said Mμreeη, "...stars do not flash."

"What do think it is?" asked Alli.

"Not a clue at this point," replied Eberhαrt, "...but I'd bet it's our destination."

"The access point?" said Jet.

"Possibly," responded Eberhαrt. "We're just too far out to know for sure."

"Anyway," said Alli, "we know the time for action is drawing near."

"You know it, sis," said Jet while slapping Alli's hand.

292

"The *Arturian* wormhole is 10 million penãrds away," announced Hɑzăr.

"I've never navigated a wormhole before, Hɑzăr," confided Tadφlŏn. Her eyes turned to Hɑzăr looking for a little emotional support.

"Me either," replied Hɑzăr reaching out for her hand. "...as long as we're together."

"Will we be harmed in any way?" asked Cołłiŋsía. "I mean...I'm a little frightened."   Cołłiŋsía leaned forward anxiously waiting for a positive answer.

"Don't worry, dear," said Tadφlŏn, "...we'll be just fine."

"This craft is equipped with automatic wormhole stabilization controls," said Jacφb.

"How are you feeling now, sir?" asked Hɑzăr respectfully.

"Better...Thank you for asking," replied Jacφb.

"Look!" Alli pointed at the viewport.

The contact was much closer now.   The gang seemed to agree it looked like a triangular-shaped rotating space platform. Could this be where the hazmats are off-loaded? It was hard to see at this distance, but there did not appear to be a receiving port for which a transport of the Werkorse class could dock their enormous hold doors. Would they just land and off-load onto the platform? Is that how it's done?   It must have taken solacles to transport and assemble this platform this far out into space.   There did not appear to be any significant structures to house a crew.

"I don't like the looks of this, Eeeb," said Julíenηe.

"Whoa," said Jerẹmy, "what's brewing here?"

"Is that a storm developing?" asked Alli.

Looking out the viewport, the gang bore witness to the swirling beginnings of a cosmic phenomenon.

"What do you think it is?" asked Julíenηe.

"It must be a...temporal vortex," answered Eberhαrt. "...Obviously, the platform is too small to off load the hazmats. This ship must be planning to traverse the vortex to some other timeline in another part of the universe."

"I don't understand," said a confused Alli. "A synthetically produced vortex would require an energy source on a galactic scale."

"I follow you," said Julíenηe. "Do you think it is naturally occurring?"

"Possibly," replied Mμreeη, "...but its occurrence would be unpredictable."

"I agree," concluded Eberhαrt. "There must be an energy source that they have harnessed in order to produce the vortex."

"In any event, guys," said Jerẹmy softly, "we're being drawn in."

As they viewed the wonder and beauty of the vortex, the I.T.S. Werkorse was being steadily drawn toward its destiny. The multi-colored whirlpool spun gently providing the pathway to another time and possibly another universe. Visually inhaling the cosmic aroma while being folded into a swirling caldron of time and space was to be lost in a spectacle of illumination, synaptic exhilaration, and mesmerizing awe. Experiencing this phenomenon for the first time had momentarily paralyzed our gang by overwhelming their senses thus leaving them vulnerable.

[FLASH! Crackle!] Our gang's senses were jarred and briefly saturated.

The ship's security, methodically searching, had been able to locate the intruders. The ship's sensors had long since detected their presence. With the bright flash and static discharge, the cosmic group of do-gooders sank helplessly to the floor. Security then carted them off to a confining space where they would be deprived of this unique experience.

CHAPTER THIRTEEN

Almost...

"Sir," said Latríŋa calling Urφch's attention to the viewport.

Urφch sat up straight and leaned forward to visually consume and examine the phenomenon. The *Sir Puŋt* commanded by Urφch was closing faster now on the I.T.S. Werkorse. Looking out the forward viewport, they observed the spectacle of a now fully formed temporal vortex. With the circumference the size of a moon, the vortex had the capacity to envelope the largest of space vehicles. Steadily, the I.T.S. Werkorse was just entering the vortex periphery.

"Wormhole?" questioned Urφch aloud.

"Possibly, sir," answered Latríŋa, "...but the erratic behavior of the ship's chronometer suggests something more."

Urφch still pondered many things. Is this an access point? Could this be how they have been able to dispose of all the hazmats? What was on the other side? Was this phenomenon natural or synthetic? Did they dare follow? Was the Uμmpάrian craft capable of enduring the forces that such an event might generate? ...Latrína is just so damn sexy.

"Reduce speed," ordered Urφch.

"But sir," said Toiletro, "...we've almost overtaken the transport!"

"We're not slowing," announced Latrína. "...The gravitational forces are already vastly stronger than our sub-light engines. If we try to resist, the ship may be torn apart."

"THIS IS THE I.T.S. WERKORSE TRANSPORT...UNIDENTIFIED CRAFT ALTER COURSE IMMEDIATELY!" crackled the communicator.

"This is Commander Urφch...we are unable to break off because of the strength of the gravitational forces. We ask for permission to dock with you."

"Latrína," said Urφch firmly, "...intercept the transport and execute emergency docking procedure."

"Yes, sir," replied Latrína without hesitation, "...increasing speed to intercept."

"NEGATIVE," replied the I.T.S. transport. "...DOCKING IN THE VORTEX IS TOO DANGEROUS. ALTER YOUR COURSE IMMEDIATELY."

"I.T.S. transport," said Urφch firmly, "...we cannot alter course. Prepare to receive us in your port hangar facility."

"Latrína...," Urφch drew his finger across his throat. "...squelch communications with the transport."

"They're still hailing us, sir," reported Latrína.

"Is the port hangar bay door opening?" asked Urφch.

"No, sir," answered Latrína, "...still closed."

"Toiletro," said Urφch, "fire a laser burst at the port bay door. They will open it. They will not risk us damaging the seal before they enter the vortex."

Toiletro quickly energized the forward cannon and fired a short pulse striking the door with ease.

"Sir," said Latríŋa, "the captain is hailing us."

"Let's hear it," said Urφch.

"WHAT ARE YOU DOING? ARE YOU MAD? IF YOU DAMAGE THE DOOR SEAL WE'LL PERISH IN THE VORTEX," screamed the captain of the transport.

"Captain," said Urφch calmly, "...we do not have time to discuss this. Open your port hangar bay door-- NOW!"

"Toiletro," said Urφch, "...with a little more feeling this time."

Toiletro again fired on the transport's bay door. This time, however, the pulse was extended and robust. Sparks flew and small fireballs were visible as the energy bursts did bore into the door's outer layer.

"Sir," said Latríŋa, "...the captain is hailing us again."

Urφch did not reply preferring to allow the captain of the transport time to ponder the lethality of the situation.

"Sir," repeated Latríŋa.

Urφch looked softly at Latríŋa's face as she awaited a response. ...her skin smooth, her eyes inviting, and her lips so tender and plush. He dearly loved this creature and his eyes shining at her transmitted his desire for her. ...she blushed.

"Toiletro," said Urφch. "Fire!"

Another energy pulse induced a plasmatic reaction ionizing most of the bay door's outer heat shielding.

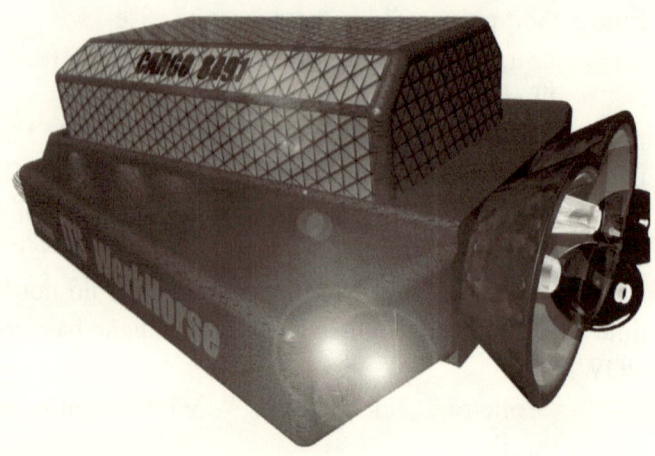

"SIR--the bay door is opening," announced Latrína.

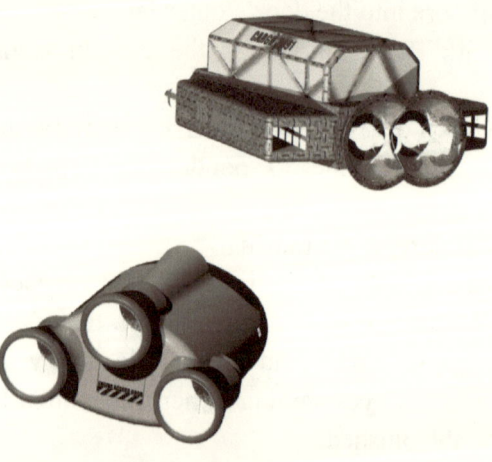

"Take us in," ordered Urφch. "Toiletro prepare to

fire our cannon at attackers inside the launch bay. Reduce power and DO NOT rupture the exterior hull! ...Understood?"

"Yes, sir!"

The *Sir Puŋt*, expertly flown by Latríŋa Pisoph, struggled to stay on course toward the bay door. Turbulence was increasing as they drew closer to the transport and the vortex. Inertial suppressors were springy at best in alleviating the vortex forces.

"Sir," said Latríŋa, "the captain says they can't keep the door open much longer."

"I.T.S. captain...I shall destroy that door if you close it!" said Urφch sternly. "...Maintain course, lieutenant."

The *Sir Puŋt* approached the bay door skewed slightly, but entered through the door fully under control. Its landing gear extending, the *Sir Puŋt* maneuvered to a landing platform and oriented itself with its forward cannon appropriately aimed at the interior entrance.

"Odd," thought Urφch aloud.

"Sir?" responded Toiletro.

"I would have thought a welcoming party would receive us."

The *Sir Puŋt* came to rest inside the hangar and all were safe. The bay door closed without incident. And yet, there was not the armed resistance that was expected.

"Breathable atmosphere is being supplied," announced Latríŋa.

"Okay, then...," breathed Urφch, "arm yourselves and stay at the ready."

Latríŋa, Toiletro, Urφch, and the only personal guard to escape with them exited the *Sir Puŋt* cautiously. Urφch motioned for the guard to take point while he followed with Toiletro in the rear. Assuming the ship's crew to be hostile, they utilized cover where possible finally reaching an upper deck lift station.

"Keep your guard up," said Urφch. He nodded for Toiletro to press the button summoning a lift.

The light flashed indicating that a lift had arrived. The door swooshed open.

[PZZZZZZZ! PZZZZZZZ!]

Laser bursts quickly found their targets burning holes deep into living flesh. The smell was all too familiar to Urφch. Bumping Latríŋa aside, Urφch rolled while discharging his weapon striking two attackers. Latríŋa, now behind a structural support, fired a barrage of energy bursts neutralizing the final attacker.

"They're dead," announced Urφch after checking the guard's and Toiletro's vital signs.

"I guess you were right to expect the captain to be angry," concluded Latríŋa.

"Shame about Toiletro though," said Urφch, pretending to be concerned.

"Don't be," replied Latrína. "...He was spying on your every move. I think he was reporting to the franchise daily."

"Damazar," said Urφch. He acted surprised at this revelation.

"I know you're not who you say you are," said Latrína. She looked directly into Urφch's eyes.

"What do you mean?"

"I know that you cannot work for the franchise," began Latrína. "...From the time you arrived at that dung hole I felt your emotional concealment. I was immediately attracted to you. The way you subtly stopped the torture of trainees, the barely noticeable continual improvement in their living conditions--*you cared about them.* And, when the two young Tellurians arrived, I thought you were almost father-like in your concern for them. You have a heart and no matter where you came from, whom you work for, or where you are going--I want to be with you always. I love you, Urφch!"

"...And I you," disclosed Urφch.

Tenderly they kissed and gazed deeply into each other's eyes.

"What now?" whispered Latrína softly. She longed to remain in his embrace.

"We must locate the Tellurians and the Uμmpάrians." Urφch lovingly kissed her forehead.

"The stabilization controls are compensating for the wormhole effects," announced Tadφlŏn, "...just as you said, Jacφb."

"It is an awesome sight," said Hαzăr.

303

"Yes," offered Cołłiŋsía, "...I have never dreamed of such an amazingly wonderful sight to behold. ...the colors dissolving into each other--exquisite!"

The *Cołłiŋsía One* approached the outer boundary of the Arturian wormhole at great speed. The crew was awe struck with this spectacular phenomenon. To traverse the Arturian wormhole was just *way* cool!

"Mom says the Arturian wormhole is a direct passageway into the Milky Way Galaxy," said Tadφlŏn.

"Has she contacted you again?" asked Hαzăr.

"No," replied Tadφlŏn, "...not yet."

"Where are we destined for?" asked Cołłiŋsía.

"The third planet from a rad located light-solacles out from the nucleus of the galaxy," replied Tadφlŏn. "The wormhole is supposed to be a direct temporal passageway to that part of the galaxy."

"Did she say what danger Eberhαrt and Julíenηe faced?" asked Hαzăr.

"She just said they would need us in the not too distant future," replied Tadφlŏn.

"I'm worried," confessed Hαzăr.

"Yeah," breathed Tadφlŏn softly.

The *Cołłiŋsía One* steadily entered the wormhole and was gone.

"Ugh...my head," groaned Jerẹmy. "It felt like I was electro-shocked or something."

"BriteLite stun grenade," responded Alli with a giddy chuckle, "...smarts a little doesn't it?"

"No kidding," he answered while taking no offence at the tease.

"Is everyone okay?" asked Eberhαrt. "...Other than the affects of the stun grenade."

"Okay, fine, yeah, we're good," came the groaned responses.

"All right then," said Eberhαrt, "...we've got to get out of here. ...Suggestions?"

"Up there," said Alli pointing.

"Hey, that's one of the vent openings that we passed earlier," concluded Jet.

"Looks like the vent will only accept you two," said Eberhαrt.

"It is small," added Mµreeη.

"What do want us to do?" asked Alli.

"It's very important that we escape and take control of this transport," said Eberhαrt. "Not only do we need to prevent them from reaching your home world, but this ship is our only way back home."

"Jet, Alli...you must escape through the vent and find a way to release us," instructed Eberhαrt.

"This transport appears to be equipped with the latest safety systems," said Mµreeη. "Possibly, activating a fire alert in this area might cause the doors to unlock automatically. This is not a brig, but a living space. It may be protected."

"It's worth a try," added Julíenηe. "...You guys going to be okay?"

"We'll be fine, Julíenηe," replied Alli. She squeezed her hand, "...don't worry."

Jet and Alli, aided by Eberhαrt, entered the duct via the small vent. Stealthily, they crawled past other crew quarters in search of an exit opportunity. Finally, finding a vent over a corridor, the two Tellurians dropped out of the duct and made their way back to where their friends were held captive.

"Psssst! Psssst!" came the sound from the hallway.

"Jet-- Alli?" Jerẹmy whispered through the door.

"We're here," was the reply. "...get ready we're going to pull the fire alert."

The alarm blared and lights flashed alerting everyone that there may be a fire. A fire aboard ship is a captain's worst fear. Most ships have a limited supply of breathable atmosphere and rely on filtration equipment to recycle the atmosphere. A fire produces contaminants that cannot be sufficiently filtered thus clean breathable air must be introduced to compensate. Therefore, extinguishing a fire is the highest priority aboard ship. As suspected, the door locks clicked open and the gang set free.

"Good job, Jet, Alli," praised Eberhαrt. "Let's make our way to the bridge."

"Here," said Jet offering Eberhαrt a stun grenade, "...we saw some on the way over. Kinda thought they might come in handy."

"You guys are just too awesome," said Julíenηe.

The gang made their way toward the forward areas dodging the ship's crew, which were frantically searching for the possibility of fire. The gang was unaware that Urφch and Latríηa had the same idea.

"Wait! Hold up, guys," warned Mµreeη. "...Look!"

The gang took turns peeking around the corner at none other than Commander Urφch and Lieutenant Latríηa Pisoph.

"How did they get on board?" whispered Mµreeη.

"I don't have a clue," responded Eberhαrt. "...Why are they here?"

"...You think they're looking for us?" asked Jet.

"Possibly," said Eberhαrt.

"Urφch and Latríηa saved us the other night," offered Alli. "I don't think they're here to hurt us."

"You may be right," agreed Eberhαrt. "Urφch was straight forward and he seems honorable."

"I say we take a chance and confront them," said Julíenηe, "...If we're right they may help us."

"What if we're wrong?" asked Jeręmy.

"Okay," said Eberhαrt, "...vote!"

"I say let's contact them," said Alli and jet.

"Yeah, I agree," voted Julíenηe."

"Me too," said Mµreeη.

"Okay," said Jeręmy, "...why not?"

"It's unanimous," announced Eberhαrt. "...Who volunteers to make contact?"

"It should be us," said Alli. "...They've known Jet and I longer than you guys."

"If you're sure, Alli," said Eberhαrt, "...we have your back."

With a nod, Jet and Alli proceeded to just walk out into the corridor and walk straight up to Urφch and Latríηa.

"Ahmmmn," Alli cleared her throat.

Urφch spun quickly with his weapon at the ready. Latríηa was quite surprised at this unexpected encounter.

"Looking for us?" said Alli smugly.

"Yes, we were," replied Urφch, "...also, your Uµmpάrian friends."

"They're close by," said Jet. "What do you want with us?"

"Nothing child," replied Urφch. "...My only concern is for your safety."

Noting Urφch's response, Eberhart motioned for the gang to follow as he moved into view to address Urφch and Latríŋa.

"Are you concerned for our safety as well?" asked Eberhart.

"I commend you on your cleaning abilities," said Urφch. "You would have earned many credits for the franchise."

"You can drop the franchise crap," said Jeręmy. "We believe that you're an undercover agent spying on the franchise."

Looking at his love, Urφch surrendered the truth.

"Yes," said Urφch, "I am a freelance agent."

"Freelance?" quizzed Latríŋa.

"I have been engaged by a coalition of planets that believe the franchise to be a small part of a larger nomadic consortium. This consortium wanders the universe harvesting planetary resources while extracting payment for illegally dumping hazardous waste on other unsuspecting worlds."

"Who is the head of this consortium and how do they dispose of the hazmats?" asked Julíenŋe.

"The consortium's leaders are still unidentified though I now believe them to be from another timeline. This belief was further evidenced when I became aware that Jet and Alli were TIA agents," answered Urφch.

"You knew?" said a surprised Alli.

"Not immediately," said Urφch, "...but noting the extraordinary skill set that you two possessed caused me to investigate you more closely. The coalition that engaged me has contacts within various intelligence agencies with the TIA being one of them."

"What I don't know is how your Uμmpάrian friends figure into this," admitted Urφch.

"We had traversed the timelines to save our own world and was returning when we were hijacked by you," said Jerẹmy bluntly.

"So you're saying that your connection to Jet and Alli is a mere coincidence," offered Urφch.

"Our meeting was certainly coincidental," responded Eberhαrt. "However, we since have learned that our grandfather is collaborating with the TIA, and consequently, Jet and Alli."

"Somehow fate has brought us all together," offered Julίenηe. "...This was not coincidental. I just know it."

"I must agree," said Urφch. "It seems that great forces have pulled us together across time and space to do battle with this evil."

"We must not fail," concluded Alli. "...We must not fail."

"The sensors are picking up multiple contacts at the wormhole's outer boundary," said Hαzὰr.

"What do you think, Jacφb?" asked Tadφlŏn. "JACΦB! What do you think they are?"

"Sorry," replied Jacφb, "my mind had wandered off."

"We're picking up multiple contacts ahead," recapped Tadφlŏn. "What do you think they are? ...Friendly? ...Hostile?"

"I'm sorry," continued Jacφb, "I don't feel well. I must retire below."

"I'll go with you," offered Coℓℓiηsίa.

"No, child," responded Jacφb. "You stay here and observe the wonder that you may never see again."

With that said Jacφb left the bridge and headed in the direction of the sleeping quarters. Hαzăr and Tadφlŏn looked at each other with an uneasy expression that neither bothered to hide. In contrast, Cołłiŋsía's innocence left her awestruck at the sights of the wormhole and not the least bit curious about Jacφb's sudden illness.

"What are you thinking, dear?" asked Hαzăr.

"I'm," started Tadφlŏn with a sigh, "...thinking about our children. I'm thinking about mom and dad. And...I'm thinking about how much I love you."

"You are just too special," responded Hαzăr leaning to kiss her, ever so gently, on the cheek.

"I am also thinking," began Tadφlŏn, "...that those are not friendly vessels up ahead. I believe Jacφb knows more than he is saying."

"I agree," said Hαzăr. "We should prepare for a battle."

"Agreed," replied Tadφlŏn. "I'll charge all weapons. Maybe you could *firmly* ask Jacφb to surrender any knowledge he might have about these vessels."

Hαzăr still did not trust Jacφb Puŋt. Consequently, Hαzăr fully understood what Tadφlŏn meant by firmly. Hαzăr rose from the co-pilot's seat, nodded at Cołłiŋsía still hypnotized by the sights of the wormhole, and headed below.

"What are you doing?" asked Hαzăr.

Jacφb looked up from where he was sitting with a small, computaterized communication device. The look on his face told Hαzăr that he might be up to something.

"I'm merely scanning for signals from the crew of the Sir Jacφb Puŋt spacecraft," replied Jacφb.

310

"I thought you were ill and needed to come below to rest," said Hαzăr sarcastically.

"Well," replied Jacφb, "...I still want to help if I can."

"I see," responded Hαzăr. "What have you picked up so far?" Hαzăr moved closer to Jacφb.

"Nothing," replied Jacφb. "It seems there is just static."

"I'm sorry, Jacφb," said Hαzăr while staring deeply into Jacφb's eyes, "...I just do not believe you."

Hαzăr took the communication device from Jacφb's hands without even a *please, may I have it?* Hαzăr quickly recalled the device's transmission history and was not surprised to see an extensive log of communication events.

"It seems my dear, Mr. Puηt," said Hαzăr, "...you are a liar!"

"Liar!" repeated Jacφb. "What would you know? ...The sacrifices that I have made for Uμmφár's people. ...a liar!"

You must not allow them to interfere, whispered the Dark One to Jacφb. ...They do not understand your plan to bring a better life to your people.

"I know," said Jacφb aloud.

"Who are you talking to?" ask Hαzăr.

"HAZĂR," yelled Tadφlŏn, "...I need you-- NOW!"

Leaving Jacφb to his seemingly schizophrenic episode, Hαzăr dashed to the bridge.

"I'm here," reported Hαzăr. "What is it?"

"Cołłiηsía just passed out again for no apparent reason," said Tadφlŏn.

Hαzăr proceeded to make Cołłiηsía comfortable.

"We've exited the wormhole. More importantly, sensors have picked up a very large transport ship and...," Tadφlŏn looked into Hαzăr's eyes. "I'm picking up the Sir Puηt's transponder signal."

"Are you sure it's coming from the transport?" quizzed Hαzăr.

"Yes," said Tadφlŏn with a hopeful look. "The signal is definitely emanating from that ship."

"Should we try and make contact?" wondered Hαzăr aloud. "Jacφb has been secretly communicating with someone...maybe it was someone aboard that ship."

Hαzăr quickly headed back to the lower deck to continue interrogating Jacφb. However, Jacφb was nowhere to be found. Hαzăr combed the lower deck, but no Jacφb. Where could he be? Did he leave the Cołłiηsía One? If so, how did he exit the spacecraft?

"I can't find Jacφb," said Hαzăr to Tadφlŏn after returning to the bridge.

"What do mean?" replied Tadφlŏn.

"He's gone," said Hαzăr. "I've searched everywhere. He's just vanished!"

"Wake Cołłiηsía then take her below and have her call out for him," suggested Tadφlŏn.

"Where...is Cołłiηsía?"

Like Jacφb, Cołłiηsía had vanished as well without a trace. Hαzăr repeated his search of the *Cołłiηsía One* several times without so much as finding a thread of their clothes.

"I don't understand," confessed Hαzăr, "...they have just vanished!"

"Not vanished," said Tadφlŏn. "They have left via a small spacecraft that was docked in the Cołłiηsía One's shuttle bay."

312

"How do you know?" asked Hαzăr. "...And why weren't we alerted when the craft left?"

"It seems that Jacφb used a security code to disable the ship's alert system," replied Tadφlŏn. "I've enabled it and I'm recalling the sensor sweep to see where they may be headed."

"How long will it take to pull it up?"

"Shouldn't take long," answered Tadφlŏn, "...once the system has been initialized again." She punched away at the console keys.

"I think I know where they went," said Hαzăr. "Look!"

Hαzăr pointed to the active sensor screen, which showed that all of the other spacecraft had converged on the transport and assumed an escort formation. Hαzăr counted seven...no eight...spacecraft including the transport.

"Sensors have identified strong energy signatures on the escort ships," said Tadφlŏn. "Likely, they're heavily armed."

"You think Jacφb docked with the transport?"

"No," replied Tadφlŏn, pointing to the replay of the sensor log. "They've docked with the largest escort ship. It has strong energy signatures. ...Must be a battle cruiser!"

"They must know we're here."

"No doubt," agreed Tadφlŏn, "...but they're ignoring us for now and are on a course heading for the third planet from that star."

"There's something else," said Hαzăr, "...the chronometer has stopped."

"Is it broken, you think?" asked Tadφlŏn. "...wait I'll run the diagnostic program and check it." She proceeded to perform the diagnostic check.

"Well?" said Hαzăr with a breath.

"...takes a bit," said Tadφlŏn. "Hang on...here. It checks out okay."

"That's odd," said Hαzăr.

"What?" quizzed Tadφlŏn.

"The escort ships are moving away from the transport!"

"No, Hαzăr," said Tadφlŏn scanning the sensors, "...it's the transport that is moving away from the escort ships. It's on a collision course with the planet!"

"We must gain control of this transport," said Urφch.

"Agreed," said Eberhαrt. "...With your help we can use these stun grenades to disable bridge security and take control."

"I've pulled up the ship's layout on this display," said Mμreeη. "Possibly, we can approach the bridge via these parallel corridors and execute our attack from two sides."

"Yes," agreed Latríηa. "Our chances of success would be enhanced."

"Here," said Eberhαrt offering some stun grenades to Urφch, "...we'll take the port side."

"Very well," said Urφch. "Good luck."

"We'll go with Urφch," said Alli.

"Be careful you two," said Julíenηe giving them a hug.

Eberhαrt and his gang began their journey along the port side corridor as Urφch led Latríηa and the

314

Tellurians along the starboard route. Each group had steeled themselves for battle.

"Here's the lift to the upper level leading to the bridge," said Mµreeη.

"Careful," cautioned Eberhαrt as he pressed the button to open the lift.

The door swished open and the lift was empty.

"Red lights are flashing," said Alli. "What does it signify?"

"I'm not sure," replied Urφch. "...We're approaching the bridge corridor."

"It's odd that we haven't encountered anyone," said Latríηa.

The I.T.S. Werkorse shuddered and creaked from an onboard explosion.

"Whoa!" exclaimed Jeręmy. "What was that?"

"I don't know," replied Eberhαrt. "...the bridge is around the corner."

Eberhαrt and Urφch's groups converged on the bridge without resistance.

"We've seen no one thus far," reported Alli.

"Nor have we," answered Eberhαrt. "Let's proceed to the bridge."

Eberhαrt and Urφch strode shoulder to shoulder to the bridge as another explosion shook the Werkorse. Electrical systems overloaded and small electrical explosions burst open panels as they made their way to the bridge through a shower of electrical sparks.

"The door is not opening," said Eberhαrt. "...Find something to force it."

"Here," said Jeręmy offering a piece of conduit that had blown free from a panel.

Urφch and Eberhαrt forced open the door to the bridge allowing Latríɳa to lob in a stun grenade. The group withdrew to cover as the grenade detonated with an intense bright light. Surely, anyone on the bridge had been incapacitated.

"There's no one here," said Latríɳa sweeping the bridge with her weapon.

"Seems everyone has left," offered Mμreeɳ.

"What do you make of it, Urφch?" asked Eberhαrt.

"I don't like this," said Mμreeɳ now seated at the tactical station.

"What is it?" asked Jeręmy.

"We're on a collision course with the planet," announced Mμreeɳ.

"The red lights and explosions," said Urφch. "They're--!"

"Ditching the ship into our world!" cried Alli.

"We have to stop it," said Jet.

"Mμreeɳ," said Eberhαrt, "...damage report?"

"Engines are off-line," started Mμreeɳ, "...the coolant pumps were turned off. The reactor is overheating causing the coolant conduits to heat and rupture. The reactor containment is failing. It's gonna go critical and explode before the ship has a chance to hit the surface!"

"We must make our way to your craft and escape," said Urφch.

"Our craft?" repeated Julíenɳe.

"Yes," said Urφch. "We used your craft to escape the franchise training base as galactic authorities were

316

making a raid. We followed the Carbonite 14 trail to catch up to the Werkorse and you."

"Talk later," said Mμreeη. "Let's go!"

The gang hurriedly made their way back down to the launch bay where they found the *Sir Jacφb Puηt* as they had left it. Wasting no time, they all got aboard and prepared to make their escape.

"Urφch, Latríηa," said Eberhαrt, "...no doubt you're more experienced at this than we are. ...If you would, please."

Latríηa slid into the pilot's seat with Urφch by her side while Eberhαrt and Mμreeη took up tactical positions. Jerεmy, Julíenηe, Jet, and Alli went below to help prepare for their escape.

"We're ready down here," said Julíenηe over the communicator.

"All systems are powered up and ready," said Mμreeη.

"Latríηa," said Urφch with a nod, "...prepare to depart."

"Aye, sir," replied Latríηa with a smile.

"Eberhαrt--blast the door!" commanded Urφch.

Eberhαrt fired the forward cannon with eighty percent power at the bay door. The resulting explosion ripped the door apart while the exhale of atmosphere into space provided the *Sir Puηt* with a boost out of the launch bay.

"We're clear," said Mμreeη. "However, sensors have detected numerous ships."

The *Sir Puηt* shuddered from an apparent energy weapon blast to the port side.

"Get us out of here," said Urφch firmly. "RETURN FIRE!"

"One engine has suffered damage," reported Mμreeη. "...It's off-line."

"We're sluggish," commented Latríηa. She initiated evasive maneuvers.

Again, the *Sir Puηt* shook as another energy explosion narrowly missed them.

"We're venting atmosphere," reported Mμreeη. "...The hull was slightly ruptured on the last near miss."

Eberhαrt steadily fired the aft cannon at their attackers. "Our weapon is doing minimal damage."

"Target their weapons!" ordered Urφch.

Eberhαrt concentrated his fire at weapon locations on the attacking ships with some success.

"Good shooting...I think the forward cannons are out on the lead ship," reported Mμreeη. "Watch it! The battle cruiser is moving into position to launch torpedoes."

"Target the torpedoes," urged Urφch.

The battle cruiser launched several torpedoes while Eberhαrt continued to fire the aft cannon in an effort to destroy them. The *Sir Puηt* shook from another energy blast and rolled slightly.

"Inertial suppressors are off-line," reported Mμreeη.

"I'm losing the helm," said Latríηa.

"Julíenηe," said Eberhαrt, "...we're losing helm control up here!"

"I'm on it," responded Julíenηe's voice over the communicator.

Julíenηe, Jeręmy, Jet, and Alli scrambled below attempting to repair the damage.

"...better now," said Latríηa. "Good job, you guys!"

"Oh my," started Mμreeη, "...more torpedoes!"

Their craft shook repeatedly with nearby detonations as Eberhαrt furiously fended off the torpedoes.

"Wait," said Mµreeη. "The cruiser is taking heavy fire from another ship."

"I see it," said Urφch looking out the forward viewport.

The *Collinsía One* was making high speed strafing passes at the battle cruiser.

"Good shooting, dear!" said Tadφlŏn. "Knock out those torpedo launchers."

"No problem," said Hαzăr confidently.

The *Collinsía One* inflicted heavy damage on the battle cruiser's torpedo launchers.

"The cruiser is withdrawing," said Mµreeη.

"Collinsía One calling Sir Puηt," said the voice over the communicator.

"Mom?" asked Eberhαrt.

"Yes, Eberhart," replied Tadφlŏn. "Your father and I were worried about you. Is your sister and her kisψm okay?"

"They're fine, Mom," replied Eberhart. "How did you find us?"

"We'll talk more after you're aboard our ship," said Hazăr. "...prepare to enter our shuttle bay."

The *Cołłiŋsia One* moved into position to accept the *Sir Puŋt*. The bay doors opened smoothly allowing the smaller craft to enter and then closed behind it. As the crew powered down the craft they could feel the *Cołłiŋsia One* roll as another explosion sounded nearby.

"Come with me to the bridge," said Hazăr who was there to meet them.

"Dad," said Eberhart.

Hazăr grabbed his son and hugged him as a tear ran down his cheek.

"It's great to see you!" said a very happy father. "Julíenŋe...."

Hazăr hugged his daughter then shook hands with the strangers that he did not know.

"Eberhart, Julíenŋe," said Tadφlŏn, "I'm so happy you're safe."

Eberhart and Julíenŋe took turns hugging and kissing their mom.

"Mom, Dad," said Eberhart, "These are our friends: Jet Scoe, Alli Oosh, Urφch, and Latríŋa."

"Our pleasure to meet you," said Tadφlŏn, "...and thank you for helping our children."

"Thanks for the rescue," said Urφch. "What of our attackers?"

"They're moving smartly toward the wormhole," said Hazăr. He motioned toward the sensor display.

"We should follow them," said Urφch. "The transport's reactor is going critical and will explode in that planet's atmosphere."

"Sensor sweeps of the planet have detected no life forms," said Tadφlŏn, "...just rocks, dirt, water, and some kind of ooze."

That ooze, thought Alli ...is primordial!

322

CHAPTER FOURTEEN

I'LL REMEMBER...

"Another seed has been sown," said Jacφb.

Yes, replied the Dark One. You have become quite an asset.

Jacφb sat in plush quarters deep in the belly of an *Armageddon Class* battle cruiser conversing with the architect of all great evil. In Jacφb's mind, the Dark One was very real and did exercise great control over him. He dare not think otherwise.

"They may not follow us," said Jacφb.

Yes, I am aware of that, agreed the Dark One. They must not make it back to their timeline.

"Why are they a threat to you?" inquired Jacφb. "They are weak and of no significance."

My dear Jacφb, began the Dark One, ...you provided them with the means to minimize my influence on the Tellurians.

"How so?" inquired a seemingly surprised Jacφb.

The A.P.E.L., answered the Dark One, ...they've altered the program.

"Surely, they lack the wisdom to--?"

The Uμμράrians are pure of heart, said the Dark One. ...The sharpness of their blade did sever my servant's head in the garden of beginnings. Alas, their wisdom came not from within, but from a former colleague, so to speak.

"A colleague," said Jacφb, "but...no more?"

He stood against me and did cast me out, said the Dark One. If the Uμμράrians return to their timeline, then they will have negated the advantage afforded me by the re-planting of this world to include my otherworldly servants.

"I see," said Jacφb now pacing. "I could not have known...."

You are not to blame, Jacφb, said the Dark One. These events are but a continued struggle between my former colleague and me.

"I understand," offered Jacφb.

I can never destroy him, confessed the Dark One. I can only attempt to destroy all that he has made. ...And so I shall. Until my time is no more...I shall pursue this endeavor to undo all that he has done or ever will do. I shall spread death, disease, despair, hopelessness, and dishonor among many by using those who may be persuaded to follow me.

"Their fate awaits them." Jacφb paused to stare at a small figurine on the table. "...En route to Uμμράr their guard will be relaxed and your assassin will strike."

There is great reward for your success and obedience, began the Dark One. You shall rule the people of Uμμράr and enjoy your every perversion. However, I remind you that if you fail--

"I will not fail...." Jacφb dropped his head.

"Any sign of them on the sensors?" asked Eberhart.

"No," replied Hɑzăr. "However, there is some interference while we're inside the wormhole that makes it difficult to be sure."

"How long will it take to traverse the wormhole?" asked Urφch.

"It took about one and one-quarter spans to come through before," replied Tadφlŏn.

"Cake, please!" Jet held his plate up in front of Julíenηe.

"Big or little?" asked Julíenηe. "...I think you want big."

"Oh yeah," smiled Jet.

The *Coℓℓiηsía One*, controlled by autopilot, sped through the wormhole at great speed. Tadφlŏn recapped their recent and disturbing experience with Sir Jacφb while the crew held a happy reunion unaware that an assassin was already onboard.

"That was a wonderful meal," complimented Latríηa. "It has been a long time since I've enjoyed one and felt this relaxed."

"To friends!" Hɑzăr held his cup high.

"There are showers below and accommodations for all," invited Tadφlŏn. "I'm sure hot baths and soft beds have been earned by you all. Please feel free to retire." She rose from the table. "Hɑzăr and I will be on the bridge."

"Thank you," said Urφch sincerely, "...for making us all feel most welcome."

"Julíenηe," said Alli, "...brush my hair and talk with me for awhile?"

"I would be honored," smiled Julíenηe. "...I'll race ya!"

Each retired below to enjoy some of the amenities that had been taken for granted not that long ago: warm showers, soft towels, comfortable beds, and puffy pillows. At this moment, it could not have been any better for a group of very tired do-gooders.

Eberhαrt quietly followed his parents to the bridge.

"Dad, Mom," said Eberhαrt softly, "...may I sit with you on the bridge for awhile?"

"Absolutely," replied Hαzăr. "It's great to be with you, Son."

"Something on your mind, dear?" inquired Tadφlŏn without looking at Eberhαrt directly.

Seems that moms will always know when you want to talk. Something was weighing heavy on Eberhαrt's chest, and he really needed to share it with the two people he loved more than anyone or anything.

"I..." started Eberhαrt then paused trying to find the right words. "Do you remember when Zewlvin's pigotar got loose from its confinement and he asked you, Dad, to help him catch it?"

"Of course," recalled Hαzăr. "I remember we chased that fool thing all over. ...through streams of water and fields of kqarne--we chased that thing."

"I had more fun than anyone I think," smiled Eberhαrt.

"You sure did," agreed Hαzăr. "When it was finally caught, Zewlvin asked me what he owed for our part in helping to catch the pigotar."

"I remember," said Eberhαrt, "...you told him nothing, and I said I would take a quarter-credit."

326

"That's right," said Hαzăr laughing. "...and after he had left, you whispered that you hoped that his pigotar would get free again!"

Eberhαrt and Hαzăr laughed until their eyes watered.

"You remember when Denz and I went to the top of High Altitude Peak to get that Utrovian celebration tree?" asked Eberhαrt.

"We were worried sick," replied Tadφlŏn. "Hαzăr and the neighbors went out looking for you two."

"That's right," added Hαzăr. "We thought you might have gone across the mountain to Groslok and became lost."

"I remember seeing you at Stondwell...and running through the stream to let you know I was okay," laughed Eberhαrt.

"What do you really want to say, Eberhαrt?" asked Tadφlŏn touching his hand.

"I just wanted to make sure, Mom, Dad," said Eberhαrt tearing slightly, "...that you know how much I love you and appreciate all that you have done for me. I know I could have been a better son...I love you both very much."

Hαzăr and Tadφlŏn gently hugged their son and kissed him. It was wonderful, the remarkable feeling of unconditional love that only parents can bestow.

"You have been a wonderful son," said Hαzăr. "We could not be more pleased with you and your sister."

"Eberhαrt...honey," started Tadφlŏn, "it is you and Julíenηe that have brought meaning and happiness to our lives. We cannot imagine our lives without you."

"You're all grown up now, Eberhαrt," said Hαzăr. "Sometimes life will not be that easy. You might feel alone, scared, and unsure of your creator's plan for you."

"But know this...," said Tadφlŏn firmly. "...your father and I love you so very much. We are sure that you can meet the challenges that life surely will present to you. Never doubt yourself...for you are a wonderful person. You will make mistakes, your heart will be broken, you will grieve, but also, you will laugh, you will be in awe at the miracle of your children, and you will enjoy a life that is full and blessed. ...We promise this to you."

"Thanks Mom, Dad." Eberhαrt hugged them both once more. "I really needed to hear that."

Hαzăr and Tadφlŏn drew each other near as Eberhαrt went below. Their son was now fully mature. Looking deep into each other's eyes, they knew that the road ahead for him was not smooth. Silently, they shared a prayer for their children and gave thanks for them and all the goodness they have been allowed to enjoy.

"EEEEEEEEEEeeeeeeeeeeeeeeeegggghhh!" Suddenly, a scream came from below.

[Pzzzzzzzzzt! Pzzzzzzzzzt!] sounded the laser fire.

Hαzăr and Tadφlŏn rushed below to find Urφch and Julíenη kneeling next to Eberhαrt and Mμreeη. Mμreeη's head rest in Eberhαrt's arms as she barely clung to life. Across from her lay the instrument of her death charred by a blast from Urφch's laser pistol. Latríηa, Jeręmy, Jet, and Alli were already scouring the ship searching for more intruders.

"Mom," said Eberhαrt. The tears were flowing down his cheek, "she's dying...."

328

Tadφlŏn did not answer realizing there were no words she could offer to lessen the pain and suffering. Mμreeη's skin was pale and purplish from the spreading poison of the serpent's venom. Her breathing, now shallow and labored, evidenced the briefness of her continued existence. Using all of her strength, she opened and fixed her eyes on her love. ...connecting with him. She longed for a life with him. ...producing children to love and nurture.

"...my pocket," whispered Mμreeη, "for you...my love."

Eberhαrt withdrew from her pocket a folded piece of paper. "Your poem...." Softly, he read...

"T'is Love I think...

T'is love I think that brought me here,
    thoughts so sweet, heart so dear,
a tender embrace, a listening ear,
    a passing glance, so sincere,

T'is love I think that kept us young,
    through solacles of life we journeyed as one,
our faith so strong that when it's done,
    we behold the face of our maker's son,

T'is love I think that brought me here,
    my fleeting breath, I feel so queer,
now hold me close, ease my fear,
    God blessed my life, with you...my dear."

Eberhart kissed her gently as his heart was being torn from his chest. With silence and dignity... Mμreeη's life force expired. Eberhart gently closed her eyes. Silently, he begged for his own death and prayed that God would forgive him for asking.

The assassin has failed, said the Dark One. Why did you send only one?

"I believed one to be sufficient," replied Jacφb.

As I told you...if you fail-- started the Dark One.

"Sir Puηt," called the voice over the speaker, "we've found them!"

"I haven't failed yet," said Jacφb. He headed quickly to the bridge.

"TADΦLŎN," yelled Hαzăr, "SENSORS SHOW NUMEROUS CONTACTS ON AN INTERCEPT COURSE."

"You must be strong, Son," said Tadφlŏn. "We need you!"

Tugging gently on his hand, Tadφlŏn helped Eberhart lay Mμreeη on a bed then ushered him quickly to the bridge where Urφch, Latríηa, and the others had converged.

"It's the same battle cruiser," said Urφch. "...They've returned to finish their assassin's work."

"Eberhart, Urφch, Latríηa," said Hαzăr, "get to the laser cannons."

As instructed, they moved into the weapons positions and began charging the lasers.

"The rest of you," said Tadφlŏn, "please take the damage control and tactical positions."

330

"Okay, guys," said Tadφlŏn firmly. "We're going to maneuver quickly between the ships. Fire on the smaller ships and let's get them out of the way before we attack the cruiser."

Tadφlŏn punched the *Cołłiŋsía One's* engines and swiftly maneuvered in and out between the hostile ships making it difficult for them shoot without hitting each other. All the while, Eberhαrt, Urφch, and Latríŋa laid waste to the enemy vessel weapons pods and engines.

"They're mixing with us, sir," said the cruiser's captain. "If we fire wildly we'll hit our other ships."

"Then hit them," ordered Jacφb.

"But sir," protested the captain.

"They are willing soldiers," responded Jacφb. "Their job is to die when it is needed. NOW--FIRE YOUR WEAPONS!"

The battle cruiser let go with salvo after salvo. Several of the hostile ships were hit while the *Cołłiŋsía One* was being attacked. Jacφb smiled slightly.

"They're firing anyway," said Hαzăr. "They've disabled most of their own ships."

The *Cołłiŋsía One* shuddered!

"Direct hit on the port side," reported Julíeŋŋe. "Alli, Jeręmy, see what you can do."

"Target their launch bay door," ordered Urφch, "Latríŋa and I will board their ship in the Sir Puŋt and overload the reactor."

"That's crazy," said Hαzăr, "...the Puŋt's damaged!"

331

"It's well enough for the task," said Urφch. "...You must trust me." Hɑzăr seemed to feel Urφch's confidence.

"Trust him," said Eberhɑrt. "...And I'm going with him."

The *Coꞁꞁiɳsiɑ One* shuddered once more as another torpedo found the port side.

"They know we're weakening on the port side," reported Julíenɳe. "Whatever we're going to do...Let's do it now!"

"Torpedoes," ordered Tadφlŏn, "...target the port launch bay door."

"Give us a chance to get the Puɳt powered up," said Urφch. "...Then skew past the port side and we'll launch into their bay."

"Be careful," said Hɑzăr, "...come back to us."

"I'm going too," said Julíenɳe jumping up and following them. "...That's a large ship. You'll need help."

"No time to argue with you," said Urφch. "Let's go!"

Urφch and the assault team hurried below and powered up the *Sir Jacφb Puɳt*.

"They're concentrating their fire on our launch bay," reported the tactical officer. "Sir, they're making a staffing run at the port side."

"DESTROY THEM," yelled Jacφb. His face was red, veins were bulging, and his eyes were frighteningly bloodshot. A scary sight if ever there was one. ...A very convincing act.

"Bring particle cannons to bear as they pass," ordered the captain. "...Their attack doesn't make sense. Tactical--stay alert."

"Urφch," said Tadφlŏn, "...we're making our pass. Be ready to launch."

"Powered up and ready," reported Latríŋa.

The *Cołłiŋsía One* rolled away from one salvo protecting her weakened port side while skewing slightly and aligning on the cruiser's port side. Tadφlŏn, pressing the engines to deliver their best, slid the *Cołłiŋsía One* into perfect alignment.

"LAUNCH NOW!" commanded Tadφlŏn. "LAUNCH NOW!"

Latríŋa punched the thrusters causing the craft to lurch forth from the launch bay of the *Cołłiŋsía One*. The *Sir Puŋt* rocketed along a direct path to the cruiser's port bay, which was missing a door. ...Kudos to Hαzăr and his torpedoes.

"SIR," yelled the tactical officer, "a ship has launched toward us!"

"They're going to--*board us!*" said the captain. "HELM! ...Hard to port! We'll ram them!"

"LOOK OUT!" yelled Jerȩmy, "THEY'RE ROLLING INTO US!"

"Fire torpedoes," ordered Tadφlŏn.

"We've got to make it," groaned Latrína in an angry voice. "...COME ON!"

The *Sir Puηt* drawing closer to the cruiser at high speed surely was going to just miss the port bay doorway and collide with the cruiser.

"HELM'S SLUGGISH," cried Latrína, "I CAN'T GET HER TURNED!"

[VA-VOOM! VA-VOOM!]

Suddenly, the *Sir Puηt* shuddered from the concurrently exploding torpedoes. The blast had damaged them slightly, but also, had bumped them into the needed trajectory to enter the cruiser's bay door.

"ALL RIGHT, MOM!" yelled Julíenηe. "OH YEAH! WHAT A SHOT!

"We're withdrawing, Urφch," said Hɑzăr over the communicator. "We'll continue our assault on their weapons pods."

"Very well," replied Urφch, "...and thanks for the nudge!"

"My pleasure," responded Tadφlŏn. "Bring my kids back!"

334

The *Cołłińsia One* withdrew to a safer distance to continue its attack on the cruiser's weapons systems. The *Cołłińsia One* had superior speed. However, the armor on that cruiser was almost impenetrable. It was now up to the assault team. The cruiser was a very large ship. Possibly, the assault team could utilize stealth to achieve their goals.

"We're going to have to get into that air lock," said Urφch.

"I'm suited up and ready," came Eberhαrt's voice over the communicator.

"See if you can gain access to the bellows air lock extension," said Urφch. "Extend it to the Puηt's access door."

Eberhαrt left the *Sir Puηt* via the lower air lock and made his way to the bellows air lock. Once there, he successfully extended the air lock bellows and connected it with their craft.

"Hurry!" urged Eberhαrt knowing that a welcoming party may soon greet them.

The team entered quickly and made their way staying clear of the main corridors to avoid detection. Using cover, hiding in vents, the team's goal was to make it to engineering without engaging the enemy. The cruiser's security teams were likely better armed and certainly unmerciful. Stealth and sabotage was the appropriate combination to destroy this vessel.

"Which way?" ask Julíenηe.

"We must get our bearing," said Urφch.

"Agreed," added Eberhαrt. "Jet, Alli...feel like some vent recon this span?"

"Thought you were never going to ask," replied Jet smiling.

Jet and Alli quickly scurried into the ventilation system to begin their recon mission.

"Let's hide quietly and await their return," said Urφch.

The team divided and moved into different hiding places to avoid being captured together.

A lengthy period had passed before Jet and Alli peeked from the vent.

"Pssssst, Pssssst," sounded Alli, "...You guys!"

"We're here, Alli," said Eberhart. He rose from cover to help them out of the vent.

"We found the ship's evac floor plan," said Alli. "...You know, the fire escape routes."

"Nice job," praised Julíenηe.

Alli and Jet presented the ship's evacuation plan layout.

"Damazar," groaned Urφch, "...engineering is two levels up and toward the aft section."

"Going to take some time to get there," said Latríηa, "...more time to get back once we begin."

"Look," pointed out Julíenηe. "They have emergency escape pods located nearby."

"Perfect," mumbled Urφch, "...they're of Carbonite construction."

"I see where you're going with this," said Eberhart. "We can have mom pick us up."

"We'll have to disable the weapons on this side," said Jerȩmy, "...or they'll destroy the pods with us in them."

336

"Okay, Latrína take Julíenηe and Alli to sabotage the reactor," started Urφch. "Eberhαrt, Jet, and Jerεmy will disable weapons on the starboard side."

"What about you?" asked Eberhαrt.

"I have other work," responded Urφch. "...Now get going."

The team split up and made their way to the objectives. Latrína and her team headed to engineering and Eberhαrt's group made their way to the main starboard weapon's node. Urφch had disappeared into the belly of the beast on an unknown mission.

"Just up ahead," said Latrína, "...stay close."

Latrína's team was entering the engineering section. Extra care to avoid contact with any of the crew was being taken.

"Okay, this is it," whispered Latrína. "We'll need to placc these charges on all of those larger coolant pipelines and that large electrical junction."

"Alli take that high position and keep watch," said Latrína. "Alert us with a whistle if someone is close to either of us."

"On my way," said Alli.

"Be careful," advised Julíenηe.

"Ready?" quizzed Latrína. "Let's go."

Alli made her way up a ladder to a catwalk of sorts to take in the big picture and keep watch. Julíenηe and Latrína moved quickly attaching the charges to the pipelines.

[Whipper Wheel!] Alli gave a warning whistle.

Latrína and Julíenηe looked up quickly to see Alli alerting them to activity just in front of them. Quickly, they took cover allowing the ship's crew to pass before moving on with their sabotage. It was slow moving. Finally, they had finished and met up again with Alli.

"Hey," smiled Julíenηe. "Thanks for the heads up!"

"Okay, guys," whispered Latríηa, "Let's move toward the escape capsules."

"Keep watch Jet while Jerẹmy and I attach the charges," said Eberhαrt.

"Wait a zliton," said Jerẹmy looking briefly at a compressed gas bottle marked M.T., "...How do you set these things?"

"Uh...Jerẹmy, keep watch while Jet and I set the charges," said Eberhαrt.

"Be cool, dude," said Jet.

"No problem, guy," said Jerẹmy. "Be careful."

Jet displayed his exceptional skills at handling explosives and moving stealthily. In no time, all the charges were attached and awaited detonation.

"Okay, guys," said Eberhαrt. "Great work! Let's make for the escape pods."

"You don't have to tell me twice," joked Jerẹmy.

You know they are aboard this ship, counseled the Dark One.

"I know," replied Jacφb. "Everything is going as planned."

What is your plan, Jacφb? teased the Dark One. I am already visualizing Cołłiηsía as my bride if you fail me.

"I won't fail," said Jacφb angrily.

Calm down, Jacφb, cautioned the Dark One, I know you're trying.

"Well now," said Urφch. He moved out from the shadows of Jacφb's quarters. "...isn't this cozy. ...just me, you, and your imaginary friend."

He does not believe in me, whispered the Dark One. Kill him now!

"Not now," replied Jacφb. "He may still be useful."

"Oh, give it up, Jacφb," said Urφch. "Do you really want me to believe that you're crazy?"

"I really do not care what you believe," began Jacφb, "...agent Urφch."

"So...you know my name," said Urφch.

"I know much," replied Jacφb.

"If so, then you know that you're coming with me," said Urφch. "You're going to pay for your evil deeds. Now--get moving!"

"You must take my sister as well...It's not safe here!" said Jacφb.

Urφch looked at Jacφb hesitantly, preparing to deny his request. Jacφb's eyes begged Urφch to agree.

"You don't say...Where is she?"

"I'll show you," replied Jacφb.

What are you doing? quizzed the Dark One. You need not go with him. Kill him now!

"In due time," mumbled Jacφb.

"Shut up," barked Urφch.

"Here," said Jacφb pressing the entry button.

"Cołłiŋsía," said Jacφb softly shaking her, "...wake up."

"Oh, Jacφb," said Cołłiŋsía, "...we mustn't go with him."

"How'd she--," started Urφch when Jacφb squelched him.

"Don't worry, dear," said Jacφb. "We're no longer safe aboard this vessel. Are we, agent Urφch?"

Jacφb spoke to Urφch in a way that made Urφch uncomfortable. Had he made a mistake to trust Jacφb? He must follow the *Believers* instructions. What were the others going to say? He felt compelled to carry out his duty though he did not want to endanger his friends. This had better work.

"Come on, let's go," ordered Urφch.

"Damazar, Urφch," said Eberhαrt, "...where are you?"

Eberhαrt paced back and forth now growing more uncomfortable. The longer they remained, the more the likelihood of their being discovered. What was Urφch up to?

"Okay," said Urφch. "Prepare the escape pods!"

"Urφch," said Eberhαrt. "Who is this slime with you?"

Eberhαrt grabbed Jacφb and began to beat the shitova out of him even though he knew it would not bring back Mμreeη. Urφch and Jerεmy intervened before Jacφb's face looked any worse.

"Get Puηt in a pod--now," said Urφch looking at Latríηa, "...and put Cołłiηsía in that one."

"But Urφch," protested Latríηa.

"You heard me," barked Urφch, "...Please, do it now!"

Latríηa proceeded to hustle Jacφb into a pod then gently helped Cołłiηsía into another one. Then she and the rest began to enter the pods as well.

340

"Wait," commanded Urφch. "...We're not leaving by pod. ...Get Jacφb out of that capsule."

Latrína looked at Urφch quite puzzled then proceeded to open the capsule allowing Jacφb to exit. Next, Latrína moved toward the capsule that Cołłinsía had entered.

"Latrína," said Urφch calmly, "leave her be. ...program the auto launch."

"But--?" uttered Eberhαrt.

"In due time," said Urφch looking at Eberhαrt. "We need to go now."

A silence ensued for a bit while the bond of trust was evaluated...*it was found to be strong*.

"Okay," said Eberhαrt, "...lead on."

Urφch, followed by Sir Puηt and the rest of the assault team, moved smartly toward the hangar bay where they had entered. Though Eberhαrt had grown to trust Urφch, he kept a suspicious eye on Jacφb. With Mμreeη's death still painfully replaying in his mind--he so wanted to hurt Jacφb Puηt. Why was Urφch saving Puηt? What was their connection?

"They've been gone for awhile now," said Tadφlŏn. "Do you think they're okay?"

"I hope so," replied Hαzăr squeezing her hand.

The *Cołłinsía One* kept its distance from the battle cruiser while surgically striking at its weapons points. The cruiser, a fortress in space, was now unarmed. With only a few defensive weapons now operating, the *Cołłinsía One* had stripped it of its offensive capabilities.

"Wha...what happened to me?"

"Oh my goodness!" blurted Tadφlŏn dashing from her seat, "Hαzăr--help, quick!"

The assault team, with Jacφb in tow, had now boarded the *Sir Puηt*.

[SMACK!] came the sound of Eberhαrt's open hand impacting with Jacφb's face.

"Eberhαrt!" said Urφch.

Eberhαrt had readied another bitch-slapping blow when....

"...she's not dead," mumbled Jacφb.

Those few words had found their way past puffy lips, dripping with blood, to ears that begged for just such a miracle. ...Another stinging strike was instantly halted.

"What did you say?" ask Julíeηηe.

"The serpent's venom was replaced with a drug to simulate death," answered Jacφb.

"If you're lying...," Eberhαrt cautioned.

"I know," interrupted Jacφb, "...You will kill me."

"We'll find out soon enough," said Urφch. "Prepare for departure."

Each member heeded Urφch's instruction but continued to ponder this new revelation hoping it to be true.

"Two engines at 70 percent," reported Latríηa, "...port engine is still offline."

"Understood," said Urφch. "...Everyone ready? ...PUNCH IT!"

The craft groaned, stumbled, and then lurched from the battle cruiser's hangar bay into space.

"Helm's very sluggish," reported Latríηa.

"Do your best," replied Urφch. "Let's hope the *Cołłiηsía One* has seen our escape."

"Hɑzăr," said Tadφlŏn, "...attend to her needs. The scanners have detected a launch."

Hɑzăr helped the now resurrected Mμreeη below while Tadφlŏn maneuvered the *Coℓℓiηsía One* to intercept the *Sir Puηt*.

"Coℓℓiηsía One to Sir Puηt," called Tadφlŏn into the communicator.

"Puηt here," came the response.

"Tell Eberhɑrt that Mμreeη has awakened," said Tadφlŏn. "I don't know how but she seems to be recovering quickly."

"That's great news," responded Urφch. "We're moving toward your hangar door."

"Hangar door opening," responded Tadφlŏn. "Welcome aboard!"

The *Sir Puηt* sluggishly entered the bay door of the *Coℓℓiηsía One*. Once inside, the doors closed and the Puηt extended her gear touching down gently. Not

343

waiting for all systems to power down, Eberhart dashed to see for himself that his beloved was indeed alive and well.

"Mμreeη," said a teary-eyed Eberhart, "...are you really okay?"

"Ah, Eberhart," said Mμreeη sobbing, "...I thought... [Sob] I would never see you again."

Eberhart and Mμreeη embraced each other and gave thanks for their second chance to be together.

"Well, I'm certainly confused," confessed Hαzăr. He gently squeezed Eberhart's shoulder.

"Yes, Urφch," said Tadφlŏn, "...maybe you or Jacφb could bring us up to speed."

"I too am a little curious," rang in Latríηa caressing Urφch's hand. Urφch gazed briefly into Latríηa's eyes,

"Okay," said Urφch, "I'll go first and then Jacφb will have to fill in the blanks."

CHAPTER FIFTEEN

Complexity...

"The escape capsule auto launch will occur in thirty zlitons when the explosives begin their detonation sequence," reported Latrína.

"I'll try to be concise," said Urϕch.

The crew gathered around to hear Urϕch's story....

"I was a counterintelligence agent within a unit monitoring intergalactic commerce. Trafficking in stolen goods, slave labor, narcotics, and etcetera was my domain. We stumbled onto what was first thought to be an operation designed to move large quantities of toxic waste across time and space for disposal. After reporting our findings to our superiors, our unit suddenly came under intense scrutiny with some of our team being arrested and accused as double agents."

"Someone thought you had gotten too close," said Eberhart.

"Possibly," said Urϕch. "Anyway, I was shortly contacted by a representative from the *Secret Society of Believers*. (SSB) I had heard of them as a child, but thought them to be a myth. Legend held that a secret society watched and waited for signs that a terrible evil would attempt to dominate and enslave the living universe. The SSB identified the Rhyuoph franchise as part of a larger nomadic consortium. This consortium sent emissaries throughout the universe harvesting planetary resources while extracting payment for illegally dumping hazardous waste on other unsuspecting worlds. I was placed as commander at the training facility in the Lotzaphii Galaxy in order to learn more about the hazmat dumping."

"I knew you were different the span you arrived," said Latrína. "...You didn't belong!"

"I tried to blend," said Urφch. "Later, I determined the hazmats brought to the facility for training purposes were of specific compositions. I did not think much of it at the time. I focused on learning the locations of the temporal access points being used to smuggle the hazmats across time. When Jet and Alli arrived, I asked the SSB to provide background reports. Apparently, the Society of Believers has contacts within many governments on many planets. I learned that Jet and Alli were TIA agents. I naturally assumed they were on the hazmat trail as well. That was good I thought. Possibly, we could help each other."

"How did you come to hijack us?" asked Julíenηe.

"As commander of the training facility, I had to keep the franchise supplied with new recruits. I made an effort to direct the recruiting toward several of the pirate infested solar systems thus helping to reduce piracy while supplying the franchise with trainees. When we unexpectedly ran upon an Uμmpárian ship with its passengers in stasis I was compelled to order its hijacking.

346

As I came to investigate you Uμmpárians and the activities that brought you into that timeline, I became concerned that the hazmat dumping was auxiliary to a larger and more terrible plan. This plan might forever tip the balance of good and evil unless action was taken."

"What made you think that?" asked Jerẹmy.

"It seemed that certain hazmat compositions went to different access points. I suspected, and as we now know, at least some of the access points led to worlds where life was developing. The hazmats were being used to alter the natural evolution of intelligent design.[28] I reported my theory to the representative of the SSB asking for additional information on the Uμmpárians. Oddly enough, Sir Jacφb Puηt's name was flagged because of numerous undocumented timeline incursions.

"How was Jacφb connected to the believers?" asked Eberhαrt.

"The SSB was well aware of the use of hazmats to affect these developing worlds. Sir Jacφb Puηt had been their earlier agent dispatched to deal with the threat. Jacφb broke off communications with the Believers a long time ago. The SSB had to consider that he might have been turned and was now in collusion with the other side. However, it was foretold to me that an opportunity to retrieve him from evil would present itself. I felt compelled to search for and did locate him on the cruiser. I'll let Jacφb clear up the ambiguities that exist," concluded Urφch.

"Yes," said Jacφb then cleared his throat, "...where to begin? Let's see...I'm not originally from Uμmpár. I came into the service of the Believers many

---

[28] Whoa! ...The natural evolution of intelligent design?

solacles ago on another planet from another timeline. My father was a deacon in the service of the SSB. From my time as a young person, I knew that my father's service was significant. He was ever vigilant... watching, waiting, and preparing for the times that evil's emissaries would penetrate into the physical world. Sometimes ministers would call him to duty and dispatch him for long periods to unknown destinations. We always worried and prayed for his safe return.

At one of those times, before he left for service, I could see a distinct level of concern in his eyes. A great number of deacons from many sects had been called to service. Before leaving, he took me to visit many of the SSB's locations apprising me of their resources should I have need of them. I remember that time.... He sat with me for a long time just holding my hand and hugging me. I was so afraid. I knew...he would not return.

Looking deeply into my eyes, he spoke of a great evil unleashed. Breaking the rules of the Secret Society of Believers, my father spoke in vivid detail about a being whose jealousy induced him to conspire against the son of God. This being and his conspirators were cast out into a domain of evil where he took up his rule. Now, he would attempt to spread evil throughout the entire universe.

First by temptation, this evil would attract followers to perform hideous and unspeakable acts in his name. Then, my father said, this would not suffice him. His jealous spite would induce him to deliver hideously sinful creatures to the physical world to prepare it for his occupation and violation. He told me that our house was chosen to deliver the adversary to the field. I did not understand until later.

Much time passed without word from my father. When I inquired with representatives of the Believers they would just say, 'Your father's courage, faith, and service is of immeasurable significance in the battle between good and evil. Yea though he may never return to this place he shall bask in the glory of our God for all of eternity.' Those words did not help that much but they sustained me. I vowed to follow in his footsteps that I too might bask in our God's glory and see my father again.

I was dispatched to Uμmpάr because the consortium had begun dumping toxic waste there. Their agents had infiltrated Uμmpάr's government and implemented a plan that would persuade the inhabitants to readily accept the hazmats."

"...Gold," mumbled Eberhαrt, "...it was gold. Wasn't it?"

"Yes," replied Jacφb. "A world many light-solacles distant produced gold as a byproduct of their energy production methods. Unbelievably, the gold is toxic to them. On the other hand, Uμmpάr does not have any naturally occurring gold deposits. The so-called gold mines were actually constructed by the Nahrμvian franchise. The mines were the receiving areas for off-world hazmats. No one on Uμmpάr has ever suspected that they are being spammed with hazmats. Subsequently, the switch to using gold as currency was a boldly, absurd plan that was implemented almost flawlessly. The franchise was ecstatic with this result. They referred to Uμmpάr as *Dumbpar*. The striving for ignorance... the gold currency.... These bizarre revelations attracted evil's attention. What better place to introduce evil's child into the physical world. Later, I would learn that Uμmpάr is precisely the center of this expanding universe. The bang, pop, fizzle, or what have you--happened at that precise location. Consequently, Uμmρár is a super-compressed fossil from the birthplace of this universe."

"So this evil you speak of is going to somehow produce an offspring?" asked Jeręmy.

"The evil I speak of *has* produced an offspring," replied Jacφb, "...Cołłiηsía Verηa Puηt!"

"I don't understand, Jacφb," stated a bewildered Mμreeη. "She is your sister; a very sweet and innocent female."

"Yes, Jacφb," said Eberhαrt. "She warned us of the Dark One. She also told us to stay in the protected areas to avoid the Dark One's incursion attempts into our psyche."

"The protected areas," responded Jacφb, "...are to protect us from her!"

"She may not even realize," continued Jacφb looking away. "...I'm just not sure. However, the Dark One utilizes her as a conduit to deliver his physical energy into our dimension. Other worlds sometime refer to this as a *possession*."

"But why did you refer to her as your sister?" asked Julíenηe.

"Because my father's seed was taken to fertilize her mother's egg," replied Jacφb.

"...Hate to interrupt," said Hαzăr, "...but the detonations have begun!"

The crew hurried to view the fireworks. Looking out the viewports, the explosions illuminated space for brief periods. The ship's instruments recorded the shock waves while long-range sensors documented the destruction of the crippled battle cruiser.

"We must go back, search for, and find the escape capsule Cołłiŋsía was in. ...or evidence of its complete destruction," said a worried Jacφb.

Hɑzăr and Tadφlŏn input a course to the source of the explosions where they would methodically search for survivors.

"Go on with your story," said Eberhɑrt.

"As I said, my father had been gone for a long, long time before I was old enough to come into the service of the SSB. When I did begin service, I gained access to certain records that indicated that my father might have been captured on Uμmφár. The records inferred that he might have been somehow compelled to serve the side of evil. They also indicated that a female had been conceived and was my father's genetic offspring. I served the SSB for many solacles concealing this knowledge. When fate placed me within the reach of Uμmφár, I embarked on my own to find her and free her from this evil if possible. ...I unwittingly fell into evil's plan.

The Dark One had waited for solacles. ...Waiting for me. As I said, it seems that Cołłiŋsía is only a *carrier* for evil. As electricity flows around a conductor and not through it, so does the evil clinging to Cołłiŋsía. God had refused to allow her to be sacrificed. Unknown to her, it seems the Dark One is free to wander as she sleeps making itself known only to those that will see."

"...the believers," said Latríŋa.

"Yes," replied Jacφb. "Only those that had been waiting and watching for so long could detect the evil's physical presence. I did find her and spirited her away to the cloaked world in a future timeline. I called this world *Sedition Outpost Alpha*. Sedition is Uμmφár tens of

351

millions of solacles into the future. The solar system is without life. I have never determined whether natural causes had produced that outcome. My followers, the CPU, and I began constructing a base of operations there. I quickly realized that Sedition would be a safe confinement for Cołłiŋsía while I designed a plan to free her and send the *prince of demons* packing. The Dark One is strong and did tempt and try me continually. A fortunate discovery has helped me to endure the onslaught even unto this time."

"Excuse me, folks," said Hɑzăr. "We've located the escape capsule."

"Yes," said Jacφb anxiously.

"It's completely intact," continued Hɑzăr. "It appears to have sustained minor damage. I think the Carbonite 14 construction helped to shield it from the intense radiation emitted by the battle cruiser's reactor."

"Possibly," responded Mμreeŋ.

"What are your instructions, Jacφb?" Urφch spoke looking at Jacφb and then the others.

"Jacφb," repeated Hɑzăr. "What do want us to do?"

"It was Carbonite 14," said Jacφb ignoring the question. "It apparently confines antiparticles though it significantly extends their life. The cinder of a world that I would dub *Sedition Outpost Alpha* was very, very rich in Carbonite 14. I used it to construct shielded areas to give me a respite from the Dark One. Though I believed the Dark One to be aware of why I constructed the shielded areas, the evil must have thought it an equal trade for longer antiparticle existence."

"Excuse me," said Mμreeŋ. "We're all aware of the four fundamental forces, but--?"

"There's a fifth," said Jacφb causing eyebrows to rise, "...and all others are unknowingly subordinate to it!"

"Say again," said Urφch.

"You're no doubt speaking of the weak nuclear interaction, the strong nuclear interaction, the electromagnetic force, the gravitational force and their wave and particle interactions," said Jacφb. "The fifth is the *Intangible Force*."

"Intangible Force," repeated Mμreeη, "...explain?"

"The four fundamental forces act upon waves and elementary particles. Energy being emitted and then absorbed by matter in small discreet units effects the interaction. They also act upon antiparticles or antimatter. The Intangible Force, put simply, is an encompassing host. The Intangible Force is the single common denominator between many universes, and more importantly, between the physical and the spiritual existence. The Intangible Force permits infinity!

For solacles, possibly from the very beginning of intelligent life, living beings have tried to account for our physical existence. We naturally seek boundaries. We want to know how far away things are, how fast they are going, and what they weigh. We have peered into space counting and identifying body after body as fools counting grains of sand in the desert. Over time, we have made predictions concerning the size of universes based solely on the volume of matter in the physical existence. We are but children seeking proof of life, proof of existence ...proof of God. The tangible is... Listen carefully! The tangible is a contamination of the intangible. The intangible is infinity, eternity, perpetuity, and so on. You do not have to consider how big it is, how fast it is going, how old it is, or what it weighs--it is *immeasurable*. It is incapable of being perceived or defined. On the other hand, the physical existence is tangible. It can be quantified, qualified, and verified. Therefore, the tangible *must* reside within the intangible."

"I'm somewhat confused," said Μμreeη. "...Even with this fifth encompassing force. How does it figure into this battle between good and evil?"

"Well, I can't say that I have all of the answers. I just do not! However, I speculate that the interface where the intangible envelops the tangible may be as a semi-permeable membrane. The tangible has a solute--the *nonbelievers*. An osmotic-like effect may be transferring evil from the intangible existence to the tangible."

"Why can't evil be transferred out of the tangible existence to the intangible," asked Jeręmy, "...did I say that right? I'm so confused!"

"Good question, Jeręmy. The reason is--there are no nonbelievers residing in the intangible existence! In the tangible existence, there are believers and nonbelievers. It is the number of believers that provide the osmotic pressure that prevents or slows evil's transfer into the tangible existence. Solacles have passed and the number of nonbelievers has grown. In other words, the osmotic pressure has weakened to a critical level. Incursions by evil into tangible existence have occurred sporadically as the ratio of believers to nonbelievers fluctuates."

"Wow, Jacφb," said Julíenηe.

"Yeah," added Eberhαrt. "That is quite a story."

"What are you going to do?" asked Jet.

"Yes, Jacφb," said Urφch. "What's next?"

"Hαzăr," said Jacφb, "...bring the capsule aboard and set a course back through the temporal vortex."

"Back through the vortex?" questioned Tadφlŏn.

"Yes," explained Jacφb. "There is a beautiful garden on the third planet from the rad."

Tadφlŏn maneuvered the *Cołłiŋsía One* into position and did retrieve the capsule.

"Looks pretty good for being blown up," said Jeręmy.

"Open it," instructed Jacφb.

The sealing clamps were released and the capsule hatch swung open.

"Where am I?" asked a bruised but safe Cołłiŋsía.

"You're fine, dear," said Jacφb. "Let us help you out and see if you're injured."

Cołłiŋsía, aided by the crew, exited the capsule. She was shaken and visibly frightened.

"Please," asked Jacφb, "...would someone escort Cołłiŋsía to suitable quarters where she might refresh herself and rest?"

Mµreeŋ volunteered and did take Cołłiŋsía to the crew quarters deck.

"Is it safe with her aboard?" inquired Latríŋa looking at Jacφb.

"For now," replied Jacφb, "...but we must not waste time."

Jacφb headed for the bridge where he was able to execute control protocols, which provided protection for all aboard.

"What have you done?" ask Tadφlŏn.

"The SSB provided me with guidance in the design of this craft," said Jacφb. "This time has been foretold and was expected. I have executed a command program that places a Carbonite 14 stasis field around Cołłiŋsía at all times."

"I get it," said Jerẹmy. "That stops the Dark One from wandering around."

"Exactly," responded Jacφb.

"I've altered course," reported Tadφlŏn, "...we're heading back to the Milky Way."

"One last thing," said Jacφb accessing yet another hidden console, "...we must visit it just before the crew of the Sir Puηt did."

"That was the world we left the A.P.E.L. on," said Julíenηe.

"Yes," replied Jacφb. "Mµreeη's serpent master is resting comfortably in the crew quarters below."

"You know about the serpent that Eberhαrt slew?" asked Mµreeη.

"Yes," said Jacφb, "...but that was only a sentinel preparing a beachhead for evil's intended invasion."

"I don't get it," said a confused Jerẹmy. "...we're now helping evil to invade?"

"We're there," announced Hαzăr.

356

The crew stood reverently in awe beholding the fledgling world. It was here that evil intended to penetrate with great force into the tangible existence.

The landing party that included Jacφb, Cołłiηsía, Eberhαrt, Mμreeη, Julíenηe, Jerεmy, Jet, and Alli shuttled to the surface and did land not far from a beautiful garden.

"It is different," said Mμreeη now stepping onto the planet's surface once more.

"Yes," explained Jacφb, "...your female has not yet been created. Only the male resides."

"Jacφb," breathed Cołłiηsía, "...what is this place? I'm frightened."

"Don't worry, dear," comforted Jacφb squeezing her shoulder. "This is a very holy place."

Jacφb led the landing party away from the garden to the place Eberhαrt and the others had called *the darkening*. There Jacφb knew that the evil Cołłiηsía was hosting would leave her in order to fulfill the agreement to battle for the souls of the tangible existence.

"Jacφb," said Cołłiηsía, "I feel funny. I'm not well."

"Just a little farther, dear," assured Jacφb, "...just a little farther."

Cołłiηsía bore more and more of her weight on Jacφb. She was rapidly growing weary. As they approached the darkening, the evil surrounding her was compelled to completely leave her. Cołłiηsía collapsed signaling to Jacφb that it was done. The darkening grew darker by a magnitude and its presence expanded tenfold.

"It is time to leave," said Jacφb. "Let us be quick!"

You have served me well, Jacφb, whispered the Dark One to Jacφb's mind. I shall remember you when I reign supreme in this tangible existence.

No doubt you will, said Jacφb in his mind. My part has been played and now I shall leave the stage where the story of good versus evil shall seek an ending.

You are hoping that I lose, stated the Dark One. You have accommodated me thus far Jacφb, but I know your allegiance is solidly with the believers. ...I have always known. God has protected you.

Then you are aware that you shall be defeated, concluded Jacφb. Repent your wickedness and beg forgiveness.

Go now, Jacφb, commanded the Dark One. You are not of this world. You and the others have no further part to play. The rules have been set and the outcome shall be determined by this planet's inhabitance alone....

"Jacφb!" said Eberhαrt shaking him, "we're ready... Let's go."

The landing party made their way back to the shuttle speedily. Immediately, upon entering the landing craft, Jacφb ordered that it lift-off and rendezvous with the *Cołłiŋsía One*. In short order, Eberhαrt and Mμreeŋ had piloted the shuttle to within visual range of the Cołłiŋsía One.

"Permission to come aboard, Captain Mom," said Eberhαrt jokingly.

"Permission granted," came mom's reply.

The shuttle was received and touched down gently. The landing party exited the shuttle and prepared to depart the Milky Way Galaxy.

"It is beautiful," commented Tadφlŏn while staring at the blue and green planet.

"Yes," mumbled Jacφb as he quickly executed commands causing the *Cołłiŋsia One* to break orbit and head for the temporal wormhole at extreme speed.

"We'll be entering the wormhole briefly," said Mμreeη while scanning the instruments.

"Is everything going to be all right now?" ask Eberhαrt.

For a brief period, Jacφb offered no response. He busied himself with the controls.

"Entering the wormhole...Now!" announced Mμreeη.

"Jacφb," said Tadφlŏn, "Eberhαrt asked about how things are going to turn out?"

Jacφb paused and looked around at each of them. Rising, he walked around, stopped, and peered out the viewport. Then he spoke....

"It seems unlikely that evil will stop pursuing the tangible existence," said Jacφb. "It is rich in precious non-believing souls. Consequently, it has been revealed to the *Society of Believers* that a battle for the souls of the tangible existence will be waged on that world--alone. We shall but spectate from afar without influence or affect. After we exit the temporal vortex, I have been warned that it shall collapse. We of the rest of the tangible existence have been forbidden to approach that world ever again. I am told that an unknowing barrier will be a warning. To come close may well mean certain oblivion." Looking at Jet and Alli, he said, "I suppose you two will be allowed to return without the knowledge of the battle that will be raging on your planet."

"But my home world is already disadvantaged," complained Alli. "Evil's offspring is already an inhabitant."

"That may be true for now," responded Jacφb, "...but I believe that God has a son and he is very competitive. I also believe that he will never forsake us."

"Well, if he's competitive," said Jerεmy, "Eberhαrt has programmed the A.P.E.L. with many challenging events."

"Yes," said Jacφb rolling his eyes a little at Eberhαrt, "...and what do you have to say about that?"

Eberhαrt looked at the others while pondering the question.

"I acted with sincerity and compassion. I certainly am not ashamed of my contribution," began Eberhαrt.

Still thinking, Eberhαrt paced a distance around the bridge before stopping to look at first Jacφb and then the others. He pulled the love of his life, Μμreeη, close. ...then he smiled.

"I am blessed with a loving family and wonderful friends...old and new. It has been a tremendous honor and a privilege to have shared in this adventure to fulfill great prophesies. On that planet, Jet and Alli's home world, a battle has been enjoined. ...For the hearts and souls of that world and all of the tangible existence. I believe with all of my heart and soul that good shall prevail. Therefore, as I...we...continue on to other adventures...I shall always remember the time when I became the designer of professional sports on that planet!"

The End

∞

Cover Design

The content previously presented may or may not be worthy of literary acclaim. That will be for you, the reader, to decide. However, from the publisher's point of view, the content is simply--*the product*. It is the essential deliverable that good folks are laying down their hard-earned cash to acquire. The author has strung together the words and laced together the sentences thus constructing paragraphs that when stacked together present a vision, a dream, or a roadmap to another perspective. This wondrous and complex literary structure deserves to be packaged carefully, thoughtfully, and in a complimentary fashion.

The serious and detailed attention given to the content packaging, *the cover,* is an important functional consideration. We believe that the cover presents the first impression, if you will, of the complexity, tone, and quality of the content. A positive first impression is desirable to several parties—the author, the publisher, and the, critically important, retailer. So when we say, "positive," we are really thinking *extraordinary!* We strongly desire that the visual aroma of the packaging whet your literary appetite.

Considering the previously stated package criteria of care, thought, and compliment, the design goal is to entice the customer to consider the valuable content inside. The cover must not only invite (...*please, kind sir ...look inside?*) but *demand (...HEY-- Yes, you! ...get back here and open this thing up!*) that the prospective buyer give consideration to that which the author has labored intensely to create, the publisher has brought to market, and the retailer has risked offering. This mission, this purpose, is fulfilled when the prospective buyer "clicks" online or "picks" from the shelf at the local retailer and thumbs the pages.

Eberhart Ghoṇadz: The Designer of Professional Sports on this Planet is a fictional story of action. Aliens and humans are doing things. They are living, loving, fighting, flying, hugging, kissing, grieving, and making a difference *out there* somewhere in the universe. We dared not to produce a cover that was static or just sitting around looking pretty. On the contrary, there was a very strong desire for the cover to be informative, engaging, and kicking butt just like the story's heroes! To that end, from the content of the back cover hook prose, the font characteristics, and the blend of colors to the flavor of the original artwork, there has been tremendous consideration.

The artwork was facilitated using computer aided design, CAD, software. The spacecraft were modeled in 3D, which affords significant advantages. For example, if the artwork were created in 2D, the laborious creation of each perspective would be required. However, with 3D models, once they are created, they may be infinitely rotated, spun, or posed in a scene. Of course, this significant advantage is not without cost. The majority of time consumed during the cover design phase was during the creation of the CAD models. The scene making effort was more straightforward.

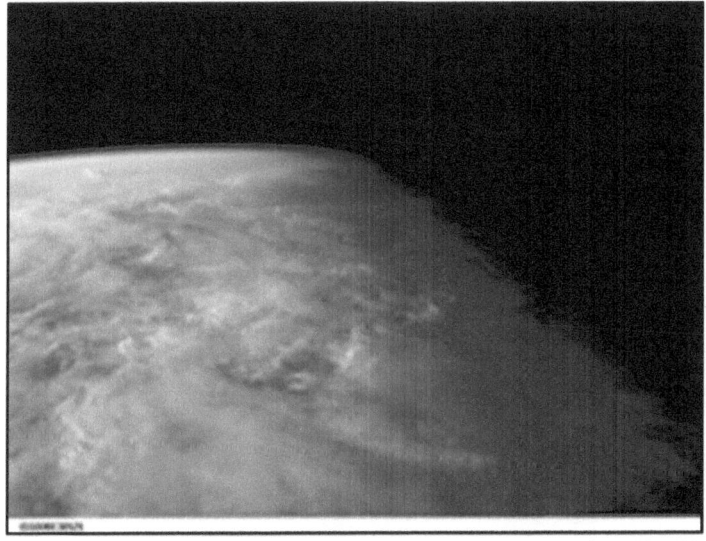

The space scene consists of a cropped planet background image, the larger *Collinsia One* CAD model, and energy torpedoes created by photo painting software. Utilizing the photo painting software, the background image was imported and placed on the base layer then cropped to the desired area. The image at that point was appropriately sized by adjusting width and height pixels/inch, the colors were converted to CMYK mode, (*they were converted to grayscale to be included in this text block*) and the resolution was adjusted to 300dpi (dots per inch) as required by our book manufacturer's digital guidelines.

CMYK is cyan, magenta, yellow, and black--the process colors. This color mode is used for images that are destined for print. The book manufacturer suggests utilizing a process color guide. The process color guide allows you to see the printed color and does list the CMYK percentages required to produce it. In contrast, images destined for viewing on monitors or video displays would likely appear better in RGB (red, green, blue) mode.

Next, we opened the graphic file containing our appropriately oriented spacecraft model.

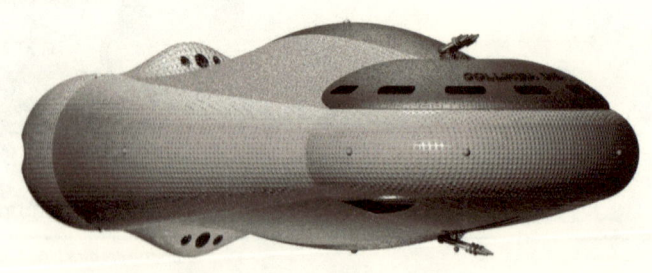

Previously, we utilized the CAD software to rotate or spin thus orienting the model and then to generate a tiff, jpeg, or other graphic file format. Additionally, the spacecraft texture and colors were applied within the CAD software. We then carve out the spacecraft or delete the background and copy it to the clipboard. Switching to the space scene background image, the spacecraft was pasted to layer one. We had complete flexibility in moving around the spacecraft to the desired location. At that point, the file was saved and then saved again utilizing a different file name. We might have wanted to start over again at that point and saving that particular instance was the appropriate way to permit that. We then went about cementing the spacecraft on layer one to the background layer. We did this by *flattening* the layers. Afterwards, there would only be one layer. Consequently, the spacecraft could no longer be manipulated independent of the background. We did this so that we may go around the edges of the spacecraft and blend it into the background by gently smudging or blurring.

The spacecraft was oriented along the right side that ultimately did become the front cover of the book. This entire graphic composes a *wrap around* cover layout. The book manufacturer generates a template based on paper type and page count that allows us to size the graphic appropriately with the desired *bleed*, or over print area, required. This image displayed on a video monitor in color is just awesome!

Utilizing photo-painting software, the energy torpedoes, solar effects, and the lights were added. We wanted to be careful with the light from the energy torpedoes. If we made the energy balls too bright and spectacular, they might have washed out the collateral image with white when printed. We typically will send the image to the printer and then adjust in order to achieve the printed best. Furthermore, there was a desire to effect motion and the evidence of some type of planetary atmosphere. To fulfill those desires, the further manipulation of the spacecraft/background interface was performed. The result became a subtle distortion around the craft. Again, viewing this on color video is excellent. Okay, we now had the basic cover graphic. This was the backbone, kick-butt action image that we could build on with graphical and informational enhancements.

The cover template provided to us by the book manufacturer did sport the layout guidelines and the barcode for the ISBN number we provided. We inserted our image and continued to build our cover. We wanted to provide some brief and catching story information on a semi-transparent panel on the back cover. And, since this
368

is a completely fictitious story, I did add some humorous pro and con fictitious reviews. Again, the entire cover must carry some weight. Next, we arranged some additional insets of original artwork. Afterward, we then chose the appropriate font characteristics. I have to say, that whether in print or on video display, the color red draws some attention. The title name at the top and the red bar across the bottom gave us a balanced feeling of attention to the product. The inclusion of the black and the yellow thin bars just above the red base bar added that pinstripe appeal. The modest blue for the subtitle and the author's name blended well with the little blue planet. We preferred a small author name font thus deferring attention to the product title. Giving consideration to online viewing, the inclusion of the number of pages and images within the text block on the cover in a subdued color was deemed appropriate. This teeny bit of information does not detract from the scene and may be helpful to that book buyer that would like to know the bulk of the product. Value adding characteristics such as the thought that thicker books look better on shelves or the addition of original artwork may influence the discriminating customer toward looking at the product may be useful information to some buyers.

The spine of the book did require some consideration. The type and number of pages between the covers determine the spine width. The spine width was calculated based on the information that we provided to the book manufacturer and was specified correctly on the cover layout template that they provided to us.

The small area of the spine gives a certain look when displayed from a bookshelf. We decided that a red title font would be too much. Consequently, the soothing blue, with a little 3D effect, was thought to be more appropriate. The small font of the subtitle was deemed easier to read with a black color. The author's name utilized a smaller font with a similar color as the title. Finally, separating the title and author's name, we placed the publisher's logo.

So there you have it. These few pages describe the creative design process that lasted weeks. Consequently, we are indeed pleased to present this take no prisoners, alien butt-kicking cover design. This may seem like an extraordinary effort.... Let us say for the record--*it is!* That effort is for our valued readers. The folks that make the decision to use their discretionary funds to buy this product thus supporting numerous other folks. You deserve no less effort! We sincerely *THANK YOU* for purchasing this entertaining, and possibly, thought-provoking product.

J.A. Justice

Please continue on to the next few pages and enjoy additional images. Again, thank you!

375

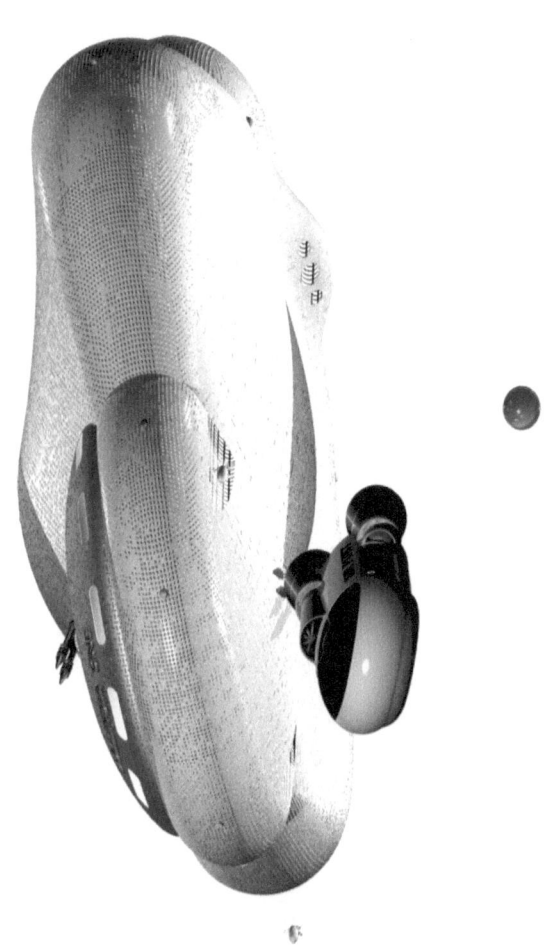

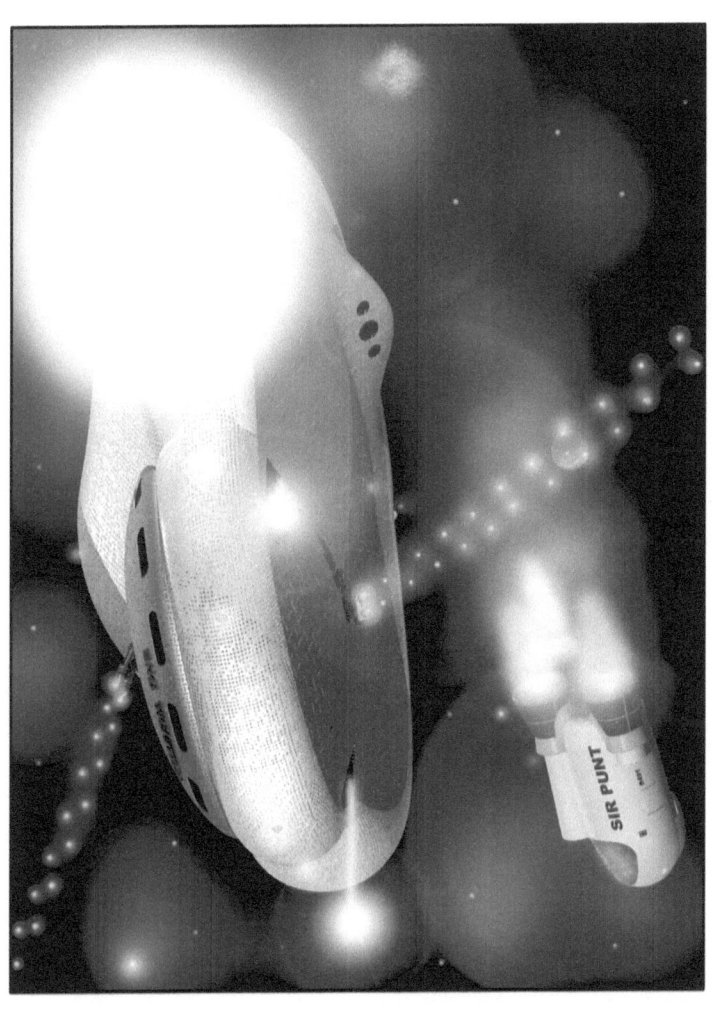